Praise for D.W. MARCHWELL *Dick Sigler Book 2*

Good to Know

Sins of the Father

D1598853

Books by
D.W. MARCHWELL

Good to Know
Sins of the Father
Falling

eBooks by
D.W. MARCHWELL

Mitchell's Presence

All available from
DREAMSPINNER PRESS

FALLING

DW Marchwell

Dreamspinner Press

Published by
Dreamspinner Press
4760 Preston Road
Suite 244-149
Frisco, TX 75034
http://www.dreamspinnerpress.com/

Cover Art by Anne Cain annecain.art@gmail.com
Cover Design by Mara McKennen

ISBN: 978-1-935192-17-6

Printed in the United States of America
First Edition
February, 2010

eBook edition available
eBook ISBN: 978-1-935192-18-3

For Andy Eisenberg

"One does not make friends; one recognizes them."
—Henrichs

CHAPTER 1

BEFORE Hank could get out the door, he heard the familiar shout of Brian's deep baritone. "Hank! Come here a minute, will you?"

Hank rolled his eyes, knowing that he was going to get another lecture about drinking the night before a climb. He squared his shoulders and tried to look contrite as he eased around the corner. "Yeah, Bri, what is it?"

"Yeah, right, like you don't know what this is about." Brian Alan swiveled his chair away from his makeshift desk in the corner room of the barge's cabin and fixed his most recent acquisition with his best boss-is-madder-than-hell glare. "You and I have had this little chat before, so can the bullshit and tell me why I shouldn't fire your ass."

Hank abandoned the contrite look for one that was more his usual style. With an arrogance and attitude that had become his trademarks in the logging business, he shrugged his shoulders as if he didn't really even need to answer. "Because I'm the best you got."

"Stow that crap for a minute and let me substitute my reality for yours, okay?" Brian raised himself to his full height of six feet five inches and was in Hank's face in only two strides. "You may think you're the best, but let me tell you that I won't hesitate to fire my best if you don't stop this next-day hangover routine." Brian poked a finger in Hank's face and smiled. "Ten four?"

"Aw, for fuck's sake, Bri—"

"I'm not talking to you as a friend, Hank." Brian crossed his arms over his chest, staring down into Hank's hesitant gaze. Hank—at only six feet three inches—knew, from many similar discussions, that Brian could teach him a sorely needed lesson, but Hank also knew that Brian wasn't about to tangle with the union just to get his message across. "You put anyone's safety at risk, and you will be out of here faster than you can spit." Brian uncrossed his arms and strolled back to his desk, not bothering to look at Hank again. "Now get your gear and get ready for the chopper. I'm coming with this morning. We're down a man."

Muttering to himself, Hank backed out of the office and headed for the door to the helipad. *I can top just as many, if not more, trees than the rest of these fuckers combined, and I'm getting shit because I want to have a little fun when the day's over. Fuck him!* As he exited onto the helipad, Hank's mood was foul and got even fouler when he noticed Roddy coming up fast.

"Listen, Roddy." Hank held up his hand to Brian's second-in-command and shook his head. "I don't want to hear it, okay?"

"Hey, man," Roddy held up his hands as if surrendering. "I was just coming over to see if you needed any help. We're already behind schedule."

"Doesn't matter. I got plenty of time." Hank jerked his head to the left towards Brian's office. "Bossman is coming with, and he ain't even sorted his gear yet."

"Actually, I sorted it for him." Roddy smiled. "You got five minutes." Roddy held up five fingers to emphasize his last statement and waggled his eyebrows, clearly mocking Hank and his most recent run-in with Roddy's best friend since junior high.

"Fuck me," Hank hissed, glad that no one was around. "Could this day get any worse?"

Hank got his gear assembled, his boots and safety vest on in record time, and was at the chopper before Brian and Roddy. As they climbed in, Hank decided to keep his mouth shut for once and try to make something out of this day. If he kept his mouth shut, he wouldn't give them any ammunition to use against him later. As Kari, the chopper pilot, guided them to their secluded piece of the forest on Vancouver Island, Hank tried to figure out what Brian had against him. *I do good work, more than anyone else. I top my fair share of trees, my cookies are always clean and precise, and I help to make the guy millions of dollars a year. What the fuck?*

As the chopper approached the landing site inside the nest of huge western cedars and cypress trees, some of them already marked from their work the day before, Hank could admit to himself that he liked to drink, liked to chase women, and even liked to rib the other guys about how much slower they were at just about everything. But he'd never gotten anyone hurt, never cost the company any money because of his off-hour pursuits. *Fuck, I've never even taken a sick day.* Even with his sensitivity to the record hundred-degree heat out here in the summer, his little bouts with heatstroke had never slowed him down; he'd be down for twenty minutes or so, go in the shade to get some rest, and then he'd be back topping trees and jigging right alongside the other men.

Shaking his head in frustration, Hank jumped out of the helicopter and headed for his section of the woods, stopping only when Brian called to him. When he turned, he felt a little relief that Brian offered him a smile and a thumbs-up. *Maybe I'm not in as much trouble as I thought.* He found himself whistling as he set off north of the landing pad to finish the trees that he hadn't finished yesterday. By his count, Hank had another ten trees to top, and then he would be done for the day, the weekend, and not have to be back here until next Thursday.

Almost an entire week, Hank thought to himself. *Find myself some nice little shapely thing—or two—and keep myself horizontal until Thursday.*

Hank approached his first tree, and remembering Brian's warning about any screw-ups, he went through the mental checklist in his head. He fastened the spikes to his boots, ensuring the straps were nice and tight around his calf muscles, checked his vest to make sure it was good and tight, and then began inspecting his gear. His rope would need replacing sometime soon—too many frayed sections—but it would get him through another season or two. His safety vest was new and didn't obstruct access to the rescue whistle at his shoulder. Even his helmet, which had definitely seen better days, had another few good seasons in it.

He clipped one end of his scare-strap on his hip harness, and winding his arm behind him as if he were about to swing at a baseball pitch one-handed, he swung his scare-strap around the trunk of the tree and caught it as it came around the other side. Catching it with ease, he clipped it into the other side of his hip harness. Planting his boot spikes into the base of the trunk, he flicked his wrists one at a time and started climbing. He'd forgotten to run the diameter at breast height of this particular trunk through the calculator, but years of experience told him the DBH was just right to ensure the load limits were observed, so he decided to keep climbing. He was never more thankful he didn't have to do Brian's job than at moments like this.

Within minutes, Hank's expert climbing had him almost fifty feet in the air and looking out at the spectacular vistas through little fluffy patches of thinning fog. Hank had never been able to understand how some people could stay stuck in concrete buildings all day, content with the little bit of greenery they'd see between cement slabs or high-rise office buildings. Before he was even in elementary school, his mother had been chasing him out of the neighborhood trees. He'd loved to climb as high as he could and see what he would never be able to see from the ground, and he still did. Hank would never admit it to anyone, but he felt free up here. And something else he would never admit to anyone was the reason why: He didn't know why, but he'd always felt more at home up here than anywhere else in the world.

A couple more wrist flicks took Hank near the first branches he would have to remove before he could top the tree. He hauled up the chainsaw that hung down on the long rope and pulled the cord, making sure to adjust the choke. As it roared in his ears, he pulled his visor down and started trimming. He didn't have that many branches to remove, but he was sure he'd spotted a widow-maker up there somewhere. He'd worry about it when he got to it. He wasn't being careless by any means, but he didn't want to lose focus this far away from any potential problems. He could hear Brian's words in his ears telling everyone over and over: "You have to concentrate your way up the tree; no use planning ten feet up when something will kill you four feet before you get there." Despite the altercation that morning, Hank was more than willing to admit that Brian's advice had saved his life on many occasions.

After another ten feet, Hank was ready to tackle the widow-maker that was stuck behind the marm. He studied the marm for a moment, wondering why these big, thick branches sticking out of the side of a tree and growing toward the sun had ever been called "school marms" in the first place. *Certainly don't look like school teachers.* He took hold of his chainsaw and began to cut away at the thick, trunk-like branch, reducing it in size. He called down before each smaller piece fell to the ground; the sound always gave Hank a rush. He backed up before his last cut with the chainsaw and screamed as loud as he could that a widow-maker was on its way down. He'd worked with plenty of guys over the years who had been injured or even killed by these wayward branches—tall enough and thick enough to qualify as small trees—that careened out of the tree tops with lethal force.

Hank breathed a sigh of relief as he set himself up to top the tree. He didn't need to send down the cookie, the little piece of the top showing his cuts and his technique, so almost a hundred and fifty feet in the air he started cutting through the trunk and sat back against his harness as he watched the top of the tree fall to the ground. *Nothing better than this feeling*, he reminded himself. *What a fucking rush!*

He set his red ribbon around and over the top of the cut trunk, the signal to the chopper pilot that this was one of the trees to take, and rappelled back down to the ground. The next tree he had to climb wasn't within clawing distance, let alone jumping distance, but if he climbed down, he could jig the trunk at the bottom with his half-inch holding wood and move on. No need to come back to this trunk and jig it later.

It wasn't until Hank was halfway up his tenth tree that he started to feel the heat. He had kept silent for most of the day, saying little in response to the playful banter that wafted over from the other guys or occasionally filtered through on his walkie-talkie, so he didn't know what the temperature was—or if he'd heard someone mention the temperature, he couldn't remember.

Must be over a hundred, Hank thought as he kept climbing, stopping more and more frequently to try to catch his breath or to lean over, uncertain if the heat was enough to make him lose the small breakfast he'd eaten that morning. He'd always ignored the comments from Brian and Roddy that drinking alcohol made heatstroke worse, but at moments like this when his guts felt like they were coming out through his nose with every breath, he wondered if they weren't right.

Hank started up his chainsaw and finished topping his tenth tree, promising himself a little nap down in the shade until his stomach stopped doing flip-flops with every inch he climbed. Hearing Brian's voice in his head for the hundredth time that day, Hank took every step very slowly. *Hell, I'm done after this. No need to hurry anymore.* His wedge was in and helped to push the tree away from him. He basked in the familiar rush one last time, stapled the ribbon around and over the top of the tree—now freed of its top—and started his descent.

Thank Christ! Now I can go find some shade and some water. He radioed to the other guys nearby that he was done with his ten and would be finding some shade to the north, away from the others, to rest for a while. He didn't get a response right away but figured Brian and the others were still pissed at him. He rappelled down, coiled his rope, and set off for the shade.

HANK was fast asleep by the time Brian arrived near his section and climbed his final tree of the day. Brian now owned the company that had once belonged to his father, and while he enjoyed the climbing part of it, he didn't much enjoy the administrative aspect. Employing and disciplining the men, having to worry about his men making enough money to provide for their families, and having to hire the helicopters—which ran about fifteen thousand dollars a day—were all more than he bargained for. But with his ex-wife Jennifer bitching and whining about alimony every chance she could get her lawyer on the phone, Brian didn't have much choice. He was in better spirits these days, though. Jennifer was getting remarried, the alimony payments would end, and Kari, the chopper pilot, had been flirting with him like crazy. Brian wasn't sure he'd pursue it, but it was nice to know that, at forty years old, he could still turn a good-looking woman's head.

Halfway up the tree, Brian saw something off to his right. *Fucking hell!* Brian started yelling down to Hank. *He said he was heading up further north!* He continued shouting at Hank, but Hank showed no signs of life. *If I have to climb down this tree to wake him up, he's gonna be shitting wood chips for a month! Seventy feet up in the air, for fuck's sake, and I have to lose this tree because he can't handle the heat!*

Brian was only ten feet down the tree trunk, thinking that he'd be closer for Hank to hear him, when he heard the familiar whirring of the blades of the Chinook helicopter. *Fucking great!* Not having any other option and wanting to be sure Hank was clear of any rotor wash the Chinook might kick up, Brian decided to claw his way to the next tree over. *I can claw over and then be at least twenty feet closer, maybe rappel down and get him outta there.* Brian took hold of his three-pronged steel claw and started letting some slack out. He let it swing back and forth about five feet below him and then tried to hook one of the stronger branches on a tree about fifteen feet away.

Yes, he thought as he felt the claw grab and hold the branch. Unhooking his scare-strap from his harness, he called down to Hank one more time. Nothing. No reaction at all. *Fucker!* Brian cursed as he slowly began to rappel over to the other tree. He reached for his walkie-talkie as he felt something give. He looked over and saw that he had not hooked his claw securely enough. He called to Hank one more time, and when he didn't get a response, he pulled the walkie up to his mouth just as the claw came loose, his body hurtling back into the trunk of the tree he'd just left. His last conscious thought was for Scott, his younger brother. *He'll be all alone now.*

CHAPTER 2

"HELLO, my name is Scott Alan. My brother is here somewhere? Brian Alan?"

The nurse looked up to see a frantic expression, and her eyes narrowed at Scott's calm tone. Her demeanor clearly said she'd become too accustomed to the yelling and the screaming of friends and relatives who would arrive once they found out a loved one had been rushed to the hospital. She offered a brief smile and consulted her chart. "I'm afraid he's in intensive care. If you'd like to have a—"

"Where is that?" Scott returned a pained and frustrated smile. "Intensive care?" He pointed down the hall, hoping for some sort of indication: a nod, words, he didn't care which. If this turned out to be like the movies and she told him that he couldn't see the only family he had left after flying nonstop from Toronto, she and Scott were going to have words. He was gearing up to explain to her just what he'd left behind. The musical was being prepared; rehearsals had been arranged. *I don't have time for this. Just tell me where my brother is, goddammit!*

"If you'd like to have a seat, I can call the doctor and he—"

"Nurse," Scott spoke softly. "He's the only family I have left." Scott let his eyes grow wide, unconcerned about showing what he was really thinking. "Please?"

"It's down the hall, turn right and—"

"Thank you very much." Scott started to walk quickly down the hall, quite sure he could find his way after turning right. "Make sure you check in at the nurse's station there!" was the last thing Scott heard before turning right and finding yet another long corridor.

"Hello, my name is Scott Alan. I'm Brian Alan's brother." Scott waited patiently for the nurse to acknowledge him. When she finally looked up, she fixed him with a perplexed look.

"Mrs. Alan is with him now. Room thirty-seven A."

"Mrs. Alan?" Scott looked back at the nurse, confusion obvious on his face. "Jennifer? You mean his *ex*-wife? They've been divorced for almost seven years." Scott turned away from the nurse briefly, rolling his eyes and whispering to himself, "I thought I was finally rid of that cow."

"It's okay, Kath." Another nurse had come up beside Scott. "I'll explain on the way."

The new nurse introduced herself as Sheila and touched his elbow as she led him to the room. She began explaining about Brian's "wife" and how she was a friend from high school. Scott wanted to turn around and tell her that Brian had finally been free of Jennifer for the past seven years. Perhaps it was the long flight or the strange surroundings—Scott hated hospitals—but he was so utterly confused now that he wasn't sure what was going on or even if Sheila knew that she couldn't possibly be speaking of Brian. As he reached to push against the door, Sheila asked him to stop, but he didn't really hear her. He was too focused on finding out if it was really Jennifer in the hospital room and if she was here for more money.

"You're not Jennifer." Scott stood with his hand propping the door open as he stared at the woman sitting beside her brother. She was petite, blonde, and had obviously been crying. She had Brian's hand in hers, her top hand caressing his brother's lovingly, but Scott didn't see a ring, no matter where he looked. "Who the hell are you?"

"Mr. Alan, please—"

"Sheila, it's okay," the petite blonde said. "I'll leave so Scott can visit with his brother."

"Not until I find out what the hell is going on here." Scott moved farther in the room, noticing in his peripheral vision that the nurse was moving toward the door. "Who are you?"

The woman raised herself from her chair and let go of his brother's hand. "My name is Kari. I'm the one who called you."

"The nurse told me his wife was...." Scott stammered, eyes narrowing, brow furrowing. "Are you two...?" Scott moved his hand back and forth between his brother and Kari.

"No," she shook her head slightly. "No, we're not." She came around the end of the bed toward Scott. "But I needed to see him, and they only allow family in, and...."

Scott listened as her voice trailed off, and the emotion in her voice announced more tears to come. Kari was in love with his brother. She loved him and needed to be with him. He could understand; Brian was very important to him as well.

"You're in love with him." It was obvious to Scott, but what he couldn't figure out was why Brian had never said anything to him. Suddenly, with a flash of clarity, Scott asked, "Does he know?"

Kari's eyes shot up to Scott's, a look that seemed ready to protest or to say that the idea was ridiculous. Scott showed her his sweetest smile, one that let her know that Scott thought the whole situation was wonderful, and she looked away and shook her head, regret quite plain on her face.

"Thank you for calling me." Scott moved beside her, the two of them standing at the foot of the bed looking down on his brother. Scott noticed for the first time that Brian's entire head was bandaged. There were tubes everywhere. The beeps of the machine by Brian's head seemed to get louder with each little detail Scott took in. "Brian will hate this. He hates having to be looked after."

"He is very independent." Kari offered a brief, humorless laugh. Scott heard her voice hitch, and he reached for her, taking her into his arms and caressing her back. "I'm sorry, but it was the only way I could see him."

"Hey, hey, now." Scott walked her over to the chair she had vacated only moments before. "I'm not going to tell anyone. Although I'm sure Sheila is a little curious about what I told her."

"Sheila and I are friends from high school." Kari sat down and peered up at Scott. "She won't tell anyone. She came in here to warn me that you were out there asking questions, obviously very upset and threatening—"

Scott reached for the second chair in the corner. "Well, it's settled, then." He offered Kari a genuine smile and put his hands out in front of him in a show of surrender. "Congratulations on your marriage." Scott winked for her and leaned back against his chair, the sudden drop of adrenaline jerking him back to exhaustion. "So, are you still registered, or should I just give you money?"

Kari huffed a little chuckle of relief. "Brian said you could be funny." She reached out and rested her hand on Scott's knee. "Thank you."

"No problem, really." Scott studied his brother's face for a moment and turned back to her. "Does he know anything at all?"

"I'm sure he suspects that I like him." Kari shrugged nervously, her eyes darting back and forth between the brothers. "He just seems more comfortable with flirting than taking it any further." Another shrug.

"Well, look on the bright side." Scott tapped his knuckled against his own skull. "We Alan men are very hardheaded, so it's probably what saved his life, right?"

"And handsome and kind and caring."

Scott looked into her sincere eyes and blushed, the heat going right to the tips of his ears. It reminded him of some of his bandmates reading out the reviews of their gigs and relishing the parts that focused on Scott's eyes or smile. Scott didn't like to think of himself that way; he was just Scott. "Oh, I'm afraid my brother got most of the handsome genes. And that's okay, because he didn't get any of the musical genes."

"He's very proud of your success." Kari's hands were worrying a linen handkerchief, twisting it back and forth as if she was trying to wring it free of tears. "He speaks of you often, of how close you two are."

"We've really only ever had each other." Scott looked up at her and smiled. "He must really like you a lot." When she blushed and looked away, Scott explained, "He usually doesn't mention me to other people. I think he's still not completely over the idea that I moved away or"—Scott shrugged, figuring he might as well get it out—"that his brother is a—"

"I know." She whispered in a quiet voice. "He told me a couple of weeks ago." Kari reached out and took hold of Scott's arm. "I have a son who's gay."

"You're married?"

"Not anymore." Kari held up a hand to show Scott what he'd already noticed. "Divorced for three years now."

"I'm sorry."

Kari offered a dismissive shrug, as if the subject wasn't worth discussing. "I was happy to get away from him." Kari peered up from under her lashes. "From what Brian tells me about your father, you'll have an understanding of what I had to live with."

Scott opened his mouth and shut it again very quickly. A slow grin spread across his face as he looked at his brother's sleeping face, a face Scott had spent so much time looking into after their mother had walked out on them. Every night, Brian would get their drunken father to bed and then come into the only other bedroom, the one he shared with Scott, and read to him. Scott looked back at Kari.

"Then he's in love with you too." It wasn't a question, and Scott beamed at Kari when her head swiveled quickly to look into his eyes. "Brian would never talk about our childhood unless he felt something for you."

Kari ducked her head, her face seeming to cave in on itself from emotion. With one hand she reached for Brian's hand, and with the other she reached out for Scott's, tears falling freely.

After a few moments, Scott patted Kari's hand. "So, Mrs. Alan," Scott tried to lighten the mood. "Did they tell you anything? Is he going to need physical therapy? Or—"

Kari pulled her hand away from Scott's and wiped at her eyes with the handkerchief. "Well, uh, Sheila's been very helpful, giving me all of the information. And like I told you on the phone, they're optimistic about a full recovery." Kari's eyes flickered briefly between the two brothers. "Sheila says that he doesn't have a concussion, there were no stitches needed, so…."

Kari looked up at Brian and smiled, and Scott felt a warm feeling for both of them. His brother had found someone, even if it was only flirting. Scott knew better than anyone how guarded Brian could be, especially after having survived Jennifer, but he hoped that his brother would learn what Kari had done for him, how special she was, and not let her get away.

"Not to worry." Scott kept his voice upbeat and his spirits hopeful. Brian had no concussion, and it seemed that the hospital staff was predicting a speedy recovery. Scott let out a sigh of relief, the exhaustion settling a little deeper into his bones. "Once he learns that I'm here, he'll work twice as hard just to get rid of me."

Kari eyed Scott suspiciously and then offered a laugh and a swat to Scott's knee. "Stop that." Kari seemed a hundred pounds lighter now that the weight of secretly caring for someone as stubborn and guarded as Brian was finally shared with the only other person who could know what that felt like. "He loves you."

"I know." Scott returned his gaze to his brother's handsome face. "I always wanted to be like him. So handsome... all the girls loved him." Scott looked back at Kari's tear-streaked face. "I'm glad he has someone again." Scott laughed inwardly as Kari blushed and looked at the man she loved. "Does anyone know what happened?"

"I'm only the Chinook pilot, but," Kari offered a brief shrug, not taking her eyes off of Brian's face or her hand out of his. "From what I gather, he was clawing his way to another—" Kari stopped and looked over at Scott. "Sorry, clawing is when—"

"You're in one tree and throw a hook to another tree and rappel over." Scott smiled wickedly. "I grew up in a logging family, remember?"

Kari held a finger to her temple, an imitation of a gun, and pretended to squeeze the trigger. "I haven't slept in almost two days."

"Since they brought him in?"

"That's right." Kari wiped at her eyes again and continued her explanation. "He was clawing his way to another tree and the claw released and he swung back—" Kari's handkerchief came up to her eyes again.

"I'm sorry, Kari." Scott took hold of her hand again and squeezed. "I get the idea. That's how our father died." Kari offered him a brief, knowing glance. "He told you that too?" Scott smiled and swatted at his brother's foot. "Give him time, Kari. He's learned to be very distrustful of women. Our mother... Jennifer...." Scott let his voice trail off, no further explanation necessary. Brian had already told her about the most difficult moments of their childhood. If he ever woke up and wasn't as stubborn as before, Scott figured he'd be going to a wedding soon. *It's about fucking time,* he thought to himself before all hell broke loose in the hallway.

CHAPTER 3

"WHAT the hell?" Scott kept his voice low but his tone menacing as he exited the room to see three men in the midst of some sort of struggle. "This is a—" Scott's voice trailed off as one of the bigger men turned to glare at him. "Roddy?" Scott's smile betrayed the intended pissed-off look that he'd planned since hearing the noise. "I should have known that you'd be in the middle of this."

"Hey, Scoot!" Roddy advanced on the shorter man and swept him up in his arms, obviously oblivious to the fracas that he been creating in the hallway. "Still weigh nothing, I see." Roddy put Scott back down and held him by his shoulders. "Don't have grocery stores in Toronto?"

"Fuck off," Scott whispered before turning to look at the other men. "What the hell is all the noise out here?"

"Doesn't matter now." Roddy fixed one of the men, a tall, handsome, panicked-looking man about six foot three, with a menacing stare and stated, "Hank was just leaving, weren't you, Hank?"

Scott looked over at the man, already feeling sorry for him. If this Hank had to work with Brian and Roddy, it was no wonder he looked as if he'd just found out that all the beer companies had decided to start manufacturing tea.

"Do you work with Brian as well?" Scott started to worry when Hank only nodded. What had the fight been about?

"Yeah, he works with us. Brian wouldn't even *be* here if it weren't for him." This from one of the shorter men—shorter than Scott, anyway. "We were just gonna show him the door."

"Why?" Scott found himself moving toward Hank, and he wasn't sure why. "You don't have to leave, Hank."

"Found the fucker fast asleep right beside where Brian was hanging up in that tree." The smaller man was ugly when he was angry. "Didn't even wake up with all the commotion of getting Brian choppered out."

"I'm sorry," Hank looked as if he was ready to cry. "I'll go. I don't want any trouble."

"Yeah," Roddy spat, "and may as well get your gear and clear out before Brian wakes up."

Scott watched, still not fully understanding what was going on. "How, precisely, is any of this Hank's fault?" Scott directed the question to Roddy and held up his hand to the smaller man when he tried to answer for Roddy. Scott watched helplessly as Hank hung his head and began to walk away. "Hold on, Hank. I'm still waiting for an answer."

"It's okay, sir, I don't want any trouble."

"Did you want to see my brother?" Scott smiled as Hank nodded.

"Listen, Scoot—"

"What, are we back in elementary school? It's Scott, thank you." Scott crossed his arms over his chest and glared at Roddy. "Can anyone tell me what Hank did?" Scott counted to ten in his head. "No? Then I guess all the fighting was for nothing." Scott spread his arms out beside him. "You created a scene and can't even tell me why?" Scott saw that Hank had moved away down the hall, and fairly quickly. Scott started walking to catch up to Hank, calling over his shoulder to Roddy and the smaller man, "This isn't over, Roddy. Nice to see some things don't change." Scott ensured he maintained eye contact with both men so that his message would not be lost on either.

"Hank, wait!" Scott glared back at a nurse who shushed him and kept walking as fast as he could. "Please, Hank?" Scott finally caught up to him by the exit. "Holy shit, you walk fast!" Scott held on to Hank's arm as he leaned over and caught his breath. "And I don't even smoke!"

"I don't want any trouble, Mr. Alan."

"So you've said." Scott looked up from his bent-over position and smiled. "And call me Scott." He blew out a final breath and stood upright. "Anyone who can get Roddy that pissed off is someone I want as a friend." Scott cringed at the look that crossed Hank's face and took hold of his arm again. "Hank, please. How could you have had anything to do with it? You were asleep, for fuck's sake." Scott let go of Hank's arm, missing the heat at once, and motioned to a bench. "Please?" Hank finally acquiesced and moved to sit on the bench beside Scott. "I'm sorry about them." Scott offered an apologetic tone. "I've known Roddy almost all my life, and he can be a stubborn piece of shit." He became pensive. "The other guy—"

"Hughy."

"Thanks. *Hughy.*" Scott spat out the name and looked back at Hank with a smile. "Well, Hughy reminds me of all the overgrown chimpanzees—with the brains to match—who used to harass me during school. I've decided not to like him." That observation got Scott a smile from Hank. "You're not really going to let them blame you for this, are you?"

"Didn't think it was my fault, but…." Hank shifted on the bench, trying to get his large frame comfortable on something that wasn't made for men his size. "I was asleep. Maybe that was the problem."

"Please," Scott thumped him on the shoulder, realizing how built he was. "My brother and father take naps out there all the time, or I should say, my father used to take naps out there all the time…. Or maybe they both used to…." Scott stopped, shook his head, and tried again. "Anyway, the point is that whatever my brother did, he chose to do." Scott offered his hand. "Not your fault, okay?" Scott felt the roughness of Hank's hand in his and felt heat slam into his face. "Come back in with me?" Hank nodded and stood up from the bench. "If they say anything, you let me deal with them, yeah?" Another nod.

Scott looked over at Hank a few times on their way back to intensive care; he was really upset by all this, Scott could tell. *Stupid pricks*, Scott wanted to yell. *How could you say something like that in front of the man?* Shaking his head as he rounded the corner, he noticed that Hank was falling farther and farther behind. He saw that Sheila, the nurse, had gotten the unruly gang under control. It wasn't until Sheila moved that Scott noticed Kari out in the hall with the other two men.

"Hey, Kari," Scott said as he touched her shoulder. "I'm just going to let Hank here in for a few minutes so he can say his piece to Brian." Scott fixed the other two men, especially Roddy, with a defiant glare and gently pushed Hank towards the room. "Go on, it's okay. No one is blaming you." Scott turned back to Roddy. "Right, *boys*?" Scott smiled inwardly as Roddy looked away in disgust and the smaller man stood, cursed, and began walking toward the exit.

When Hank had gone in and closed the door behind him, Scott rounded on Roddy. "And you call yourself a man?"

"Hey, Scoot, what the—"

"I don't want to hear it." Scott pointed back at the room. "He's a person, Roddy." Scott hissed at the downcast look that Roddy had adopted. "How could you? My brother is in there, and maybe Hank played some part in that, but we both know how stubborn and rash my brother can be, so just let it go." Scott planted himself in the chair between Kari and Roddy. "Accidents happen, you know, especially when you're a stubborn perfectionist like Brian. It's not like, even if Hank did something, he did it on purpose."

"He's a fuck-up, Scoot." Roddy had tried to whisper these last words, but Scott turned at the whooshing sound that the door made. Hank was standing there, his expression just as pained as before. Scott closed his eyes as he realized that Hank had probably heard. "He's always showing up drunk or hung over, not checking the DBH, so we have to do twice as much work—"

Scott looked away from Roddy to see Hank moving quickly down the hall, and Scott found himself on his feet, chasing Hank for the second time. Scott finally caught up to him, but Hank's reaction was much different from before.

"Just leave me alone, okay?" Hank stood outside the hospital, pulling his arm out of reach so Scott couldn't grab it this time, his mood hardening into defiance. "They're never gonna stop blaming me for shit, so just let it go, okay?"

"No." Scott tried to make himself feel taller. "No, I don't think I will." Scott raised his eyebrows, daring Hank to take him on, just as he'd done with his father so many times. "Did you have a good visit?" Hank nodded and looked down at his boots. "Listen, Hank, I know my brother, and there is no way he would ever blame someone for making a mistake."

Scott moved a little closer to Hank when an orderly pushing a wheelchair opened the automatic doors and moved past them. "Just give it time, okay?" Scott smiled wryly. "I don't know if you've noticed, but these loggers can be a little stubborn and passionate about stuff."

"I've noticed, yeah." Hank offered a small smile. "I should get home."

"Promise me you'll come back to visit?" Hank turned as he walked and offered Scott a salute. "If you don't, I'll come and find you." Scott held up his fists. "And then I'll have to embarrass myself by showing you I can't fight." Scott noticed Hank give a little chuckle and walked off to his truck. *Doesn't seem like a fuck-up to me. A little shy, maybe, but not a fuck-up.*

Scott made his way back into the hospital, wondering what Hank's story was. Scott often found himself observing people and making up stories or poems. They made good material for his songs—both the people and the stories. He'd left home when he was eighteen and headed first to Calgary and then to Toronto, determined to make a success of himself both as a singer and a songwriter. It had taken him almost twenty years, but he'd done just that. His songs were being sung by some of the biggest names in the business. Hell, some of the biggest names in the business were even commissioning songs from him. He had more than enough money in the bank and a nice group of guys he played with regularly, although he was never really fond of the name they'd chosen for themselves: Dragonfly. He'd tried to have it vetoed—who wouldn't?—but he'd lost the battle in the end.

Scott found no one in the hall and returned to Brian's room to see Kari alone beside Brian. "Where'd Roddy go?"

"He was pissed, so he went home."

"At me, I hope?" Scott slumped into the chair. "I swear if he does anything to Hank, I'll—"

"Hank is a bit of a wild man, Scott." Kari took her hand from Brian's and wiped at her eyes again. "I know it's not nice to say, but I wouldn't be surprised to learn that Hank—"

"Oh for chrissakes," Scott huffed, "if I have to take on every one of you, I will." Scott leaned forward, suddenly feeling very tired and angry.

"Even if he did, it was an accident, right?" Scott rubbed his hand over his face. "He didn't mean to hurt Brian."

"Of course not," Kari sighed. "But meaning to and actually doing don't make much difference to these guys."

"Well," Scott countered, "from what I remember of these guys, they used to support and help each other." Scott eyed Kari warily for a moment, wondering just how much Brian had told her. "Listen, Kari, I know Roddy and I know my brother. My brother has turned out to be very similar to our father." Scott held up a hand when he thought Kari might protest at the comparison. "I'm not talking about the drinking or the attitude, but I am talking about the stubbornness, the inability to see past what is right at the end of his nose. He's not a liar, but I've seen him be belligerent to people just because he thought they deserved to be knocked down a peg or two." Scott stopped for a moment and gathered his thoughts. "And Roddy? Well, I'm sure I don't need to tell you how much growing up that asshole needs to do."

"Brian has often said that you take after your mother." Kari laughed a little, tension easing out of her jaw and forehead. "Roddy?" Kari nodded. "He can be a bit of a loose cannon."

"I've never been fond of the gossip, but I will tell you this." Scott leaned forward a little and whispered, "When Brian wakes up, make sure to get him to tell you about his and Roddy's high school graduation." Scott waved his hand in the air and leaned back in his chair, knowing that if he had to tell the story, it would be the end of him. "Now!" Scott swatted playfully but lightly at Brian's leg again and started listing his inventory. "The doctors are hopeful. He's got me, and he's got you...." Scott stopped and lifted his hands, palms up, in front of his chest. "He'll be back telling us all what to do in no time."

"I hope so, Scott." Kari stroked Brian's hand gently, as if her mere presence would somehow revive him. "I have so much to tell him... even if he doesn't feel the same way." Kari looked over at Scott. "What was I so afraid of? So what if he doesn't feel the same way."

Scott suddenly realized something. "Um, I don't mean to be rude, but didn't you say you have a son? Shouldn't you go and see if he's okay or something? I can stay, and I'll call if there's a change."

"Justis is eighteen already." Kari didn't take her eyes of Brian this time. "He's in university. In Calgary."

"Eighteen?" Scott whistled. "When did you have him, when you were twelve?"

Scott delighted in the first real laugh from Kari since he'd arrived. "I was nineteen. Married my high school sweetheart and got pregnant right away." Kari's mood brightened a bit, or so it seemed to Scott. "First mistake in a marriage o' plenty."

"The husband or the pregnancy?" Scott laughed.

"The... Brian?" Kari was off the bed in an instant, leaving Scott to wonder if he'd overstepped his bounds. And then he saw his brother's eyes open.

CHAPTER 4

"HEY, big brother." Scott stood on the other side of the bed from Kari. "You didn't tell me you got married." Scott watched as his brother's eyes fixed on Kari and a smile ghosted across his lips.

"You had us worried, Brian." Kari's voice was barely a whisper. She was obviously struggling to keep herself together. "Can you talk? Do you want some water?"

"What happened?" To Scott's ears, his brother's voice sounded raspy and weak. "What are you doing here?"

"I wasn't expecting a fanfare or anything, but how about a 'Hi, how you doing?'" Scott leaned over the railing and planted a big, soft kiss on his brother's cheek. "Do you want us to get the doctor? Are you in any pain?"

"Don't... know," Brian struggled to get up, but Scott held him in place. "Jesus, my head. What happened?"

"Actually, we were hoping...." Scott looked over at Kari, who couldn't take her eyes of Brian's face. "We were kind of hoping you could tell us. Seems Roddy and Hughy are about ready to lynch Hank."

"What?" Brian looked from Scott to Kari, his gaze finally settling back on Scott. "What are you talking about?"

"Never mind." Kari said and cast a pleading look at Scott. "You need to rest."

"I'm going to go find the doctor or the nurse." Scott gave a sly grin to Kari and squeezed his brother's hand. He slipped out the door, retrieved his cell phone from his pocket, and headed outside to check his messages. He'd told his bandmates surprisingly little before he left, but now that Brian was awake and seemed out of danger, he decided he should call and let them know. He waited until he cleared the inner doors before turning on his cell phone, hoping the cool morning air would help to relax him. He'd almost finished dialing when he shut his phone again and approached the lone figure sitting on the bench, his head in his hands. "Hank?"

Hank turned, startled like a deer, and looked up. "Sorry, I couldn't sleep."

Scott could see that Hank had been crying. "You don't have to apologize to me." Scott slid onto the bench beside the big man and reached out tentatively to rest a hand on his shoulder. "Brian's awake." The look of relief that spread across Hank's face at that moment made Scott smile and stroke Hank's upper arm. "It's okay, Hank. He'll be okay."

Scott was startled for a second when Hank's meaty hand came up and covered his. As Hank leaned back against the metal rails that formed the back of the bench, Scott heard him sigh and, Scott assumed, let go of all the anxiety and frustration the last few nights had brought him. "Have you slept at all since the accident?"

"Not really."

"You need to get some rest, Hank." Scott took his hand back and stood up facing Hank. "He'll be fine. Go home, let your wife or your girlfriend make you a nice breakfast—at," Scott checked his watch, "five o'clock, and then get some sleep. Okay?" Scott studied the haggard expression on Hank's face and stopped to consider his suggestion. "Do you have anyone to take care of *you*, Hank?" Scott hoped that the answer was yes, but he somehow had the impression that Hank didn't let people in all that easily.

"No," Hank shook his head and looked down at his hands. "There's no wife or girlfriend." After a few awkward moments, Hank looked up quickly and then back down at his hands and added, "I live alone."

Scott saw Hank's shoulders slump a little, and his heart broke a little for the poor man. *With friends and coworkers like those, it's no wonder Hank was alone during this crisis.*

"Okay, look," Scott started, clapping his hands together and waking himself up a little more in the process. "Here's what we're going to do." Scott pointed to the hospital entrance. "I'm going to go talk to a doctor, if I can find one, and then you're coming home with me. I'll make us a big breakfast, and then you can crash. How does that sound?" Scott kept his smile bright and his mood cheerful. The thought of this guy not having anywhere to go except a lonely apartment made Scott want to take care of him. "No arguments. That's what we'll do. Don't go anywhere, okay?" Scott didn't wait for Hank to argue. He walked back into the hospital and went to find a doctor.

After almost fifteen minutes of searching and ten minutes of trying to convince the doctor to use much smaller words, Scott was able to put his mind to rest about his brother's condition and any possible complications. The doctor made it clear that Brian would be required to stay in the hospital for at least another two days so that some final tests could be done to ensure that there would be no permanent damage. The doctor was certain that Brian would have a nasty bump on the side of his head but was not concerned about anything more than a really bad headache for a couple of days. Of course, the doctor was quick to add, Brian should be kept away from operating heavy machinery and from driving for at least a week or two until the medical professionals had gauged his recovery as sufficient.

Armed with the information, Scott checked in one last time with Kari and Brian, smiled ebulliently as he saw them both sleeping, Brian in the bed and Kari in her chair, and wrote them a little note explaining where he would be and when he would be back at the hospital, being sure to let Brian know that he'd taken his house keys. *Even without me, Brian will have a lot to look forward to during his recovery*, Scott thought happily as he looked over at Kari. *Maybe she can even cook.* He cringed as he remembered his teenage years and Brian's cooking.

HANK was where Scott had left him, although he had decided to stand and stretch his legs for a bit. Muttering his apologies for having taken longer than anticipated, Scott pointed out his rental truck to Hank and told Hank to get in. It took a few more minutes to squash Hank's protests about needing a ride, but Scott wouldn't hear of Hank driving in his overtired state. "Besides," Scott pointed out as he pulled the truck out of the parking lot and headed to Brian's house, "I need someone to help me with all of this luggage and my musical equipment."

Scott had to rely on Hank's directions to Brian's house, Scott not having been back for a visit since just after Brian sold the family home and moved to the new subdivision in Duncan. He'd been somewhat saddened at first about the loss of the family home but had finally realized that with Brian being on his own, there really wasn't any reason that Brian shouldn't start over fully. Jennifer had never really been happy in the house where Scott and Brian had grown up, constantly complaining that it was too small and that there was never enough closet space, something that had never worried either brother. Brian was far too fond of jeans and flannel, and Scott had never really been one for spending money he didn't have on five pairs of jeans and a few drawers full of sweaters when one or two of everything would suffice. Scott had never considered himself or Brian cheap; they were just frugal, thrifty even.

"Okay," Scott smiled over at Hank when the truck came to a stop in the driveway. "You pop the cover on the truck bed, and I'll get the house unlocked." Scott climbed down out of the cab and shut the door, calling over to Hank, "I'll be back in a minute to help you." Hank didn't say much, and Scott figured it was because he was so tired. Hank only nodded and set to work. Scott got the door unlocked, flipped on some lights and headed back to help Hank.

"How long you staying?" Hank hefted two of the big suitcases over the side of the truck bed and then reached back in for the long, rectangular black case. "What kind of guitar is this?" Hank was holding up the long, rectangular case that housed Scott's keyboard and seemed to be studying it carefully as if it were some foreign object that he had never seen before. He seemed wary of it, not certain whether it would bite him or just hiss at him.

"The kind with black and white keys," Scott teased, and was pleased to see a small smile spread across Hank's tired face. "It's my keyboard." He bent over to grab the two larger suitcases and grunted as he lifted them. "Kari called me in the middle of the night and told me Brian was in the hospital. My mind wasn't really working right, so I just threw a bunch of crap into the suitcases. I didn't really know how long I'd be staying." Scott nodded toward the house, feeling like his arms were coming out of their sockets from the weight of everything he'd brought with him. "Now that I know he's going to be fine, I feel kind of silly that I brought all this stuff."

"Sorry." Hank made his way to the house, his smile fading slowly as he stopped a few feet from the back door to the house, causing Scott to stop quickly behind him. "You sure this will be okay with Brian?" Hank turned and looked at Scott, who was loaded down with the two suitcases and his leather messenger bag half-filled with unfinished songs he'd tried working on during the flight. "I mean, I'm not even sure I still have a job." Hank started moving again, backing up into the foyer, and put down the case and the one suitcase he had been holding under his arm.

"Hank, listen to me." Scott put his items down beside Hank's load and stood up straight, trying to offer Hank a solemn and meaningful answer. "If you've worked with my brother for long, you'll know that he can be a real pain in the ass, but you'll also know that he's fair and doesn't hold grudges." Scott closed and locked the back door to the house, turned off the foyer lights, and pointed up the stairs. "So, quit worrying about it until it actually happens, okay?"

"Not as easy as you make it sound, Scott." Hank followed as Scott led him to one of the spare bedrooms. "How can you be so sure?"

"Listen to me." Scott took a deep breath and smiled as he heaved one of the suitcases onto the bed and took the other one from Hank. "I've known Roddy all my life, and if he could be forgiven for some of the shit he's caused my brother over the years, you won't have anything to worry about." Scott clapped Hank on the shoulder and pointed to the other spare room. "Now, take off your coat, go wash up, and I'll meet you in the kitchen."

"Why are you being so nice to me when Brian could just turn around and say it's all my fault?" Hank was removing his coat slowly, his face a study in confusion as he stared at Scott. "I mean, I appreciate what you're trying to do and all, but—"

"I'm nice to everyone." Scott smiled and offered a wink. "Although, I'll tell you that what Roddy and what's-his-face pulled at the hospital has me rethinking opening the door to them." Scott pointed towards the bathroom. "Now, go wash up and meet me in the kitchen."

Scott watched for a second as Hank threw his coat into the third bedroom and walked slowly, dejectedly into the bathroom. Hank didn't bother closing the door, and when Scott heard the water running, he headed for the kitchen. He was pleasantly surprised to find a mostly full fridge with enough ingredients to make bacon, eggs, and hash browns. They wouldn't be real hash browns, though, more like quartered baby potatoes baked in the oven. Scott knew he didn't have the energy for making real hash browns. He didn't know if they had a proper culinary name, but he just called them hash browns anyway.

As he prepared the skillets and the cookie sheet for the bacon and the hash browns, he thought again of calling Toronto. He did the math to figure out how many hours ahead they were and figured that three hours' time difference meant that the boys were probably up already. And if they weren't, too bad.

He fixed the eggs and covered the skillet while he waited for the bacon and potatoes, pulling out his cell phone again and dialing. Both Jake and Marc lived in the same house as Scott, so he would be able to let both of them know with one phone call. Jake picked up on the third ring.

"Hey, Jake, it's Scott.... Yeah, everything is fine here. Nothing major, looks like just a bump on the head, no stitches or concussion, so.... No, didn't get any sleep on the plane; too worried. Don't know how long yet, but I'll call as soon as I have a better idea. Well, you want me to call Rankin and see if he can fill in on those gigs?" Scott checked the oven as he chatted with Jake about some of the upcoming gigs next week—gigs that Scott would probably miss—and turned when he heard the footsteps. "Let me figure it out. I promise you won't lose any gigs, okay? Listen, I've got to go.... Yeah, thanks for letting him know for me. Okay, I'll call you later today." Scott pocketed the cell phone and looked over at Hank, giving him a big smile. "Well, you look better."

"I'm sorry about your gigs." Hank sat at the table. The look on his face seemed to reinforce Scott's idea that Hank was usually the scapegoat for Roddy's and what's-his-name's frustrations. Scott couldn't put his finger on anything at that moment, but he had the feeling that Hank's still waters ran deep. He just knew that there was something under any swagger or bravado that Hank had shown his colleagues. Scott was willing to bet big money on that.

"Hey." Scott waved a hand in the air. "Don't worry about anything, okay? I'll figure it out." Scott checked the oven and then leaned against the counter. "Besides, I'm glad to be away from there for a while. Kind of gets to me sometimes."

"Must be exciting, though, living in Toronto." Hank blinked a few times and held his hand over his mouth when a yawn overtook him. "I mean, all those clubs, all the girls?"

Scott didn't know what to say. He'd always known he was gay and had never thought of Toronto as a place where his social life would improve. He didn't live downtown and didn't go to the clubs, except to those where he was performing. In lieu of a proper response, Scott just shrugged and asked Hank if he wanted juice or coffee.

"Juice is fine." Hank yawned again and chuckled a little when Scott looked over at him. "Sorry, didn't know I was so tired."

"Up for two whole days with no sleep and all that guilt eating at you?" Scott opened his eyes wide and turned to get the juice out of the fridge. He poured two big glasses that he'd found in the dish drainer beside the sink and put the glasses and the juice carton on the table. "I'm surprised I didn't find you asleep on that bench." Scott returned to check on the oven.

"I really appreciate you being so nice to me, man." Hank lifted his glass as if in a toast and drank half of it before setting it back down.

"Pffft." Scott shrugged exaggeratedly, as if the conflict that had prompted the invitation had never happened at all. "Couldn't stand what they were saying back there—and right in front of you." Scott stooped one more time and retrieved the potatoes and bacon from the oven. Sprinkling some salt and pepper on the potatoes, Scott found two plates in the cupboard and loaded them up, Hank's more than his own. "There," Scott announced as he put the steaming plate in front of Hank. "You want toast?"

"No, thanks." Hank protested softly and then added, "This is good." Scott put the extra bacon onto a plate lined with paper towels and tried to remember where the cutlery was hidden. He found the drawer with the knives and forks, took out two of each, handed one set to Hank, and then sat down.

"Man oh man," Scott groaned. "I had no idea how tired my feet were until I sat down just now." Scott picked up his fork and scooped up some eggs, stopping just short of his mouth. "What's wrong?"

"Don't know what I'm gonna do if I lose this job."

Scott put his fork back down on the plate and took a deep breath. "Do me a favor, Hank?" Scott felt a little guilt that maybe he'd not listened intently enough, had maybe been too flippant with Hank's concerns. Who knew, really? Maybe Brian *would* fire him. "Eat, get some sleep, and then we'll worry about it later, okay? You need some sleep, man. You're worrying over nothing."

Hank pushed his fork around the plate a few times, finally spearing some eggs and popping them into his mouth. "'S good, Scott."

Scott sighed silently. Hank might actually take his advice this time and leave him alone. He shrugged—amazed at the feelings Hank stirred in him—finished chewing, and then smiled at him. "Well, thanks, but it's kind of hard to screw up scrambled eggs or bacon."

Hank snuffed a little laugh at that comment. "Funny, I manage most days."

Scott's laugh came out like more of a snort, and he chewed a little more slowly. There was something that drew him to Hank. He didn't know whether it was because of Hank's expression, the kind that told the world he felt defeated or misunderstood, or whether it was because he had the impression that Hank would normally be the life of the party, but Scott found himself feeling for him. He studied the slumped shoulders, the drawn and fatigued features that, at any other, happier time, would probably sparkle and shine. He wanted to know more about this man.

"This going to get you in trouble?" Hank had practically inhaled his eggs and was finishing his last piece of bacon. Scott reached over to the kitchen island and grabbed the plate of extra bacon. Tilting the plate over Hank's, he let the remaining strips slide off, smiling to himself as Hank blushed a little at the attention and nodded his thanks.

"No." Scott put the empty plate back on the island's granite counter and turned back to smirk at Hank. "Would you be upset at your brother for helping someone?"

"'S different." Hank folded a piece of bacon and popped it, whole, into his mouth. "Don't have a brother."

"Sisters?"

"Two."

"Older?"

"Younger."

"So," Scott grinned at having pried this much information from Hank. "You're the eldest?" Hank nodded and finished his orange juice.

"Here," Scott reached for the carton and refilled Hank's glass with juice. "Are you from here?"

"Thanks." Hank took a healthy swig of his juice and wiped his mouth with the back of his hand. Scott felt a tinge of guilt. He could hear his mother's voice reminding him that he should have found some napkins and put them out for a guest. "From Coquitlam, originally."

"How'd you end up on the island?" Scott got up and took the paper towel roll off its holder and returned to the table, offering Hank a couple of squares. "Doing this, I mean."

"Never wanted to do anything but this." Hank gave a bashful shrug to his shoulders. "Work outside with my hands, out in the open air."

"Did you always want to be a logger?" Scott put his fork down and crossed his arms over each other on the table.

Hank ate the last of the bacon, finished his juice, and leaned back in his chair, rubbing his stomach. Scott couldn't help but look down, admiring the trim waist and big hands. They were large with long, thick fingers and just the right amount of hair. Scott pulled his eyes back up when he realized where he was staring.

"Not specifically. I started out as a logger, mainly summers, then started working for fire and rescue, and then one day, I dunno, I guess I thought this would be more exciting." Hank stood and collected his plate and cutlery and held his empty hand out for Scott's, giving him a satisfied look. "Only fair I clean up."

"No, you should go sleep now." Scott took Hank's plate from him, grateful that Hank had told him so much in one sentence but regretting the look of embarrassment on Hank's face. *Maybe I shouldn't be asking so many personal questions.* "I'll clean up." Scott was grateful that he didn't have to fight Hank on this one, suddenly feeling a little drained himself. Food always did that to him. "What time should I wake you?"

"Don't worry about it." Hank shrugged as he headed out of the kitchen and stopped at the hallway entrance. "If I get up, I'll just head home."

Scott felt a little bit panicked at the thought of being alone in the house. There was still so much he wanted to learn about Hank. "Are you sure? You don't have to go. I grill a mean porterhouse." Scott dragged out the last word, an enticement that Hank would surely not be able to resist. "But hey." Scott laughed to break the tension. "No pressure, right?" Scott turned but suddenly realized something. "Oh, Hank? I forgot to ask. Do you need something to sleep in? Oh, and throw your clothes out on the floor there. I'll be doing some of my own laundry." Scott lifted his arm a little and pretended to get a whiff of something awful. "May as well do it all together."

"Sleep in the raw." Hank started to unbutton his shirt. "But I'll take you up on the wash. The machine at my place has been broken for a couple weeks now." Hank removed the shirt, revealing a well-muscled pair of arms and a wide expanse of chest, all straining against a tight-fitting white T-shirt. As Hank pulled it off and revealed his impressive and hairy torso, Scott felt as if he might drop everything he was holding, the impulse to reach out and touch as strong as his urge to keep breathing in Hank's scent.

"Jeans are okay for now." Hank ducked his eyes as he let the shirt and T-shirt hit the floor, and then he looked back up. "Thank you, Scott." Hank's hand reached up to scratch the back of his neck, his eyes fighting to maintain contact with Scott's. "For everything."

"You're welcome." Scott stood, hands full, smiling at Hank. He couldn't help but feel a twinge of envy for the girlfriend or the wife that Hank would one day have—those beautiful eyes, the long lashes, the slight pinking of skin as he accepted and showed gratitude for any help that was given. *What would it feel like to wake up with those eyes shining down on you? What I wouldn't give to feel those arms close around my shoulders as we watched the game or just sat looking at the stars.*

Scott knew it had not been an easy couple of days for Hank, and he was pretty convinced that Hank probably didn't know how to ask for or accept help, but Scott made sure he was going to do whatever he could to make Hank feel that he had at least one person on his side.

CHAPTER 5

ONCE the dishes were stowed away and the dishwasher began its low, hypnotic whirring, Scott decided to take a shower and clean away a couple days' worth of grime and travel. He quickly sorted through his luggage and found a comfortable pair of sweats and a long-sleeved T-shirt and laid them out on the bed, already looking forward to putting the comfortable clothes on. Scott didn't really consider himself a slob. He could look drop-dead gorgeous if he put his mind to it. No, Scott considered himself one of those function-over-form people; why dress in jeans if all he was going to be doing was lounging and dozing in and out of consciousness for the next few hours? Clean, comfortable, well-worn sweatpants and a loose-fitting cotton T-shirt were to him now what hot chocolate and clean sheets after playing in the snow all day had been to him when he was ten years old. Nothing felt better. Nothing made him feel easier in his own skin.

It felt, despite his brother's accident, as if he were at his secret cabin, the one that only Scott knew about, the one where he went to spend a few weeks every couple of months to do some writing, some relaxing, some soul-searching. He found himself staring absently at the third bedroom, wondering what it would be like to share the cabin with someone, the lazy days sitting around in just shorts during the hot, muggy summers in Muskoka or in front of the fire during the cold weeks he'd spend, alone, around Christmas and New Year's. Of course, Scott was quick to remind himself that he never told anyone about the cabin for a reason, the same reason he'd bought the cabin in the first place. He'd written his first major hit and, although it had been recorded by another singer, had realized how much money there was to be made when movies and television commercials wanted to use the song or even just the melody. He'd made more than half a million dollars off of that one song and had gone straight away looking for a nice secluded place to be by himself, the hassles of living among millions of other people gone for a little while.

It was a nice fantasy, though, thinking that he might want to try another relationship. He hadn't been in one for more than five years, his career and the gigs starting to become too frequent for him to maintain any kind of a normal social life. Scott had found himself spending most of his free time writing songs, sometimes with Jake and Marc, sometimes without. The three of them had become somewhat inseparable, their lives intertwined and dependent on each other. They were good friends, but they were also roommates, something that Scott would always be very grateful for. The three of them understood each other, and Scott was always a little wary of introducing anything into that particular mix that might change the dynamic. Jake and Marc were straight and didn't have a problem living with a gay man, but still, Scott didn't want to push things. He was happy with the arrangement. It gave him plenty of time, something he definitely needed now so that he could finish the musical. Each of them—he, Marc and Jake—had decided, for now anyway, to concentrate on their music, both collective and individual, and the gigs.

Which reminds me, Scott sighed as he dried himself off and reached for the sweats and the cotton T-shirt. *I have to call Rankin to see if he can fill in for me.*

He headed out to the kitchen again, trying to put enough distance between his voice and Hank so as not to wake the poor man up, and checked to see if he had Rankin's number on speed dial. After a couple of rings, Scott found himself leaving a message for the other singer to call him back as soon as possible, listing a few of the dates for the upcoming gigs.

Scott would never admit it to anyone, but he'd always felt a little jealous of Rankin. The guy was about ten years younger and was a trained singer, gifted with an amazing range and capable of singing any kind of song someone could throw at him. Scott was a great interpreter of songs, but Rankin was a true singer. Where Scott got by on pulling people into the feel of a song, Rankin was able to wow them with a clarity and purity of tone that Scott could only dream of. In fact, Scott had thought many times of asking Rankin to take his place in the trio permanently in order to focus on songwriting full time.

But Scott had never gotten around to doing it. He'd always been too—scared wasn't necessarily the right word—hesitant to let go of something that had been such a big part of his life for so long. After all, he'd reasoned, if you don't have something to replace what you lose, then it's kind of stupid to let it go. But with only a couple of big solos and the finale of the musical left to write, Scott was hoping that the musical would be a huge success. It would set him on the road to being able to write full time, for sure.

It seemed to Scott that he'd just disconnected the call when his cell phone started chirping. He spoke to the other singer for about five minutes. Rankin readily accepted the additional gigs and offered to do more. After listening to Scott's explanation that he was looking for more time to devote to writing songs, Rankin very quickly agreed to consider becoming a permanent part of the group.

Scott chuckled to himself over the rapid response, but he knew that, although incredibly gifted, Rankin wasn't what anyone would call a go-getter. He was more of a people person, preferring to spend his time chatting with people, learning about them. Scott had very briefly toyed with the idea of a romance with Rankin but had decided against it, finding that the younger man lacked a certain hunger in his consumption of life. Rankin would make someone very happy one day, but it would never be Scott.

After speaking with Rankin, Scott was quick to call Jake and Marc and let them know that he would be gone for a while and that he had the gigs covered, and that Rankin would be taking his place until further notice. Marc wasn't particularly happy. Rankin didn't read music all that well, so Marc had to play the songs for him and then Rankin would learn them by ear. Scott placated the two, reminding them that it would only be for a few weeks until Brian was on his own two feet again. Scott didn't like lying to them, and it wasn't technically a lie, but he still had some things to sort out in his head before making any final decisions. Dragonfly had been a big part of his life for almost ten years, and he didn't want Marc and Jake to think they'd been abandoned. Still, Scott was growing tired of the grind. He missed having a social life, going out to movies, sitting in a restaurant for hours staring into the eyes of someone special. He hadn't had that for so long that he wondered sometimes if he would be able to hang onto it when it did find its way into his arms.

He turned towards the bedroom, thinking he'd heard Hank's voice. He quickly pocketed his cell phone, wondering if Hank had called him. It sent a little thrill through him to think that Hank would need him for anything. Scott tiptoed down the hallway, not wanting to wake him by barging in, especially if Hank was just grumbling in his sleep. He pushed the door open a little and peeked in. His eyes first saw that Hank was fast asleep, his facial muscles seemingly overactive for someone so sound asleep.

Must be a good dream, Scott smiled and then froze as Hank turned over, the sheet that had barely covered the muscled body falling to Hank's waist to reveal a perfectly tanned and hairy chest, and an equally tanned and impressive belly, flat and heaving, the corded muscles of his abdomen rippling, as it dawned on Scott that it was probably not a dream at all.

Scott felt foolish for not realizing that Hank, during his first sleep in days, would most definitely have some sort of nightmares about what the poor man had come to see as his fault. He felt even worse when he realized he didn't know what to do about it. The little voice in his head told him to back away from the door and go get some sleep of his own, but he knew that wouldn't be happening after staring at this beautiful man half-naked, his head tossing from side to side as he relived something real or imaginary. Finally, Scott made a decision.

He was backing away from the door, closing it gently, when he heard Hank's voice mutter the word "no," followed by some unintelligible gibberish

Scott opened the door and saw Hank sitting up in bed, his hand running over his face. "Bad dream?" He stood in the doorway, expecting Hank to shake it off and tell him he was fine, but he was surprised when Hank looked up and tried to smile for him.

"Yeah, I guess."

"I've got some over-the-counter sleeping pills if you'd like." Scott shrugged, not sure of anything else he could offer. "Can I get you a glass of water?"

"Sure," Hank yawned and moved quickly to cover his mouth. "Thanks."

"No problem." Scott left the door open and moved swiftly through the kitchen, collecting a tall glass and filling it with filtered water from a jug in the fridge. When he returned, he found Hank sitting on the edge of the bed, the sheets pooled carelessly around his waist. Scott flushed a little, the heat moving quickly to his neck and cheeks, as he entered the room and noticed that Hank had nothing on underneath the sheet—the cloth stopped short of covering the far leg.

"Here, hopefully this can get you back to sleep." Scott held out both hands, small blue gel cap in one and the glass of water in the other.

"Cheers." Hank smiled wanly and gulped the cold water, handing the glass back to Scott.

"I'll get you a refill and leave it on the bedside table." Scott turned to go. "In case you need another of either."

"I don't want to be a bother." Hank fixed the sheet around his waist more snugly and looked around the room. "Maybe I should head home before the pill kicks in." His eyes scanned the room, his brow furrowing when he did not seem to find what he was looking for. "Forgot, my clothes are probably still in the wash, huh?"

"You could," Scott conceded. "If you really want to go, I could lend you something?" Scott watched Hank shift a little on the bed, his eyes unable to focus on any one thing for more than a couple of seconds. As he opened his mouth to tell Hank he was welcome to stay, Hank looked at him and shrugged.

"You're sure I'm not in your way?"

Scott was convinced at that moment that Hank didn't really want to leave. Scott couldn't help but think that this must be what it was like to have kids: present them with an option they don't really want and watch as they try to figure it all out in a matter of moments.

"You're welcome to stay, Hank." Scott waited for a moment. "I'll get you those refills, okay?" Scott turned to leave when he saw a slight nod from Hank, but Hank's low, whisper-quiet voice stopped him.

"Scott?"

He turned and offered a sly smile to Hank but didn't say anything. The few moments spent standing in the doorway seemed to be endless, but Scott waited patiently for Hank to say what was on his mind. After what felt like an hour, Hank nodded at Scott.

"For as long as you like." Scott felt a warm shiver spread through him, like the kind he got just before a performance, and added, "I'll wake you up before dinner." Scott backed out of the room, watching Hank stretch back out on the cool sheets, and closed the door. *What is it about that man that makes me want to protect him, make him feel like he's not alone?*

Scott didn't have an answer to his question, and he wasn't necessarily bothered by the fact that he found himself going out of his way to protect a man who was as straight as they came, no possibility of anything other than a friendship. But as he sauntered back to the kitchen to refill the glass and to palm another sleeping pill, Scott found a little comfort in the fact that it would only be a friendship, at most. What with Brian coming home in a day or two and the burgeoning relationship that his brother would have with Kari—if his brother allowed it, that is—Scott was okay with the idea of having someone for himself during his visit, gay, straight, or otherwise.

He returned to place the pill and the refilled glass, and, as he stood for a moment at Hank's bedside, Scott found a smile creeping across his face. He watched Hank turn on his side, muscled back shifting with his breathing and his hands relaxed on the pillow beside his tanned and rugged, unshaven face. Hank was an outsider here, if the treatment he received at the hands of Roddy and What's-his-name was any indication, just as Scott had been with his music before he left.

He had found himself thinking about that as he drove to the house, familiar sights forcing his brain to recall long-ago events and forgotten people. Perhaps he and Hank would form a friendship while Scott was here. Perhaps Scott would find a kindred spirit in Hank, someone who would understand what it felt like to be the one thing that doesn't belong with the others. Scott chuckled to himself as he rummaged through the freezer and the fridge. Sesame Street and "which one of these things..."— he hadn't thought about that in so many years.

It had not been a difficult childhood by any means. Despite losing their mother when they were still in elementary school, Brian and Scott had been pretty happy children. It wasn't until they were teenagers that their father had started finding comfort in the bottle, not spending as much time with either of his sons as he'd used to. The two brothers had spent many a night, once they had managed to pour their father into bed, discussing what had happened to cause such a drastic change in his behavior. Even years after the death of their mother, neither Scott nor Brian had been able to determine any reason for their father to be so unhappy with his life, and despite many attempts to turn the tide of his drinking, they'd had to watch him drink himself into an early grave.

As he settled on the couch, Scott made a mental note to go and visit Brian before dinner. He hoped that Hank would want to go with him, just to put his mind at ease, but he'd go alone if that's what Hank preferred. All of the activity and the uncertainty of the last few days, his brother being injured, the long flight, the showdown at the hospital, and his inexplicable need to keep an eye on Hank seemed to be catching up to him now. He briefly thought of pulling out some of his music to work on but then decided against it, letting his body sink into the overstuffed cushions of the sofa. The last thought he had before drifting off was of Hank. He hoped that Brian wouldn't confirm Roddy's and What's-his-name's suspicions about Hank being responsible for Brian's injury.

CHAPTER 6

HANK drifted in and out of a fitful sleep. He didn't realize where he was when he awoke several hours later, but a fleeting memory of Scott reminded him of the kindness he'd received. *Weird, that.* Hank smiled to himself, confused as much as relieved. *A perfect stranger going out of his way to help me.* It wasn't the kind of treatment that Hank had been expecting or could remember receiving all that often. It felt good to have someone in his corner, someone looking out for him.

He settled back against the warm sheets, his blunt, square fingers coming up to rest on his muscled chest, idly scratching at an imagined itch. Hank had never been one to look gift horses in the mouth, but he wondered why Scott would do this for him. Hank was accustomed to having girls do whatever he wanted—he knew he was handsome and he knew his way around the bedroom—but he felt a little odd being cared for by another guy.

He was pretty sure that the guy was gay, but Scott wasn't what he'd thought of as *gay*, Hank's only experience being long ago, one drunken night with his co-captain of the football team in high school. Since then, Hank had only come across the odd one here or there in a bar. There was that younger brother of the blonde—*What was her name?*—he'd been seeing last year, but Scott wasn't anything like him. The blonde's brother had this annoying habit of letting his wrists drop or planting a hand on one out-thrust hip. It was creepy and had always made Hank lose focus later on when he was trying to give the blonde a good ride.

Of course, the blonde had teased him over and over that he'd lose focus because Hank was probably really gay and that's why it bothered him so much. He could still see that long, pink fingernail waving in his face while she teased him and taunted him. Hank always figured that she did it to get him to give her the pounding she'd been wanting. Whatever her motives, it was one of the major reasons that Hank had stopped calling her.

He shook his head at the memory of her going down on him before she'd get on all fours begging for it, finding his hand wandering all by itself to his throbbing cock. As he remembered the heat and wet of her mouth, he stroked himself absently, wondering if it was true what she'd always teased—that gay men gave the best head. She said she'd learned a few tricks from her younger brother about satisfying men in bed. Another one of the reasons he'd stopped calling: Who wanted to talk about some chick's gay brother's sex life when he had his tongue halfway up her pussy?

Hank had admitted to himself on more than one occasion that he might be bisexual, and he'd even seen one or two fellow loggers or firemen over the years that got him thinking back to that night in high school, wondering if it *had* been just a one-time thing. But Scott? Physically? Hank imagined that if he was going to try again with a guy, it would be someone big and burly, someone like himself. But Scott had something. There, just under the surface, Hank could see so much more beyond the ready smile and the generosity.

Rolling onto his side, he pulled the sheet up under his chin and found himself wondering what Scott was doing, if he'd managed to get any sleep. He still felt a little guilty about spoiling the man's return home. *Of course, if it hadn't been for me, the guy wouldn't have had to come home to find his brother all busted up.* He shook off that thought as soon as he remembered what Scott had told the guys in the hospital, but he was still nervous about what Brian might have to say about it all. Hank wasn't really looking forward to seeing Brian so soon, but he was pretty sure it would be better to do it sooner rather than later. If he was going to be out of a job, he'd need to start looking.

If Hank was honest with himself—something he tried to avoid at all costs—he'd been considering moving back to Coquitlam and the fire department for the past couple of months. He had no girl, no family in these parts. The only thing that had kept him here for the past ten years was heli-logging. He was a good logger, had been a damn good fireman, but he'd hung on to this job for a lot longer than he'd stayed with the fire department because there was just something about being out in the open air, climbing the two-hundred-foot cypress or cedar trees and topping them. Hank had taken to it faster than anything else he'd ever tried. But he had to admit that his cocky and arrogant attitude, a trait which got him plenty of play with women, didn't seem to go over too well with the other loggers—or firemen, for that matter.

Hank was tired of being labeled as reckless, careless, and too egomaniacal. He was good, probably the best, at most everything he tried, so why shouldn't he live that way? At first, Hank had always assumed it was just jealousy on Roddy's and Hughy's parts, but now, what with Brian being injured, Hank began to think that maybe they'd been right all along. So, as he pushed the sheet away from his torso and moved to sit on the side of the bed, Hank made a promise to the logging gods; *If I don't get fired, I'll show them that I can be the best at everything—logging, safety, all of it.*

He listened for a minute and then stood beside the bed, reaching for his jeans. He would go and get his stuff out of the laundry, wherever it was, thank Scott for being there, and head to the hospital. If he had to eat a little crow to keep his job, that's what he'd do. And after Scott going to bat for him in front of the others—something he couldn't remember anybody ever doing for him—he'd make damn sure that Scott wasn't disappointed in him.

Pulling the door open gently, not wanting to risk waking the man up in case he'd finally managed to fall asleep, Hank wondered what he might be able to do for Scott as a way of saying thanks. If he still had a job—or hell, even if he didn't—he still had another couple of days off. Maybe Scott would like to go camping. Hank hadn't been to the family cabin since his father had passed away last year; maybe Scott would like to go… unless Brian needed him around here. Hank decided to ask Scott later, to make sure the man knew how much he'd appreciated the support and the friendship.

"Hey," Hank whispered when he saw Scott jump up from the couch with a muffled shout. "Sorry, didn't mean to scare you."

"'S okay, Hank." Scott rubbed at his eyes with the palms of his hands and then stood to stretch out the muscles of his aching back. "How you feeling?"

"A lot better, thanks." Hank fidgeted with the waistband of his jeans, hoping this wasn't going to sound like he was asking for a date. "Listen, I just wanted to say thanks to you for being so nice, and—" Hank held up his hand when he saw Scott wave his hand back and forth and open his mouth, ready to object. "I was wondering if, after we see that Brian's okay, you might want to go camping." The words rushed out of his mouth at such a speed that Hank wasn't sure Scott had understood them. He stood waiting for Scott's answer.

Slowly, Scott's lips curled into an easy grin. "Camping as in cabin or camping as in tent?"

"WHICH do you prefer?" Scott was relieved, and a little happy, to see a little playfulness in Hank's expression.

"Tent." Scott did not hesitate. "I have a cabin in the Muskokas, so it'd be a nice change to spend… How long are we planning?" Hank held up two fingers as Scott came around the couch and peered at the clock on the microwave. "Definitely a tent, then," Scott nodded his head vehemently. "I haven't done the tent thing since…I don't when. But listen, I was going to go see Brian in a couple of hours anyway." Scott shrugged and put his hands out, palms up. "Why don't you come along?" No one would have been able to miss Hank's tension level rise dramatically at the question, so Scott reassured him that nothing would happen.

"If you're sure." Hank threw his arms out to the side, as if what he meant to say was that Scott would have to accept the blame for any fallout.

Scott pushed himself away from the counter where'd been leaning. "Okay, you've got five minutes to get yourself presentable." *Like he's not right now!* Scott's libido was starting to get very loud. A couple of days in the wilderness with Hank… Scott couldn't wait. "Unless you want to shower first."

"If you don't mind?" Hank was already unbuttoning his jeans. "Wash away the last couple of days."

"Okay." Scott showed a lopsided smile. "You've got ten minutes."

Hank returned the smile and rubbed the stubble on his cheeks and chin. "How about fifteen, so I can shave too?"

"Hank?" Scott's tone was playful and impatient at the same time. "Do whatever you need to do and meet me out here when you're done." Scott placed his hand on one broad shoulder, the electricity of the touch making him lose focus for a moment, and leaned against Hank's body to push him forward. "Now go, and then I can get your clothes out of the dryer." Scott watched for a few moments while the muscles in Hank's arms and back started doing a little dance beneath the tanned flesh. He looked away quickly, the fear of being caught more powerful than the desire to follow and watch to make sure not an inch of that body was left untouched.

ONCE in the bathroom, Hank shaved quickly, willing his hands not to shake at what he thought would be the upcoming confrontation with Brian. He'd already decided that if he had to eat a little crow, that's exactly what he would do. He just hoped that he wouldn't have to do it in front of Scott. As he let the steam from the hot water soothe his body and his mind, Hank wondered suddenly if the phone call Scott had made about the gigs was to a boyfriend or a lover. And he didn't know why, but that thought left him feeling a little disappointed. Maybe Scott wasn't interested in him. Maybe the attention Scott had been giving him was because Scott was just a decent and generous guy.

With his face smooth and free of a couple of days' worth of stubble, Hank stripped naked and stood under the hot spray of the shower, his muscles soothed but his mind still unable to focus on where, precisely, he wanted all of this to lead. A few moments ago, he was content to wonder just about his job. But as he soaped his tired body, he wasn't really sure that he wanted to settle for just the job now. Hank hadn't had a lot of friends since he'd made the move to the island, and he found himself feeling a little conflicted. Scott seemed to him what a friend was supposed to be, and that made him happy. But Scott also had a life back in Toronto and would eventually go back to it. That thought made Hank decidedly less happy.

After drying himself off with the thick, thirsty towels that made his own look shabby, Hank grew frustrated with himself over these kinds of thoughts. *Scott's not here for you, you idiot.* Hank felt the need to remind himself that he had more important things to worry about than when Scott would go back to his own life. *This,* he scolded himself as he pulled on his boxers, *is why people think you're a screw-up! Focus on keeping your job and not on whether or not Scott wants to be your friend!*

He stepped out of the bathroom in a halo of steam to find Scott in his borrowed bedroom. While he'd been in the shower, Scott had stripped the bed, replaced the linens with a clean set, and was laying out his clean clothes for him on the freshly made bed. As Hank took in the scene before him, he couldn't help but regret not having given over his jeans for washing. They weren't that dirty, but it would have added that little bit more to the thought of climbing into clean clothes after his nice, hot shower.

"Sorry." Hank chuckled and reached out and put a hand on Scott's shoulder when he realized he'd startled the shorter man. "Didn't realize I was so stealthy."

"It's okay." Scott finished laying out Hank's T-shirt and button-down and then tossed Hank his clean socks. "I don't think it's that you're stealthy as much as I tend to zone out far too easily."

"I am sorry, Scott." Hank caught the balled-up socks and worked them open. "I keep thinking that this is all my fault, and then there's your missed gigs, and—"

"Listen, Hank." Scott clapped Hank on the shoulder as he squeezed himself between the door and Hank's muscled frame. "They've done gigs without me before, and what happened to Brian was an accident." Scott smiled as Hank turned and narrowed his eyes exaggeratedly. "Unless you're telling me that you sabotaged his claw?"

"Okay, okay," Hank chortled and pushed playfully at Scott's shoulder. "I'll stop. I'll be out in a couple of seconds."

SCOTT threw himself into the doorframe at Hank's playful push, delighting in the smile that spread across Hank's face. He still wasn't sure what all the fuss was about in regards to Hank being the cause of Brian's accident and didn't really understand how Hank sleeping a dozen yards away could have caused his brother to become so careless. He was determined to find out before the day was over, if for no other reason than to be able to head back to Toronto feeling a little less compelled to be so protective of a man he'd known less than twenty-four hours.

Scott made sure to lock up after Hank had left the house dressed in his clean socks, T-shirt, and button-down and hopped in the rental. When he got in the car, the smells of the laundry detergent, shampoo, and something that must be uniquely Hank hit his senses like a velvet boxing glove, the pleasant and heady aromas forcing Scott's eyes closed as he inhaled deeply. Before fitting the key into the ignition, Scott couldn't help but wonder how sensual it would be to let his nose and tongue trail over every inch of Hank, to let his senses lead him to those tender, sensitive spots where Hank's scent would be the strongest, the most potent.

Before shifting into reverse, Scott adjusted himself in the bucket seat so he wouldn't be so blissfully uncomfortable with those thoughts. He knew he wouldn't be able to control them, so he would have to be content to minimize the discomfort of his groin having a mind—and will—of its own.

They drove mostly in silence, Scott checking his route with Hank every couple of minutes, reassuring himself that he remembered the way to the hospital correctly. Scott couldn't help but notice that when Hank did speak, there was a hesitant, nervous tone to his voice. He didn't know what would happen and couldn't guarantee Brian's forgiveness, if there was anything to forgive, but Scott felt the need to reassure Hank again. So, as he pulled into the visitor parking lot at the hospital, Scott put the car in park and turned to face Hank.

"I don't want you to worry about this, okay, Hank?" Scott resisted the urge to reach out and soothe Hank with a hand to his arm or his thigh, especially when he noticed the big thigh bouncing with nervous anticipation. "I'll help you in any way I can," Scott promised with a smile. "Even if my brother turns out to be as pig-headed as our father."

"Okay."

Scott turned and had his hand on the door, ready to open it when he felt Hank's hand on his shoulder.

"Scott?" Hank hesitated for a moment, his eyes darting to the windshield and back. "I… I want… I was serious about going camping, you know?" Hank didn't seem to be able to look at Scott. Shifting his eyes to the console, he added, "It'll be nice to have… I've never really had a lot of friends."

Scott's heart melted a little at the lost look on Hank's flushed face, and he wondered how much courage it must have taken for some big, bad logger to admit something like that. He reached out and patted Hank's shoulder.

"Well, you've got one now, Hank." Scott winked playfully before exiting the truck. "But I warn you. You may change your mind when you see how useless I am when it comes to pitching a tent or starting a fire."

Hank laughed, relief showing in his green eyes. "Lucky for you I don't have a problem with either."

The walk to the hospital room seemed longer for some reason. Scott wasn't really sure if it was because he hoped he hadn't offered any false hope to Hank or because he was suddenly realizing that Brian might not be as forgiving and trusting as he'd once been. Cursing Brian's bitch of an ex-wife one final time, Scott eased the door open gently, not wanting to disturb Brian or Kari, quite certain that they would both still be fast asleep. He found that his brother was alone. Kari had probably returned home to shower and change her clothes. He turned to smile at Hank, who was only a few inches behind him, giving him a thumbs-up to try to ease the worried expression he found on that handsome face. Both men entered the room slowly, uncertain if Brian's eyes were closed in sleep or in boredom. Scott noticed that the television wasn't on and that, other than Brian's breathing, there were no other sounds in the room.

"Morning." Scott stepped closer to the bed as he saw Brian's eyes open and his head swivel in their direction. "How you feeling?"

"Got a bitch of a headache." Brian smiled up at his brother. "But other than that, I'm good."

Scott moved to his brother's side and took his left hand between his own. "Yeah, the doctor said you'd have a whopper of a headache for a few days." Scott petted his brother's forearm for a moment and then asked, "Has he come in to see you, explain anything to you?"

"This morning," Brian grunted as he tried to sit up further on the bed. "He came in and explained to me and Kari what to expect."

"Where is she?" Scott looked around the room, not seeing any evidence that Kari was nearby. Her purse was gone and the blanket she'd used last night to cover herself was folded neatly on the chair she'd occupied since Brian had been admitted.

"Home. Asleep, I guess."

"Uh huh," Scott teased. "Did she leave on her own or did you send her home?"

"I sent her home." Brian blushed a little at the tone of Scott's question. "She doesn't need to stay and worry about me."

"Even if she wants to?" Scott didn't wait for an answer. He already knew what the answer would be. "I think she's kind of sweet on you, big brother."

"Yeah, whatever."

Scott noticed Brian's gaze shift to the door and turned to see Hank trying to take up as little space as possible. "Hank's here."

"So I see."

Scott couldn't really tell by his brother's tone whether Brian thought Hank's being there in the room was a good thing or not, but he didn't really care. Scott knew that his brother was every bit as stubborn as their father, but he'd made a promise to Hank to help with that, and that's what he was going to do. Patting his brother's forearm one more time, he turned to look at Hank. Scott sighed heavily.

"Okay, then, I've had this awful craving for bad vending machine coffee, so I'm going to go find some and let you two talk." Before he left his brother's side, Scott leaned over the railing of the bed and kissed Brian's cheek, whispering, "He's been worried about you. Give him a chance to explain, at least." He stood back, watching Brian's eyes flit between his baby brother and one of his loggers. Satisfied that his brother wouldn't do or say anything rash, Scott stopped by Hank long enough to give him a warm smile and pat his thick, muscled shoulder. Without a word, Scott hoped to convey his faith in Hank's ability to do or say what he needed to in order to alleviate the guilt that the big man was feeling.

HANK watched as the door closed, his hands rubbing absent-mindedly over the front of his jeans. His eyes turned back to see Brian's restrained glare. *Even if I have to eat a little crow*, Hank reminded himself as he stepped further into the room.

CHAPTER 7

SCOTT sat alone at the little white table just inside the door to the cafeteria and offered his thanks for not hearing any alarms or fist fights coming from the general direction of his brother's room. That must be a good sign. He didn't know how long he'd been sitting there, nursing the same cup of godawful coffee, and wasn't sure if he'd actually been able to come to any conclusions about his brother. Had Brian become ornery enough to take out his current situation on the man whom everyone else assumed had put him there? Or was he was still the same sweet and kind man who'd always looked out for his younger brother? Scott was pretty sure of the answer; his brother would listen to whatever Hank had to say.

He smiled at the random memories of his big brother—how he'd tuck Scott in just as their mom had done and then read him a bedtime story, or how Brian always tried to comfort Scott during the fierce thunderstorms that would blanket the region in the spring and the fall. Scott huffed out a one-note laugh when he remembered how Brian had tried so patiently to teach him how to start a campfire. As he leaned back in the uncomfortable fiberglass chair, his right leg bouncing so fast it made the chair squeak in protest, he was pretty certain that if everything Brian had gone through with Jennifer hadn't changed him, then Hank wouldn't have to worry about a thing.

Scott was so lost in thought that when a hand landed on his shoulder, he just about jumped out of his skin. "Jesus Christ!" Scott muttered when he saw Hank's smiling face looking down on him. "So, from the smile, I'm assuming that you still have a job?"

Hank dropped into the seat opposite Scott and shrugged, the smile still firmly planted on his face. "For now, yeah."

"For now?" Scott couldn't help but notice that his leg wasn't bouncing anymore. He wondered why briefly but pushed the thought away to concentrate on Hank's smile and what it meant.

"Yeah, for now." Hank leaned back in his chair, the squeaking much more noticeable under his imposing frame, and his grin grew even wider. "You were right." Scott leaned forward a little and studied Hank's handsome face, his eyebrows lifting on their own. "He was really cool about it all. I mean"—Hank's hands came up to emphasize his point—"he was pissed, that's for sure, but more at himself than at me."

"Thank Christ!" Scott let out a breath that he hadn't realized he was holding. "I mean, I was pretty sure, but...." Scott finished his coffee, grimacing at the bitter taste the cold seemed to lend to the awful sludge, and stood. "Okay, I'm off to see what my brother needs, and then I'm going home to start dinner." Scott looked up into Hank's emerald green eyes and couldn't help but smile. "You want salad with your porterhouse?"

"Hey, Scott, listen," Hank started. Scott felt his stomach drop as he realized that maybe Hank didn't feel the need to hang around anymore, now that he knew his job and his boss were going to be okay. "I know you've got stuff to do, and I'd only be in the way—"

"Hank?" Scott looked directly into Hank's eyes and felt a little mischief creep over himself. "Are you telling me it's over between us?" Scott grinned up at the reaction he got from Hank, delighting in the slow creep of pink rising up from the big man's neck. He reached out and slapped Hank's bicep. "Dinner is at seven. If I see you, great. If not...."

Scott shrugged and backed out of the cafeteria, wondering if it would be a good thing if Hank didn't show. Scott could work on his songs instead, and that was a good thing, but not having Hank there would make the house feel so empty. He waved at Hank one last time and turned down the hall toward his brother's room, his fingers crossed as he willed Hank to show up for dinner.

"So?" Scott raised his eyebrows as he entered his brother's room. "I don't see any blood, so it must have been a pleasant conversation?"

Brian rolled his eyes and balked. "I don't know if I'd use the word pleasant, but, yeah, he was okay."

"I'm glad." Scott settled himself on the edge of the bed, pushing at Brian's legs. "Remind you of anything?"

Brian laughed a little and then put a hand to his head. "I'm surprised I didn't turn out gay, what with all the time you spent in my bed when we were growing up."

"Hey," Scott protested and pushed his brother's legs some more. "I can't help it if thunderstorms scared me."

"I know," Brian reassured, pushing his knee against Scott's thigh. "I was just teasing."

"I know." Scott looked adoringly at his big brother and put his hand in Brian's. "So, why didn't you tell me you'd gotten married?" Scott let out a few peals of laughter when he saw Brian's cheeks flush and his eyes dart away. "Oh, come on, now. You can't tell me you didn't notice how much she's in love with you."

"I noticed," Brian conceded in a whisper.

"So?" Scott continued to push tenderly against Brian's thigh. "Why did it take this for you to realize it?"

"I guess I've always known, but…." Brian lowered his head slowly to the pillow and looked over at his baby brother. "Well, after Jennifer—"

"That," Scott barked, "was seven years ago."

"Doesn't mean I still don't feel it." Brian's face became somber all of a sudden, and Scott tried to think of something to cheer him up. Before he could think of anything, Brian's hand reached out to cover his. "Remember what it was like when Mom died? How long it took you before you could sleep in your own bed?"

Scott looked down at the big hand covering his and felt his lips curl into a sad smile at the memories that her name brought. "Yeah, I remember." After a few moments, he met Brian's eyes and added, "But that's not the same thing, big brother."

"Maybe not." Brian closed his eyes and sighed, "But it's the same feeling of loss, the same… I don't know… the same feeling of disappointment."

"I know." Scott patted Brian's hand absent-mindedly as he remembered how crushed Brian had been at the failure of his marriage. "But that doesn't mean you stop trying, does it?"

Brian opened his eyes and offered a resigned smile, his words something of a mix of a whisper and a sigh. "No, I guess it doesn't."

"Okay, then." Scott patted his brother's hand one last time and then raised himself off the edge of the bed. "It's settled. I'll get you settled at home, and then you'll invite Kari over for dinner." Scott offered his big brother a wink and then added, "Of course, if you want her to come back for a second date, you'll have to let me cook."

"Fuck off." Brian laughed and then placed a hand on his forehead, his eyes closing at the sudden sharp pain behind his eyes.

"I'm going to go get some more of that lovely coffee. You need anything?"

"Just water."

"Here." Scott reached to the bedside table and found the pitcher empty. He was in the bathroom letting the water run a little colder when he heard Kari's voice just outside the bathroom door. He waited until the pitcher was full before exiting to see Kari's hands stroking Brian's cheek, her face a study of relief and contentment.

"Good morning, Kari." Scott beamed at the flush on his brother's cheeks. "He won't say it, but he missed you."

"Weren't you going to get some coffee?" Brian's glare was a lot less menacing when he had that stupid, lovesick grin on his face. Scott showed Brian his tongue and asked Kari if he could get her anything from the cafeteria.

"Oh, by the way, Kari?" Scott shot over his shoulder as he left to find some more coffee. "Brian was just telling me how much he'd love to have you over for dinner when he gets out of here."

Scott was still giggling to himself over the look in Brian's eyes when he entered the cafeteria. His smile disappeared just as quickly when he found that Hank was still there, seated in the same hard plastic chair, his chin perched on top of his hand as he stared out the window—at what, Scott couldn't tell, but he could see a strange, faraway look on his face.

"Hank?" Scott called, but saw no reaction. "Hank?" Scott's voice was a little louder. Finally, Hank turned, and Scott's chest tightened at the sparkle in the green eyes and the way the smile got a little broader. "I thought you were going home?" Scott lowered himself into the uncomfortable chair again and let himself get lost in the way Hank's eyes never left his.

"Yeah, I was just going." Hank leaned back in the chair and took a deep breath, as if he had just awoken from some sort of dream. "I was just thinking. Kind of got lost in it, I guess."

"Can't be your job," Scott offered casually. "I know you can't still be worried about the others blaming you even if Brian doesn't, but if you feel like sharing or talking it out with someone...." Scott let the thought finish itself and stood up again, certain that what had Hank preoccupied wasn't anything too serious. Scott took a few steps towards the coffee pots at the end of the cafeteria and turned. "Kari's in with him right now. Did you know about them? About Kari's... interest?"

"Hard not to," Hank sighed as he lifted himself out of his chair. "We were all wondering what was taking Brian so long in returning the favor."

Scott shrugged and jerked his head to the side. "Well, once bitten and all that."

"Yeah, I guess." Hank raised his hand as if to say goodbye and then stuffed both of them in the pockets of his jeans. "I'll see you tonight? Seven, you said?"

"Yeah, sure," Scott tried to control the butterflies in his stomach. "Whenever." His heart threatened to beat out of his chest as he saw Hank smile and offer him a wink. He watched Hank walk down the hall and was suddenly reminded of some movie he'd seen once where the man watched the woman walk away. The inner dialogue of the man had claimed that if the woman turned around, she wasn't interested in only friendship. Fidgeting with the coins in his moist, nervous hand, Scott waited to see if Hank would turn around.

When Hank didn't, Scott found himself trying not to care. Turning toward the coffee machine, he counted out the correct change and wondered if he would ever be able to admit to how much he had wanted Hank to turn around. He missed Hank turning to look at him before the tall, handsome logger turned the final corner to the parking lot.

CHAPTER 8

"I KNOW I'm early," Hank huffed as he struggled with the grocery bags in his hands. "Tried going home and getting some sleep, but I started cleaning the place, and before I knew it, I had energy to spare."

Scott wiped his hands on the dish towel, swooping in to take the bags from Hank's hands so he could put them on the counter. Scott wouldn't admit it, but he'd spent most of the day cleaning Brian's house as well, the need to impress Hank becoming a low, insistent whisper in the back of his brain, and even then he'd found the time to finish one of the solos for the musical.

"Here," Scott offered as he tried to get the bags free of Hank's big hand. "Okay, wait... open your hand and let... there you go." Scott laughed a little at the production they'd made of it, and hoped Hank didn't see him blushing because of the prolonged excuse to touch Hank's hand. Scott was never sure why, but he'd always had a weakness for long, blunt-ended fingers with just the right amount of hair on them. Maybe it was because he was a musician and used his own hands for work or maybe because he, in his more indecent moments, would wonder what those kinds of hands would feel like on his sensitive flesh.

"Thanks, Scott." Hank put his remaining bags on the counter with the ones Scott had taken from him and then let out a big breath, his hand coming up to swipe at his forehead. "Guess I could have done it in two trips, huh?"

"What is all this, Hank?" Scott stepped back as Hank started unloading the grocery bags. "You didn't have to bring anything. I've got everything we need right here."

"Ah, perhaps." Hank hummed as he raised his eyebrows inquisitively. "But do you have this?" Hank pulled the plastic bag away to reveal two tall, slender brown bags.

"Brown paper bags?" Scott mocked as he threw his hands up in the air.

"No, smartass," Hank grinned. "This?" Hank pulled the brown bags away to reveal two bottles of wine; Scott saw one white and one red. "Told the lady at the liquor store what I needed them for, and she told me I couldn't go wrong with these."

Hank handed the bottles to Scott and then stood back, so obviously proud of his treasures that Scott didn't have the heart to tell him that he didn't drink wine. "Well, thank you, Hank," Scott said after deciding he'd have to go ahead and have at least one glass with Hank. He didn't want to offend such a nice gesture. Scott turned to place the two bottles on the counter when he heard the bags rustling again.

"Or this?" Hank pulled two loaves of freshly baked bread out of another bag. "I didn't know which you'd prefer, so I just got both of them." Scott took the two loaves, almost laughing now, when he heard Hank clear his throat. "Or this?" Hank produced a large plastic container that housed a thick cheesecake. "It's a cheesecake!"

"I can see that." Scott laughed at the look on Hank's face, as if Hank had been the first person to discover the dessert. "What flavor?"

"Uh," Hank took the container back and studied the label.

"You didn't look before you bought it?" Scott was having difficulty containing his laughter now, unable to think of anything other than what Hank would be like on Christmas morning.

"It says chocolate raspberry and truffle." Hank grimaced a little and looked over at Scott. "Isn't that a mushroom?"

"It's actually a tuber," Scott announced as he carefully stowed the container in the fridge. "And very expensive." Scott stepped back to the counter and regarded his dinner guest with a quizzical look. "Hank, you didn't have to do all of this."

"Needed to thank you somehow." Hank flushed slightly and busied himself with emptying the rest of the grocery bags while Scott stood and looked on, shaking his head slightly.

"Well, this is...," Scott said after a few moments, feeling slightly dumbfounded. "Thank you.... very much." Scott returned to the stove to check on the mashed potatoes. "Of course, you realize," Scott offered over his shoulder, "that neither one of us will be able to move if we eat all of this."

"No worries," Hank said with a distracted air while he tried to fold the paper bags that had housed the wine bottles. "We'll take the rest of it camping or leave it all here for Brian." Hank gave up trying to fold the paper bags and shoved both of them into the plastic bags. "Is Brian going to be okay if you take off for two days?" Hank moved around the peninsula-style counter so that he was eye-to-eye with Scott and not behind him. "I mean, we can postpone if you need to stay here and—"

"Actually," Scott said as he looked over at Hank with a sly grin. "When I went back to the room, Kari was reassuring Brian that coming over and checking on him wouldn't be any problem for her." Scott leaned back against the counter behind him and gave Hank a little smile. "So, being the bratty little brother that I am, I made sure to mention that there is an unused third bedroom, you know." Scott opened his eyes wide as if to say, *What else could I do?* "Just in case she was too tired to go home."

"Oh yeah?" Hank let out a little chuckle, probably at the thought of Scott being so involved in trying to get Brian and Kari together. "What did Brian say to that?"

"Don't know." Scott was laughing now as he picked up the potato masher and set to work. "Didn't stick around to find out."

"I bet you were hell on wheels when you were younger, huh?" Hank had his considerable arms folded over his chest, and Scott couldn't help but wonder whether the hairs covering Hank's forearms would be soft or coarse.

"Me?" Scott responded seriously. "God, no. I was too shy and quiet back then. Scared of my own shadow."

"Really?" Hank guffawed. "I have trouble seeing that."

"Well, that was then," Scott said as he took a little rest from mashing the potatoes. "I've seen a lot and done a lot since then, so there's not too much that still scares me anymore." Scott blew out a lungful of air and started mashing the potatoes again, cursing himself for not letting them boil long enough.

"Here," Hank whispered as he came around to stand behind Scott. "Let me do that before you pass out."

"Hey!" Scott scolded, but he stepped aside just so he could watch the muscles in those forearms flex and relax. "I may not be big like you and Brian, but I can be pretty scrappy, you know."

"Oh," Hank huffed and nodded in agreement. "I have no doubt about that."

"Okay, good," Scott nodded his head once, glad that he'd made his point. "Well, I'll go put the steaks on, then." Scott pushed up his shirt sleeves and turned towards the patio doors. "How do you like yours?"

"Bloody." Hank grunted while he made quick work of the stubborn potatoes. "Did you boil these long enough?"

"You know," Scott mused sarcastically, "in some cultures, guests actually compliment the chef." With his eyes firmly planted on Hank's grinning face, Scott pushed open the patio door, congratulating himself on a perfect exit. And if he hadn't forgotten the lighter on the counter, it would have been. He ignored Hank's boisterous laughter and the teasing glint of those beautiful green eyes when he had to go back to retrieve it.

Standing out by the gas barbecue, Scott found himself wondering about the camping trip; he wasn't sure if it was such a good idea to be alone with this man for two days. Scott didn't know if Hank had figured out his preference yet, but he definitely knew that it would not take him very long to fall for Hank and fall hard. It was more than just caring for him now. There was an easy flow to their conversation, an effortless interaction that came from knowing that there were no expectations other than a friendship. And Scott wasn't sure he wouldn't fuck it up, eventually. He'd never been a hound dog, never chased after anyone before, but then again, he'd never met anyone quite as mesmerizing as the man who was standing in his brother's kitchen.

"Need help with that, too?" Hank stood, with his arms folded over his chest, looking down at Scott as he tried to ensure that he'd been successful at lighting the barbecue. The smile spread across his face, slow and easy, as Scott glared at him.

"Get outta my way, you big tree stump!" Scott pushed past Hank and went to the fridge to retrieve the steaks, forcing himself to ignore the fact that Hank had let his hand fall to the small of Scott's back as he passed. *It doesn't mean anything*, Scott told himself, *just Hank feeling free after the last couple of days worth of stress.* As he headed back to the patio with the steaks, he hoped that that was all it would boil down to, not really sure if he'd have the strength to refuse anything more.

"So, why Toronto?" Hank asked as he turned from studying the view beyond Brian's backyard. "I mean, couldn't you have been able to write songs from Duncan?"

"I guess." Scott concentrated on the sizzle that the steaks made when he laid them over the grill. "But it wasn't so much that I was going to Toronto as I was leaving *here*." Scott turned, empty plate in his hand, and added, "Not that I had anything against Duncan, but... I don't know, I was looking for something else, something... somewhere I could be...." Scott wasn't sure how to finish the sentence he'd started, not really sure anymore why he'd felt such a burning desire to leave his hometown.

"Yourself?" Hank had moved into one of the deck chairs, his intense green eyes focused solely on Scott, who wondered just how much Hank wanted to know about him and, if he found out, just how much he'd miss the guy when he took off. Scott didn't know Hank well enough to judge him, but he did know Hank's type. And Hank's type always had a problem with the queers.

"Yes, where I could be myself," Scott agreed readily. He held up the empty plate and asked, "Can I get you anything?"

"Do you mind if I have a beer?"

"Of course not." Scott squinted at Hank's sheepish grin. "But don't you want any wine?"

"Not really," Hank confessed. "I'm not much of a wine drinker." Scott's laughter gained momentum as he felt his face contort into a twisted mass of clenched muscles. "What's so funny?" Hank looked like he was was still trying to figure out what he'd said wrong when he raised himself out of his chair and walked over to where Scott stood, halfway inside the house and halfway out. "What? Tell me."

"Sorry," Scott sputtered when he could take in a decent breath. "I was wondering how to tell you that I don't really like wine either." Scott's laughter erupted again as he watched Hank's eyes widen and then heard the deep bass voice offer an infectious laugh of its own.

Hank sighed finally, "Well, isn't that a kick in the rubber parts." He followed Scott back into the house.

"So, why did you get *two* bottles of wine, then?"

"I don't know." Hank rounded his shoulders as he pulled out one of the barstools hidden underneath the peninsula overhang. "You just seemed like the classy, wine-drinking type to me."

"Me?" Scott laughed. "Jesus, somewhere, right now, my mother is rolling over in her grave laughing hysterically at the irony of it all." Scott's laughter subsided, and he leaned against the counter to explain. "When I was growing up, my mother used to get so mad at me 'cause I would always be rolling around in the dirt or I'd be trying to eat everything with my hands." He shook his head, amused by the memories of his mother. "She had such a hard time trying to instill any kind of manners into us." Scott turned around and opened a drawer to get the bottle opener. "She had much more success with Brian, but with me?" Scott opened the fridge and pulled out two beers, popping the tabs off both and handing one to Hank. "The only classy thing that took for me was the piano. And she wasn't happy about me playing it after I'd been outside making myself all dirty. She used to make me come in and scrub myself from head to toe before she'd let me touch it." Scott held up his bottle to Hank. "To the classy, wine-drinking types."

Hank laughed as he brought his bottle to Scott's. "At least you look the part now. Maybe that's enough for her."

"Yeah," Scott sighed before gulping down some of his beer. "Maybe. Just maybe."

"Were you young?" Hank asked, his voice low and quiet. "When she died, I mean."

"I was ten. Brian was sixteen."

"I'm sorry, Scott."

Looking over at Hank's face, Scott fell just a little bit further, wanting to reach out and reassure him that it all seemed like a lifetime ago. Instead, he whispered a quiet "Thank you" and leaned back against the counter again. After a few moments of silence, Scott announced, as if he'd just remembered, "Oh Jesus, you like yours rare." Without waiting for any sign of Hank hearing him, he rushed around the peninsula to check on the steaks. Flipping them quickly, he went back in to find that Hank hadn't moved. He studied the big, muscled, very broad back as he came back in announcing that he hadn't ruined the steaks and took up his vacated spot against the counter.

"Can I ask you something personal, Scott?"

"Sure." Scott cringed, wondering if this would be the end of whatever kind of friendship they'd been headed for. When Hank didn't speak again for a few seconds, Scott took pity on him. "You want to know if I'm gay?"

Hank looked up, a slight smile on his face. "No," he said and shook his head. "I figured that much out, but…." Scott saw the look of amusement on Hank's face and decided to allow him some time to ask his question. "How did you know? I mean, how did you know that you preferred men to women?"

"And I thought you were going to ask a difficult question," Scott teased and then took another long swallow of his beer. "I figured it out in high school," he announced proudly. "And," he added after a few moments, "I've never been with a woman, so…."

"Then how do you know that you're not missing something?"

Scott laughed, more at the memory of Brian asking something very similar ten years ago than at Hank's confused and bewildered expression. "Have you ever wondered what you're missing by not playing the piano?"

Hank's brow furrowed; he'd certainly not anticipated this comparison. "Well, no."

"Then how do you know that *you're* not missing something?"

"I'm not interested in playing the piano." Scott stifled a small laugh as he saw understanding light up those beautiful green eyes and relax the furrow of that tanned forehead. "So, you're not even slightly curious?" Hank asked after a few seconds. "You're not even a little curious about what it would be like with a woman?"

"Nope!" Scott took another long swallow and found his beer empty. "You ready for another?" Scott chuckled to himself as Hank downed the last of his own beer and handed the empty bottle back to Scott. "Everyone knows what they want, what turns them on, you know, so I don't need to take it for a test drive to know I don't want it."

Hank let go a full-bodied laugh with his deep, bass voice. "No, I guess you don't." Hank held up his beer to Scott. "Here's to playing the piano."

Scott smiled and brought his bottle to Hank's. "And to knowing what you want before you test drive it." Scott felt the heat slam into his face when he saw the waggle of Hank's sunkissed eyebrows. Pulling the bottle away from his suddenly dry mouth, Scott fixed Hank with his gaze. "You mind if I ask you something personal?"

"'Course not," Hank laughed. "But you should know I'm not the kind to kiss and tell."

"I'll keep that in mind." Scott leaned back against the counter, his lips losing the smile from a moment ago. "Does it bother you? I mean, if you don't want to go camping now, I'll understand. Not every straight guy—"

"I asked you to go camping after I'd already figured it out." Hank said as he looked directly into Scott's eyes. Hank raised his beer again in a silent toast. "So, no, it doesn't bother me. At all." Scott saw Hank open his mouth and shut it again, just as quickly; Scott couldn't help but wonder what Hank had wanted to say. As he drank his own beer, Scott considered asking Hank but decided against it. No use in ruining what had turned out to be a very happy surprise of an evening.

CHAPTER 9

THE green glow of the alarm clock's LED lights was mocking him. Scott was convinced of it as he entered his second hour of not sleeping. He didn't understand it; he'd had a wonderful evening with Hank, said goodbye more than three hours ago, and hit the sack, completely exhausted, just after midnight. Yet, here he was, wide awake at—he hit the button to project the time onto the ceiling, silently cursing whoever invented that little trick—three fifteen in the morning. *I stand corrected,* Scott thought as he rolled onto his side. *My fourth hour of not sleeping!*

He wondered, for the hundredth time, what had caused such a shift in Hank's personality. He definitely enjoyed it, but his brain was stuck on why there'd been such a drastic change. Hank had been jovial, funny, and witty, just as Scott had assumed he would be without the weight of Brian's injury and the potential loss of his job hanging over him. But there'd been something else in his playfulness that left Scott feeling... what? Concerned, curious, uneasy?

Disgusted and frustrated, Scott heaved himself out of bed and went to find the sleeping pills. He just hoped that the alarm clock would be loud enough to wake him from the drug-induced slumber he was looking forward to. It would be a busy day tomorrow: pick Brian up at the hospital, check to make sure everything at the house was ready for him, call Toronto again to find out how the gig last night had gone. *Funny,* Scott scoffed out loud in the empty kitchen. *I didn't even remember the gig until after Hank had left.*

He decided not to wonder too long on the reason why and popped only one pill in his mouth and chased it with a full glass of water. As he eased himself back onto the bed, he promised that he wouldn't play that stupid game with himself, the game he'd always played as a kid when he couldn't sleep where he'd look at the clock and do the mental math to figure out how many hours of sleep he'd get if he fell asleep within the next five minutes.

He closed his eyes and let his mind envision a completely blank screen, nothing on it at all. He let out a slow exhale and refused to admit that images of Hank kept popping up on the screen; they didn't count if he pushed them away within a couple of seconds. He tried the trick that Rankin had taught him about counting his breaths to the count of four and then counting backwards from four to one. "Goddammit," he muttered under his breath when he found himself at sixteen, too distracted by the thought of being in a tent with Hank. *My own personal heater—with fur.* Scott giggled at the thought and pulled the pillow over his face. *Maybe if I deprive my brain of enough oxygen, I'll just pass out.*

He looked over at the clock as he rolled onto his other side. *Son of a bitch!* He huffed through gritted teeth when he found himself calculating how many hours of sleep he'd get if he fell asleep right then. He brought his legs to his chest and kicked them out wildly, sending the sheets and the duvet flying off the end of the bed, figuring that if he was cool enough, he might be able to fall asleep faster. "Pathetic," he muttered to himself when he realized that he just needed to relax enough and let the pill do its thing. *Maybe if I just go with the thoughts....* He let himself think about Hank's forearms, his hands, his beautiful green eyes and how it would feel to fall asleep next to that warm, hairy chest. He knew it would never happen, but there was no harm in using it as a tool. *Yeah,* he thought finally. *A tool, a sleep aid.* He dismissed the little voice that called him pathetic and continued to picture Hank's beautiful smile and easy swagger. He felt his body relax into the mattress as he thought of the camping trip to come. He'd be as close to Hank as he'd been tonight but in a space the size of this bed. He pushed away the thought that he would do anything inappropriate, reminding himself that he'd been camping with plenty of straight men and had never done anything even remotely unseemly. He chuckled to himself as the little voice reminded him that he'd not been even slightly attracted to those men. Not like he was to Hank.

He inhaled deeply, his mind recalling the smell of Hank's shampoo, the smell that had been left behind on Hank's shirt before he tossed it in the washing machine. Scott had always freely admitted to his partners that he was far more interested in the sensual than the sexual. There was something he found incredibly erotic about learning the places that would make them gasp or cry out or shiver. He'd always been much more taken by the sounds of sex than the actual acts themselves. He wasn't averse to the acts, of course, but he found it much easier to get going when there was a sensual connection already established, a connection like being mesmerized by emerald green eyes or wondering if the hair on the man's forearms was coarse or soft or closing his eyes and hearing the soft laughter from someone with such a deep voice or even anticipating the feel of rough, muscled hands as they skimmed over his skin.

Scott found himself focusing on Hank's hands and voice. What would it be like to have those hands searching out his most sensitive spots while that voice soothed and caressed his ears with whispered words of encouragement and affection? It was the last thought that Scott could remember having before the alarm clock trumpeted him awake at seven o'clock.

Leaning over, his skin chilled from almost three hours with no duvet, he slapped the alarm clock and lay back on the bed, his hands rubbing vigorously to reheat his arms and legs. Slowly, he sat up and rubbed his eyes with the heels of his hands, wondering why the beer hadn't made it easier for him to sleep. Before heading to the bathroom to shave and shower, he laid out his jeans and T-shirt.

As he scrubbed his scalp with his fingernails, trying but never succeeding to massage his scalp like his barber did whenever he went for a haircut, his mind thought about his brother and what he would need when he got home. Brian had always been independent, but not being allowed to drive for a week or two would definitely put a cramp in his brother's need to get back to the office and obsessively take care of all the details that came with running his own business.

Scott was debating cancelling the camping trip or at least postponing it when he heard the familiar tune playing from his cell phone. As he dried himself off, he decided to let the call go to voice mail. He looked at his face briefly in the mirror and decided he had at least another day before he would need to shave again. Scott's inability to grow a beard had always been the source of much amusement between Brian and their father. Of course, neither of them would understand what it was like, since both his brother and father had found it necessary to shave twice a day.

He slicked his hair back with some gel, thanking his mother for his dirty blond locks, and threw the wet towel over the curtain rod. Once he was dressed, he checked his cell phone and found he'd missed a call from Hank. Debating with himself for all of five seconds about whether to call the man back right away or wait until after breakfast, he flipped open his phone and listened to two rings before he heard Hank's low growl.

"Hey, it's Scott. You called?"

"Just wondering if you needed any help with your brother this morning."

"Sure," Scott said through a smile. "But I'll warn you that he's a really awful patient."

"Can't be any worse than when he's pissed at me at work... can it?" Hank didn't sound so certain he wanted to help now.

"Probably not." Scott laughed at the change in Hank's tone. "But if you want, you can come over later and visit him."

"Nah," Hank dismissed the suggestion. "I'll come and help anyway." Scott heard something bang, as if Hank was closing a door or a window. "What time are you going?"

"In about an hour?"

"Sounds good." Hank knocked on the door and Scott started laughing when he realized that Hank was just outside. "Want to let me in? I brought coffee and muffins." Scott flipped his phone shut and ran to the back door, opening it wide to see Hank still had his phone clutched to his ear. "Did you just hang up on me?"

"Get in here, you." Scott stepped aside and watched Hank ascend the small flight of stairs, wondering why he hadn't invited Hank to accompany him to the hospital. "It's really nice of you, Hank, but I'm pretty sure there's no more room in the fridge."

Hank turned from his task of opening the cupboard to find a plate and offered a smile as he opened the box and started pulling out the muffins. "Didn't know what you took in your coffee, so I just left it black. Figured you had all the stuff here to fix it up the way you like."

"Black," Scott growled as he found himself being pulled towards the two cups on the counter. "Which one is it?"

"Either." Hank presented Scott with the stacked plate. "I drink mine black, too. Muffin?"

"Maybe later." Scott sipped his coffee and leaned back against the counter, losing himself in the smell and taste. "I think I'm still full from last night."

"I was wondering where you were putting all that food." Hank put the plate back on the counter and reached for a tea towel to cover the untouched muffins.

"You don't have to wait for me, Hank," Scott protested mildly, still lost in his coffee. "I'm not really a morning person, so if you're hungry, have at 'em."

"Maybe later," Hank echoed and popped the plastic lid off of his coffee cup, inhaling deeply before he brought the cup to his lips. "You look tired."

Scott wasn't sure if the comment was made out of concern or out of a mild sense of disgust over his appearance. Deciding to concentrate on the former, he took another sip of his coffee and offered, "Yeah, I had trouble getting to sleep."

Hank didn't offer anything more, content to sip his coffee and check his watch from time to time. "What time is Brian expecting you?"

Scott turned slightly to check the clock on the microwave. "In about half an hour, give or take."

Hank nodded. "Then maybe a couple of days of fresh air will have you sleeping better."

Scott put his cup of coffee under his nose and inhaled deeply. "God, let's hope so." He took a healthy swig of the dark liquid and exhaled heavily. "I feel like I haven't slept in about a week."

"Don't worry," Hank said and smiled softly. "We'll fix that."

Scott's heart fluttered a little bit at Hank using the word *we* and suddenly feeling a little nervous, glanced back at the clock and announced that it was time to go. Hank wondered out loud at the need to take both trucks and suggested that they take his. Scott was still feeling a little stunned at the potential implications of Hank's being there so early in the morning and his words, so he just went with the idea, not really knowing how to protest or even if he wanted to protest.

Scott sat in Hank's truck, admiring how clean it was. The dashboard had that shiny, just-wiped sheen to it, the windshield was spotless, and there wasn't so much as a speck of dust on the plush floor mats. It seemed obvious now why Hank had made the suggestion, and Scott found himself wanting to say something, to acknowledge Hank's efforts. "Is your truck always this immaculate?"

"No." Hank looked over with a sly smile on his face, and Scott was suddenly at a loss for words.

"Some woman is going to be very happy that she found you one day." Scott looked around, avoiding Hank's glances. "Even Marc, who's completely OCD with cleanliness would admire this cleaning job."

"Marc?"

"Roommate and member of our little trio."

"Oh," Hank muttered, his fists tightening a little on the steering wheel.

"Honestly, Hank," Scott enthused some more as he continued to study the interior. "Even he wouldn't be able to find any dirt in here."

"Is he—" Hank hesitated, his voice trailing off. "Is he a real neat freak?"

"To say the least," Scott huffed as he let himself sink back into the leather bucket seat. "He drives us all crazy at least three times a week with his cleaning schedule."

"Us?"

"Marc and Jacob and I."

"Is Jacob a roommate too?"

"Yeah," Scott drawled as he turned to look at Hank. "The three of us are *Dragonfly*." Scott announced the name of the trio with a flourish, feeling foolish. "God, I hate that name."

"So." Hank seemed to be trying not to laugh out loud at the name. "I take it you're not a metal band?"

"Very funny," Scott leaned over to swat at Hank's shoulder. "No, we're a jazz trio, mainly."

"Do you ever perform your songs?"

"Sometimes." Scott looked over at Hank again, wondering when he'd ever explained about being a songwriter. "If it's got a jazzy feel to it."

"You know," Hank said and looked out his own window, avoiding Scott's eyes as he pulled into the hospital parking lot. "'But for You' is one of my favorite songs."

Scott's hand froze on the door handle as he turned to look at Hank, who had already exited the truck's cab. If he'd had a moment to think about it, Scott would have been able to rationalize that Brian had probably regaled his crew with tales of his famous songwriter brother. The song had seen more than its fair share of airtime and had even been used in several movies and even a greater number of commercials over the years, but it made the flush of that success come rushing back to him when he heard Hank admit to it being one of his favorites. Scott lowered himself out of the cab and caught Hank as he came around the front of the truck.

"That was my first big hit, you know." As he fell into step alongside him, Scott looked over at Hank and wondered what else the logger knew about him.

"I know," Hank explained. "It's all Brian could talk about for weeks."

"Really?" Scott knew Brian was happy for his success, but he had never known that his big brother was bragging about him like that.

"He's really proud of you, Scott."

Scott didn't respond, not really knowing what to say. He felt a surge of emotion as he approached Brian's hospital room, a wheelchair waiting outside of the room. "Oh Christ," he groaned as he heard his brother's voice complaining about the wheelchair. "Here we go."

"I told you I'm fine." Brian's face was red and his temper had crested. "I'm perfectly capable of walking."

The male orderly's voice was stern but soothing. "Sir, it's hospital policy."

"Brian, please?" Kari was there as well, her voice soft and coaxing, and Scott could tell what kind of a mother she'd been. "It's hospital policy." Kari looked over to Scott as he entered the room.

"Good morning!" Scott stepped further into the room and stood beside his brother, feeling dwarfed by Brian on one side and Hank on the other. "Well, I see you're back," Scott sighed as he looked over at Kari and rolled his eyes dramatically. "That didn't last long. I think I like you better unconscious."

"What's Hank doing here?"

"Hank," Scott cautioned, "is here to make sure you get in the chair." Scott looked back at Kari and gave her a surreptitious wink. Turning to the frustrated orderly, Scott offered his thanks and assured the man that they would make sure Brian used the chair. "So," Scott said finally, standing mere inches from his brother. "Are you going to go quietly, or do I have to show them how I always won fights when we were kids?"

Brian looked at his brother with narrowed eyes, his lips moving without any sound. After a few tense moments during which Scott wasn't sure he remembered "the move" anymore, Brian finally huffed his assent and lowered himself into the chair. Muttering barely audible obscenities the entire way, Brian vacated the chair at the first available opportunity and turned to Scott. "Where the hell is your truck?"

"Hank is driving us." Hearing nothing from Brian, Scott turned to Kari. "Do you want to come with? Hank bought muffins this morning."

"I have my car here, thanks." Kari pointed somewhere off to her right. "I'll be over a little later, if that won't be any bother."

"Not at all." Scott chuckled. "It'll give us time to shoot him full of horse tranquilizer." Scott wondered if Kari was only seeing this side of Brian for the first time, but then he remembered as he followed Hank and Brian to the truck that she worked with him. *She's probably already seen him at his worst,* Scott chuckled to himself. *And still fell in love with him.* Of course, Scott was also quite certain that she'd also seen his charming side as well, the Brian that had always taken care of his younger brother, sometimes at the sacrifice of his own wishes.

CHAPTER 10

"IT'LL be fine," Scott reassured Kari, hoping with every fiber of his being that it would be. "I promise. Now." Scott pointed to his wrist, even though he'd forgotten to put on his watch this morning; he'd been kept pretty busy by his grousing big brother. "Dinner will be at seven. So you go home and rest. I promise I'll beat him into a better mood by then." Scott delighted in Kari's relieved smile and waited for her to pull out of the driveway.

He stormed back into the house to find Brian flipping mindlessly through the hundreds of television stations. "Why aren't there any games on?"

"Because it's only ten o'clock in the morning?" Scott reached over Brian's shoulder and grabbed the remote, turning off the television and rounding the sofa to glare at what he'd come to realize was his "baby" brother. "Are you trying to drive her away?"

"Give me the remote, Scott." Brian's voice was low, the kind of low that used to let Scott know when they were younger that Brian meant business.

"No." Scott put the remote in his back pocket and planted his hands on his hips. "Not until you tell me what's gotten into you." Brian didn't even bother to look up let alone answer, his mouth pulled into a tight, white line. "She came all the way over here to see how you were doing, and you barely said two words to her." Nothing. "Brian?"

"What?" Brian finally looked up at his brother. If Scott had to guess, the smile on his own face only served to fuel the fires of immaturity.

"I want an answer."

"And I want the remote."

"I asked first."

"What are you, twelve?"

"Are *you*?"

"Bite me!"

"Nice," Scott laughed, unable to control himself, almost reduced to tears by the scene in which he now found himself. "That answers my second question."

"It's just...." Brian huffed, his hands fiddling with the drawstring of his sweatpants. "I can't even drive myself for two more weeks."

"And that's her fault?"

"No."

"Then what?" Scott tossed the remote back to his brother and sat down on the other end of the sofa. "Tell me, Brian." Brian reached for the remote but didn't turn on the television.

"It's just not the kind of first impression I wanted to make."

"First impression?" Scott scoffed at the way his big brother's mind worked sometimes. "She's already in love with you, for fuck's sake." Scott nodded as Brian's headed pivoted. "So I'm guessing that the first impression you did make was a pretty good one."

"Did she...." Brian's hands went back to the drawstring. "Did she tell you that?"

"She didn't have to." Scott picked up a cushion and tossed it at Brian's legs. "We women know these things."

"Shut up," Brian laughed. "You're not a woman."

"Hey," Scott corrected, his own laughter echoing his brother's. "I'm just repeating what you used to call me after I told you."

"I never called you a woman!" Brian growled, tossing the cushion back at Scott.

"Oh, that's right." Scott narrowed his eyes and tilted his head, as if in stern concentration. "You just told me that you'd have to start telling people you had a sister."

Brian stifled his laughter as he remembered that night, when Scott had finally confessed to something Brian had surely known all along. "I was just kidding."

"I know," Scott assuaged as he scooted closer to his brother, wrapping one arm around Brian's shoulder, careful to avoid his head. "I know I haven't said this nearly enough, big brother, but I love you." Scott noticed the flush of Brian's cheeks. "And I was the luckiest kid in the whole world to have you taking care of me and looking out for me." Scott kissed Brian's temple, softly.

"I love you, too, Scooter."

"Good," Scott said as he raised himself off the sofa and turned to study his brother. "Because Kari's coming over for dinner, and if you don't behave, I will make sure that a certain baby picture of you finds its way to the bulletin board in your office."

"Blow me."

"No thanks," Scott winked. "I prefer men who can drive themselves." Scott hadn't really anticipated Brian feeling well enough to move that fast. Before he knew what hit him, Scott was face down on the sofa, Brian's hand pushing his face into the sofa cushions, lifting his head up occasionally so he could breathe.

"If—" Scott huffed out in short breaths. "If—you—hurt me—you'll have to cook—for Kari—and then—you'll be arrested—for culinary—homicide." Scott felt Brian let go of his head, delighting in his brother's insane giggles. "You're the only forty-year-old that giggles like a schoolgirl."

"What was that?" Brian pushed Scott's face back into the cushion. "And where is this spectacular move you threatened me with at the hospital?"

"Oh," Scott warned. "It's coming. I'm just not angry enough yet."

"Right." Brian released his grip on Scott.

"Honestly, though." Scott massaged his wrists and stretched to pop his back. "You should seriously consider voice lessons. I mean—" Scott started running to his room when he saw Brian's face grow evil and wicked. "She obviously hasn't heard you laugh yet, has she?"

Scott made it to his room just in time to close the door, but he was laughing so hard that he couldn't keep Brian from forcing open the door.

Brian may have been recently injured, but he still had five inches and at least fifty pounds on Scott. As Brian tackled him onto the bed, Scott could not find it in himself to stop teasing. "As soon as she hears that laugh of yours, not being able to drive will be the least of your worries."

Brian had Scott on his back, his knees pinning his brother's arms to the mattress. "Now," Brian cautioned, his voice low and menacing. "I think someone owes me an apology."

"Yes, you're right," Scott conceded. "But how can we make genetics apologize?" Scott felt the first flick against his ear before he'd even finished the questions. "No, no," he whined. "Not the ear thing!" Scott bucked and pulled and pushed, but it was no use. "Okay, okay, I give."

"Apologize," Brian said and then quickly raised a finger, ready for another round of ear-flicking. "And make me believe it."

"I'm sorry." Scott couldn't help the laughter escaping his restrained chest, tears forming in his eyes as he saw Brian's finger descend for another bout of torture.

"I didn't believe that one. Care to try again?" Brian raised a hand before Scott could speak. "And remember," Brian menaced through clenched teeth, "what used to happen if I didn't believe you the second time."

Scott opened his mouth in disbelief. "You wouldn't dare."

"Try me!" Brian cocked his head to the side, licked his finger and pretended to swirl it inside of his own ear. "Now, make me believe it."

"Brian." Scott tried to straighten his face. *For some reason, this was so much easier to do when we were teenagers.* "I am very sorry that you are a freak of nature—" Just before Brian could slick his finger, firmly intent on following through with his threat, Scott threw his legs up in the air and managed to get Brian in a scissor hold. "Ah ha!" Scott trumpeted, his voice full of strut and swagger. "And you were feeling pretty safe in the belief that I'd forgotten how to do this." The air whooshed out of Scott when he felt Brian's fist connect with his stomach, his legs coming up instinctively to his belly. "Oh, fuck me," Scott wheezed. "You always were a cheater."

"You say cheater," Brian gloated, as he stood beside Scott's bed and rearranged his T-shirt and sweatpants. "I say superior fighter."

"Okay, then," Scott grunted as he rolled to the edge of the bed. "Next time? I'm going for the gonads."

"Okay." Brian seemed amused. "But just remember, you'll need both hands."

"Pig." Scott sat up, feeling somewhat energized. He was glad to see that his brother was feeling better enough to fall back on the standard jokes of their youth. "So, what should I make for dinner?"

"Whatever, you know I'll eat anything."

"God," Scott rolled his eyes. "You're thick!"

"And long."

"Eww." Scott followed his brother out to the living room and sat beside him on the sofa. "Seriously, Brian, this dinner is about Kari." Scott looked over at Brian and reached a hand to tame Brian's cowlick. "Are you interested in her?"

"Have you seen her?" Brian pushed Scott's hand away and looked over at him, realizing what he'd just asked. "You know what I mean. She's something else."

Scott sat up on the edge of the sofa, just staring for a few seconds. "Then why have you never asked her out?"

Brian shrugged, his hands finding the remote and turning on the television. "I just wasn't sure I wanted to go down that road again." He glanced over at Scott sheepishly and then returned his eyes to the television. "Didn't think I was ready."

"Then this is a good thing?" Scott tried to grab the remote, but Brian pulled it out of reach too quickly. "You're okay with me pushing you two together?" Another shrug. Well, if Brian wasn't objecting, Scott would consider that his approval. "I was thinking barbecue."

"Sounds good."

"And we have some leftover cheesecake too." Scott stood and then stopped. "Or do you think I should buy something fresh?"

"Leftovers are good." Brian waggled his eyebrows. "She's a low-maintenance kind of gal."

Scott strolled to the kitchen and started surveying the contents of the cupboard, trying to figure out what would impress Kari the most. As he formulated a menu, he heard Brian yell something about Hank. Without really thinking, he popped his head up out of the fridge and asked, "What about Hank?"

"I said why don't you invite him over?"

"To your dinner date?"

"Well, since you're going to be here," Brian groaned, "it's not really much of a date, is it?"

"Do you want Hank here?" Scott was a little confused by the suggestion. He didn't really understand why Brian would want Hank here on tonight of all nights.

"I sometimes worry about him, you know," Brian confessed. "He seems kind of lonely to me. I wonder if that's not where the bravado comes from. Maybe he needs more friends. The non-sexual kind, I mean."

"Yeah, maybe." Scott closed the fridge and started writing the list of supplies he'd need. He pulled the piece of paper off the pad and grabbed his keys.

Before heading to the grocery store, Scott dialed Hank's number, surprised when he heard the deep bass voice after only one ring. He explained Brian's suggestion, omitting the part about Hank seeming lonely and in need of friends. He was surprised again when Hank readily accepted the invitation. *I'd like to be more than just his friend,* Scott whined to himself. *But I can live with this for a couple of weeks.*

Ignoring the little voice that told him he was too old to contemplate summer flings anyway, he drove to the grocery store whistling the tune he'd been working on for almost two months. As he pulled in the parking lot of the Safeway just off Island Highway, he found himself with a possible bridge between the first two verses. And then, realizing he'd forgotten to call Marc and Jacob, he pulled out his cell phone to update them on his plans.

CHAPTER 11

HANK had been the first to arrive, dressed in dark slacks and a crisp, freshly pressed white button-down. His attire had elicited a surprised whistle from Brian. Kari arrived moments later, dressed semi-casually in a pair of beige slacks and a loose-fitting blouse that had elicited a whistle from Scott, which in turn earned him a glare and a smack on the back of the head from Brian. The brothers, dressed only in jeans, had each excused themselves quickly enough to put on something more appropriate for their respective guests.

The dinner had gone over very well with everyone, Scott accepting the congratulations with ease and with a satisfied grin. He had inherited the duties of cooking for his father and brother when they all found themselves without a wife and mother, and he'd become quite adept at it in a very short amount of time. He was sure that it was one of the reasons he enjoyed living with roommates so much, the habit of cooking for three being too hard to shake. Kari had been especially appreciative of the wine, although she barely made a dent in the two bottles Hank had bought two nights before. Brian and Hank preferred beer, and Scott, who had been busy serving and fetching, had barely consumed his first beer before the dinner had given way to dessert.

Only two hours after finishing their dinner and with Kari and Brian sitting in the living room enjoying the conversation that centered on work, Hank had suggested that he and Scott take a stroll along the river. It wasn't until Scott was outside after cleaning up most of the dinner mess that Hank explained that he'd started to feel like an eavesdropper. Scott confessed to finding the whole situation incredibly sweet and romantic, although he did also have to confess that he hadn't thought far enough ahead to what he would do once Kari and Brian wanted to be alone.

Dressed for the beautiful summer night, Scott and Hank strolled to the end of Palahi Road and headed south to Moorefield and then west toward Somenos. The evening air was cooler than usual, and the streets seemed to be filled with children playing and laughing. Hank stopped momentarily as they neared Moorefield to scoop up a baseball and throw it back to the small throng of boys who watched the ball sail over their heads and land, quite neatly, in the pitcher's mitt.

It wasn't exactly romantic, but as he walked beside Hank, Scott felt a twinge of jealousy for the woman who would one day find a way into Hank's heart. He was kind, attentive, good-hearted, and didn't have a problem with gay men; what more could a woman want? Of course, Scott ignored the nagging question that he'd been wanting to ask Hank for the past couple of hours: *Why aren't you married yet?*

Scott figured firstly that it was none of his business and secondly that it might very well be a sore subject for his new friend. In fact, it might be the reason he'd wanted to vacate the house after dinner. *Maybe,* Scott thought to himself as they approached the middle of the river, *Hank had tried to grab Kari for himself, but had gotten shot down.* He remembered what a bear Brian had been when he'd spent so much time pining over certain girls in high school only to be refused even a first date. *Straight men,* Scott laughed to himself, *can be so high maintenance.*

There hadn't been too much conversation during the stroll, so when Scott heard a whistle and turned around to see what, if anything, was wrong, he was surprised to have found himself so lost in his own thoughts that he'd neglected to notice Hank stopping about ten feet behind him. Hank was grinning as if he could sense Scott's embarrassment and leaning against the back of a bench just beyond the pedestrian corridor. Scott walked back slowly, Hank's eyes trained on him, the grin still firmly planted on his face.

"You know," Hank laughed, "I *was* going to wait and see just how far you got before you realized you were alone."

"Trust me," Scott assured him, willing the heat from his face. "I probably would have been in Sooke by the time I noticed."

"Sooke is that way," Hank chuckled as he pointed to the south. "We're heading north." Scott just rolled his eyes, as if to say *See what I mean?* Which drew out more laughter from Hank. "What's got you so preoccupied?" Hank turned slightly, leaving one hand on the back of the bench and bringing the other to rest inside his trouser's pocket. "If you don't mind my asking?"

"Nothing, really," Scott lied. "I was just hoping it works out for the two of them." Scott shrugged, not really sure if Brian would let Kari in. "Especially for Brian. He's been really lonely since the divorce." Scott appreciated that Hank didn't offer any observations. Sitting down on the bench, Scott added, "About a year after the divorce, I was even ready to move back here just so he would have something other than work."

"Why didn't you?"

Scott closed his eyes and shook his head slowly. "That was six years ago, and...." Scott turned to see Hank still studying him. "And," Scott sighed, "I was a selfish prick." Scott continued before Hank could protest. "The trio was still fairly new, and it seemed like whatever time I didn't spend promoting or arranging gigs, I wanted to spend composing."

"That's not selfish!" Hank countered.

"Maybe not," Scott agreed, although halfheartedly. "But it sure made me feel like a selfish prick."

"Trust me." Hank finally sat next to Scott and gave him a playful push against his shoulder. "Selfish is not going to your sister's wedding reception because you have the opportunity for a three-way with two stewardesses."

Scott stared for a moment, finding himself oddly heated by the thought and also quite disgusted on Hank's sister's behalf.

"Really?" Scott didn't know why he was laughing when he saw Hank nod and lower his head at the same time. "Wait a minute," Scott pulled his head back at the thought that had just hit him. "You drove to Victoria for a three-way?"

"No," Hank shook his head, face still serious, and Scott felt even more like a prick when he noticed that this particular memory might not be a happy one for the big logger. "Originally from Coquitlam, remember? Sister's wedding was in Vancouver."

"Was she pissed?"

"No," Hank admitted, "but my dad was."

"But still." Scott clapped him on the shoulder like he'd always imagined straight guys would do when they heard about such an adventure. "That must have been some night, huh?" Scott realized his joke fell short when Hank only shook his head. "I'm sorry," Scott lamented after a few moments. "I was trying to make you feel better."

"I know. And thanks." Hank turned on the bench, resting his forearm over the back of the bench. "You seem to be doing that a lot lately."

Scott turned at the observation and found he didn't have anything to say. He raised his eyebrows and gave a slight shrug before looking back out across the expanse of green grass. Scott could feel Hank's eyes boring holes into the side of his face. He wanted to say something, but he couldn't think fast enough or clearly enough knowing that Hank was studying him like that.

He finally turned and asked, "I meant to ask you how you and Brian settled everything back in the hospital." Scott raised a hand quickly. "That is, if you don't mind telling me? Don't want you giving away any logging secrets." Scott offered a stupid grin to cover his second failed attempt at humor.

"You probably know just as much about that as I do." Hank laughed, which made Scott feel a little less self-conscious. "There's nothing much to tell," Hank sighed as he stretched out his long legs in front of him. "I told him that I was going to do whatever it takes to help him and the company." After a few moments, Hank added, "No more drinking the night before a job, no more making Brian regret hiring me. Just… prove to him, I guess, that I'm worth keeping around."

"He thinks you're lonely." Scott realized that the words were out of his mouth before he could censor his thoughts and tried to minimize the damage. "I mean, Brian is worried that you're—oh shit, please don't be angry. I shouldn't have said that."

"It's okay," Hank chuckled, and Scott relaxed a little. "He's usually right about everything, so no hard feelings." Hank brought his legs back in and rested his forearms on his thighs. Scott noticed the stretch of Hank's muscled back against the thin fabric of his shirt. "Truth is," Hank admitted slowly, "I guess I have been pretty lonely out here most of the time."

"I know the feeling, Hank." Scott didn't know where that admission had come from, but he did know that it was the truth. Just because he lived with two bandmates didn't mean he hadn't had moments of watching other people be happy and attached and wondering when it would be his turn. "I used to tell myself that I liked to be alone so that I could concentrate on my writing. But—" Scott suddenly found the back of his hand quite fascinating, unable to look up. "It's actually the other way around." Scott leaned forward, his elbows resting on his knees, his voice soft when he spoke again. "Are you?" He glanced over at Hank. "Lonely, I mean?"

Hank nodded, and Scott felt the return of that overwhelming urge to kiss and soothe the handsome face.

"One day, Hank," he whispered through a sincere smile. "You'll meet the right woman, and she'll end all of that for you."

"Maybe that's been the problem. Maybe I should be looking for the right *person*." Hank looked over at Scott, who flushed as the meaning behind his words sank in.

Scott sat there, not really knowing what to make of the comment. He had figured that Hank's admission of not having a problem with Scott's being gay had been the logger's way of trying to put him at ease, but now...? Scott was suddenly very aware of some of the other observations and comments that Hank had made since they'd met and wondered if he shouldn't bring up the subject again. Scott was startled when Hank suddenly slapped his own thighs and stood up. "Okay, then," Hank announced. "I don't know if it was me or you that started this meeting of the Whiners Club, but I vote we adjourn and go plan our camping trip."

"Lead the way." Scott laughed when he stood up and fell in stride beside Hank. "And for the record," Scott whispered as they exited the little park, "it was you."

"Yeah," Hank sighed. "Might as well blame me. Everybody else does."

Scott pulled his arm back and landed a punch to Hank's ample deltoid, raising his eyebrows when Hank stopped walking and brought up a hand to soothe his shoulder.

"What was that for?"

"The meeting was adjourned." Scott brought up a finger in warning. "No more self-pity."

"That hurt!"

"I told you," Scott reminded, backing away quickly. "Scrappy." And even though he tried to outrun him, Hank had him in a headlock before Scott had managed to get to the end of the street where Hank had parked. And secretly, Scott delighted in the opportunity to run his hands over whatever muscles he could reach.

CHAPTER 12

"YOU'RE sure you'll be okay?" Scott asked for the hundredth time as he stood in the kitchen, his eyes darting around to ensure that Brian would have everything he needed.

"Yes, mother!" Brian huffed, trying to contain his bemused annoyance. "I'm quite self-sufficient, you know."

"Please," Scott chastised, his eyebrows furrowing. "You have a hard enough time looking after yourself without a head injury." Scott waved away the next protest. "Don't think I didn't notice your cupboards full of Kraft Dinner."

"What's wrong with macaroni and cheese?" Brian spread out his hands beside him on the sofa, not even bothering to look back. "It's a good source of protein."

"Right," Scott laughed. "If you're a small cat!" Scott patted his pockets to check that he still had his cell phone. "Okay, Hank'll be here soon. You have my cell phone if you need it, right?" Without waiting for acknowledgment or any asinine comments Scott continued to go over his checklist. "We'll be back by noonish on Wednesday. We're only an hour away, so if you feel sick or—"

"Jesus, Scooter," Brian leaned his frame over the back of the sofa. "Would you just go and have some fun. You're like an old woman."

"God," Scott sighed as he closed his eyes. "No wonder dad drank when you were a teenager."

"What was that?"

"I said you're my favorite brother!"

"Bite me!" They both heard the car horn as Hank pulled into the driveway. "Now go!"

"And remember," Scott cautioned as he grabbed his backpack and headed for the door. "If Kari comes over and decides to lower her standards, I left some condoms in your dresser drawer!" Scott closed the door just in time, laughing as he heard the hollow thud of the remote against the solid wood. He laughed even harder when he heard Brian yelling for Scott to bring the remote back to him.

"What's so funny?"

"My idiot brother," Scott laughed as he tossed his backpack into the backseat of the cab. He could barely contain his laughter as he told Hank about the warning he'd given to Brian about the condoms.

"So they're a couple?"

"Oh yeah," Scott reassured through the smirk on his face. "After we got home from our walk last night, I came in to find Kari gone and Brian absolutely reeking of Chanel No. 5. So unless he's decided to attract a different kind of partner, I'm pretty sure there was something going on."

"Good." Hank nodded. "I'm glad for them."

"Me too." Scott settled into the soft leather of the seat, relaxing himself for the hourlong drive that would take them to French Beach on the west coast of the island. As he sat back, content to let Hank do the driving, Scott found himself staring out at the scenery, something he hadn't really thought he'd miss as much as he found he had.

The TransCanada highway twisted and turned through the green valleys, and the entire area on both sides of the highway seemed to be a sea of tall, majestic trees. He pulled his sunglasses off the top of his forehead and sat up a little, feeling like he'd never really looked at his home province when he lived here. He'd been so anxious to leave, to find what he thought would be something better. What he'd found, however— despite a respectable amount of fame and a lot of money—didn't seem as impressive as the Cowichan Valley. He couldn't help but wonder what French Beach would be like. If it was half as impressive as this, he wasn't sure he would be satisfied with only two days.

"Hey?"

Scott turned at the sound of Hank's voice, and felt the familiar tightening of his chest when he took in the long legs covered to mid-thigh by Hank's baggy cargo shorts and the cheerful smile that had taken hold of that ruggedly, handsome face.

"Where'd you go?"

"Sorry." Scott shook his head. "I was just wondering why I was in such a hurry to leave this place all those years ago." Scott put his sunglasses back on the top of his head and sank back into the leather seat. "It's funny, isn't it?" He let his head loll to the side, his eyes fixing Hank's stubbled jaw line. "No matter how long you're away, home always seems to be better when you come back."

"Is that regret I'm hearing?" Hank lifted his own mirrored sunglasses and offered Scott a cheeky smile. "'Cause if it's self-pity, I owe you one."

"No," Scott mused distractedly. "It's just...." Scott lifted himself to sit properly again and made an impulsive decision to tell Hank what had been on his mind for almost a year now. "I've been thinking about composing full time." Scott held out his fingers, one by one, as he rattled off his reasons. "I mean, I have more than enough money—"

"Must be nice," Hank teased.

"I don't really like performing, never have—"

"Then quit."

"I've never been overly fond of Toronto and the gray winters—"

"Ooh, sorry." Hank grimaced and turned to Scott. "We get those here, you know. Or have you forgotten already?"

"That's different."

"How so?"

"I don't know." Scott shrugged. "It just is."

"Fair enough." Hank nodded and then glanced at Scott. "So," he questioned, "what's stopping you, then?"

"Fear, I guess."

"I thought you were scrappy." Hank held up a hand when he saw Scott's hand come up. "Careful, I'm driving."

"Baby!"

"Seriously, Scott, what's stopping you?" Hank repeated as he steered the car back into the sun's rays and reached for his sunglasses. "I mean, it would be kind of nice having you here all the time. We could go camping. We could go skiing… go see a movie."

"It *would* be nice to have a social life outside of Dragonfly," Scott agreed readily, and then added, "God, I hate that name."

"And I'm sure Brian would love to have you back home."

"Nah," Scott huffed. "He's like a dog with a bone when he's dating."

"Yeah, sure," Hank redirected. "But by then, he might be married."

"That would be nice, yeah, but…." Scott turned slightly to face Hank, his mind trying to figure out how to phrase his thought without seeming too bitchy. "Does it make me a bad person if I'm glad that he never had kids with Jennifer?"

"Why would that make you a bad person?" Hank glanced over again, his face an expression of confusion. "I mean, I never met the woman, but I've never heard anyone say anything nice about her."

"Man," Scott sighed loudly. "She was a Class-A bitch." Scott shook his head, disgusted to find himself giving her any thought at all. "It would be nice to have a few nieces and nephews, though."

"What if Brian doesn't want kids? And Kari's kid is already grown, so…."

"That would be a shame."

"You could always have your own."

Scott scoffed at the idea. "Yeah, right!" Scott found himself laughing at the thought of him waking up in the middle of the night to change diapers. "I'm the kind of person that should never be given that kind of responsibility."

"Then why do you want Brian to have any?" Hank's brow furrowed even more, the look on his face a strange mix of bewildered and amused.

"He'd make such a good father." Scott stared distractedly out the window. "He's such a nice guy… so much love to give." Scott looked over at Hank, suddenly aware of having said that out loud. "I mean, he was always there for me, and… I don't know, I guess I always hoped that there would be some little miniature version of him running around who I could spoil and take on trips and who would call me Uncle Scotty." When

Hank looked over with a smile, Scott asked, "What about you? Aren't you anxious to get married and have kids?"

"No."

Scott felt the answer like a rush of wind, wondering if the terse answer was Hank's way of closing the subject. He decided to let it drop and settled back against the leather one more time, counting the telephone poles like he used to do when they'd go on family vacations. He leaned over and turned on the radio, glancing at Hank, who only nodded and smiled.

When he awoke, the radio was turned off and Hank wasn't even in the truck. "Hank?" Scott jumped out of the cab and looked around, his hand coming up automatically to shield his eyes from the bright sun.

"Hey, sleepyhead." Hank came around the back of the truck, his T-shirt tucked into one of his back pockets, a fine layer of sweat covering his torso and neck, his dark chest hair glistening under the midday sun. "We're just over here."

"Why didn't you wake me?"

"Don't worry," Hank warned. "There's still plenty left to do."

Scott grabbed the backpacks and the canvas bag that housed the tent and followed Hank down a little winding trail to their campsite. Stopping when he saw that they were right on the water, Scott asked cautiously, "This is French Beach?"

"No." Hank shook his head, the devious smile on his face confusing Scott even more. "French Beach is about five miles that way." Hank spread his arms out wide, legs planted firmly on the rocky beach. "This is better than French Beach. It's more secluded here. Not as many tourists."

"Hank?" Scott exhaled. "We *are* tourists."

"You know what I mean."

Shaking his head, Scott set to fixing the tent. He had just about figured it out when he felt Hank's hand on his shoulder while the other reached around and twisted some little piece of wire, causing the tent to fly out of Scott's hands and land, ready-made on the rocky shore. As if Hank hadn't thought of it, Scott turned, offered his thanks and then asked, "Isn't this going to be a little hard on our backs?"

"That's why," Hank laughed and pulled out a second canvas bag, "I brought this." Hank handed the canvas bag over and then turned to go lock up the truck. "I forgot the pump, so you'll need to blow it up." Scott nodded his agreement, knowing full well that Hank hadn't forgotten the pump. Scott had been the one to bring it down to the shore.

Within a half hour, the tent was filled with the inflatable air mattress, two sleeping bags, and two pillows. Scott's arms and hands were screaming in protest at the manual air pump that he'd had to use to fill the mattress, but he found some relief by putting them in the cool ocean water that would be only yards from their tent. As he was wondering if what they were doing and where they were was legal, he heard the rocks being disturbed behind him. From his little perch, squatting at the shoreline, he called over his shoulder, not even bothering to look around, "Don't even think about throwing me in."

"Spoil sport." Hank came up beside him and squatted down, thrusting his hands into the water and dousing his face and neck.

"I should tell you, though," Scott started, hoping he could pull this one off with a straight face. "That I had a really terrifying experience one time when Brian pushed me in the water and... I... well, I've been sorta scared of drowning ever since." He didn't look over to see Hank's reaction, convinced that he'd crack up if he did.

"Hey, Scott." The earnest note of Hank's voice made Scott feel like an asshole for what he was planning, but he kept his head down, "I wouldn't do anything like that. Promise."

Scott stood up and muttered a muted "Thank you," and as Hank stood alongside him, planted both of his hands on Hank's sweaty chest and pushed as hard as he could, shouting "Sucker!" as he watched Hank's surprised expression be swallowed up by the ocean. Scott knew he would be repaid in kind, but he couldn't resist. He was still laughing, his hands on his hips, when he saw Hank raise himself slowly out of the water. "Hank?" Scott kicked off his shoes and waded into the water when he saw the grimace of pain on that handsome face.

Hank kneaded his lower back with one hand while he pushed the hair out of his eyes with the other. "Water's not as deep as it looks, I guess." Hank's voice was strained, as if he could barely get enough air into his lungs.

"Oh fuck, Hank, I'm sorry." Scott was ready to offer a massage to help ease the pain he'd caused when he saw the look on Hank's face. He tried to move away, but Hank grabbed him around the waist and had him over his shoulder, fireman-style, within seconds. Hank's only answer to Scott's feeble apologies was the word "Payback."

Scott watched as Hank stood guard over their little stretch of the beach, both men neck deep in the ocean. He resisted Scott's promise of a massage, of cooking whatever he wanted, and even managed to resist Scott's pathetic attempt at an apology. He was, however, amused at Scott's profanity when Hank's only response had been to laugh at what Scott had considered to be a sincere apology.

After catching Scott when he tried to escape and do an end-run around him, Hank had easily taken hold and hoisted him in the air, laughing at how much fun he was having tossing Scott back into the ocean. But when Scott grew too tired, Hank stepped aside and let the smaller man head back to the beach, reminding him that apologies weren't supposed to be perforated with snorts of laughter.

CHAPTER 13

"YOU could have drowned me," Scott groused, not laughing as hard as Hank was. Occasionally throughout dinner, Scott noted that Hank's shoulders would start bouncing up and down. The first time, he'd asked to be let in on the joke only to be reminded of what Hank called his "Shamu impersonation." "What if I really had had a traumatic experience as a child?"

"Sucks to be you, then," Hank laughed as he sipped his coffee by the fire and stretched out over the rocks.

"Did I really hurt your back?"

"No." Hank winked and held up his hand to stop any protests. "But I did owe you one."

"You're lucky I'm such a good sport."

Hank laughed even harder, his hand gripping his stomach as he tried to spit out the words. "Good sport? I believe you called me an overgrown Neanderthal, but with a smaller braincase." Hank sat cross-legged and counted off the other half-dozen insults that Scott had thrown his way, his laughter increasing with each insult.

"It was said with great affection, if that counts for anything." Scott held up the coffee pot and topped off Hank's metal camping mug. "No, seriously, I'm sorry. I can get carried away sometimes. Thanks for being such a good sport."

"Anytime." Hank held up his mug. "Especially if you make those cheese-stuffed hoagies again tomorrow."

"There's still two left, if you want them." Scott reached into the cooler as Hank just shook his head.

"No," Hank snickered. "As it is we're gonna have our own horn section in there tonight."

"Eww," Scott winced. "Why is it always the bathroom humor with the straight guys?"

"As opposed to," Hank chastened through his smile, "lies meant to trick people as part of a ruse?"

Scott attempted to look wounded as he withdrew the imaginary epée out of his shoulder. "Touché," he grimaced as he feigned death, delighting in Hank's low growl of laughter. "Well," Scott pronounced after a few moments of silence. "I'll get these dishes washed up, and then I'm going to sleep."

"Leave 'em," Hank said as he sipped his coffee. "There's only the coffee pot and a couple of mugs. I'll do them and be in shortly."

"Deal," Scott said as he smiled and stretched and then made his way to the tent. "You might want to do some squats or something… to, uh, tire out the horn section."

"I'll do my best, boss." Hank saluted and gathered the coffee pot and mugs, rinsing them in the basin of water left over from the dinner dishes and throwing the dirty water into the bushes.

"Shit," Scott spat and slapped his forehead. "That reminds me. I have to call Brian to see how he's doing." Ignoring Hank's admonishments to leave the poor man alone, Scott flipped open his cell phone and headed toward the truck to see if the signal was any better. He was gone for only a few minutes when he returned to see the mocking look on Hank's face. "You were wrong. There was this huge ten-alarm fire right down the street, and Brian had to be evacuated. We should leave right now to make sure he's okay."

"Scott?"

"What?" Scott protested. "It's the truth, I swear."

"What did I do before logging?"

Scott stuffed his phone in his pocket and looked over, his expression contrite. "Don't tell me. There's no such thing as a ten-alarm fire, is there?"

"Oh no," Hank reassured him, "there is. But while each fire department is different, in Coquitlam, a six-alarm fire meant that just about every engine was needed." Hank swallowed his laughter. "So, if there was a ten-alarm fire in Duncan, I'm thinking that would mean the whole town was on fire."

"I'll be sure my lies are more believable in the future." Scott bowed and escaped into the tent, leaving Hank alone by the fire.

HANK stretched out by the fire to finish his beer, settling back against the rocks, squirming until he felt his back fit more easily into the hard surface. He'd found his mind wandering, quite often, back to what Scott had said about how he missed his hometown. Hank hadn't been born here and hadn't even lived here for as long as Scott had before he'd left to make his fortune in the music business, but lying out under the stars, he couldn't imagine living anywhere else.

He'd been willing to promise Brian anything to keep his job, having consoled himself with the possibility of returning to the fire department in Coquitlam, but he was glad that Brian had been so decent about the whole situation. Scott had been right, after all. Of course, why wouldn't Scott know his own brother? And there was the added bonus of having Scott here for a little while, anyway. As he closed his eyes, his hands coming to rest behind his head, Hank found himself planning another little trip with Scott, not even sure whether Scott was moving back or not. It didn't really matter, though. Hank let himself think about spending more time with the person he was pretty sure was the first real friend he'd ever had.

"HANK?" Scott pushed against Hank's chest, softly at first and then a little harder. "Hank, you fell asleep out here, and the fire's out." Scott smiled when Hank finally opened his eyes. "Come inside before you freeze."

Hank groaned as he felt his body protesting the sudden change in position. "How long was I out?"

"About an hour." Scott stood beside the tent, holding back the flap. "Come on. I've got your sleeping bag all ready for you."

"I sleep on the left." Hank teased as he stooped down and crawled into the tent.

"Well, then," Scott placated sarcastically, "throw your pillow to the other end, and then you'll be on the left."

"That's not right." Hank leaned back on his heels as he stripped off his T-shirt and then shimmied out of his cargo shorts. "Oh, I forgot to get the clothes that were drying."

"Look behind you, you big Sasquatch."

Hank did and smiled over at Scott, who was crawling into the sleeping bag, his eyes already closed. "Thought I was a Neanderthal?"

"Say 'good night', Hank."

"'Kay."

Scott turned off the Coleman lamp and looked over at Hank's peaceful face. He closed his eyes and listened to Hank's steady breathing, falling for Hank a little bit more.

SCOTT woke up to the sound of the seagulls and the waves, such as they were, lapping at the rocky shore, content to stretch out, his toes and fingers making a familiar cracking sound. It was the sound that Scott's joints made when he'd been in such a deep sleep that his body had barely moved all night. He had a vague memory of Hank tucking the sleeping bag around him securely and telling him to go back to sleep, but he dismissed it as wishful thinking. Scott put on his shorts and a new T-shirt and decided not to worry about his hair—everyone had bed head when they went camping, right?

When he peeked out of the tent, dawn had long since come and gone and had left in its wake a day as sunny as the previous one. He saw the coffee pot on the Coleman stove and wondered how long it had been sitting there. Deciding that any coffee was better than no coffee, he stood up and stretched again, hearing only a few cracking noises this time. He steered himself in the direction of the coffee and grabbed a mug on his way.

"I can make you some fresh if you want?"

Scott turned and waved at Hank sitting by the shore and then poured himself a coffee, smelling just how strong it had become. He took a slow sip, feeling himself wake up just a little bit more. As he made his way over to the shore, he thought he should probably bathe first, but then he was at the shore and seated already, so he chose to wait until he would be able to brave the cold water.

"Sleep well?" Hank asked, tossing another little stone into the water.

"Like the dead, thanks." Scott gulped some more coffee and groaned his approval. "Your coffee is better than mine."

"Thank you." Hank gave a quick bow and studied Scott for a moment. "I wasn't sure when you'd be getting up. Otherwise, I would have had bacon and eggs waiting for you."

"Sorry," Scott yawned. "You should have woken me up." He looked absently at his wrist, noticed he hadn't put his watch on, and then leaned over to grab Hank's wrist. "The day's almost half over."

Hank chuckled, "It's not even nine thirty in the morning yet."

"I usually don't sleep this late."

"I thought that was the whole point to this camping trip." Hank squinted over at Scott. "You know, you not having slept in a week, and all."

"Just ignore me," Scott pleaded. "I'm not a morning person."

"'Kay."

Scott took a deep breath and wondered whether the musky scent was the outdoors or Hank. "Have I thanked you for this yet?"

"A couple of times, yeah." Hank nudged his shoulder. "And you're welcome."

"I do miss the ocean."

"Speaking of," Hank looked down at his hands, his voice a low rumble. "When are you due back in Toronto?"

"Ticket's open, so... whenever." Scott wouldn't have bet money on it, but he thought he saw Hank's whole body relax at that answer. "Why?" Scott teased. "You going to miss me?"

"Yes." The answer came so quickly and with such conviction that Scott wondered if his sleepy brain had merely constructed the answer it wanted to have. Scott looked over to see Hank's green eyes staring directly into his. "I was thinking last night how much fun it would be to hang out with you." Hank looked back at the ocean. "You make me laugh. You don't let me take myself too seriously."

"I'll miss you, too." Scott wondered if Hank would miss him at all if he knew that Scott was falling in love with him. "And as for the rest of it," Scott chided, his eyes glinting with amusement. "You only have one life, Hank, so you've got to go out there and live it like there won't be a tomorrow." Scott finished his coffee and leaned over to rinse his cup in the ocean, swishing it around a few times and then dumping it out on the beach. "You, of all people, should know how fragile life is."

"I know." Hank allowed with a heavy exhale. "It's just hard putting up with all the... crap from Roddy and some of the others."

"Well, there are options," Scott counseled. "Just focus on the promise you made Brian. That should keep your mind off of Roddy and the others and the crap, right?"

Hank nodded and then looked back out at the ocean. "Would you mind if I called you sometimes?"

Scott used every ounce of self-control he had not to reach over and kiss the worried look off of Hank's beautiful face. "Of course you can!" Scott felt his stomach rumble and looked up to see Hank's expression. "Feed me and you can have anything you want."

Hank hopped up and held out a hand for Scott, but he just stayed seated. "I'll be there in a minute." Scott nodded towards the water, "I'm debating whether or not hygiene is really necessary while I'm out camping."

"Okay." Hank urged, his tone full of warning, "But be careful out there; I think I saw fins this morning while I was washing up."

"Are you kidding me?" Scott stood up quickly enough that he almost lost his balance on the uneven, rocky surface. Finally, he saw the smirk on Hank's face and relaxed visibly. "That's not funny, man! Do you not remember the movie *Jaws*? Christ, left me traumatized for years."

"Seriously, Scott," Hank appeased. "When was the last time you heard of a shark attack in Canadian waters?"

Scott whined, "Yeah, well, that doesn't mean I can't be the first."

"Jeez, I thought you were scrappy?"

"Fine." Scott threw back the flap of the tent, wondering why Hank was laughing so hard. *It's not that funny.* He rummaged around for the soap and came back out. "But if I get eaten out there, I'll haunt you forever."

"Go get 'em, Scrappy!" Hank laughed even harder when Scott flipped him off, and when Scott stripped down to his birthday suit, he called, "I wouldn't worry! Unless they're looking for a toothpick to clean their teeth!"

WHEN Scott returned to the tent with a towel around his waist a few moments later, Hank studied Scott's body up and down. Scott started twisting and turning to see what Hank was looking at. "Just checking for bite marks," Hank taunted and almost dropped the frying pan of eggs when Scott threw the towel at him. Hank lobbed it onto the makeshift clothesline and called to Scott to hurry or his bacon and eggs would get cold.

Scott and Hank ate mostly in silence except for the occasional moan from Scott about even Hank's eggs being better than his. Hank delighted in the praise, but it made it that much harder to realize they only had one more night together. Hank would be back at work, living out on the barge while Scott looked after Brian's house for another couple of days or another week at the most, and then Scott would be gone.

"Hey?" Scott kicked at Hank's sandal. "What? No more jokes at my expense?"

"I was thinking," Hank lied, "that we should go for a nature hike this afternoon."

"Is that safe?" Scott swallowed his last bit of bacon and put his plate down by his feet. "I mean, what if someone comes and steals your stuff?"

"They won't," Hank assured him. "Most people don't know about this, and we're at least five kilometers from the highway. Besides, I've done this plenty of times."

"As long as you're sure," Scott cautioned. "Maybe we should at least put the food in the truck so the animals don't get at it." Hank nodded, finished his own breakfast, and stopped to pick up Scott's plate. "I'll do that. You cooked; I'll clean."

Hank disappeared into the tent, reappearing just as Scott finished drying the few dishes they'd used and put them back in the large plastic container, figuring they may as well stow these in the truck along with the Coleman stove and other valuables. As he hefted the plastic container, he turned, headed for the truck, to see Hank standing there with a towel draped over each shoulder.

"You're not going to throw me in the ocean again, are you?"

"Ah, I believe"—Hank's tone was stern but gentle—"it was you who threw me first. And no, I'm not going to throw you in the ocean."

"I thought we were going hiking?"

"We are." Hank grinned and left it at that.

It took them only ten minutes to stow everything in the covered bed of the trunk and another five to put on their hiking boots. Still wondering if everything would be safe from thieves who might stumble on their campsite, Scott bit back his desire to ask about that one last time and followed Hank through the trees to a well-worn path littered with scenic views of the Strait of Juan de Fuca.

SCOTT felt like he'd walked about twenty kilometers by the time he felt the pace beginning to slow. He pulled out his cell phone, intent on calling Brian to check on him, when Hank reached out and grabbed it.

"You called him last night."

"So?" Scott held his hand out for his cell phone, debating whether or not to go after it when he saw Hank put it in his pocket. "I'll go in there and get it." Scott shook his head in frustration when he saw Hank turn and present him with the pocket.

"Go ahead."

"Hank, come on," Scott begged. "I just need to know he's okay."

"He's fine, Scott," Hank assured him. "Now leave the man in peace, will you?" Before Scott could think of any other valid arguments, Hank took off down a path to the right and halted them both. "This," Hank announced proudly, throwing the towels down onto a collection of boulders and stepping aside to reveal a crystal clear pond, "is why I brought the towels."

"Wow," Scott whispered as he took in the little pond the size of a Jacuzzi nestled in a cove of miniature cliffs of varying heights and colors. "It's so clear." Scott's voice was full of awe at the sight before him.

"Thought you'd like it."

"It's so...."

"Yeah," Hank affirmed, "it is." Hank dug into his backpack and pulled out a Tupperware container with the leftover hoagies from the night before. "Hungry?" Hank didn't wait for an answer before pulling out a couple of bottles of water and a thermos full of coffee.

"When did you do all this?" Scott stood before Hank, pointing at the little impromptu picnic that Hank had made on the rocks near the towels. "And how long have we been walking?"

"When you were asleep," Hank squinted up at him, the pleased look on his face obvious. "Don't know, forgot my watch."

"Should we eat first or wash off the sweat?" Scott pointed to the tempting pool.

"What would you like?"

"Actually," Scott said, already pulling off his T-shirt, "I'd like to cool off first." He laid his T-shirt out beside the towels on the boulders and then took off his boots and socks, stepping carefully across the dirt strewn with jagged pebbles to stand knee-deep in the refreshing water. Letting out a sigh, he turned to see Hank discarding his own clothing but looked away quickly when he saw that Hank was removing both his cargo shorts and boxers at the same time. Scott backed out of the water, removed the rest of his own clothing, tossed them near the boulders, and dove in, letting the fresh water soothe his heated skin. When he surfaced, he noticed that Hank was up to his waist in the water, his hands dipping into the pool and sluicing the liquid over his bronzed skin.

"This is so relaxing." Scott sputtered as he cleared the hair out of his eyes, realizing that his feet touched the bottom; the water only came up to his chest. "I can't believe I've never been to this part of the island."

"I love this place," Hank commented before lowering himself slowly into the water. "I found it just after I first moved to the island."

"How often do you come here?" Scott waded backwards, his back settling against a smooth bit of rock at the far end of the pool. Hank made his way over to where Scott was, covering the small distance in two or three strides. Scott was hypnotized by the way the water moved around Hank's large frame and the way it made his skin glisten and sparkle. He brought his hand up to wipe his face before he got caught staring.

"As often as I can."

"It must be nice for...."—Scott waggled his eyebrows—"those special ladies you're trying to impress?"

Hank sank to his neck in the water and Scott felt their knees touch under the water. Hank stroked absently at his hair, smoothing it away from his face. "I always come out alone." Hank's eyes were very earnest, his eyes boring holes into Scott's overheated skin.

"You've never brought anyone out here?"

"Just you."

The words were so faint that Scott wasn't sure if Hank had said them or if the water and the air had mixed to create some sort of pressure change near his ears. Before he could think fast enough to move away, to tell Hank he didn't believe him, he felt Hank's hands on his thighs, the fingers pressing into his skin like hot coals. He wanted to protest, to tell Hank that he wasn't sure about this, but the words wouldn't come. He couldn't get his lips to do anything but wait.

As Hank moved one hand to the small of his back, Scott could feel the air rush out of his lungs moments before he felt the other hand slide gently up the back of his neck and into his hair. He looked for some sort of reassurance in Hank's eyes. He needed to know that this wasn't a mistake, a trick of some kind. It seemed like he spent an eternity staring into those brilliant green eyes before Hank lowered his lips to cover Scott's. Feeling the heat of Hank's body molding to his own, smelling the musk and maleness that was so unique to this gentle man, Scott finally allowed his hands to respond. His eyes fluttered closed as his mouth was covered by

Hank's, the gentle licking and probing of Hank's tongue drawing an uncontrollable whimper from somewhere deeper than his own body.

Hank pulled his lips away only long enough to smooth wisps of hair from Scott's face and to wrap Scott's long legs around his waist. As Scott saw the depth of desire in those green eyes, he realized he didn't need to worry anymore about how much it would hurt when he finished falling. He'd never imagined, never even considered the possibility that Hank would be there to catch him.

CHAPTER 14

"YOU realize," Scott sighed as he put his dinner plate beside him on the rocks and looked over at Hank's happy, smiling face, "that, eventually, we're going to have to talk about what happened back there."

Hank's smile faded as he dropped his fork onto his plate, the clattering sound loud and foreign to Scott's ears after the afternoon he'd spent with Hank in the little pool. "Does it have to be now?"

Scott inhaled deeply, catching Hank's eyes as they stole a look at his face in the dying light of the best afternoon of Scott's life. "No," he assuaged, wanting to reach out and comfort Hank but not daring to. "I guess not."

"I'm not—" Hank's voice seemed strained, as if he were about to divulge a secret long hidden. "I'm not using you, Scott."

Scott came off the little log that they were using as a bench and settled himself in front of Hank, his hands coming to rest on Hank's knees. "I never thought you were, Hank." Scott put his hand on Hank's cheek and let it trail down along his jaw line. "But...," Scott said after a few moments. "You're not gay." When Hank didn't look up, didn't respond, Scott asked hesitantly, "Are you? Is that what this is about?"

"No!" Hank looked up then, his features twisting at the implication in Scott's last question. "I don't know," Hank admitted after studying Scott's friendly smile.

"You can trust me, Hank," Scott soothed, his hands resting on Hank's muscular thighs and feeling the tension that his questions must be causing. "I don't want to see either of us hurt."

"I couldn't control myself," Hank confessed after a moment. He put his hands over Scott's, stilling them while he tried to find the words. "You're not the first man I've… but you're the first where alcohol wasn't involved."

"Uh." Scott tried to hide his smile. "Thanks?" Scott finally laughed when he saw the edges of Hank's full lips twitch into a relieved, lopsided smile. "Hank, please believe me," Scott continued, moving back onto the log so that he could wrap one arm over Hank's broad shoulders. "That I'm not sorry it happened, but…." Scott stroked his back, hoping to ease some of the tension and worry out of Hank's clenched muscles. "Well, you should know that I'm starting to… develop feelings for you." That was a lie; he was in love with Hank, he knew that and had known it from their first kiss, but he wasn't ready to admit it. He was still hoping that he would be able to recover some dignity if Hank realized he had only done it because he was lonely—and maybe scared.

"Really?" Hank's arm came around Scott's waist and pulled him closer, Hank's look of grief replaced with a genuine smile.

"What do you mean, 'really?'" Scott wondered just what kind of life this man had lived up until their meeting. How could a man so perfect, so handsome, so funny, so tender, possibly have such low self-esteem?

Hank's response was to shrug and pull Scott a little closer. "I know I'm not ugly, but—"

"I'm not even talking about the physical stuff, Hank—which is very impressive by the way. I'm talking about how kind and gentle and attentive and funny and—"

"You think I'm funny?"

Scott reached over with both hands and let his long fingers glide over the stubble and the fine hairs near the beautiful green eyes. "Hank, I know you think I've been helping you, but you've been just as much help to me." Scott nodded when he saw the disbelief cloud Hank's eyes. "I'm serious, Hank. I never really felt attractive. I mean, I know I'm not ugly," Scott echoed, "but there's never been anyone who made me feel like you did this afternoon."

"I know this will sound funny." Hank blushed and looked away. "Since we're both men, but holding you, kissing you… it made me feel like a man. You made me feel like a man."

Scott wasn't really sure what that meant, but he was sure Hank had meant it to be a compliment. "You *are* a man, Hank." Scott leaned over to kiss his lips, Hank accepting it eagerly. "A beautiful, kind, generous, wonderful man."

Hank licked his lips after the kiss and put his forehead to Scott's. When he pulled back briefly, it was to look into his eyes and ask, his voice a mere suggestion in the cool evening breeze, "Can you stay a little longer in Duncan?"

Scott's immediate thought was for the musical. He would need to get back soon before things started to fall apart—or worse, fall off schedule. Scott dismissed that thought and answered the question with another kiss, his tongue seeking permission against Hank's warm, moist lips. He heard Hank groan as his tongue moved into the warmth, Hank's teeth nipping lightly at his tongue and swollen bottom lip. His own moans urged Hank to reach for him and soon he found himself straddling Hank's thighs, the large, work-hewn hands caressing his thighs and back and cheeks. He groaned when one of those hands found its way to cup the back of his head, pulling it gently so that Hank could whisper something in his ear. He shivered when Hank told him he wished he'd brought condoms, stifling a little giggle of happiness at the thought that Hank wanted this to happen. He freed himself from Hank's tender grasp and stripped naked outside of the tent before entering.

He unzipped the sleeping bags and laid them out as if one were a sheet and the other a comforter, his cock already hard and leaking. He felt the cool rush of wind when Hank drew back the flap and entered the small space, his clothes having joined Scott's outside the tent. Hank knee-walked over to Scott and pulled the smaller man up so that their bodies touched from lips to knees. Scott felt the heat pressing into his belly, his desire to feel it and taste it so hard to ignore, but it was up to Hank to lead—wherever this went.

Scott heard Hank take a deep breath and then felt Hank's hands on his face. Scott lost himself in the feel of the rough, calloused skin and the soft, wet kisses to his neck and mouth. Hank moved one hand to rest against Scott's lower back. There was no pressure, no urgency, just a hand to make sure there was constant contact. When Hank's lips found his ear and the deep voice whispered for Scott to lie down on his back, Scott knew it wouldn't take much before he would finish. He didn't have the advantage of cool water to help him stave off the inevitable result of being so close to Hank this time.

Hank was on his knees, his legs nudging between Scott's thighs. Scott looked up and was convinced that he'd never seen anything more beautiful, more sensual than the look in those eyes, the slight heaving of Hank's belly as he breathed, or the slight curve to that uncircumcised cock. Hank was definitely bigger than any man he'd ever been with before, but Scott had never wanted anything more. He reached between his own thighs as he felt Hank's hands behind his knees, pushing them up towards his chest, and stroked a hand down the length of the silky shaft. He closed his eyes when Hank whispered his name. He felt his legs being coaxed around Hank's waist, and then the handsome face was only inches from his. Hank's elbows found a comfortable position near his shoulders. Scott felt the calloused skin brush against his face and move back to smooth away the hair from his eyes. Hank's hair fell against Scott's lips as Hank began to explore his neck, his warm lips bringing out even stronger shivers of delight as Scott felt the heat build in the pit of his stomach. Scott turned his head and inhaled the scent that was all Hank's, the smell of shampoo and soap mixed with the smell of their two bodies making Scott's vision blur a little around the edges.

Hank seemed to spend hours exploring Scott's neck and shoulders, sucking and nipping at the tender, heated flesh. Unable to wait any longer for the little bit of additional friction, Scott locked his ankles together over the strong back and pressed up into the firmness of Hank's belly, his breath hitching when he felt the initial contact between the soft, velvety hairs and his own swollen cock. He thought he heard Hank chuckle briefly before the big man brought his hands up to bookend his flushed face. "Where's the ten-alarm, Scrappy? We got plenty of time."

"Hank," Scott sighed, unable to think of anything else but crawling inside of Hank.

"You want me to take the edge off?" Hank didn't wait for an answer. He put both of his hands under Scott's back and hauled him up so that he was once again perched in Hank's lap. Hank leaned forward as he pulled Scott closer to his chest, their lips meeting in a tender yet impatient kiss. Scott heard a moan coming from one of them when Hank's hand slid down and wrapped around both of them, the leaking tips supplying more than enough slick. Scott pulled his lips away to warn Hank he was close, pressing their foreheads together when he saw the lustful, faraway look on Hank's tanned face.

He reached down with one hand, his fingers stilling Hank's frenetic pumping, and let his finger find Hank's tender head, tracing a path around it under his foreskin. He felt Hank shudder and watched as Hank's eyes closed, feeling the heat spray up to coat both of their chests and bellies. He fisted himself while muttering nonsense to Hank about how beautiful he was when he came, how pretty his eyes were when he let go. Hank's lips devoured his, and he felt himself getting closer, feeling his belly tighten in anticipation. As he heard the rumbling whisper urging him to come, he felt Hank's fingers probing at his crease, and when Hank told him how much he wanted to be in him, Scott's head fell forward to rest on a muscled shoulder, the feel of those calloused hands and the sound of that bass voice easing him down gently from his own release.

He didn't move his head right away, content to nestle his face against Hank's neck, his tongue darting out occasionally to taste the salt and the heat. He felt Hank's pulse spike a little when he let his hand fall between them, gently gripping and stroking him. When he felt a shudder pass over Hank, he looked up and placed a gentle kiss on his cheeks. He smiled when Hank opened his eyes and moved to disengage himself from his seat atop the thick thighs.

"This must be killing your knees," he joked and released his hold on Hank.

"Don't," Hank whispered and tightened his grip around Scott's waist. His lips found their way to an ear and begged, "Not yet?"

"I thought you tough guys didn't like to cuddle?" He left a trail of kisses along Hank's jaw line.

"Not so tough, I guess." Hank reached out and slapped playfully at Scott's ass. "You're ruining this for me."

"Sorry," he whispered into Hank's ear and pulled the solid frame closer to his chest. "You're just the right amount of tough for me, Hank." When he heard their breathing slow, Scott pushed away just enough to look at Hank's smile and said, "Come on. Your legs must be cramping. Time for bed." He backed off of Hank's lap and grabbed a pair of boxer shorts, wiping at their bodies and then pulling the top sleeping bag back so Hank could climb in, the big hands clinging to him and pulling him in to lie alongside.

"It's too early to sleep."

"Who said anything about sleeping?" Scott propped his head on one elbow and let his hands stroke the silky hairs that covered Hank's muscled chest. "So," he asked cautiously, "who was the first?"

Hank's head lolled to the side, and he grinned at Scott. "A friend in high school." Hank snaked his hand underneath Scott's arm to caress his back, chuckling to himself as the squirming it caused brought Scott closer to him. "We were both on the football team, and we liked to get drunk on the weekends and... one Saturday, when his parents were out of town, we...." Hank waggled his eyebrows and then asked, "Who was your first?"

"Well," Scott teased, hands stilling over Hank's heart, "compared to you, I was a late bloomer." Scott cleared his throat, already embarrassed that Hank would learn just how much later he'd bloomed. "I was twenty-five and living in Toronto by that time."

"That's not so late," Hank soothed as he continued to stroke Scott's back, his hand coming up to squeeze Scott's neck gently.

"Yeah." Scott felt a shiver pass through him as he felt the hand comb through his hair. "Says the man whose first time was when he was eighteen."

"Seventeen."

"Don't interrupt!" Scott scolded as Hank laughed. "I met this guy at one of the gay bars down on Church Street, and he seemed nice and I was still new there, and well, I guess, a bit lonely, so...." Scott sighed and felt the inevitable flush of embarrassment wash over him. "When he asked me back to his place, I went."

"Did you enjoy it?"

"No," Scott huffed. Then he amended, "Well, I liked the kissing—"

"That hasn't changed," Hank goaded as he waggled his eyebrows again. "And may I say that you're very good at it."

"Behave," Scott slapped at the defined chest and finished his answer. "I guess it wasn't that I didn't like it, I was hoping that it would have been more... sensual... like you do it."

It was Hank's turn to blush as Scott leaned over and kissed his lips. "I do like to kiss."

"Lucky me." Scott brought his top leg up so that it rested between Hank's legs, the rest of his body making full contact with Hank's. The kisses were sweet and tender, nothing urgent in them except the desire for another. But when Hank brought his other arm across to take hold of Scott's hip, his big frame turned onto its side, and then Scott felt one of those muscled thighs push between his legs. He reached down and took hold of Hank's growing erection, absolutely amazed at such a rapid recovery time, and pinched the foreskin just as Hank's tongue found his.

As they touched and explored and enjoyed their last night beside the calm ocean waters, Scott found himself wanting to tell Hank that he'd fallen in love with him, that maybe some people thought of Hank as a fuck-up, but that he knew Hank was so much more. Scott had always guffawed loudly at the novels or songs he read about people falling in love so quickly—*That's why the divorce rate is so high,* he explained to anyone who argued with him—but he was starting to understand why "But for You" had been such a big hit. He could write sappy love songs with the best of them, but he found it ironic that the first song he'd written, after a broken relationship with a man he'd found to be everything he'd thought he was looking for, had proven to be oddly prophetic.

CHAPTER 15

"Dɪᴅ you have fun?"

Scott looked over at his brother, not really sure how to answer. "Yeah, but all that hiking and swimming really makes you tired." Scott sorted his laundry, quickly assessing which items needed hiding. He gathered the small pile into a neat little ball, wrapped it in a towel and headed for the laundry room. He got as far as the door to his room.

"Do you think I'm an idiot?" Brian still stood, arms folded over his chest, his big frame leaning against the door jamb.

"Which answer will get me to the laundry room?" Scott tried to laugh it off, not certain if his brother was asking what he thought he was asking.

"Scooter!" Brian's posture became defensive, like it had so many times when they were younger. His brother was ready to provide some sort of lecture. "Do you really think that's such a good idea?"

"I'm a big boy," Scott argued. With a grin he was incapable of hiding, he added with a stage whisper and a waggle of his eyebrows, "And so is Hank."

"Oh, for fuck's sake, now who's the pig?" Brian moved aside and walked to the kitchen, planting his hands firmly on the counter. "You know this will end badly, right?"

"How can it end badly when it hasn't even begun?" Scott lied and stood at the door to the laundry room. "What are you really worried about, Brian? That one of your *men* might actually be gay?"

"You know I don't give a shit about that stuff!" Brian's back was up now, and Scott decided to let the subject drop. He knew all too well how his brother reacted when backed into a corner. "I've *never* cared that you're gay."

"Then what's wrong with a harmless weekend between two consenting adults?" Scott didn't bother looking over his shoulder as he filled the washing machine and spun the dial for the twenty-minute cycle. "You're making too much out of this."

"Scott," Brian cautioned, "I know Hank. I've worked with him for almost five years."

"Okay, Brian," Scott countered. "So tell me about Hank."

"Scooter, look," Brian leaned back against the counter, his hands rising and falling to hang lifeless at his side when he couldn't find the words to continue. "I don't want to see you get used... or hurt."

"Did you ever think, Brian," Scott asked as he approached his brother slowly, "that maybe I'm the one doing the using?"

"Scott?"

"I'll be in my room if you need me." Scott didn't wait for a response, hoping his indignant exit would be enough to halt his brother's concern. He really didn't want to have to analyze this; he knew he was probably making the biggest mistake of his life, but being near Hank was like a drug. He was sure he loved Hank, and if he thought about it too much, dissected every word and movement, he was sure he'd find himself doing what he always did: pushing Hank away because of fear of being hurt. He knew that Brian was only looking out for him, but if he'd always listened to Brian instead of following his heart, he'd be stuck here climbing trees instead of living in Toronto and doing what he'd always dreamed of doing.

He was still sitting on the edge of the bed thirty minutes later when he heard the knock on the door.

"Scott," Brian asked calmly. "May I come in?"

"Of course you can." As the door opened, Scott began. "I know you're just trying to protect me, and you probably do know Hank better than I do, but I don't need protecting, Brian." Scott felt the bed shift as Brian sat down beside him. "You're my brother and I love you, but I want this. I know it may not go anywhere, but I don't care." Scott looked over at his brother's concerned expression. "He makes me happy. He's kind and funny and passionate and—" Scott stopped when he saw his brother shake his head. Scott laughed at his brother's squeamishness. "Maybe it's only temporary, and maybe I'm an idiot, but I've done plenty of stupid things before."

Brian put a hand on his brother's shoulder and pushed himself off the bed. "Kari's coming over later today."

"Should I go to a movie or something?"

"Of course not," Brian smirked. "Unlike you, I have some self-control."

"Yeah," Scott quipped, "I remember the lecture about that from when I was fourteen."

"Well, what did you expect," Brian winked. "We were going through so much toilet paper, Dad thought we were the ones tee-peeing all those houses north of Allenby."

"Ewww," Scott groused. Then he heard the chime of his phone and reached for it. He muttered a "hello," still grateful for his brother having come after him, just like he'd always done, and heard Hank's deep, gravelly voice. "You get home okay?"

"Of course," Hank assured him. "Listen, I was wondering if you wanted to come over tonight, you know, for dinner?"

"Do I need to bring anything?"

Scott waited for a few moments, ready to repeat the question when he heard, "Toothbrush?"

"Dinner, huh?"

"I was trying to be a gentleman."

"What time?"

"Six-ish?"

"I'll see you then. Oh," Scott added at the last minute, remembering that Kari was coming over and Brian's warnings about being hurt. "Kari's coming over to visit with Brian, so I don't know about staying all night."

"We'll work around your schedule, then."

Scott disconnected and flipped his phone shut, walking out to the living room to find Brian on the sofa watching a baseball game. "So," he said after a few minutes. "How are things with Kari?"

"Fine."

"Oh-oh," Scott mocked. "Did she find out about your hairy back?"

Brian looked over, and Scott could tell he wanted to smack the grin off his face. "I do not have a hairy back."

"I'm sure some women find that sexy." Brian didn't take the bait. "So," Scott pushed, "are you gonna ask her to go steady?"

"Are you always like this after you get laid?"

"I don't know." Scott poked at his brother's shoulder. "Ask me tomorrow."

"And I'm the pig?" Brian looked over, his expression stern. "Are you at least careful?"

"Yes, Mom." Scott picked up a cushion and tossed it at his brother. "Can I ask you something?"

"I'll tell you about Kari when there's something to tell."

"No," Scott huffed. "Do you want to have kids?"

"Only if I'm married," Brian said and turned the television off. Turning to face Scott, he asked, "Why?"

"I worry about you sometimes." Scott sat on the edge of the sofa. "I worry that you're not happy."

"And having kids will make me happy."

"You know what I mean."

"Scooter," Brian smiled, "if it's meant to be, it will happen. But at the moment, my business is going well, I'm providing work for some good men who need to support their families, and I have a famous brother who—*thank God*—doesn't visit very often." Brian tossed the pillow back at Scott and reminded Scott about his laundry before heading to the fridge to fix himself a sandwich.

HANK checked the pot roast; it was the only thing he'd ever learned how to make. He'd done nothing but curse the foods study class he'd been dumped in as one of his options, having registered too late to get his first choice of auto shop. But with company coming, he found himself thanking that haggard old woman who'd insisted on making him pay attention to the actual recipe.

With only a half hour to go before he anticipated the knock on his door, he surveyed the dining room quickly. He figured he wouldn't need to light the candles until Scott actually got there, thereby sparing himself the embarrassment of having to go out and try to find another tablecloth if the candles had time to melt—and ruin—the only one he had. Ticking off each item as he scanned the room, he checked the stove, figuring the steamed vegetables would need another couple of minutes, and headed for the shower.

He opened the door to the oversized shower and then turned to study his scruffy face in the mirror, smiling as he remembered Scott telling him how much he liked the feel of rubbing his cheeks against Hank's unshaven ones. Hank felt a stirring as he thought about how so very definite the man was in his likes and dislikes; it helped to take the guesswork out it for Hank. He didn't mind figuring things out for himself every once in a while, but it revved his motor when his partners could tell him what they wanted. And Scott could certainly get his motor revving.

He took a deep breath as the hot water sluiced over his neck and back. He wouldn't have time to stay in for his usual ten or fifteen minutes, but maybe he could convince Scott to join him later. He stopped his hand from traveling too far south at the thought of what he'd like to do to Scott once he got that tall, lean body under the hot water and focused on rinsing off the soap and shampoo. He wouldn't have time to dry his hair, but letting it air dry seemed to leave it soft anyway, and the softer his hair, the more often he would find Scott's fingers sliding through it.

He glanced at the clock as he ran the towel over his body and hurried to throw on a nicer pair of shorts and his favorite well-worn button-down. He didn't remember if he'd told Scott to dress casually or not, but he hoped they wouldn't be wearing anything for too long anyway. Hank couldn't really remember the last time he'd invited anyone over for dinner. It had to be years by now, and even longer since he'd felt this nervous about it.

He shoved his size twelve feet into his slippers and exited the bedroom just in time to hear the two knocks in rapid succession at the door. He let out a breath as he grabbed the knob and twisted, pulling it open to find Scott holding two six-packs of beer and a worried look on his face.

"Brian figured it out."

Hank had barely had time to register a smile before Scott blurted out the news. "What?" Hank hoped the question sounded more inquisitorial out in the open than it did inside his head.

"Don't worry," Scott soothed, handing the beer to Hank and kicking his shoes over by Hank's. "I told him that it wasn't serious, it was just a fling."

"Oh," Hank muttered, not sure whether it was an excuse or the truth. This evening hadn't started as Hank thought it might. "Take a seat. Dinner's almost ready. You want a beer?"

"I'd love one." Scott moved over to the sectional and let himself sink into the overstuffed cushions.

"So," Hank started, handing over one of the last Heinekens to Scott. "You didn't deny it?"

"I tried, but," Scott shrugged, "he told me he wasn't an idiot, that he could tell." Scott's stopped the beer bottle just short of his lips. "You're not upset, are you?"

Hank sank back on the sectional and laughed, shaking his head. "Nah," he lied. "So your brother knows I play for both teams. No big deal. He's only my boss."

"You think Brian will care." Hank didn't hear a question at the end of the sentence. Scott put his beer on the coffee table and leaned forward. "Brian's not the type to do anything about it, Hank."

"It's not Brian I'm worried about." Hank fidgeted in his seat and found a stray thread on his shorts to pick at.

"Do you want me to go?"

"What?" Hank thought at first that he hadn't heard the question and then realized he had. "No, of course not." Hank reached over and stroked Scott's bare forearm once, twice, and then pulled the smaller man onto his lap, letting his hands find their way to the waistband of Scott's jeans. He didn't encounter any elastic and pushed his hands further down the firm globes of Scott's ass before grinning against Scott's lips. "You're not wearing any underwear."

"I was being practical." Scott pressed himself against Hank's abdomen as he arched his back and pushed his hand into the leg opening of Hank's shorts, offering a sly smile of his own. "What's your reason?"

"You." Hank flipped Scott onto his back, grabbing a few of the cushions and tossing them aside. "Every time I think about you and your skin, I run out of room in my boxers."

"Maybe you shouldn't think about me, then."

Hank felt Scott's hands at the waistband of his shorts and felt himself leaking already. "We only have about ten minutes before the roast is done." Hank sucked in a quick breath as he felt Scott's finger find its way between his foreskin and the head of his prick, moving it slowly around and then up and over the slit. "That particular move is not easy to forget." Hank saw Scott pull the same finger out and press it gently against his lips, Scott's mouth opening when Hank took the finger in and gently lapped at the tip.

When Scott pulled his finger out and repeated the move, Hank was convinced that the dinner would burn, especially when Scott put the finger in his own mouth this time. Hank felt the growl before he heard it and lowered his lips to cover Scott's and then slowly lowered his body to cover Scott's torso. Bracing his elbows beside the sinewy muscle of Scott's shoulders, he let one hand cradle Scott's long neck while the other hand fisted in the soft, fair hair, pulling on it gently so that Hank could suck and nip at Scott's sensitive throat.

SCOTT heard the smack of lips and kisses against his neck and felt his jeans growing uncomfortable, his erection straining against the zipper. He let his hands trail away from Hank's back and slipped them between their bodies so that he could release some of the pressure.

"We should stop soon, Hank." When Hank stopped kissing up and down his neck and looked into his eyes, Scott brought his hands up to push back the wayward chestnut waves and smiled. "I didn't bring a change of clothes."

Scott felt Hank's head drop down beside his, a heavy sigh Hank's only answer; Scott wondered if he would even have anything to lend the logger—he was at least three or four sizes bigger. "My fault," he heard Hank mutter into his sensitive neck. "I should have reminded you."

"I can't stay the night anyway, so…."

"Why do I suddenly feel like I'm back in high school?" Hank pushed himself up so that his arms were braced on either side of Scott's head, his expression resigned and melancholy.

Scott laughed and pulled Hank down to give him a quick kiss. "There'll be other nights," Scott whispered just as the buzzing from the kitchen signaled that the roast was done.

Hank sat back on his heels, not even making a move to rescue the roast from the oven. "When?" He freed his legs from underneath him and stomped to the kitchen. "I'm back out for three days starting tomorrow."

"Hank?" Scott had moved to the doorway of the kitchen, his chin perched on top of one of the swinging gates. "I'm not asking for anything but what we have tonight. And," Scott pushed through the door as Hank let the steaming pan drop onto the cutting board, "I don't think it's wise for us to take this too quickly. I mean," he drew up next to Hank and let his fingers curl around the nearest bicep, "this is still new for you and you're worried about the other guys as it is—"

"But I just found you—"

"I'm not going anywhere, Hank." Scott tossed the hair off his forehead. "You asked me to stay for a while, and I'm more than willing, but at some point I have to go back to Toronto."

"And what about us?"

"What about us?" Scott asked. He leaned in to feel the warmth of Hank's body against his own. "Do you want there to be an us?" Hank answered him by wrapping him in his arms and kissing his forehead. "Good," Scott chuckled when the stubble tickled his eyebrows. "Then we'll figure it out as we go along."

CHAPTER 16

"YOU'RE a very good cook." Scott was lying on the sectional with his legs across Hank's thighs. "It was wonderful, thank you." He jumped a little when the calloused hands trailed lazily over the soles of his feet.

"Are you ticklish?" Hank laughed as he pulled one foot up and let his fingers glide over the warm flesh. Scott smiled at him and tried to pull his foot away. "Let's see," Hank drawled as he held Scott's ankle. "Your neck, your sides, your inner thighs and now your feet." He let go of the ankle and stood up, his arousal evident, and held out a hand. He managed to get the man to his feet with one quick pull and then, with Scott caught in his arms, began walking backward to the stairs. "I wonder what other parts are that sensitive."

"I think you've found them all now."

"You don't mind"—Hank kissed the tip of his nose—"if I check for myself, do you?"

"Not at all." Scott complied, his hands finding their way under the soft cotton shirt. "Is this a solo mission or do I get to return the favor?"

Scott's heels hit the first stair and he stopped. He brought his hands out from under Hank's shirt and began to undo the buttons, tilting his head to one side as Hank's lips caressed his neck.

"God, I can't think when you do that."

Hank brought one hand to the back of his neck and massaged lightly while his lips continued their journey to the sensitive flesh behind Scott's ears. Scott moaned and finished unfastening the last button, his hands sliding the shirt over Hank's shoulders and arms. Bending his head, his mouth found a nipple and began sucking and laving intently, delighting in the deep growl it brought out of Hank.

"Oh, baby," Hank moaned. "You've got the sweetest mouth." Hank's hands slid down along Scott's belly when he switched his attention to the other nipple, taking hold of the T-shirt and lifting it over Scott's head in one swift movement. "No change of clothes," Hank reminded him and popped open the tight-fitting jeans with one hand while his other reached immediately for Scott's erection. Scott helped him discard the jeans as he pulled on them with one hand.

Down on his knees, finally watching the jeans pool around Scott's long, toned legs, Hank brought his hand up to the flushed belly and pushed Scott back onto the stairs. He reached down and pulled off the denim, letting the backs of his hands trail up the soft, blond hairs of Scott's thighs until he could gently push his hands against the backs of his knees. When his head descended to lay a wet trail of kisses along Scott's inner thighs, Scott whimpered and slid his hands into Hank's hair. "Can't wait for the bedroom, baby."

Scott hissed when he felt himself enveloped in the warmth of Hank's mouth. He laid his head back on the step as Hank's tongue swept over the sensitive head, and when he felt himself drawn in by the suction, the only thought that came into his head was the name of the man who was giving him so much pleasure.

"Hank," Scott panted as he opened his eyes and saw himself fall out of that mouth. He began to feel dizzy and euphoric when he watched and then felt the tongue slide around his sac and stop finally at his entrance. First, a few tentative flicks of the tongue, then a few licks, each more forceful than the last. His hands came up to cover Hank's, encouraging and stroking—he had no ability to speak anymore. The sensation coursing through him was too much, and the sight of Hank's head pulling away, Hank's eyes fixed on his hole made him insane with desire. He didn't want to come yet. He had wanted Hank to be seated deeply inside him before he lost control and let himself finish.

Scott heard his own panting, his breathing so ragged; he knew he was close, but he didn't want to stop. He saw Hank watching, captivated by the sight they must have made. Scott's head fell back onto the step; he was certain that Hank couldn't possibly be enjoying this more than him.

"Come for me," Hank whispered and then took just the purple head into this mouth, letting it fall out so he could kiss it and then taking it back into his mouth. When he felt Scott's hands slide back into his hair, he had to have known it was time. Hank took Scott as deep as he could one last time and let his teeth drag slowly over the swollen head before tonguing the slit. He swallowed the entire length and then repeated the movements, finding a rhythm until he felt Scott's hands curl into fists, the urgency of his grip the final signal. "That's it, Scrappy," he growled as his stubble rubbed across Scott's balls. "Come for me. Come for me so I can fuck you."

Scott heard the words, none of them really registering. But when the sensation of Hank's stubble against his testicles came again, Scott opened his eyes to see himself in Hank's mouth, those green eyes staring at him, demanding for him to come. The hot breath as Hank exhaled across his belly made him feel like his insides were on fire. The sensation of the stubble became so intense that Scott did not experience the same usual series of events; they all happened at once, and he cried out as the hot, creamy ropes exploded from him.

He heard Hank telling him how pretty it all looked. He couldn't see; his eyes wouldn't seem to focus. Scott felt his legs shake as Hank lowered them to rest on the step. When he opened his eyes, he saw that Hank was already out of his shirt and was lowering his shorts, kicking them off to the side. Scott took in the sight of the slight tan line, wondering briefly where Hank would go to sunbathe nude, and then his eyes focused on the foreskin. He'd never been with an uncircumcised man before, and the idea of learning how to use it to give Hank pleasure started him hardening again.

"God, Hank," Scott sighed, the sight of what he'd been wanting for almost a week too much to bear. "You're so fucking gorgeous." Scott tried to sit up, but his legs were still too shaky. It made him wonder what would happen when Hank did finally fuck him.

With Hank's help, Scott moved to a sitting position and immediately felt Scott's hands move around to squeeze the firm muscles of his ass, that sweet mouth kissing its way down Hank's treasure trail. He stared in amazement as he watched the entire thing disappear into Scott's silky wet mouth; no one he'd ever been with had been able to take the entire length, not without gagging. He let his head fall back as he felt Scott nuzzle into his lower belly. He looked down again at the spectacle, unable to look away.

"Oh fuck, I could come just watching you do that." Hank brought his hands up to caress the soft, blond hair, careful not to push too hard into Scott's mouth. As soon as he felt the familiar heat licking up and down his spine, he pulled Scott up and kissed him soundly. He still had plans for the rest of their evening, and none of them involved coming quite so soon.

"I wasn't finished," Scott complained as Hank pulled him up. He'd planned on saying more, trying to slide back down to finish what he'd started, but Hank had him in a bear hug, covering his lips and neck with kisses.

"I'm not finished either," Hank growled and lifted Scott's legs, wrapping them around his waist. He took the stairs slowly, feeling for the flat surface of each step as he reached below Scott's ass and started pushing against his hole. "Not even your mouth will distract me from what I've been waiting for," he whispered against Scott's neck.

Finding his way to the top of the stairs, Hank was in the bedroom within a few easy strides and lowered their bodies to the bed. After another round of kissing and sucking his way up and down Scott's neck and shoulders, Hank pulled back and straightened up to stare down at the fair, sensitive skin.

"Roll over," he commanded and watched as Scott positioned himself with his ass in the air, his forehead resting on his forearms. As Hank bent to flick his tongue across the heated flesh, Scott's eyes rolled back in his head and he felt himself grow hard and hungry with the need to be taken by this man.

Just as he was thinking of begging Hank to do something, anything, he heard the familiar sound of a pop-top being flicked open. Unable to control his curiosity, he craned his neck to look behind him and saw a knowing grin on the handsome face. He heard Hank ask if he was ready and nodded, his breath forced out of him as he felt one slick finger slide easily into him. He let his head drop down onto his forearms again, trying to focus his breathing as he listened to Hank's soft, heated words of encouragement.

Scott did as he was told, relaxing, letting himself be opened and explored. He pushed back slowly onto the two thick fingers and then arched his back when Hank found his prostate and rubbed it slowly. He didn't know how many times he begged Hank to fuck him before that deep voice became raspy with passion, the thick fingers pulling out.

Scott turned one last time to see Hank rolling the condom onto himself and then positioning his tall frame to give him what he'd asked for. "It's so hot, Scotty, like an oven in there. So good, so tight."

As Hank pushed in very slowly, his hands came up to caress Scott's back. Scott could feel the calluses exerting a faint, unbearable pressure along his spine before moving off to trail along his sides. When Hank was fully seated, the feel of hands on Scott's back was replaced with the delicious heat of tender kisses landing on his shoulders and neck. He could feel Hank's hands push through his hair, moving it out of the way, so that he could kiss as far as he could reach.

It seemed like an eternity that their two bodies were joined, neither of them moving, no friction happening. Finally, Scott pushed back slightly and whispered only one word, "Move," and he felt strong hands grip his shoulders, thumbs stroking the sides of his neck. Hank pulled out slowly and then pushed forward again, his thrusts becoming more energetic. Scott used his arms to push himself up, hoping the change in position would help him take the length and girth more easily, but he let his arms collapse when he felt the overwhelming tapping against his prostate with each slow, deliberate snap of Hank's hips.

Neither spoke, and Scott found the silence intoxicating. There were only the muted, yet insistent, grunts from Hank each time he pulled out and Scott would try to grip against the loss, or the plaintive gasps from his own mouth each time he felt himself stretched by the rhythmic roll of Hank's hips.

Scott could feel the roiling deep in his belly and felt Hank reach down to wrap both of his arms around his waist, pulling the skin of his back against Hank's sweat-soaked chest. He concentrated on the breathless cries the shifting caused in Scott and let his hands smooth over pecs and belly and then back up again. He squeezed the lithe body to his own, his lips and teeth biting into Scott's shoulders and neck, losing all control as he listened to Scott calling his name over and over. He felt the long, slender fingers reach back to rest on his hips, urging him to go deeper, faster.

"Come with me, Scott," he whispered against the soft shell of Scott's ear, his hand sliding down the heaving belly to wrap around his erection.

He pulled only once and then let his thumb trail over the exquisitely soft head, stopping to press against the slit, and then his own erection felt as if it was gripped in a vice as Scott exploded all over his hand and forearm.

Scott let the waves ebb, and he let Hank's hands lower him to the bed and lost himself in the heated breath that flowed across his sweaty neck and shoulders. He felt Hank pull out slowly, feeling the final stretch of his muscle. The weight of the man on his back and the conflicting sensations of cold and hot as Hank's sweat-soaked and hairy chest hovered mere inches above him were obliterated by the sudden, unexpected caress of Hank's unsheathed cock between his ass cheeks. Scott lifted his hips slightly, his cheeks separating enough to allow Hank to settle in between them. He pressed against Hank and turned his face to the side, the warm, moist lips taking hold of his earlobe.

Scott continued to push against Hank, squeezing his cheeks each time Hank pushed his throbbing cock forward. He reached out to find a hand, and when he interlaced his fingers with Hank's, he felt the muscled and sweaty body stiffen, the roars sounding more like pain than pleasure. Hank's thrusts slowed and Scott could feel the air make the come on his backside feel cold. He shivered slightly at the sound and feel of Hank.

Hank let himself down slowly onto Scott's back, their breath leaving their sated bodies noisily and quickly.

"Jesus, fuck, Scotty," Hank panted into Scott's shoulder. "I've never come like that in my life." Scott wanted to ask, *Not even with the stewardesses?* but didn't since the comment might remind Hank of skipping out on his sister. For once, Scott had no quips or teasing remarks. So in a moment of weakness, he said what had been on his mind since Hank had carried him up the stairs.

"My turn," Scott murmured as Hank rolled off his back and lay on his side. Turning on his side to face Hank, he pushed gently against the tanned and bulging shoulder. "You need to teach me what to do with your foreskin." Scott pushed tendrils of chestnut hair out of Hank's eyes and off his forehead. He saw Hank's eyes, dazed and cloudy, flutter shut when Scott took him in hand. "Are you too sensitive right now or"—Scott planted a very tender kiss on Hank's heaving chest—"do I get to play?"

"No." Scott noted Hank's grin. "I'm only sensitive just before, especially if the foreplay is that good." A slow, happy grin ghosted across Scott's face and then he slid down the bed until he was licking playfully and carefully over and under Hank's foreskin. Scott could feel Hank comply with his wordless instruction, a push against his hip. Scott rolled Hank onto his back, and parted his legs slightly and began to tease Hank's foreskin gently with fingers and lips.

"Don't be afraid to chew on it, bite it a little," Hank whispered. Scott's eyes met his lover's intense stare, hoping Hank was as turned on as he was. He heard Hank's breathless words: "Gently... yeah, oh fuck... Scotty."

"Are all uncircumcised cocks this sensitive?" Scott darted his tongue in and out of the slit, one hand finding its way to cup and squeeze Hank's sac.

"Dunno," Hank panted. "Don't know anybody else's but mine." Hank let his hands slip through Scott's wet dirty-blond hair and chuckled. "Do that thing with your finger again."

Scott slid his finger in between the foreskin and the sensitive mushroom head of Hank's cock, the resulting grunt accompanied by an almost-painful gripping of his hair.

"Jesus, Scrappy." Hank let his head fall back as his dick responded to the attention Scott was giving it. "I've never had anyone get me up again so quickly."

Scott moved himself so that his head was lying on Hank's hip. "It's so thick and beautiful and warm." Scott did not look up when he spoke; instead, he moved his head slightly forward until he could dart his tongue out a few inches to touch and lick and kiss. After Hank was hard, Scott cupped Hank's sac, squeezed gently, and pressed his balls into his body. "Do you wear cologne?"

"Sometimes." Hank pulled his hands away and folded his arms to prop his head up, wanting to see everything Scott was doing with his mouth. "Why?"

"Your smell is so...." Scott looked up from under his lashes and then put his mouth back down on Hank's dick. "Musky and... addictive."

There were a few moments where neither spoke, Scott too focused on learning what made Hank crawl out of his skin. Hank's eyes were closed, Scott noted, but his breathing didn't seem to indicate he was sleeping. Finally, Scott turned his head to kiss the tip of Hank's cock, his tongue darting into the foreskin to lick the slit one last time. "When are you back?"

"Probably get back either Saturday, late afternoon or evening," Hank answered without opening his eyes. "We're driving down to the south to do some windfirming, but I don't want to have to do that drive twice a day, so...."

"I know I used to know what that was," Scott muttered as he climbed his way up to rest his head beside Hank's.

"Topping the exterior trees, the ones closest to the edge of the forest, and then cutting off branches so they're standing firmer in the wind. Won't knock 'em over like dominoes."

"So they stand firmer in the wind," Scott repeated, his lips kissing along shoulders and biceps. "Guess that's why it's called windfirming, huh?"

"Should I go for the easy joke here?" Hank rolled onto his side and threaded his arm between Scott's head and the mattress, staring into sleepy eyes. "Or should I just kiss you senseless?" Hank craned his neck around to look at the clock on the bedside table. "For the next three hours."

Scott leaned in, brushing his lips against Hank's, hoping his choice was clear.

Hank took him twice more, in various positions and in various places around the townhouse, before Scott was able to pull himself—literally—away and head back to his temporary home.

THE first thing Scott noticed when he arrived home, just after eleven, was that Kari's car was still parked in front of the house. When he tried the door and found he wouldn't have to use his key, he got his second surprise of the evening. Walking through the door and up the stairs, he could see that the television was on, but that the screen was frozen. One of them must have hit the pause button for some reason. He didn't recognize the movie, but he definitely recognized the sounds. He tried to tiptoe noiselessly down the hall, but the floorboard—the one Scott had mentioned to his brother over a year ago—creaked. He cringed and turned around to see two heads pop up over the back of the sofa, not really sure which of the three adults was more embarrassed.

Scott shot his brother a look as Brian tried to shield Kari, as if Scott was some unknown voyeur and hadn't even considered that he'd never seen these feelings growing between the two of them.

"Sorry," he cringed in their direction, not really wanting to focus his eyes anywhere too specific. "I'm just going to my room now."

Neither of the love birds said anything at all, mercifully. It was one thing knowing that your brother had a sex life, but an entirely different matter to have a ringside seat. As he walked quickly down to his room near the end of the hallway, Scott tried to remember if he'd brought his headphones with him, although he was quite sure that he'd single-handedly doused whatever fire had been kindled tonight.

He didn't bother to exit the bedroom. Whether it was out of fear or simple courtesy, he couldn't exactly determine. Scott was sure, however, that tomorrow morning his brother would have something to say about it.

CHAPTER 17

THE morning light peeked through the little space between the blind and the window casing as if it were an impatient child waiting to see when his parents would awake. The small sliver of light allowed Scott to open his tired eyes slowly and adjust to another day even though it was the first day he would be without Hank. As he lay there, content to let his mind and body remember the previous night's passion, Scott was thinking only about whether he would hear from Hank before his three-day windfirming task was done. Hank had said he would, but Scott was remembering all the years he'd lived with his brother and father; when they'd been out in the forests, hundreds of miles away, they'd rarely had time to call. Of course, Scott wasn't only curious to hear about Hank's day; he was also thinking that the phone call would be a sign—a clear sign—of Hank's interest. Scott hoped with every fiber of his being that this wouldn't turn out to be just a casual fling, like he'd told his brother, but the start of something deeper and meaningful.

Scott had become accustomed over the years to convincing himself that brief was best when it came to his romances; he would get bored, or the other man would become far too needy. Two days ago when Hank had made the first move, Scott was already making the deals in his head about how he would handle all of this, how he would be mature and recognize the opportunity for what it was: a chance to explore Hank's body, to find a release for the many months Scott had done without any kind of meaningful contact.

It was easier to think of this period as being in months even though the truth was it was going on two years since Scott had felt any kind of connection like he'd found with Hank. And, he reminded himself over and over as he got up and headed for the shower, Hank had been the one to make the first move. There had been something in him that Hank had wanted. And Hank had wanted it many times since he'd first brushed their lips together in that little pool near French Beach.

He padded out of his bedroom and headed for the kitchen for his first cup of coffee, noticing that Brian's bedroom door was open and that the bed had been made. He didn't think anything of it at first until he reached the counter and saw the note. Brian had gone into the office. Scanning the note quickly, Scott couldn't help but wonder how, precisely, his brother had gotten to the office; he still wasn't allowed to drive himself. He tried to ignore the little voice that told him that Brian had always been the responsible one and took the few stairs leading to the back door two at a time, relief flooding him when he saw Brian's truck still parked in front of the garage. Relieved, but still wondering how his brother had managed to get to the office, Scott trudged back to the kitchen and poured himself a cup of coffee, not really minding that it must have been sitting there for hours. After popping the mug into the microwave for a minute or two, he leaned back against the counter, sipping lazily and thinking about what he would do with his day.

He'd promised Hank that he'd stay on for a little while longer, and he wanted to, if for no other reason than to see what would become of their little affair, but the slow realization of having nothing to do and no friends was giving Scott that sinking, useless feeling that he detested. He could do more work on his songs, but his daily life had been such that he'd never really been able to do that for more than a few hours a day, the rest of his time having been devoted to meetings or rehearsals for the trio. After fixing the coffee maker to brew another pot of coffee, he headed to the bathroom while he tried to come up with something other than cleaning to occupy his time. If there was one thing Brian didn't need help with, it was cleaning. The house was almost immaculate. The only cleaning and arranging he needed to do was because Scott wasn't as neat and orderly as his brother.

He was shaved and showered and drinking his second cup of coffee, sitting at the little kitchen table with his sheet music spread out in front of him and his keyboard powered up and ready for some attention when he heard the phone ring. He stared at it for two rings and then decided to let the machine get it. When he heard Brian's voice call him after the beep,

Scott picked up the cordless phone lying on the island and greeted his brother.

"Hey, Brian."

"Was wondering when you were going to get up."

"I'm up," Scott laughed, the old routines from their childhood still firmly fixed. "As a matter of fact, I'm even shaved and washed."

"Good." Brian offered a slow chuckle. "Listen, I've got a few problems to take care of, and then I'll be home."

"No problem." Scott yawned. "I'm just doing some writing." After a few seconds, he said, "So, how did you get to the office? I mean, I noticed your truck is still here."

"Kari picked me up this morning," Brian said, his voice low, almost a whisper.

"Oh." Scott wondered if Brian was trying to avoid curious ears that probably hovered nearby in the office. "I'm sorry about last night, Brian, I didn't know—"

"Don't worry about it. You didn't know." Brian let out a little sigh. "Actually, I didn't know it would happen either, so...."

"I'm happy it did." Scott smiled, knowing his brother would hear it in his voice. "Happy for you—and Kari, of course."

"Thanks, Scooter."

"So," Scott started, planning on changing the subject. He knew how much Brian was embarrassed by the topic of his own love life. "What do you want for dinner?"

"Whatever," Brian said. Scott could see his brother shrugging his shoulders, easy-to-please as always. "I should be home around three or four this afternoon. Okay?"

"See you then." Scott disconnected the phone, turning his attention back to his keyboard and his sheet music.

He'd managed to finish finding the bridge to the one piece that had been haunting his thoughts for the past couple of months, jotting the notes and chords down as quickly as he could. He heard the familiar chime of his cell phone coming from his bedroom. He punched the power button on the keyboard and covered the distance within a few seconds, picking up his cell phone off the dresser and seeing Hank's name on the display.

Without realizing he was smiling, Scott flipped open his phone, wondering why Hank would be calling him.

"Hey, Hank."

"Hey," Hank sounded as if he were smiling, too. Of course, Scott rationalized to himself as he waited for more than that one word, maybe it was just wishful thinking on his part.

"How's the cutting going?"

"It's going well." Hank laughed, his deep, sexy voice sending shivers radiating out from Scott's spine. "Didn't call you to talk about windfirming, though."

"I know," Scott blushed. "Are you alone, or…?" Scott knew what *he* wanted to talk about, but he wasn't sure Hank wasn't surrounded by at least three other loggers.

"For now, yeah Why?" Hank's voice was teasing. "You want to have phone sex or something?"

"No," Scott corrected. "I was just wondering whether you'll be able to talk… you know… about… stuff."

"Rather have phone sex than talk about… stuff."

Scott could hear the serious tone in Hank's voice, but he knew they weren't going to have phone sex.

"So," Scott drawled as he recovered from the thought of how just Hank's voice in his ear as he stroked himself would get him off. "What would you like to talk about?"

"Don't care," Hank sighed. "Got another three or four hours out here, and then we'll be heading back to the hotel."

"Are you on schedule?"

"For now."

With those two words, Scott could tell that Hank's voice had changed radically. He wasn't sure whether there was a problem with the other loggers or whether the weather had started to make it difficult to climb, but Scott found himself in new waters here. He didn't know whether he was allowed to ask Hank about certain questions. "Is… is it the weather, or are the other guys—"

"I'm on schedule." Hank sighed heavily. "But there's some problems with Roddy."

"What kind of problems?"

"He's making some pretty bad calls out here." Hank's voice was strained. "We got a new greenhorn out here working with us today, and Roddy's been spending most of his time... I don't know... goading and harassing the poor guy."

"Did you call Brian?"

"I can handle it, Scott." Hank's tone let Scott know that he shouldn't mention anything to Brian either. "I'm going to keep an eye out for the new guy, let him know that he's doing okay for his first big job."

"Okay," Scott nodded. "And Hank? You know I wouldn't say anything unless you asked me to, right?"

"Of course," Hank said. "It's just...." Hank sounded very far away as he tried to find the words. "I told Brian he wouldn't have to worry about me anymore, so I got a lot to prove, you know."

"Absolutely," Scott agreed.

"Need to make sure he knows I'm not going to disappoint him anymore. Need to handle this myself. Do whatever it takes, so everyone knows I've changed."

Scott couldn't help but imagine that Hank was referring to more than just the change in his work ethic. Was Hank also talking about his budding relationship with Scott? "Will you call me when you get back to the hotel?"

"Was hoping you'd ask me that."

"Yeah?" Scott felt himself flush at the innuendo in Hank's voice.

"Might be late, though."

"Doesn't matter." Scott shook his head, the idea of having to wait another two days for Hank to be in his arms again suddenly oppressive and stifling.

"Maybe...." Hank's voice trailed off. "You can find someplace... private?"

"What for?" Scott teased, his face a study in innocence.

"What—" Hank's voice rose a little and then Scott could hear a slow laugh building. "Thought maybe we could discuss the role of women in seventeenth-century Russian literature."

"Oooh," Scott drawled. "Sorry, that's not my area of expertise."

"Smartass."

"Do you have any other topics in mind?"

"A few," Hank whispered, his voice going straight to Scott's groin.

"I'll be waiting," Scott assured him. "Take care of yourself, Hank?"

"Always do."

"I mean," Scott redirected, "don't let Roddy goad you into doing anything... unsafe."

"Not gonna happen," Hank promised. "Got someone waiting for me. Need to get home by Saturday night."

"Be safe, Hank." Scott wanted to make some teasing remark about the possible identity of the someone waiting for Hank, but he couldn't bring himself to ruin the moment. Scott had his answer, and it both terrified him and thrilled him.

CHAPTER 18

HANK disconnected the call, the harness making his growing erection uncomfortable in his loose cotton workpants. It was something new for him, these feelings that were growing inside his chest whenever he thought about Scott. He'd never been really good at expressing his feelings, but something about the man made Hank feel like he could. What was even more surprising to Hank was the realization that it wasn't scary. In the past, with women who'd started to talk about commitment and making a decision about a future with him, Hank had always felt his chest tighten as if there were a harness around it as well. But not when he thought about talking to Scott, about holding him, making love to him. It all felt like the most natural thing in the world.

"Fuck you!"

Hank looked over when the harsh words reached his ears. Chris, the greenhorn, was about seventy feet up in the air, and Roddy was on the ground at the base of the same tree, making crying sounds and goading Chris to go higher in the tree. "What difference is another three feet going to make?"

"Whatever, man," Chris yelled. "I ain't getting paid enough to risk my life."

"Fuckin' pussy, man!" Roddy laughed as he kept taunting the greenhorn.

Hank walked over slowly, assessing the situation; if Roddy was being reckless, he'd have no choice but to report all of this to Brian or the Falling Supervisor. As if the thought were enough to conjure up the man,

Hank looked over as a red F150 pulled up alongside the other parked trucks.

"Roddy?" Hank called over when he was about ten feet away, wanting to wipe the smirk right off the man's face. When Roddy turned, Hank nodded his head once in the direction of the truck.

"So?" Roddy shrugged his shoulders and turned his face upward again, his taunts calling up to Chris. "Come on, you dumb fuck, we'll be out here all night if you don't get your shit together."

"Maybe you want to do some work then, huh, Roddy?" Hank was almost within reach of the man, not really sure what he was going to do when he was right beside him. "Otherwise we *will* be too far behind by tomorrow."

"Go fuck yourself, Hank," Roddy spat. "Greenhorn's got to learn how to obey his superiors."

"What makes you think that's you?" Hank had a glint in his eyes, knowing that Gord, the Falling Supervisor, was standing only six feet away, taking it all in.

"*Back off*, Hank!"

"Chris!" Hank yelled up, noticing how Roddy jumped just a little bit at his booming voice. "Why don't you come down after you're finished there?" Hank brought a hand up to shield his eyes against the setting sun, noticing Chris nodding. Before he could bring his hand down back to his side, he saw Roddy pull back his arm and prepare for a roundhouse. Hank felt like laughing at the trouble that Roddy was going to find himself dealing with if he actually followed through. Hank took his left foot and planted it behind his big frame, watching the fist coming at him. It all seeming like slow motion to him. It didn't take much effort to pull his head back and watch Roddy's fist smash against the tree. Hank heard the chilling sound of bones crunching and then heard Roddy screaming in pain.

"You looking to lose your job, Roddy?" Hank took a step forward, his right leg hooking under Roddy's left and bringing the smaller man's leg out from under him. "If you know what's good for you, you'll stay there while Gord checks on your hand."

"Fucking piece of shit," Roddy hissed, clutching his bloody hand to his chest. "Goddamn fucker!" Hank could only smile at Roddy's ramblings. He wasn't about to say or do anything else unless Roddy got back up and started swinging again.

"Thanks, Hank," Gord said as he got back from Roddy's truck with the small medic's kit that all Level Three First Aid medics had to carry with them. *Ironic,* Hank thought to himself. *Our first aid guy decides to punch a tree.* "If it's broken, I'm not sure we'll be able to finish this job in time." Gord kneeled down beside Roddy, looking back up at Hank.

"We'll get it done," Hank smiled down, although he wasn't sure he was smiling to reassure the Falling Supervisor or because Roddy's hand looked broken. *Karma,* Hank thought and then went to join Chris when he saw the greenhorn was finally out of the tree.

"He okay?" Chris was coiling his climbing rope and looking as relieved as Hank about Roddy's possible absence over the next two days.

"Who cares?" Hank winked at Chris and moved to the next set of trees. "Even if he's hurt, we still got another three hundred trees to do." He pushed his helmet further up his head. "And only two more days to do 'em."

"We can't do that with just the two of us!"

"Yes." Hank smiled. "We can." Hank looked down at the greenhorn and pointed to the watch on his wrist. "We got another thirty hours of daylight over the next two days, and I got somewhere to be Saturday night." Hank pulled his harness straps tighter into the creases where legs met groin and pushed his helmet and visor back down over his smiling face. "Now," Hank intoned, as if he were about to launch into a sermon. "If you don't want to climb any higher than what you've been doing, that's fine, but you need to start figuring out how to relax when you're up there."

"I'm not—"

"Chris," Hank soothed. "I'm not interested in riding you like Roddy does. I'm trying to help you here." Hank checked his chainsaw and his boots and then looked back up. "You're good, kid, real good, but you're tighter than a drum up there." Hank smiled to show that he was actually trying to help the greenhorn. "Try thinking about something that makes you loose and happy."

"Like what?"

"Whatever it is that makes you loose and happy," Hank laughed, not really sure how this particular piece of advice had any holes in it. It seemed fairly obvious to Hank.

"What do you think of when you're up that high?"

"The view." Hank shrugged. "The beauty of where we're living." Hank pointed to where Roddy was sitting up while Gord bandaged his hand. "How what goes around comes around." Hank chuckled to himself and offered a gentle slap on Chris' shoulder when he noticed the greenhorn smile, his small, compact body already seeming lighter and a little freer of anxiety. Of course, there was no way for the greenhorn to know that Hank also thought of a certain long-legged blond waiting for him back in Duncan. Nobody needed to know that but Hank.

It was another three hours in the dying light before Hank had managed to do most of Roddy's share of the trees, although he had been smiling the entire time. Another two days without Roddy and then an entire week with Scott... Hank was at a loss to think of another time when his luck had been this perfect. He couldn't help but throw a little shit back at Roddy. From high up in his tree, Hank hadn't been able to resist waving as Gord loaded a still-pissed Roddy into the truck for the return trip to Duncan, Roddy flipping Hank off until the red F150 drove out of sight.

"Hey," Chris said as they headed back to the hotel in Hank's truck. "I never thanked you for helping me out back there."

"Don't mention it." Hank smiled as he doused the truck's lights and headed for his room. He watched as Chris headed to his own truck. "You drive careful tonight." Hank figured there was someone special that Chris was needing to see tonight. Lord knew, if it wasn't a two-hour drive to Duncan, Hank would be driving back to see Scott. "Wind's supposed to pick up, so we might have some fallen trees around by tomorrow morning."

"Yeah." Chris raised his helmet in a mock salute. "My grandma's been worried about me too. Nice to know there's two of you now." Hank laughed and locked up his truck, impatient to get to the shower and his cell phone—and Scott.

He allowed himself to picture moments like this, moments where he and Scott might travel together, might go visiting some of the places around Canada and the U.S. that Hank had always wanted to see but had never really found the proper motivation to make him draw up the plans.

Maybe Scott could be that motivation. He dropped his gear by the door, the smile on his face growing exponentially as he got closer and closer to stripping and heading for the shower.

He knew he'd need to take the edge off before talking to Scott tonight; he didn't really mind shooting early, but he wanted to last at least fifteen or twenty minutes. Scott had always been so in control of himself that Hank had found himself having to think of dirty socks or church sermons just so he would be able to keep from ruining their times together. Hank had never seen himself as out-of-shape or in need of any work on his stamina, but being with Scott made him realize that being with men was a lot different than being with women.

Like Scott's mouth, for one. Hank moved under the water, his hand stroking absently at his chest and moving slowly down his belly as he thought about how Scott could take him into that sweet mouth all the way down to the base. He'd never been with any woman who'd been able to deep-throat like Scott could. He found himself rock hard within seconds, the image of those kiss-swollen lips wrapped around him burned into his brain forever. Hank couldn't, even if he tried, think of anything that was sexier or hotter than those beautiful eyes looking up at him as Scott's mouth worked up and down his shaft. Hank threw his head back when he remembered those long, skilled fingers probing at his hole, darting in and out during the blow job and cried out as he felt his balls tighten. He braced his legs as his hand pumped another two or three times, his release spilling down the drain. His hands came up to either side of the shower head and he had to take a couple of long, slow breaths to calm down a little. *Damn,* he muttered as he took the soap in his hands and cleaned himself from head to toe.

He didn't take too much time to dry himself off and only swept his fingers through his wet hair, exiting the bathroom stark naked and heading to lie back on the bed. He reached for his cell phone and punched a button, his hand retracing the journey it had just taken while he waited for Scott to pick up.

"Hey, baby," Hank smiled into the phone when he heard Scott's greeting. "What are you wearing?" His chest tightened a little more when he heard the man laughing; he was sure he'd never heard a sweeter sound.

"What are *you* wearing?"

"Nothing."

"Really?" Scott's voice rose about an octave. "You're naked?"

"Isn't that how phone sex works?"

"You're asking *me*?"

Hank chuckled to himself and brought his free hand back behind his head. "So," Hank sighed, happy just to be talking to Scott. "What did you do all day?"

"Well," Scott said slowly, "I did some writing, thought about you, did some laundry, thought about you some more, did some cleaning, thought about you again, and oh yeah, thought about you."

"So," Hank teased. "You didn't think about me?"

"No, not really." Scott's teasing tone disappeared, and Hank could hear the serious tone take over. "What about you? Things go okay?"

"Sure." Hank's brow furrowed, wondering if he sounded like he'd had a rough day, because the truth of it was, he'd a fucking awesome day. "Why'd you ask?"

"Brian told me that Roddy was pulled because of an injury." Scott didn't ask the question that Hank could hear lurking just below the surface. "Are you? Okay, I mean?"

"Am now that I'm talking to you."

"Hank."

It was just a whisper, but Hank heard the message. It was crystal clear and loud in his ears. Hank was sure that this was what he would replay in his mind in the shower tomorrow night. "It's been a good day, baby. You don't need to worry about me."

"Really?" Scott's voice seemed to lose some of its worried tone. "There were no fights or anything?"

"Nothing I couldn't handle, Scott... honestly." Hank cleared his throat and brought his hand back down to his chest. "Now, what *are* you wearing?"

Twenty minutes later, Hank had returned from his second shower, a smile on his face as he doused the lights and wondered what he'd be dreaming about.

CHAPTER 19

HANK heard the chirping of his cell phone and rolled over to look at the alarm clock. He'd set it for six, and if it hadn't woken him up in time.... A sigh of relief flooded him when he noticed that it was only five forty-five. After cursing whoever was on the other end for a moment, Hank wondered if maybe Scott was calling for a repeat of last night. Hank was pretty sure, judging from the breathless panting, that Scott had really enjoyed their conversation last night. It had taken Scott a little longer to get into it, but Hank had found the whole experience to be almost as hot as having the man there in the room with him.

He reached for the phone and spared a look at the display. Brian? *What is he doing calling me now?* A feeling of dread washed over Hank's sleep-warmed body as he thought that maybe Scott had said something to Brian. He shook his head, knowing that Scott wasn't the type to gossip, and flipped open his phone.

"Hey, boss," Hank tried to sound like he was awake.

"Morning, Hank." Brian's voice was tense, strained. "Spoke with Gord yesterday after he brought Roddy back. How far behind are we?"

"We aren't," Hank answered plainly.

"What?"

"We aren't behind."

"How.... What do you mean?" Hank wanted to laugh at the disbelief in Brian's voice; the boss was usually so calm and collected.

"Chris and I managed to make up for Rod—" Hank stopped himself and swiped a hand over his face. "For the problem yesterday."

"Wait," Brian called, a little too loudly for Hank's ears. "You weren't cutting in the dark, were you?"

"No." Hank felt his face screw up at the thought of him doing something so irresponsible. "Managed to get it all done before the sun went down." It wasn't a complete lie; Hank and the greenhorn had done maybe one or two trees in very low light, but they'd had enough to make sure they could see what they were doing.

"I don't…." Hank wasn't sure he liked Brian being at a loss for words. He'd gotten far too used to the solid, take-charge boss he'd been afraid of for so many years. "Can't thank you enough, Hank."

"No problem." Hank downplayed it all. "Took me a while to get Chris to relax, but he's going to be a damn fine logger real soon."

"I won't forget this, Hank," Brian stated plainly. "In fact, when you get back, come and see me when you've got a minute. Have something I want to speak to you about."

"Sure, boss," Hank nodded, yawning into the receiver. "Anything serious?"

"No." Brian laughed. "Not this time. Well," Brian added after a few seconds. "It could be, but good-serious, you know."

"Sure, boss," Hank repeated and wondered if it was too early to call Scott.

He decided against calling Scott and was out and in his gear before six thirty, waiting for the greenhorn to show up so that they could make a huge dent in the remaining two hundred and some trees left to do. Come hell or high water, Hank was determined to get home on time. As great as the phone sex with Scott had been, he wanted the real thing. He *needed* the real thing within the next couple of days, or he would go crazy thinking about those lips, that sweet, sweet mouth, and the look in those beautiful eyes when Hank was inside him. He was thinking about the camping trip when Chris pulled up in his truck.

"Sorry." Chris grimaced as he slung all of his gear over his shoulder and ran over to Hank's truck. "My grandmother wouldn't let me leave until I ate a second helping."

"Yeah?" Hank was laughing as Chris flung all of his gear into the bed of the truck and hopped in the cab, a little paper bag on his lap. "Well," Hank said as he started the truck and pulled it into gear, backing out of the parking lot. "It's good to have someone looking out for you."

"Like you?"

Hank looked over at Chris' earnest expression and chuckled. "I was thinking more of your grandma, but yeah, me too."

"I told her about what you did for me yesterday," Chris mumbled, "and she gave me something to give to you. Made me promise that you'd get it." He picked up the bag and positioned on the console between the two bucket seats.

"For me?" Hank let his eyes dart down to look at the bag, a few little grease spots starting to show near the bottom of the bag.

"Chocolate chip cookies." Chris looked out the window as he said it, and Hank couldn't help letting out a slow, easy laugh.

"Well," Hank sighed when his laughter subsided. "You be sure to thank her for me."

"I will."

Hank had to hold on to the urge to reach over and brush the hair out of Chris's eyes. The poor kid had already turned a thousand shades of red just explaining about the cookies. Hank didn't have it in him to give the kid a good ribbing. "How old are you, anyway?"

"Twenty-two," Chris stated boldly and looked over, his eyes shifting nervously between Hank and the windshield. Hank raised his eyebrows in disbelief. Chris's cheeks pinked, and he looked back out of the passenger's side window. "In two months," he added in a much softer tone.

"Twenty-one," Hank mused, more to himself than to Chris. "Can't even remember what the hell I was doing at that age."

"What about you?"

"Thirty-five," Hank said, not really sure if that's what Chris had been asking.

"And what about someone to take care of you?"

"Why do you think I want to get this done?"

"Oh yeah." Chris put a finger at his temple, playfully pulling the imaginary trigger. "Forgot, sorry."

Hank didn't feel the need to respond, his hands clutching the steering wheel a little tighter at the thought of Scott.

"So," Chris asked after a couple minutes' worth of silence. "What's the plan today?"

"Same as yesterday," Hank announced, looking over, a little confused. "Get out there and do another hundred, hundred and fifty by the end of daylight." Hank offered a reassuring smile and put his focus back on the road. "That way, we can both get out of here by Saturday afternoon."

"So," Chris asked tentatively, "you live in Duncan too?"

"Yeah. Got a nice little townhouse near downtown." he added after a couple of seconds.

"Cool."

"That where you're from?"

"Originally, yeah," Chris answered. "But my dad left me and my mom when I was nine, so we had to move back down here so my grandparents could help us."

"Sorry to hear that, kid." Hank thought about his own rocky history; he'd had a father growing up and hadn't fared any better than Chris. His father had never been abusive or overbearing, but Hank had always been unsure of how to win his father's approval. If he thought about it, he could remember a lot of good times they'd spent together as a family, but there'd always been that undercurrent of unspoken disappointment when Hank didn't get very good grades in high school or injured himself too early in the football season or brought home a girl that didn't quite measure up somehow. He'd tried to figure it out while he was in high school and for many years after that, but he'd finally come to realize that maybe his father had just been one of those people who felt a general disappointment with life.

"Sorry," Chris said, and Hank realized he'd been daydreaming and looked over at him. "Did I say something wrong?"

"'Course not," Hank chuckled softly, shaking his head. "Funny business, huh? Family, I mean."

"Sure is." Chris smiled and went back to looking out the window. "After a couple of months, though, Mom seemed happier, and I was glad to be able to spend so much time with my grandparents, so...."

Hank filled in the rest of the sentence on his own. "Like I said," Hank said after a few moments. "Good to have someone to look after you."

"Yeah." Chris nodded his approval as Hank pulled into the makeshift parking spot he'd carved out yesterday. "Well." Chris raised his eyebrows and his hand to show Hank his crossed fingers. "Hopefully, I won't slow you down today."

"Hey, Chris," Hank called, coming around the back of the truck to drop the tailgate. "Quit worrying about that kind of stuff, okay? Just take it one tree at a time and keep thinking about how much closer you'll be to eating more of those cookies, yeah?"

"Okay." Chris laughed as he grabbed his gear and followed Hank out to the clump of trees that would keep them occupied for the next twelve hours.

CHAPTER 20

TRY as he might, Scott could not get back to sleep. It was just past six in the morning, and the only thought in his head was that Hank would be home in less than twelve hours. Looking back, he couldn't honestly say where the last two days had gone. He'd been so worried about how he would fill his time after leaving Hank's condo. He'd tried, in vain, to get any serious writing done. So what had he done to occupy his time?

But at that moment, when he heard Brian puttering in the kitchen, readying the coffee maker and emptying the dishwasher, Scott couldn't remember one blessed thing he'd done to occupy his time. Or, more truthfully, if he could pull his mind away from a particular pair of well-muscled and bronzed pair of arms, he might be able to remember something other than the feel of Hank's arms around him or the way their bodies seemed made for each other.

Abandoning all hope of ever getting back to sleep, he wiggled his feet into his slippers and padded out to see if he could help his big brother with anything. Brian was already showered, shaved, and dressed and waiting for Kari to pick him up. Scott made his way to the counter, not even annoyed by the steady dripping of the coffee maker that had not yet filled the carafe with enough liquid to make one full cup, and leaned against the counter.

"What's that look for?" He looked up when he heard the deep voice of his brother. Brian was thumbing his way through the newspaper, his knowing grin all the signal Scott needed to know that Brian had already sensed his good mood. Scott said nothing as he pulled a bowl out of the cupboard and studied the cereal boxes, trying to decide between something with bran or something with oats. "Just casual, huh?"

"What?" Scott chanced a glance and saw the big smile on Brian's face. "Oh yeah." Scott waved off the comment. "Of course it is."

"Okay." Brian's sarcasm oozed as he made two syllables seem more like five or six. "You remember the time you got into Dad's whiskey and I found you passed out in your bed?"

"Yeah," Scott answered, suspicious but very curious as to where this particular anecdote was leading. "So?"

"Scooter." Brian pushed himself up and away from the small kitchen table and rounded the island to stand a few feet from his younger brother. "Scoot, you know I've always been able to tell when you're lying to me."

"I'm not lying," Scott insisted. "It's nothing—" Scott stopped and laughed when he saw Brian looking at him from under his thick lashes. He watched helplessly as Brian made the signal for Scott to tell the truth: a quick sweep of his index finger forming a circle over his heart.

"Okay." Scott stopped studying—or pretending to study—the generic cereal choices and turned to face his brother. "You think I'm a fool, don't you?"

"Scooter," Brian chided through a warm but guarded smile. He took the three steps necessary to pull his brother into a rough hug and sighed, "I don't think you're a fool." Brian kissed the top of Scott's head and then moved away. "But." Brian's handsome face still held a smile for his younger brother. "I do think you might be in for some heartache."

"You know," Scott launched into an immediate, possibly innate, need to contradict everything his brother said. It was, Scott was most certain, a remnant of having been raised by Brian for most of his teenage years. "I don't know why you guys are so hard on Hank. He's kind and sweet and funny and—"

"I have nothing, I repeat, nothing against Hank."

"Then what is it?" Scott threw his hands up in the air, his exasperation clear. "What makes you so sure he's going to hurt me? Is it," Scott softened his voice, "because he's just realizing he might be gay?"

Brian didn't say anything for a moment, and Scott knew he'd been right in his assessment. He threw up his hands again, but Brian cut him off.

"Look, Scooter, you've been out for a long time, and I don't want to see you... I don't know... have to deal with someone who's afraid, who won't be able to give you, well, what you deserve."

"Ah." Scott's shoulders slumped as he looked at his brother nervously fidgeting with the cell phone attached to his belt. Scott moved closer to his brother and punched playfully at his shoulder. "You can stop worrying about me, you know. I'm all grown up, and if this doesn't work out with Hank, hey." Scott raised his eyebrows and cocked his head to one side. "It'll have been a hell of a ride."

"And on that note." Brian backed up at Scott's laughter but only got two steps before Scott had him in a bear hug.

"Oh, come on, big brother," Scott's arms came free as Brian used his considerable upper body strength to break the hold. "I'm sorry!"

Brian backed up even more, fanning the air in front of his nose. "Still don't brush your teeth in the morning, I see!"

"Not until after I eat, no." Scott moved away from Brian as he heard a car door slam. "Your girlfriend's here."

"Scott." Brian raised a finger. "Don't!"

"What?"

"You know damned well what!" Brian gathered his papers and stuffed them into his briefcase, looking back up when he heard the clicks of the latches. "You leave her alone; she doesn't know what you can be like yet."

"I remember that speech!" Scott trailed after his big brother like he'd done on so many nights when he was only in elementary school and Brian had already begun dating. "You only ever told me that when you were serious about the girl."

"I was serious about all of them," Brian called over his shoulder and then shut the door after turning to give Scott a little wink.

HANK knew he was pushing the speed limit a little; the signs read 110 km/h, but he figured if he added ten or fifteen to that, the RCMP would probably never stop him. *Surely,* he rationalized to the empty cab, *they have better things to do?*

It was already past three in the afternoon, all of the trees having long been trimmed, topped, and the entire area cleared. He'd packed his bag the night before so that he'd be able to take off right after he got the okay from the Falling Supervisor. He'd tried to clean himself off as best he could, but he was really hoping that Scott could help him do a better job. He was fifteen minutes away from a nice, hot shower, and with any luck, he'd have some help washing the hard-to-reach places.

His cell phone broke him out of his lascivious thoughts. He'd called Scott about ten minutes before and left a very blunt message about where he was hoping Scott would be when he pulled up to his condo.

"Hey, Scott," Hank smiled despite himself. "You got my message?"

"Yup!"

"Can you make it?"

"Yup!"

"Do you have a change of clothes?"

"Yup!"

"You going to say anything else?"

"Yup." Scott chuckled. "But I'll tell you when you get to your place."

"When are you coming over?"

"Already here," Scott whispered, his voice low and sexy. "Just waiting on you."

Hank pushed his foot to the floor when he saw the sign announcing that he was now entering Duncan. "Give me five minutes." He cursed the third set of red lights and then turned his truck onto Church Road; his condo was the last on the left. He pulled up beside Scott's truck, hopped out of the cab, grabbed his gear from the back, and ran for the stairs, stopping suddenly when he saw Scott leaning against the front door, his eyes fixed on his watch.

"Six minutes," Scott teased. "I was ready to go home."

"I would've come and dragged you back here." Hank dropped his gear at the door, pulled out his keys, and unlocked the door, pulling Scott through to the little foyer. He heard the whoosh of breath leave Scott's lungs as he picked him up and brought their lips together. "Don't move!" Hank commanded as he deposited a breathless Scott on the first step to the upstairs and returned to throw all of his gear inside the door. When he heard the click of the lock, he turned around and Scott was gone. "Hey!" Hank yelled as he took the stairs to the bedroom three at a time. "I told you not to move!" He stopped in his tracks when he saw Scott, stark naked, standing at the foot of the bed.

"Hey." Scott shrugged and tried to move past the bigger man. "I was just trying to move things along, but if you want, I'll go back down and wait."

"Smartass," Hank huffed and grabbed Scott around the waist, pulling him into his solid frame, their lips finding what they'd lived without for almost three days. Hank felt Scott's tongue pushing against his lips and moaned loudly, more turned on than he thought he'd be at this sexy but slight man taking the lead for once. He let his hands skim down Scott's back, the smile at the shiver it caused cut off by Scott's insistent tongue. He felt those long fingers in his hair trail down his back and land, finally, at the button and zipper of his workpants. He pressed into Scott's hand as he used one hand to pull at his T-shirt, freeing it and pulling it over his head. The momentary parting of their mouths and tongues had him gasping for air, wanting somehow to crawl inside this man he was holding.

Scott took the reprieve as an opportunity to free Hank from his pants and boxers. He fell to his knees, his hands pushing both layers of cloth down Hank's legs. He rubbed his cheek against Hank's erection as he lifted one foot to free Hank's feet from the trousers and boxers.

"Shit," he muttered when he realized that neither of them had planned far enough ahead to remove Hank's work boots. He put one hand against the tanned, hairy belly and pushed Hank's big frame up against the wall, his mouth descending to take Hank in as his hands found the laces and began pulling. There was nothing sensual about Scott's attentions to the swollen erection. It was all lust and need and wanting. He looked up as he freed Hank's other foot from its boot and, mouth still eliciting those deep growling sounds from the big logger, Hank felt Scott's hands come up and pull him closer, his fingers digging into the firm flesh.

"Baby," Hank panted. "Don't want to come yet." Hank reached down and pulled the shorter man up, pressing him into his body with two hands centered in the small of Scott's back. He rubbed against Scott, needing friction but knowing that too much would spoil all the plans he'd made over the past two hours traveling toward this moment. "Okay," Hank finally said, using his hands to still both of their flushed and sensitive bodies. "Shower, now." Hank grabbed at Scott's shoulders and spun the slight body so that he was behind it, his erection pressing into the crease of Scott's ass. "Need you, Scott."

"I'm here, baby, all yours." Scott was pulling one of Hank's hands up to his mouth, his lips and tongue laving and sucking on Hank's thumbs and fingers.

"Oh yeah, fuck." Hank began to walk them forward, towards the shower, not really sure if what he was actually hearing the doorbell. "Are you kidding me?" Hank released his hold on Scott's body as he planted both of his hands on his hips. "Who the hell could that be?"

"Ignore it," Scott pleaded as he wrapped himself around Hank, his long legs lifting to encircle the trim waist. "I swear if you go, you'll have to answer the door with me like this." The doorbell sounded again, and Hank easily picked up the clinging body and deposited it in front of himself.

"Ah, fuck," Hank muttered as he grabbed his shorts and pulled them on. "You get in the shower while I get rid of them." Cursing as only a horny man who'd been delayed yet again could do, Hank took the stairs two at a time and had the door open in no time, his glare—he hoped—communicating his refusal to whatever was being sold. He swung the door open, sparing a glance back up to his bedroom. He didn't hear the shower. As he turned back to the open door, he thought about yelling about not hearing any running water and then froze.

"Brian?"

"Hey, Hank," Brian smiled. "Bad time?"

"No," Hank lied. "Come on in."

"Thanks." Brian nodded and took a step inside the door. "Listen, I'm sorry to come unannounced, but this wasn't something I wanted to discuss at the office."

"What'd I do now?"

"Huh?" Brian looked up and saw the panicked look on Hank's face. "Oh shit, nothing, sorry." Brian took a moment to school his features and then looked back at Hank. "Listen, Gord has decided to accept an offer to run the operations for another logging firm in Vancouver, and well, he told me how you managed to keep this job on time, and how you handled Roddy, and…." Brian offered his hand. "I wanted to say thanks and to offer you a promotion to Falling Supervisor." Hank's face fell; he heard Brian's laughter and reached out to accept the offer of a handshake. "It'll be probationary, of course, and well, I figure I've finally got the opportunity to reward you instead of bitch you out."

"But...." Hank's smile dropped a little. "What about Roddy?"

"That," Brian sighed, pulling his hand back and letting it rest on his hip, "is a subject for another day."

Hank could tell that his boss didn't really want to discuss it. It was probably a sore subject, what with how Roddy had been acting lately.

"Fair enough," Hank nodded, not willing to push his luck.

"Okay, then." Brian moved to the door, his hand on the brass knob. "Oh," he said, snapping his fingers. "Don't forget about the first aid training on Wednesday."

"Brian?" Hank was grateful. "I meant what I said to you back in the hospital."

"I know you did, Hank." Brian offered his hand once more. "And I appreciate it." After taking his hand back, Brian pointed to something on the other side of the door. "Well, listen, Kari's waiting, so...."

"Yeah, sure, okay." Hank felt flustered all of a sudden; he wasn't sure what to make of all this.

"And," Brian said as he pulled open the door, "if Scott asks why I was here, tell him I wasn't checking up on him." Hank accepted Brian's smile and offered his own, ignoring the embarrassment he felt.

Hank found himself back in the bedroom but didn't really remember walking up the stairs. *Did I just get a promotion? Did Brian just thank me for helping keep the job on schedule? And for handling Roddy?* It all seemed so surreal; one minute he was thinking about what he wanted to do with that toned, silky smooth body of.... *Oh fuck!* He shot off the bed and turned to head toward the bathroom and found Scott standing, hand on hip, by the bathroom door. "I... I, uh...."

"I heard." Scott smiled. "Congratulations!"

Hank opened his mouth to try to say "Thank you," or something like it when he suddenly found himself on his back, spread out across the king-size bed, his arms full of Scott. "I can't believe it," Hank sputtered as Scott's kisses covered his face and lips. "One minute I was thinking my job was gone, and the next…." Hank grabbed the trim waist and, in one move, had that smiling face directly under him.

"I told you he's a good guy," Scott scolded playfully. "I told you he didn't hold grudges."

"There's only one thing that could make this day better," Hank announced as his hands found their way to either side of Scott's face.

"And what's that?"

"If I actually, finally," Hank stated, wrapping his arms around Scott's waist as he tugged him off the bed, "get to have a shower!"

CHAPTER 21

"I'M PROUD of you." Scott was lying on his side, his hand finding its way to play with the dark, silky hairs on Hank's muscular, tanned chest. He looked down at Hank's handsome face. The big man's eyes were closed, but Scott knew he wasn't sleeping. Slowly, Scott saw the eyes open and a small grin ghost over Hank's kiss-swollen lips.

"Yeah?" Hank shifted so that he could lean over and kiss Scott's neck.

"I overheard Brian on the phone with Gord this morning." Scott stretched his arm across the broad chest and let it come to rest on Hank's far shoulder, offering a little squeeze. "Brian was incredibly grateful—and maybe just a little surprised—that you were able to keep the job on schedule."

"I made him a promise." Hank's lips were leaving wet, sloppy, loving kisses along Scott's neck and shoulders. As if he was unhappy with the small, insignificant distance that separated him from his lover, Hank reached out and pulled Scott on top of his body. "He could have just as easily fired me."

Scott squirmed for a moment until their bodies fit together just perfectly. "Well," he sighed after he let his head rest on his hands, palms flat over Hank's heart. "I just wanted you to know that while I was listening, I couldn't help but fairly burst out of my skin knowing it was you they were talking about in such glowing terms."

"Glowing, were they?" Scott reveled in the feel of Hank's fingertips caressing his spine; he heard Hank chuckle a little devilishly as his body shivered and squirmed.

"Yes." Scott smiled down at the emerald green eyes. "They were glowing." He moved his palms and bent his head to press his lips against Hank's warm skin. Lifting his head again, he saw a look of quiet contemplation on the handsome face. "And I'm very proud of you."

With a deftness and economy of movement that shouldn't have surprised him anymore, Scott felt Hank place one hand behind his neck and one hand at his lower back and roll both of them so that Hank was settled on top of him, the look on his face so sincere and earnest that Scott wasn't sure whether it was that look that knocked the breath out of his lungs or the fact that Hank's two-hundred-and-thirty-pound frame was on top of him. "Thank you, baby."

"Was I getting too heavy for you?" Scott teased, bringing his legs to either side of Hank's hips and letting his feet rest on the muscled backside.

"Nah." Hank smiled and kissed the tip of Scott's nose. "I can handle a hundred and sixty pounds."

"Ah, one eighty, thank you." Scott's protest was cut off almost immediately by Hank's roving hands.

"One eighty, bullshit!" Hank was using his index finger and thumb to grab at Scott's sides. "You're nothing but sinew and muscle."

"Yeah," Scott agreed as he giggled and tried to avoid the strong fingers. "And muscle weighs more than fat."

"And you have no fat and just the right amount of muscle, so where's the one eighty come from?"

Scott let his arms fall off to the side, tired from so much exertion earlier in the evening. "Okay," Scott conceded, "so I may have rounded up."

"From what?" Hank was laughing, his big arms pushing himself up so he could position his elbows on either side of Scott's head. "One sixty?"

"Okay." Scott huffed and pushed his face into the crook of Hank's neck and shoulder, "I admit it. I'm one sixty four." Scott let his head fall back against the mattress and sighed. "Hello, my name is Scott A., and I'm a scrawny weakling."

"Hello, Scott A." Hank was smiling down at him, the look in his eyes making Scott feel as if he were ten inches taller and one hundred pounds heavier. "My name is Hank B., and I think you're absolutely perfect." Hank stroked his hands over the soft blond hair, his eyes trailing lazily over Scott's wide-eyed expression.

"Thank you, Hank B." Scott leaned up and snatched a kiss from Hank's lips, feeling the press of swelling erections between their bodies. "Hey, wait a minute!"

"What?" Hank stilled his hands, concern evident on his face.

"Oh my God!" Scott slapped at Hank's shoulders.

"What?" Hank rolled onto his side, not sure whether he was crushing Scott or if there was something more seriously wrong.

Scott rolled over to keep contact with the broad chest and pushed his face against the point where chest met rumpled sheet. "I'm a slut," Scott groaned.

"What are you on about?"

"I've slept with you three times now." Scott was shaking his head, his hair tickling the sensitive skin on the underside of Hank's upper arm. "I'm going to spend the night with you," Scott whispered when he finally lifted his head up. "And I just realized I've never asked you your last name."

Hank backed away, stifling the urge to laugh, and held out his hand. "Henry Isaac Ballam."

Scott took the hand in both of his and turned it to kiss the sensitive palm, feeling Hank flinch when he placed a few slow kisses. "Scott Michael Alan. Please to meet you, Henry."

"The only other person who's ever called me Henry is my mother."

"So," Scott asked tentatively as he rolled a little closer, their bodies pressing together and responding to the touch almost immediately. "You don't like being called that?"

"No," Hank said as he shook his head. "It's not that." Hank pulled Scott on top of his body again, his hands tracing lazy circles. "Everyone has always just called me Hank." He brought one hand up and pressed Scott's soft lips to his. "And besides, *Henry* just doesn't sound sexy when you're yelling it out in a moment of passion, you know?"

Scott teased at Hank's collarbone with his lips and tongue. "Maybe if we try it in different languages?" He looked into Hank's eyes and muttered, "How about Heinrich?" He laughed when he saw Hank's face contort and twist into an expression that could only be construed as disdain. "How about Henri?" Hank's expression seemed to convey he was thinking about it for a moment and then he gave one quick shake of his head. "How about Enrico?" Another shake of the head. "Enrique?"

"How about," Hank whispered slowly, deliberately. "What you called me just before your brother showed up?"

Scott squinted and furrowed his brow. *I've never called him anything but Hank, haven't I?* "I called you something other than Hank?"

"It's okay." The expression on Hank's face was like a physical punch to Scott's gut. He felt his head being drawn down to rest against Hank's shoulder. He'd obviously forgotten something that Hank had found to be an important development in their relationship. He'd been so careful to remember everything, every word that he uttered to this man. He didn't want to scare Hank, but he needed Hank to know how much this all meant to him, that he needed this as much as Hank seemed to need it. "Are you hungry?" Scott shook his head against the warm skin of Hank's shoulder, his brain running at a thousand thoughts per second.

"I'm sorry, baby." Scott pulled his head up to see the smile spread across Hank's face. "That's it?" Scott beamed at him, relief washing through him like a good shot of bourbon. "You liked that, huh, baby?" Scott squirmed a little, pushing their dicks together and grinding their hips together. Scott pressed their lips together, their tongues finding each other almost immediately as Scott continued to squirm and press and grind. Scott brought his hands up to thread into the tousled waves of chestnut, delighting in the sounds of lips coming together and pulling apart, of quick, panting breaths before their mouths found each other again, and of two bodies memorizing what brought pleasure to each other.

Finally, Scott pulled his head away from Hank's, his lips tingling and his lungs burning for more air. "I," Scott panted, "was really worried there for a minute." Scott heard himself swallow hard and looked down at the grin on that handsome face. "There are a lot of things I've wanted to call you, but I wasn't sure if, you know, you would... well... like them."

"Such as?"

"Well," Scott started as he rolled off of Hank's body and pressed against his side, his hand trailing up and down the flat belly and firm pecs. "Like *baby*—"

"That's my favorite so far." Hank rolled onto his side and pressed their bodies together, his hands defining their usual path up and down the soft skin of Scott's back. "What else?"

"Handsome?"

"I'll take it." Hank smiled and kissed soft, warm lips. "What else?"

"Gorgeous?"

"Anything else?" Hank asked before stealing another kiss.

"Sexy?"

"I like this game," Hank chuckled. "Anything else?" Scott shook his head. "Okay," Hank announced and wrapped his arms around the smaller frame. "*Baby* is still my favorite, but I can live with the others too."

"You're weird," Scott muttered against the scruff on Hank's neck.

"But in a handsome, gorgeous, sexy way, right?" Hank released his prisoner and scooted to the end of the bed, reaching back around to pull Scott off by the ankles.

When they were both standing, Hank reached out and brought his hands to either side of Scott's face, leaning down and kissing his lips so gently and tenderly that Scott felt dizzy with a renewed passion for this man. He felt Hank's hands find their usual spots between his shoulder blades and on the small of his back while Hank nuzzled his earlobes and then trailed kisses along the tender skin where neck met shoulder. "Baby?"

Hank pulled his head away, his hands not budging an inch, and looked into Scott's eyes.

Scott had come so close to uttering the words he was sure would ruin this wonderful evening and any evenings that might follow. He wanted so desperately, so passionately, to tell this man that he was falling in love with him, but he couldn't get his brother's voice out of his head. What if this was just a casual fling for Hank? What if Scott was the one who was foolishly hoping for something more?

"I was hoping I could talk you into another shower." Scott smiled as Hank started backing up to the bathroom, willing his face to show anything but confusion and disappointment at another lost opportunity.

"This is nice," Scott whispered in Hank's ear as the two of them stood holding each other. The usual frenzy of bending and licking and kneading and grabbing and rutting was gone. Of course, it could have been that it was already past eleven at night, or it could have been that they'd made love at least five times—possibly six, but Scott wasn't sure that the third time could be counted. He hadn't realized that Hank's feet were an erogenous zone. Or it could have been any number of reasons that popped into Scott's mind as he let his head settle safely in Hank's big hands. But no matter which reason he settled on accepting, he knew what the real reason was: He was in the arms of the man he'd fallen for over and over again during the past week.

There had been so many moments when Hank had surprised him. At first, Scott had been quite pliant and happy to go with the flow that Hank's frenzied appetites had set. But somewhere within the haze that had invaded Scott's memories, he couldn't remember anything but the tender touch of Hank's lips, the feel of his chest hair as it caressed his skin and nipples, the smell of something that was uniquely Hank, and the sounds of the deep, bass voice as it whispered little endearments. And when Hank washed his body, not missing an inch of his skin with wet, tender kisses, and dried him with one of the large, plush bath sheets, and then finally wrapped his arms around him, the two of them snuggled under clean crisp sheets, Scott knew only one thing for sure: If Hank asked him to stay and never return to Toronto, Scott would not refuse him.

HANK awoke to a cold nose pressed against his shoulder, as if Scott had tried to wedge it in between the warm skin and the pillow. He couldn't help but smile at the irony of how this perpetually cold man had so thoroughly melted his heart and made him feel like he wanted to protect him and stay in bed wrapped around him for the rest of his stay. And then there was that. *How do I ask him to stay, for good? How can I tell him what he's come to mean to in so little time? Is all this just because he stood up for me, made me feel like somebody actually saw something no one else did?*

Hank wasn't even sure he understood it all. He'd never anticipated that the urge to kiss Scott in that little pool back at French Beach would lead to the intensity of the feelings he was experiencing right now. *Where did they come from?* It wasn't that Hank had always assumed he was straight, but rather that he'd always just assumed that he would one day marry a woman and have children and become a grandfather and lead the kind of life that his parents had—the kind of life that most other men lived.

He shifted to lie on his side facing Scott and felt the lithe body snuggle closer to him, the cold little nose pressing into his chest as he stroked the messy blond mop of hair that still smelled of shampoo and caressed his fingers as if he were stroking a cat. He smiled at the snuffling that Scott did in his sleep and wished that it all didn't have to end soon. After another couple of days—days they would spend mostly apart—Scott would have to go back to his life in Toronto. And Hank would have to remember so many things; he would have to remember how to come home to an empty apartment and not feel so alone, or how he used to occupy his time before falling into bed alone. Hank had always known that he could be attracted to men, but he'd never given any thought to the possibility of falling in love with one.

Is that what this is? Do I love him? The little voice that answered him was the same voice that had always told him that it was okay to sleep with women and never call them again, the voice that told him that drinking himself sick the night before a climb was no big deal. *Nah, it's not love, it's opportunity; you knew he found you attractive and you scratched an itch—his and yours. Nothing more.*

Hank hadn't really realized or spent too much time wondering why that little voice had seemed to have disappeared over the past week. *Is that what love is?* Hank wondered as he heard the purring coming from the man whose back he was stroking so absent-mindedly. *Maybe love is nothing more than wanting to ignore that little voice, the one that wants me to think only of myself.* He closed his eyes as his cheek caress the soft locks and felt his lover's arm curl over and around his waist, long fingers resting at the small of his back. *A lifetime of this.* Hank pulled him closer, snuggling him against his chest, and whispered softly into Scott's messy, silky mane, "How could anyone not want a lifetime of you?"

CHAPTER 22

HANK'S eyes drifted open when the sensations on his belly became too irresistible to ignore. "Morning, baby," he croaked, his hand finding its way to soothe the warm, sensitive skin of Scott's back. "Whatcha doin'?"

"Tummy rub," Scott stated matter-of-factly, not moving his head from Hank's chest.

"Hey," Hank pouted. "Does a kiss come with that?"

"Of course." Scott smiled and shifted so that he could let his lips find Hank's. "Morning, handsome."

"Feels good, baby." Hank let his head fall back, his arms coming to rest under his head and cushion it as he looked back down. Scott's head now lay on his shoulder, but his warm fingers continued to move slow circles over Hank's belly.

"Okay," Scott announced suddenly and pushed himself up so that he was kneeling on the bed, his butt resting on his heels. "Roll over."

"Huh?" Hank's right eye peeked open, a small, bewildered smile on his face as he stared down at the devilish grin on his lover's lips.

"I never got to give you the massage I promised you last night. So…." Scott made the universal signal for *roll over* and then reached into Hank's bedside table for cinnamon-scented oil. "I always wondered why you smell of cinnamon all the time." He knee-walked his way back to straddle Hank's slim hips, positioning himself so that he was a bridge over the backs of Hank's hairy, muscled thighs.

"Do I?" Hank looked over his shoulder.

"Don't worry." Scott squirted the viscous liquid onto one palm and then rubbed his hands together vigorously. "No one else could smell it... unless they were... you know...." Scott let his hands leave featherlight touches over Hank's muscular ass.

"That's not what I was thinking," Hank protested a little too loudly, uncertain if the heat in his face was from the touching or the thought that Scott had already figured out why he'd been worried.

"Of course it wasn't," Scott soothed as he began pushing his hands up Hank's back, his fingers playing at a nonexistent piano as he felt the solid mass of muscle begin to relax and unknot. "God, Hank, are you ever tense." Scott pushed his hands all the way up to the cap of each shoulder, his own belly and erection making points of contact against Hank's warm, slick skin. "I'm going to have to do this more often. Your back is like bricks!"

"Sorry," Hank muttered through a little sigh.

"Why...." Scott laughed a little. "Why are you apologizing?"

"'Cause," Hank grunted as Scott's capable fingers bore down and kneaded his firm flesh. "Oh, Jesus wept!" Hank's eyes came open as he felt the knuckles of Scott's fingers begin to make slow circles into the muscle tissue.

"Hurt?" Scott stopped.

"God, no," Hank panted, "keep going."

"Yes, sir," he acquiesced and leaned down to kiss the small of Hank's back. "Whatever you like, sir."

"Careful," Hank cautioned, his voice becoming lazy and his words slurred. "I'll hold you to that."

"Yes, sir," Scott repeated. "You can hold me to anything you like, sir."

Hank pushed up with his left hand against the mattress and peered over his shoulder. "Keep talking like that and you won't be finishing this massage."

"Oh-ho," he chuckled. "Have I awakened your dominating alter ego?"

"No," Hank whispered slowly and let himself fall back against the mattress, hoping that Scott wouldn't see the blush creeping across his face.

"Are you blushing?" Scott let his body fall onto Hank's warm, relaxed back. "What? Tell me."

"Of course I'm not blushing." Hank balked and moved his head so that it was more or less buried in the pillow.

"Please, baby?" Scott was placing lazy little kisses across Hank's shoulders as his hands started to massage Hank's heated scalp. "You can tell me... please?"

"No," Hank grunted into the pillow. "You'll make fun of me."

"Henry Isaac Ballam!" Scott lifted his body up so that he straddled Hank's thighs again. "When have I ever made fun of you in bed?" He positioned himself so that he was now between the amply muscled legs and began kissing each of Hank's buttocks, his tongue darting out now and then to taste the cinnamon oil. "If I promise not to make fun of you, will you tell me?" Scott felt the muscles in the cheeks tense as Hank pushed himself to one side.

"Promise?" Scott released the little pout he'd put on for effect and made a cross with his fingers over his heart. "Okay," Hank agreed and raised his body so that he was seated in front of Scott. "It's not the dominant side you've awakened, baby," Hank said as he blushed and darted his eyes between Scott's hands and eyes.

"You mean...," Scott whispered as his hands smoothed over muscled thighs. For the briefest moment, he saw the glint in those beautiful green eyes and the sly grin that ghosted over Hank's red lips. Scott pushed himself against Hank so that they both fell back against the mattress. "I've... I just figured that you were a top." Scott's mouth covered Hank's, the kisses urgent, sexual, and bruising. "Oh baby," Scott sighed when he pulled away. "But I don't want you to do it if you're not ready."

"I want to, but...." Hank felt the heat slam into his face, his neck, his ears as he tried to admit to wanting something that he'd never been able to ask for, let alone allow anyone to do. "It's just... I've never... But with you... I want to... now."

Scott's fingers found their way, instinctively, into Hank's chestnut waves, his hands coming to rest on either side of the beautiful—and bashful—face. "Oh, Hank," Scott crooned, at a loss for anything else to say.

They lay there for a few minutes, wrapped in each other's arms, their lips and tongues repeating movements they'd come to find familiar yet exciting and new. After a moment or two of the urgent kisses giving way to more tender and sensual ones, Scott's lips and soft touches reassuring Hank that he didn't need to be afraid or hesitant anymore, they found themselves lying down again. Hank guided Scott's hips to rest in between his parted legs, the slow yet demanding movement of their erections against each other echoing the delicious probing of lips and tongues and hands. Hank raised his knees so that Scott was caught between his muscled thighs, a slight tremor the only sign that he wasn't sure he wanted it to happen right at that moment.

"Here," Scott whispered against Hank's earlobe as he nipped and sucked, nudging Hank to lie still. "I want to see your face, make sure I don't hurt you."

Scott let his hands trail slowly up and down the flat, hairy belly as he slicked his fingers with the massage oil. He sat beside the large, prostrate frame of his lover, one muscled leg wrapped around his waist, as his hand found its way to Hank's heated hole, one finger tracing slow and deliberate circles around the ring without entering it. He could feel Hank clench and tighten, one powerful hand shooting out to seize Scott's forearm while the other found a fistful of sheet.

"It's okay," Scott soothed. "I won't do anything you don't want me to." Scott continued to rub Hank's stomach, encouraging the big man to relax. "You're so beautiful, Hank." Scott smiled at him, wanting him to see how much he was enjoying this. "Want you to know what it feels like when you're inside me." And with that, Scott pushed his middle finger forward and breached Hank's ring of muscle.

"Oh fuck," Hank hissed as his head came off the pillow.

"Breathe, baby," Scott encouraged and saw Hank finally let go of the air he'd been holding in anticipation. "That's it, baby, breathe for me." Scott petted the furry belly and pushed his finger a little further when he felt Hank's muscles relax a little more. "It'll get even better, Hank." Scott leaned over, forcing Hank's leg to move closer to his chest, opening his hole a little more.

"Oh God," Hank panted, his upper chest and face flushed with desire. "Oh God, Scott," he whispered as he closed his eyes and breathed a little more rapidly, his eyes fluttering shut as Scott's thumb began to caress the area just under his ball sac.

Scott smiled and continued to offer Hank words of encouragement. "Breathe, baby," Scott warned with a whisper. "Just remember to breathe—"

"Fucking hell!" Hank's eyes shot open and his muscles clenched around Scott's finger. "What the fuck was that?"

"That was your prostate." Scott smiled and kept reminding Hank to breathe. "Did you like that? Did it feel good? You want me to stop?"

"God, no no no," Hank repeated as he moved his head back and forth, his eyes fluttering shut, then open, then shut again. "Oh sweet Jesus," Hank whispered, his lips coming out to moisten his dry lips.

Scott pushed against Hank's leg again and lowered himself so that he could lick along the underside of his lover's engorged cock. "So beautiful, baby," Scott said against the heated and sensitive flesh as he stopped the circular caresses over Hank's belly and brought that hand to pinch at the sensitive foreskin; his finger remained inside the tight heat as he licked and pinched and massaged and kissed. "Breathe for me, baby," Scott reminded as he slid two fingers inside Hank very slowly.

"Scott, Scott," Hank babbled as his hands fisted in the sheets. "I'm gonna come."

"Yeah, Hank," Scott said. "Want to see your face, want to feel you squeeze my fingers when you come for me." He continued to give his attention to Hank's throbbing erection as he slipped two fingers all the way inside, his middle finger tapping once or twice on Hank's prostate. He nipped at Hank's foreskin with his teeth, gently at first and then with a little more pressure. Scott could tell that Hank was close; his breathing was getting more and more urgent, his belly was heaving, and his legs were drawing up towards his chest. "Come for me, baby," he hummed as he slipped his mouth over the sensitive head. "Want to taste you."

"Oh...." Hank's rough, gravelly voice drew out the one syllable for what seemed like minutes. "Fuck, baby, fuck, fuck...." Scott saw Hank's eyes open and look down at the sight of his long, thick cock being swallowed whole.

Scott looked up and saw Hank's eyes glazed over with lust, the large hands almost trembling with the desire to climax. With one final thrust of his fingers, Scott began rubbing and tapping against Hank's prostate while his mouth descended one last time to take in the entire length and girth of his lover. He heard Hank call his name one last time before he felt every muscle in the solid frame tense and bear down to ride out the release. Hank's breathing was ragged and uneven, as if he'd gone for a run that was a few miles too long for him. Scott returned his hand to Hank's belly and began rubbing again. Hank took it in his own hand and hung on, not letting go until he'd spent all he had to give down Scott's willing throat.

Scott removed his fingers slowly, waiting until Hank's breathing had found a much more even pace. "Did I hurt you?"

"Oh fuck, Scott." Hank reached down and pulled Scott up to lie on top of him. "That was fucking amazing." Hank wrapped his arms around the slim, sinewy shoulders, his lips searching for Scott's. "I've never... felt anything... so intense... in my life." Hank kissed and panted against Scott's smiling face.

"That's what you do to me, baby, every time you fuck me." Scott smoothed his hands over Hank's cheeks and forehead. "Nothing better than having someone you love inside you."

Scott realized what he'd just said and his face froze in horror; it's one thing to engage in a harmless fling—everybody knows the rules and observes them—but it's completely unacceptable to change the rules halfway through the game; that's how people get hurt, lost, confused. His cheeks heated as he suddenly found the sheet quite fascinating. He wanted to look up and to tell Hank that's not what he meant; he hadn't meant it like that; *it's just a figure of speech.*

"You...." Hank's eyes were searching, blinking rapidly. Scott could only imagine Hank's mind working furiously, wondering if he'd just heard what he'd thought he heard. "You...." Hank rolled them so that they were on their sides, his hands pressing against the small of Scott's back, his eyes opened wide. "You love me?"

"I...." Scott started and then realized how right it all felt, even if Hank couldn't say the same to him. He'd never felt this before, and it didn't seem right to lie about it, to try to take it back. "I do, yes," he whispered as he looked into those beautiful green eyes. "I love you, Hank." Scott was on his back within a few moments of his confession, Hank's body pressing against him, holding him safe, and Hank's swollen lips pressing against his. "I don't mean for you to—"

"I think I'm in love with you too." Scott could see Hank trying to resolve his own feeling. *Is he wondering how this could all happen in only a week?* Hank's elbows braced against the mattress, he smoothed his hands over Scott's hair, both hands coming to cradle his head. "I've never felt this way about anyone, Scott." Hank kissed him gently, purposefully. "I've never wanted anything as much as I want you... want this."

Scott closed his eyes at the words, the terror of the past few days, of the idea of trying to convince himself that he could handle this even if it was only a casual fling suddenly evaporating as if it had been only a thin and transient fog suspended between him and what he'd always wanted to find.

"So," he asked cautiously, "what now?"

"What do you mean?"

"Will you wait for me?" Scott blinked, wondering if he could bear to hear anything except that Hank would do anything to be with him. "Until I can move back here, I mean?"

"You mean…." Hank's face threatened to split in two from the grin spreading across his face. "You'd move back here," he whispered, "just to be with me?" Scott nodded, slowly, delighting in the awe-filled expression on Hank's face. "Oh, Scrappy." Hank kissed him soundly. "I'm going to make you so happy. Be everything you want me to be, do anything to make you proud of me, of us."

"I already am, Hank." Scott pressed his mouth against Hank's, his tongue tracing a slow, wet path across Hank's smiling lips. He felt his body being pulled closer to his lover's, his mind at rest and able to concentrate on the weight of Hank's solid body pressing against his, Hank's head nestled against his, murmuring three little words that he knew would change his life forever.

CHAPTER 23

"GOD, these towels are so soft." Hank couldn't help but grin with satisfaction at the approval in Scott's sigh.

"Just bought them," Hank announced proudly and smiled down at him as he began to pat and rub. "And I just got them out of the dryer before you manhandled me into having a shower with you."

Scott laughed, his voice full and vibrant in the clean, white bathroom. "Yeah," he chuckled as he took another towel and began to return the favor. "It was quite a struggle to get you in there with me." He rubbed gently and kissed Hank's chest. "But if anyone asks, I'll be sure to let them know how valiantly you fought to protect your virtue."

"Do you know we spent almost the entire day in bed?" Hank closed his eyes as Scott worked the towel over his wet chestnut hair. "I can't remember ever staying in bed for the entire day." Hank took the towel out of his lover's hands and threw it on the counter. Bending with his knees, Hank put his hands on the back of Scott's thighs and lifted the lithe body so that he was sitting on the counter with Hank's slim hips between his legs. Hank's hands stroked up and down the smooth, flawless skin of Scott's back, catching sight of it in the fogged-up mirror. *You make me so happy, Scott.* It was the only thought that circulated in his brain. He wanted to say it over and over until Scott was sick of hearing it, but instead he said only, "Your skin is so soft. I'll never get tired of touching you."

"You're such a romantic, Hank." Scott wrapped his arms around Hank's back and brought them up to hook over his shoulders from behind.

"And I'll never get tired of you touching me." Scott straightened his back and reached up with his lips, and Hank obliged him eagerly.

Hank brought his hands up to rest against the long, muscled neck, his thumbs stroking absently along Scott's jaw line. He couldn't help but think of the confession he'd made to Scott; it hadn't scared him to tell Scott he loved him. And that's what scared him. Hank broke the kiss and looked into Scott's bedroom eyes, hooded and expectant.

"We have to eat, Scrappy," Hank sighed, "or we're not going to have enough strength for you to ravage me again."

"Okay," Scott pouted, his hands falling away to rest on the counter. "But as soon as we're done...." He held up a finger, a warning and a promise all at once.

They padded down to the kitchen and began fixing sandwiches, their shoulders or hips brushing against each other as they worked to prepare their first meal in almost ten hours. They joked with each other and they listened to each other. Scott recited items, making a list of groceries they'd need to get before Wednesday, and Hank listed the days he would be off and the days when he would have to go to work. It was easy, comfortable, and a welcome change for each man to have someone else beside him who had no desire to control or to whine about things neither could control. Scott had seen his fair share of relationships end due to his work schedule, and Hank wondered why he'd never known that a relationship with a man—well, maybe it was just Scott—would be so... freeing.

"Okay," Scott said as he finished chewing his BLT. "So I'll go and get the groceries tomorrow morning, and you make sure you're here when I get back."

"Okay...." Hank looked over, his brow furrowed. "Or I could give you a key." Hank reached out and stroked Scott's forearm. "Or I could come with you." Hank noticed the hesitant expression on Scott's face and thought he'd have a little fun; he pulled back playfully, a mock look of horror on his face. "You're ashamed, aren't you?" Hank delighted in the confused look on the younger man's face. It was as if he couldn't decide to be concerned or amused by Hank's sudden playfulness. "You're ashamed to be seen with a lowly lumberjack, and you don't want me to go with you."

"What the hell are you talking about?" Scott's eyebrows were knitted as he laughed and lifted himself out of the chair to go fill the bowls on the counter with ice cream and fruit salad. "Have you had a seizure or something?"

"Admit it," Hank whimpered. "The magic is over already, isn't it?"

Scott turned and showed Hank a look of concern. "Oh my God," he whispered, so over the top that Hank's expression changed; perhaps he'd gone too far and now Scott really was concerned about something. "I've heard of this happening, but... I... I... never thought I'd see it actually happen."

"What?" Hank's hands were rubbing absent-mindedly at his face. "What's wrong?"

"Of course, it all makes sense, the incoherent thoughts, the crazy mood swing...." Scott placed a bowl in front of Hank. "You've actually gone and fucked your brains out!" Scott sat quickly as Hank finally understood that Scott had turned the tables on him, making him the butt of Scott's own playfulness. Hank noticed the younger man was still giggling. He lobbed a grape at Scott, catching him right in the center of his forehead.

Hank smiled as he watched Scott wipe away the grape juice from his forehead and picked up another grape, this one also aimed at Scott's head. "Think that's funny, huh?"

"No." Scott's lips trembled with the effort to keep a straight face.

"No, what?"

"No, I don't?"

"No, what?"

"No, way?" Scott seemed to appear flustered at the frown that Hank was wearing. "No, sir?"

"That's better." Hank harrumphed and dug into his melting ice cream. He almost had the spoon to his mouth when he felt something wet and cold hit his nose. He lowered the spoon and looked over at Scott, who was inexplicably fascinated by the plain white tablecloth. "What was that?" Hank's eyes were wide, his expression patient and menacing all at once.

"I'm sorry?" Scott looked up, his features schooled, his voice dripping confusion.

"Did you just throw food at me?"

"No," Scott answered, his face a study of indignation. "I think you have me confused with a certain lumberjack sitting at this table."

"Okay, then." Hank took a scoop of ice cream.

"Hank?" Scott was already up at moving away from the table when he saw how he was holding his spoon. "Don't!" Scott ran for the stairs, but he was too slow. "Hank? Please?" Scott was squirming underneath the big hands, his body held firm between powerful thighs. "You'll get your carpet all dirty."

"I'll rent a shampooer tomorrow," Hank shrugged.

"My clothes!" Scott snapped his fingers. "I only have a couple of T-shirts with me."

"I have a washer." Hank grinned. "*And* a dryer."

"Is there anything I can do... to... stop you?" Scott's voice was husky, sexy, and seductive as he brought his hands up to Hank's waist, his fingers finding their way underneath the cotton fabric, his eyes promising everything and anything. The relief that washed over Scott's face as Hank began to move his hand, still holding the spoon, back and away from their position just over Scott's face.

"No!" Hank whispered the word, slowly and seductively. He smiled menacingly when he noticed the look on his lover's face change from one of relief to one of realization. He laughed as he reached for the elastic of Scott's boxers and was quickly pushed out of the way as Scott came off the stairs and began to dance around the living room in an effort to remove the dollop of ice cream from his boxers. Hank was enjoying the sight more than he'd thought he would.

"Okay." Scott approached the kitchen sink as bowlegged as a cowboy who'd spent his entire life on an overweight horse. "That was just rude." He grabbed some paper towels, pulled open his boxers, and began dabbing at the ice cream blotches, his head flicking up and back to remove the hair from his eyes. He stared at Hank. With his serene smile and the spoon moving back and forth slowly from bowl to mouth, the man was a study in quiet contemplation. "Now I have to take another shower."

"That *is* a shame." Hank shook his head and lifted himself off his chair, bowl in hand, and walked into the kitchen. "Truce?"

"I'll tell you what, baby," Scott said as he tossed the paper towels in the garbage bin. "Why don't you ask me that at two o'clock tomorrow morning when you're tied to the bed and I'm shoving ice cubes up your ass?"

"You flirt." Hank chuckled as he swept Scott into his arms. "If it'll make you feel better, I'll lick you clean in the shower."

Scott pulled back a few inches and looked up at Hank. "I'm listening."

"And then...." Hank's lips found the sensitive spot where shoulder met neck. He brushed his stubble over it and then soothed it with his tongue. "I'll dry you off." Hank's voice was but a mere whisper now, and he could feel Scott's body responding to the anticipation. "And then fuck you 'til you walk like that all day tomorrow."

"Hmm." Scott pulled away completely and walked past Hank towards the stairs, removing his T-shirt and boxers. "Tempting," he stated matter-of-factly. "I'll let you know my decision at two tomorrow morning." He had meant to go with a saucy wink, but Hank chasing him up the stairs could be just as much fun, he figured.

IT WAS almost midnight by the time Hank collapsed beside Scott's sated and flushed body, his own body covered in sweat and matted hair. Hank pulled him against his body, well aware that they should be getting some sleep, but he didn't want to close his eyes, didn't want to have to end the day. It was a perfect day. They'd talked, played, made love at least a half-dozen times, and even started talking about plans—in the shower just after dinner—for the future. Hank had surprised even himself when he'd been the one to mention Scott moving in with him or finding a house together. But Scott had surprised him even more when he'd said that he'd leave the decision up to Hank. *I can write anywhere, Hank,* is what Scott had said to him in the shower.

Hank leaned over and kissed the top of Scott's head, not sure whether he was asleep yet or not and not really caring. Scott was in his bed and in his arms, and that's what mattered to Hank the most. He'd found someone who loved him, believed in him, wanted to be with him, and he wasn't going to ask too many questions or make too many demands. For once, Hank was going to let everything fall where it may. And with Scott beside him, letting things fall where they may couldn't be anything but good.

CHAPTER 24

SCOTT awoke as he heard the flush of the toilet, his mind not registering for a moment that he was alone in bed. He rolled over and spread out in the heated space that Hank's body had created and took hold of the pillow. As he curled up with the pillow between his folded arms, inhaling the only scent he could ever remember making him this happy, he heard Hank's familiar whistle getting louder. He watched the big, graceful, beautiful body walk toward him. Hank's lips curved into a sweet smile, and Scott stretched out on his back, his toes and fingers clutching at air as he worked to awaken his body fully. He couldn't help but bring his hands to his stomach protectively as Hank settled his naked body on the edge of the bed.

"What time are we going to the grocery store?"

"Whenever." Scott yawned.

"Well." Hank pulled the sheet down Scott's body and licked his lips seductively. "If we go soon, we'll have the whole afternoon to do something... fun."

"Hmmm." Scott yawned and stretched again when he felt Hank's hand define a line between his hip bone and his neck. "Fun, huh? Anything specific in mind, handsome?"

"Could be, sure," Hank whispered as he hooked his hand under Scott's neck and brought their lips together. "Balls...." Hank licked at Scott's lips. "Holes...." Hank brought his other hand to the small of Scott's back and moved his lips to nibble on Scott's earlobe. "Wood...."

He brought both hands together at the nape of Scott's neck, his breath hot and moist on the smaller man's lips. "Iron...."

"Keep talking like that—" Scott pulled his head back and looked at the grin on Hank's face. "Wait, iron?" It took another couple of licks of Hank's tongue against his neck and ears before Scott finally clued in. "Oh shit," he huffed. "Are you talking about golf?"

"Of course." Hank feigned indignation. "What did you think I meant?"

"Golf? Really?" Scott fell back on the bed and rolled over, turning his back to Hank. "I don't think I like you anymore."

"Actually," Hank soothed as he pushed his naked body closer to the warm, silky-smooth back. "I was talking about mini-golf."

"Okay," Scott squirmed and wiggled as he felt the hair on Hank's muscled chest tickle the sensitive skin of his back. "But I still don't like you for getting me all hot and bothered and then—"

His words were cut off when Hank pushed against his shoulder and had him flat on his back with Hank's chest hair now tickling his own chest. His hands went instinctively to the broad back, delighting in the play of muscles as Hank used his powerful arms to suspend his own body a fraction of an inch above Scott's. He felt Hank's lips on his. The kisses were tender and gentle. He arched his back, intent on bringing their leaking erections closer together. He was quite sure that if Hank didn't start grinding or creating some sort of friction, he would crawl out of his skin. He tried to reach between their bellies, to encourage some sort of progression, but Hank lowered his hips and trapped his hand where it lay, hovering somewhere north of their belly buttons.

"Hank, baby," he whispered against the freshly shaven cheeks. "Please, please, I want you."

"Will you forgive me," Hank muttered between kisses, "for getting you all hot and bothered... if I... fuck you stupid... right now?"

"Anything," Scott pleaded. "Please, Hank, fuck me." Scott's voice was hoarse, a mere whisper against the chestnut waves; he felt the silky strands against his lips as Hank's mouth moved across his cheek to his temple. He heard the air being pulled into his lungs when Hank snapped his hips, sending his engorged shaft between Scott's legs, nudging his perineum. "Oh fuck, baby, want you... so much." He felt the cool air on his cheek as Hank raised his head, his eyes hooded and full of lust. He watched, enraptured, as one big, powerful arm supported the muscled torso, and then felt Hank grab his right leg, bringing it up to rest on Hank's left shoulder. Scott threw his head back and his body responded when Hank's finger began to circle and massage his entrance.

"Can you reach the oil?"

Scott shook his head; he didn't think he had any muscles that would respond except the one that Hank was rubbing and pushing against. "Let me," Scott pleaded as he reached for Hank's hand, pulling two fingers into his mouth and wetting them. He felt the trail of saliva slip from the fingers as Hank pulled them back and took his hole. "Hank, oh God, Hank," He panted and looked into those beautiful green eyes.

"Ooooh, so tight, Scott. It's like an oven in there." Hank looked down at his lover. "Touch yourself, baby." Hank's eyes grew dark as he watched his lover wrap a fist around his engorged and leaking cock. "My beautiful baby," Hank whispered against the wrist that Scott was trailing across his cheek.

"Oh, Hank," Scott sighed as he arched his back and pushed himself down on Hank's thick fingers. "Yours, all yours—can't get enough of you." Scott let go of his own shaft and caressed Hank's sides, reveling in the feel of the muscles as they contracted and relaxed under his palms.

"Need you, Scott." Hank removed his fingers slowly and reached toward the dresser, his fingers trembling ever so slightly from the strain of holding himself up for so long. "Can't believe you're mine," he whispered as he bent down to scorch Scott's lips with a searing, claiming kiss. His needy, hungry tongue pushed past Scott's swollen lips, his fingers finding their way back into the heat he'd claimed as his own. Hank resisted the urge to struggle as he felt Scott's body press up into his, the small, lithe body rubbing and searching frantically for friction, for anything that would bring about release.

"Now, Hank, please," Scott panted against Hank's hungry mouth, his desperate and impatient hands pushing against Hank's hips to align them between his own thighs. "Fuck me, baby. Please, fuck me."

"Jesus," Hank hissed as he felt Scott's feet pulling urgently against his ass. "So fucking hot when you're horny, Scrappy." Scott saw the smile on his lover's lips as Hank rolled on the condom, slicked his fingers. Hank lined himself up against Scott's entrance and slowly pushed in. Scott wanted him so badly, desperately, at that moment. But there was something different in the way they were making love at that moment; there was something less primal, less playful. Neither of them seemed to be thinking, as they had before, about his own need to get off. Hank was so completely focused on pleasing him; he seemed to lose his rhythm and stopped, his eyes searching Scott's sweaty, flushed face.

"Hank." Scott barely heard the word that issued from his heated mouth; his lips were on fire from the kissing, his body alive and throbbing and nothing more than an instrument that only Hank could use to produce the sounds he was making. With that one word, Scott felt the soft chestnut waves fall forward and caress his chest as Hank bent over to kiss his chest, lick his nipples, and then rejoin their lips. Hank pulled up slightly and searched Scott's eyes, neither of them speaking—neither of them needing to. Scott closed his eyes and arched his back. He whispered Hank's name one last time and then felt the big body rear back, Hank's hands maintaining a firm hold on Scott's ankles as he snapped his hips over and over.

"Scott," Hank growled. "Soon, gonna... soon." Hank's arms reached around and encircled Scott's thighs, fixing them in place while he pistoned in and out of the delicious, intoxicating heat of Scott's ass. "Come with me, baby, come... come...." Hank was grunting and rutting like a man possessed.

Scott touched himself, his thumb teasing its way over his slit only once before he felt himself clench against Hank's thick shaft. He cried out Hank's name when he felt Hank's entire body tense under his thighs and felt Hank's teeth and tongue find his calf, Hank spilling into the condom with a seemingly endless number of thrusts. Scott thought that perhaps he would pass out if it didn't end soon. The emotion, the release, and the thought that this gentle giant of a man could love someone like him made Scott dizzy with the desire to crawl right inside of him and never come out.

Hank released Scott's legs after kissing and snuggling them against his chest and guided them to the mattress, his gaze fixed intently on Scott's rosy cheeks and hooded eyes. He lowered himself slowly so that their bodies were aligned from head to toe, his face nuzzling the skin on Scott's neck, his lips offering lazy, sated kisses on whatever skin they could reach.

"Forgive me now?" His hand crept across the flat belly and started petting when he felt the little laugh that pushed against his hand. "I didn't hurt you, did I?"

Scott rolled onto his side, first pushing his hair out of his eyes and then gently sweeping Hank's off the sweaty forehead. His smile was serene, his eyes contemplative, and his voice was low and husky. As he stroked the side of Hank's face, Scott whispered, "Did you mean it? That I'm yours?"

"Every word, Scott."

He felt his chest tighten at the look on Hank's face and at the meaning behind those words. He'd never had anyone want him that much, never had anyone claim him like that before. There were so few moments in his life when Scott could honestly say he remembered every word, every feeling, every emotion, or even what he'd been thinking, but this was one moment in his life that he would never forget. He'd known that Hank was a man of few words and that it might even be difficult for him sometimes to open up, to allow someone inside of his heart, maybe even to relinquish some of the control that he'd felt he needed. And from the first time he'd watched Hank at the hospital, prepared to slink away and accept responsibility for something he hadn't even known he'd done, Scott knew that these particular waters ran very, very deep. But there they were, arms and legs entwined as Scott listened to the sound of what he'd always thought he'd never have. He was looking into the face of the first and only man he would ever love.

"Baby?" Hank raised himself up on one elbow and looked down at Scott, his hands caressing away the moisture on the flushed and heated cheeks. "Oh God, I did hurt you!"

"No," Scott protested and pulled the palm of Hank's hand to his lips. "Just...happy," he whispered as he closed his eyes. "Just happy, that's all."

Hank stayed propped on his elbow and guided his hand to Scott's waist, pulling very gently so that their bodies were pressed firmly together. His lips found themselves next to Scott's ear, and his voice was strong and sweet when he whispered, "I love you, Scott."

Scott closed his eyes and kissed Hank's shoulder, his hand over the center of Hank's chest. "I love you, too, Hank."

Hank pulled back a few inches so that he was looking down at Scott's sleepy eyes. His tongue snaked out and teased at a sweaty shoulder. "Enough to do the grocery shopping tomorrow?"

"We'll do it whenever you want." Scott laughed and pushed playfully at Hank's chest. "But if I can't walk tomorrow, you're doing it all yourself!"

"Well," Hank kissed the shell of Scott's ear again, pulling the sheet up over their bodies; he felt the shiver pass through Scott's body. "Maybe," Hank teased as he grabbed a handful of Scott's ass, "we'll just have to make sure we're both walking funny, so no one is only staring at you."

Scott's head popped up, his lips stopping their exploration of Hank's skin. "Only if you think you're ready, baby."

Hank smiled sweetly. "Told you," he said as he kissed the tip of Scott's nose. "I want to be everything to you." Hank's mouth covered Scott's, and he traced the contours of teeth and gums and tongue, his cock stirring again. "I want to feel you inside me, baby."

Scott pushed against Hank's chest and they rolled together until Hank was underneath him, Scott's hips finding their way between Hank's spread thighs. "You're so beautiful, Hank." Scott hummed against his lips, his tongue resisting the urge to start everything over again. "So kind and gentle and sexy and handsome and—"

Hank sighed as he shook his head. "I don't think anyone has ever seen the things in me that you do."

"You're who I've been waiting for, Henry Isaac Ballam." Scott propped himself on his elbows and looked into the orbs of green, his hands stroking the sides of his lover's face. "You're absolutely perfect to me."

"Even though I hog the covers?"

"You do not," Scott laughed. "I hog the covers, but it doesn't matter since you're a natural heat source."

"Even though I snore?"

"I can sleep through anything."

"Even though I'm not rich and famous?"

"I've got enough money for both of us," Scott harrumphed. "And being famous isn't everything."

"Even though—"

"Even though, Hank." Scott silenced him with a kiss that let Hank know the discussion was over.

CHAPTER 25

SCOTT was the first to wake Wednesday morning, the alarm buzzing near his side of the bed. He rolled over, noted the early hour, and hit the snooze button, perhaps a little too forcefully.

"Hank?" Scott pushed against the warm, broad back beside him. "Hank," he called a little louder. "It's time to get up."

"Mmmungh." Hank grunted and rolled onto his stomach, pulling the fluffy down pillow over his head.

Scott resisted the urge to laugh at how surly Hank was this morning and decided to try a different method to get Mr. Grumpy out of bed. He lifted the sheet so that he could move his body slowly over toward Hank, and when he was close enough, he snuggled his body onto the warm lump of flesh.

Scott lifted the pillow hiding the chestnut waves and whispered into the sensitive flesh of Hank's neck, "We have nine minutes to snuggle before you have to get ready for your day of first aid training."

Hank's hands reached out in a futile attempt to find the discarded pillow and then snaked down the bed to his sides, his hands coming to rest finally along Scott's hips. "Don't wanna get up yet." Hank turned his head to the side, eyes still closed, and showed an exaggerated pout.

"Well," Scott bargained, "if you get up now, I'll have time to give you a tummy rub."

"Hmmm," Hank murmured as he wiggled his body so that the smaller man fell snugly into all the right places. "What time is it?"

"It's almost eight," Scott whispered, his lips and tongue dotting the thick, tanned neck with wet, sensuous kisses. "You don't have to be there for another hour."

"If I skip shaving," Hank reasoned, "I'd only need ten minutes to shower and five to drive there."

"Okay." Scott lifted himself off the prostrate body and rolled to sit on his side of the bed, his feet dangling over the edge. "I'll go make breakfast and wake you up again in thirty minutes."

"Huh?" Hank rolled over in time to curl one arm around his waist. "Where you going?"

"I thought you didn't want to get up yet?" Scott knew what Hank had meant, but he couldn't get enough of hearing the words come out of those full lips. He let himself be dragged back so that his back was to Hank's chest, the silky hairs tickling his back.

"Not what I meant," Hank grunted into the nape of Scott's neck.

"I know," Scott admitted and tried not to shiver at the warm breath that ran across his neck and shoulders.

"You're mean," Hank pouted as he pulled their bodies closer.

"I am?" Scott asked, already turning his body around to lie face-to-face with his lover. "I guess that means I'll have to make it up to you." Scott kissed the tip of Hank's nose and watched it wrinkle.

"Tickles."

Scott continued to touch his lips to Hank's forehead and cheeks and chin. He was so incredibly content just to lie there in Hank's arms and do whatever he could to keep the low, purring sounds coming from the sleepy body. He stroked lazily at the forearm that encircled his waist, his eyes drifting shut as Hank lavished his neck and shoulders with gentle kisses. When the alarm sounded again, he felt Hank pull away and sit up in the bed and throw his legs over the side.

"Just think of it like this." Scott smiled as he lifted himself up and crawled over to lean against Hank's broad back. "You go and put in your three or four hours learning how to save lives, and," he smiled against the skin of Hank's back, "I'll be here when you get back, naked and waiting."

"Great," Hank muttered as he pulled Scott to sit on his lap. "Now I'll be rock hard all day."

"Well," Scott teased as he squirmed, pushing his ass down onto Hank's growing erection. "Just think of something else...like dirty gym socks or sleeping with Roddy."

"You really are mean." Hank huffed as he slapped Scott's ass.

"I make it up to you." Scott backed away from Hank's lap and stood a few feet away. "What would you like for breakfast?"

"You." Hank leered. "In the shower, right now."

"Now that"—Scott turned and sashayed to the bathroom door—"I can make."

Scott waited under the big showerhead, the hot water sluicing its way over his sore muscles. It wasn't the amount of time that they'd spent in bed that was the only source of his aching muscles, although the two of them had definitely spent more time in the bedroom than in all other rooms—or outside—combined. Scott was feeling particularly sore this morning because they'd been go-kart racing on Monday and then spent a good couple of hours golfing yesterday. He'd thought that they were going to do mini-golfing, but, at the last minute, Hank had decided that they should try golfing nine holes at the ritzy course down the street from Hank's condo. Hank had, of course, explained and reassured that it would all be just for fun, but the entire afternoon had shown a side of Hank that he'd found to be frightening and playful at the same time.

Hank had been patient and very generous, but when they'd found themselves being overtaken by a few of the more serious golfers, Hank had become rather insistent that Scott 'try harder" to keep his balls on the fairway, or "try to at least make par." Scott had had to stifle his immediate impulse to burst out laughing at the look of distress on his lover's face when he'd asked to be reminded of what "making par" meant. And, Scott could admit to himself now, he'd played a little fast and loose with some of his questions, wondering out loud why it was called a green or who had ever thought to call it "bogey," just to see the reaction from the very competitive Hank.

Scott didn't have a competitive bone in his body. It was obvious to Scott now that Hank did. Scott didn't imagine it would create any problems between the two of them, but he could see Hank not getting what he wanted as a potential problem. Hank had always been very sweet and kind to Scott, but their two afternoons participating in sports-like events had proven to Scott that Hank was used to winning and to being the best at whatever he tried. Scott, on the other hand, had learned his limitations long ago. Growing up with Brian and their father had permitted Scott to come to grips with his weaknesses. And more importantly, Scott had determined early on what he wanted to work on improving and what was not really all that important.

As he turned the faucet a little to the left, knowing that Hank would want the water even hotter, he heard the click of the shower door and felt Hank's heat long before the muscular arms came around his waist and pulled him back into the broad, hairy chest. Hank's hand smoothed its way up his smooth chest and settled along his jaw line, turning his head slightly so that Hank could plant a wet, passionate good-morning kiss on Scott's wet lips. Scott turned in Hank's embrace and settled their bodies together, paying close attention to lining up their erections, his hands skimming along the freshly shaven jaw. "So smooth, baby," he whispered against Hank's eager mouth.

Hank's hands trailed down the wet skin of Scott's back and cupped a cheek in each hand. "I never did ask you if you like the hair." Hank pulled his face away in anticipation of Scott's answer.

"I love hairy bodies," Scott admitted, a slight blush coming to his cheeks.

"If you don't," Hank said between kisses, "I can always shave."

"*What?*"

"I said—"

"I heard you," Scott barked his astonishment. "Don't you dare!"

"Really?"

"Yes, really," Scott echoed. "I can't believe you'd think I'd want you to shave it off."

"I didn't think that," Hank smiled softly. "I just wanted to be sure. Women don't tend to like the hair."

"I," Scott articulated, "am not a woman. And I love my man with hair." As if to emphasize his point, he drew his hands up and over the dark, wet hair that covered Hank's chest. He felt himself grow even harder as his fingers jump when Hank flexed his considerable pecs. "Doesn't that itch when it grows back?"

"Like a son of a bitch!" Hank laughed and put a hand behind Scott's head, pulling their mouths together for a searing kiss. Their tongues played together for a few moments when Hank pulled away a few inches.

Scott could tell that Hank wanted to ask for something but didn't have the words. "What do you need, baby?" He had a good idea what Hank wanted, letting one hand find its way to the crease at the top of the strong, solid ass, but he waited for Hank to ask.

"Will you suck me while you put your fingers...?"

Scott didn't know whether it was the hot water or the hesitation that made Hank's skin flush, but he wasn't going to make Hank say all of the words. He brought one hand up to cup Hank's balls while he brought the other around to find Hank's entrance from between his spread legs.

"Lean back, baby," Scott advised as he tongued the slit of Hank's erection. When Hank was leaning against the white ceramic tile of the shower wall, Scott pushed one finger inside while his thumb pressed and rubbed and smoothed the area just behind Hank's balls.

With his hand still wrapped around the base of Hank's dick, Scott ran his tongue along the underside, feeling the heat and the little ridges of veins and arteries and finally slipping in between the gorged head and the foreskin. He heard Hank suck in a quick breath and then felt the big hands smooth their way over his head. Not being terribly selfish when it came to pleasure, Hank's calloused fingertips teased and stroked the sensitive area around Scott's ears and throat. And when Hank's fingers descended to caress and pinch his nipples, Scott moaned and took Hank's entire length and girth to the back of his throat, grunting a few words and shaking his head slightly from side to side.

"Oh yeah, fuck, baby." Hank sighed and let his head fall back against the shower wall, his hands coming back up to the sides of Scott's face, his fingers playing with the soft lobes of his lover's ears. "Sweet mouth, such a sweet mouth."

Scott withdrew the one finger and replaced it with two, delighting in the sounds of pleasure this caused in Hank. He could do this for hours and had often thought that he preferred this kind of sensuality to the grunting and pounding. But anything and everything they did together was incredible, and Scott would never get enough. As his knuckle grazed Hank's sensitive gland, he moved his hand from the base of the swollen erection to cup one of Hank's ass cheeks, pulling and encouraging Hank to thrust into his mouth. He opened wide when he felt the cheek flex and press forward, taking all of his lover into his mouth and still wanting more. No man had ever made Scott feel so sexy, or wanted. No man had ever given Scott this kind of pleasure before, in or out of the bedroom.

"Oh Scott, gonna come," Hank warned.

But Scott didn't move, didn't *want* to move. The first jets of ropy heat hit the back of his throat, and he swallowed, his own sense of pleasure heightened by the musky and salty taste of Hank's seed. After three or four more snaps of Hank's hips, Scott took a few minutes to lick and tease, resisting the urge to smile at the spasms that rocked the big, strong body. He finished cleaning Hank and stood to share the taste between their two mouths. He loved that Hank was so sensitive after coming, loved that this big, muscled lumberjack could be reduced to uncontrollable convulsions from a few minutes inside Scott's mouth. Of course, he also realized that Hank was just discovering what it felt like to have someone inside him, what it felt like to have someone tease and tap and massage his prostate. It was something that Scott would always remember—this feeling of being the one to give Hank such pleasure for the first time. Hank hadn't been too eager to be fucked the other day, but Scott was nothing if not patient.

"Jesus, baby," Hank panted as he wrapped his arms around Scott's body. "That was fucking hot! Watching you swallow like that."

"Well," Scott rested his chin on the hard muscle of Hank's shoulder. "I'm glad I could help you find a better mood."

"Fuck me, baby." Hank guffawed and kissed the top of Scott's wet head. "You always know what to do to get my motor running."

"Wash up." Scott leaned up for a gentle kiss. "And then come down, and I'll make you breakfast." It would need to be a quick one, but Scott would make sure his man got an even better start to the day.

CHAPTER 26

"JESUS, fuck me!" Brian threw down his pen and pushed himself away from the table. "Roddy!" He started walking towards the double doors that Roddy had thrown open just a few moments before.

Hank sat there, shaking his head, pen in hand. He'd arrived in such a good mood, but Roddy's antics were beginning to take their toll after the incredible start to this day. It was a condition of every heli-logger's employment that they maintain certification in first aid. Roddy knew that. So why was he pulling this arrogant move yet again at what must be his fifteenth first aid course? Every year, Hank realized, Roddy would pull this kind of stupid tantrum, delaying the time that each of the other twenty loggers could be spending with their families or doing something other than sitting in the basement of the community recreation center learning how to use an EpiPen or how to tie a sling around someone's shoulder.

He laughed to himself a little and caught Chris, the greenhorn, grinning and shaking his head. Hank couldn't help but notice that Hughy, Roddy's partner in crime, shot him a dirty look when he let loose with a little chuckle at the absurdity of the situation, and he felt a little surge of pride—or was it power?—when Hughy was the first to avert his eyes. Some of the others, more seasoned than either Hank or Chris, seemed to be taking it all in stride. There were a few conversations about something other than what everyone could hear erupting here and there, but when everyone heard Brian raise his voice, their smiles disappeared. Brian was making it clear that if Roddy wasn't back in that room by the count of ten, Brian would not be able to use him on any future jobs until his certification was valid and up-to-date.

The count to ten seemed to last far too long, and Hank heard some of the other men grumbling about how they had to put up with Roddy's "fucking attitude" every year. The instructor, Hank noticed, was taking it all in without showing any outward signs of having to wait—again—for Brian to reign in one of his men. His name was Matthew, and Hank was sure he was new. At least he didn't look familiar. What Hank did notice, however, was the striking resemblance the man bore to Scott: dirty blond hair, bright eyes, tall and slight but hard-bodied. Hank had been caught looking more than once and was certain that, were it not for his size, he'd be in serious trouble for coming on to the strikingly beautiful man. He wasn't coming on to the man, not in any way that was conscious on his part, but there was no way the instructor would know that Hank already had the perfect partner at home, waiting—maybe even naked—for him to get home. The perfect partner who cared about him, loved him.

At moments like these, listening to Brian and Roddy scream at each other, or when he'd driven over here after hearing those three little words from Scott this morning, Hank was frustrated to find himself thinking about what he'd do when his little Scrappy had to go back to Toronto. It wasn't that Hank didn't believe Scott wouldn't come back as he promised. It was more the realization that Hank would find himself alone again. Sure they could talk on the phone, and Scott had promised to come back—and for that matter, Hank could hop on a plane for an extended weekend—but he couldn't seem to let himself forget all of the other times in his life when people had failed to keep their promises, the times when something had always seemed so much more important to them than spending time with him.

It was, Hank was certain now, the reason he'd always ended things with the women he'd dated. He'd never begrudged any of his bedmates the freedom to do whatever they wanted, but he'd always found himself at a loss when he seemed to need them the most. He was aware that he'd always had difficulty asking for what he wanted or what he needed. He could recognize that he wasn't perfect by any means. But when it came to trusting people enough to follow through on promises, Hank had always grown tired of the ping-ponging thoughts in his brain. It was like the whole debate about the chicken and the egg. It was a constant source of frustration and fatigue for him: *Do I not trust someone because so many have let me down, or do I let people down because I don't think I can trust them?*

As he asked himself the same question for the millionth time, he felt more than heard the double doors swing open. He averted his eyes when Brian entered the room. He knew better than to get in the boss's way when he was red-faced and his eyebrows were practically vertical. He'd been on the receiving end of that stare more times than he could count. But now he noted with a perverse sense of glee that it was Roddy who had pushed all the wrong buttons. Hank was finally not responsible for making all of these other men—men who had chosen a job that had them climbing, enjoying the outdoors, and pushing their bodies to their limits—sit around with their thumbs up their asses and their brains in neutral.

Hank leaned forward, ready to listen to the rest of the derailed lesson, and planted his forearms on the table when he heard Brian pull back his chair with such force that the sound of metal scraping across the concrete floors made almost everyone wince.

"My apologies, Matthew." Brian placed himself gently in the chair and pulled it forward. "You won't be having any more problems from any of my employees." Hank heard the emphasis on the last word. It was Brian's way, he was sure, of making sure that everyone there knew that they were as easily fired as hired.

The lessons continued, and Hank made sure to pay attention to everything for the expected test at the end of the day. After another ninety minutes, Matthew suggested that they break for lunch. No one had any objections to a shorter lunch. That way, everyone agreed, each of them would be out sooner than the scheduled end time of four o'clock that afternoon. Hank certainly wasn't going to argue the benefits of getting home sooner and found himself rushing to his truck to get home to see Scott. He was almost at his truck when he heard Brian calling his name.

"Yeah, boss?" Hank stood beside his truck, his stomach suddenly in knots. Was this his boss that was coming to speak to him or Scott's brother?

"Listen, Hank," Brian started, the back of his thumb rubbing against his forehead. "I don't know that I can trust Roddy with being the third-level medic anymore... I mean with the accident last week and Gord leaving...."

Hank wondered what any of this had to do with him. It was fair to say that he and Brian had usually been at odds and had never seen each other as confidants, but something in the boss's voice had Hank thinking that Brian might be asking for his help. "You want me to take over?"

"I'm not gonna force you or anything." Brian shrugged. "But I've been thinking that it would probably make more sense... I mean, considering your background as a fireman and all."

"Yeah," Hank smiled. "No problem." Hank nodded a couple of times when he noticed Brian's shoulders relax a little more. "It makes sense, you know... considering I could probably teach this course."

"Thanks, Hank." Brian offered his hand, gratefully showing his relief that Hank had come through for him again, and shook like the grateful boss he was. "Listen," Brian returned his hand to his pocket and took a step back. "I know you and Scott probably have plans and all, but I was hoping you two might like to come over for dinner tomorrow night." He removed his hand again and brought it up to his chest, palm out in a sign of understanding. "Kari's going to be coming over, and she wants to cook something special for Scott being so nice to her when I was in the hospital."

Hank's immediate thought was that it had seemed like a different lifetime, the one where he'd been convinced that Brian would fire him for having caused the accident. But he'd never really believed he'd caused it, and Scott had been so wonderfully kind to him even as a complete stranger that he dismissed the thoughts of blame and smiled at Brian. "We don't really have any plans, but I'll ask him." Hank shrugged. "I'm pretty sure he'll want to come."

"I haven't seen him in a couple of days now." Hank thought he might have seen a faint blush creep into Brian's tanned face. "He's been absolutely relentless with the phone calls to make sure I'm okay, but...."

"Well," Hank chuckled, "then I'll say yes right now and make sure I drag him with me."

"Okay." Brian smirked. "Sounds good."

Hank nodded at Brian and turned to his truck, turning before his boss got too far away. "Hey, Brian?" When he turned to look back, Hank took a deep breath and asked, "You're okay with this, right? I mean, if you think this might cause some problems between us, I don't want...." Hank didn't know where he was going with this particular declaration. He suddenly realized that there was nothing that would—or could—keep him away from Scott. "I don't want you to think that I'm just... you know...."

"Hank," Brian said softly as he came back to stand in front of his new Falling Supervisor. "I'm not gonna lie to you and tell you I don't have my doubts, but Scott is capable of making his own decisions." Brian punched Hank lightly on the shoulder. "Besides, if you haven't already figured it out...." Brian shrugged, his grin growing wider. "Scott can take care of himself."

"I've noticed." Hank snorted. "And Brian?" He held out his hand when Brian turned to face him again. "I just wanted you to know that I consider myself the luckiest man on the planet to have him in my life." He'd been meaning to say something like that to Scott but couldn't bring himself to do it. It sounded so corny and sappy. But hearing it out loud as he said it, Hank realized that it was the truth. It wasn't corny or sappy at all.

"He's very special, Hank." Brian smiled sweetly and then snorted. "Drives me screaming up the wall sometimes, he's so stubborn, but he's the nicest person I know."

"Yeah." Hank grinned as he felt the heat creep into his cheeks. Just thinking about Scott could usually disarm Hank in a way he'd never experienced before. "He's really something special, that's for sure."

HANK was almost late getting back to the training session but managed to arrive just before Chris and with enough time to chat with Matthew. And if Chris hadn't walked in just as Hank realized that Matthew was a shameless flirt, well, Hank wasn't really sure what he would have done to keep the tall, blond instructor from thinking he was available. Hank didn't care if the other guys knew that he was with Scott, but he certainly wasn't going to go out of his way to give them yet one more thing to harass him about. And more importantly, he certainly didn't want to think that Roddy and Hughy would be smart enough not to make any rude remarks about Scott. Even though Scott was the boss's brother, Hank had worked long enough with both Roddy and Hughy to know that they'd make their voices heard. Neither of them would have any qualms about making the occasional—or frequent—snide or insulting remark about Scott.

And besides, Hank thought to himself as he waited for the rest of the loggers to return, it was kind of nice having Scott all to himself. He didn't really want to share Scott with the outside world just yet. It was new and exciting, and they'd have to admit to it sooner or later, but Hank was hoping that it would be much later. Hank liked the feeling of being the most important person in Scott's life right now. The rude, homophobic remarks would come soon enough, so, Hank reasoned, why not enjoy it as long as he could?

When everyone had returned from lunch, Roddy and Hughy making a point of arriving almost twenty minutes late, Matthew proceeded to introduce the afternoon's activities: hands-on experience with the various medical treatments they'd discussed all morning. And when Matthew called on him to be the "victim" for the third time, Hank wasn't sure if Matthew understood that it made him a target for the likes of Roddy and Hughy. But he'd made a promise to Brian and more importantly, Scott, so Hank stepped forward and lay on the floor.

"Okay," Matthew began while he let his hand rest on Hank's heated forehead. "Hank has fallen. You don't know how far the fall was, but you need to prep him for transport. First steps?"

"Check his pockets for cash," Hughy whispered to Roddy.

Matthew issued an exasperated laugh as Brian turned to glare at the two men. "After that?" Matthew asked again, patiently.

"Brace his neck?" One of the other men in the room asked.

"Good," Matthew praised. "And once his neck is immobilized?"

"Transport?"

"Excellent," Matthew congratulated. "Okay, so if you can all come around here, we'll practice lifting our victim."

Each of the men stood and made his way to where Matthew and Hank were in the middle of the tables that formed a rectangle around the edges of the room. Matthew asked several of the men to position themselves by Hank's shoulders, hips, and legs while he stayed by Hank's head. After issuing a count of three, the men began to lift Hank a few inches off the floor.

Hank felt himself being lifted, wishing more than anything that Roddy and Hughy had been chosen to stand and observe. But realizing that he would be lifted more than once so that each man got a turn at practicing the lift, Hank decided to grin and bear it. He listened with his eyes closed to the soothing sounds of Matthew's instructions as he felt himself being lifted higher and higher. He wouldn't find out until later that he'd actually been three or four feet off the ground when Roddy and Hughy had exchanged a look and then decided to let go of his hips. All he really remembered about that split second was the pressure of the other hands grabbing and pushing his body while Matthew's hands prevented his head from smashing against the concrete.

As he sat up, more confused than anything, he heard Brian's stern voice telling Roddy and Hughy to pack up their stuff and to go home. He would schedule another opportunity for them to get their certification. And until then, he heard Brian state—much more calmly than he would have if their positions were reversed—they wouldn't be getting any calls for work from him. He watched Brian turn away from the two men, neither offering anything but expletives, and move toward him, asking him if he was hurt or if he wanted to go to the hospital to get checked out. Hank waved away the concern and couldn't help but feel tremendous empathy for Brian.

None of the men left were surprised when the rest of the afternoon's lessons passed by without incident or delay. They each passed their final evaluation and had a tiny, wallet-sized recertification card in hand and were out the door shortly after three o'clock.

Hank was home and back in Scott's arms fifteen minutes later. He would have been with his lover sooner, but he'd had this crazy impulse to stop and buy some massage oil—strawberry, Scott's favorite fruit. He didn't know when he'd learned that, but he'd repeated it to himself enough times for just such an occasion when he'd need to remember it.

CHAPTER 27

SCOTT collapsed onto Hank's muscled chest and tried to get his breathing under control. He could still taste the strawberry oil on his tongue, mingled with the taste that was purely Hank. For Scott, the combination was quickly becoming a flavor he was wondering how he'd live without for however long it would take him to uproot his life and move back to Duncan.

He knew that he would need to leave soon. The musical was nearing completion—he had worked most of the day and only had the finale to finish—and then would come the long haul of finding the right actors to play the various roles. If need be, he'd told himself all day while Hank was away learning how to save lives, he'd let the producers and the director deal with all of that. Sure, he had a lot of money invested in this project, but he wasn't about to let it take over his life, especially now that he'd found a life he'd never thought would ever be his.

"Scrappy?"

Scott looked up to see Hank's flushed and handsome face, beads of sweat lingering and pooling in that little dip where his clavicles met under the prominent Adam's apple.

"Yeah… uh…." Scott frowned and then gave a lopsided smile. "How come I don't have a pet name for you yet?" He saw Hank shrug and roll his eyes playfully and then rolled off to lie beside his lover. "How about Bunny?"

Hank let go a belly laugh, his big frame making the bed bounce and Scott's toes vibrate. "Bunny?"

"Yeah." Scott began kissing his way up to Hank's mouth. "You know, Paul... Bunyan... Bunny," he stated matter-of-factly as his lips reached their intended destination. "I like it!"

"Hmm... well, I don't," Hank returned the kiss, increasing its intensity and smiling against Scott's swollen lips. "So," Hank asked as he rolled onto his side to wrap Scott's cooling body in his arms. "Why not 'Ox' then?"

"Because you're not an animal?"

"And what's a bunny?" Hank seemed confused, like he was missing something in the logic. He reached down and pulled up the sheet to rest over top of their bodies, delighted that Scott kept pulling himself closer and closer to his warm body.

"How about Hanky-panky?"

"Or...." Hank kissed Scott's forehead. "How about just Hank?"

"But I want to be able to call you something that's just for me. Something...." Scott brushed his hand down Hank's side and over the front of one thigh, letting it come to rest between Hank's legs, his forearm resting comfortably against the warm flesh of Hank's groin. "Something that I can scream out while you're... you know...."

"While you're....you know?" Scott blushed as Hank chortled and pulled him even closer, his chin resting against the top of his sweat-soaked hair. "This shy man I'm with right now? Is this the same man who just had three fingers up my ass and was deep-throating me?"

"When you're fucking me into the mattress." Scott pulled his hand forward a few inches and cupped Hank's ball sac, smiling inwardly when he felt the muscular thighs spread for him so easily. He looked up into Hank's eyes. "Better?"

"Than anything I've ever known, baby." Hank chuckled and kissed the tip of Scott's nose. "Okay, then, a pet name for me.... Hmm." Scott began to fondle his lover, a sigh issuing forth from Hank almost immediately. "Jesus, Scott, I've never come so many times in my life." Hank rolled onto his back, and Scott worked at bringing him fully erect again. "It's only eight, and already we've each come three times."

"See?"

"See what?" Hank looked over, obviously not getting the trail of his lover's thoughts.

"Three times in four hours," Scott said, as if that would make it all seem so clear. "Another reason for 'Bunny'...." He noticed the wide-eyed stare and added, "The Energizer bunny? It works on so many levels"

"I love you so much, baby." Hank brushed his lips against Scott's, not moving them but just letting them rest there, heat resting against heat. "You just go ahead and call me anything you want, okay?"

"Okay." Scott beamed. "And I love you, too, Bunny."

"Except Bunny."

Scott let out a sound that was a cross between a laugh and a grunt of disappointment and huddled a little closer to Hank's body. "I'll think of something... eventually."

"And I'm sure I'll love it as much as I love you, Scrappy." He pulled him even closer until Scott was almost on top of him again and kept dotting any skin he could reach with kisses. Hank lay there, his eyes closed while his brain raced ahead days, weeks, months into the future. He wanted to know when Scott would be back, would move in with him, would start to see him as a priority for his time and his attention. But in the end, Hank settled for having Scott with him that moment and the next and the next. He didn't want to ruin this by asking too many questions, pushing too hard, or wanting too much too quickly. Hank would do what he'd never been very good at doing: he would trust that Scott meant every word and come back to him as quickly as possible.

"Poochiesnookumface?"

Hank opened his eyes when he heard the whispered word and regarded Scott's hopeful expression. "You can't think of anything shorter?" Hank rolled onto his side to let his bicep snuggle under Scott's head. "I mean, really, I'll be asleep by the time you finish saying it."

"Cuddlemooglie?" Hank shook his head. "Schnookumdumpling?" Another shake of the head. "Doodlesnookums? Smoochiecakes? Moopielips?"

Hank could barely contain his laughter. "Okay," he snorted. "Now I know you're just having me on."

Scott harrumphed and pouted.

"Perhaps you're trying too hard?" Hank brought a hand up from where it was resting on Scott's thigh to stroke and soothe his back. "It'll come to you... when you're ready."

"Tarzan? Prince? Pumpkin? Ace? Stud?"

Hank decided to silence him with a kiss. He let his tongue trace the outline of the full lower lip before seeking entrance slowly and playfully by touching both lips and then retreating. In that kiss, Hank was trying to find the courage to ask for something he wanted from this beautiful, playful, passionate man. He let his hand stroke down Scott's back and swoop slowly around to the front where he took the growing erection in his hand. "Baby?"

"Hmm?" Scott's eyes were closed while his fingers tickled and nipped and pinched at the deliciously sensitive nipples on Hank's perfect pecs.

"I want...." Hank kissed his lips one last time and brought his mouth around to whisper in Scott's ear. "I want to feel you inside me."

Scott pulled away, perhaps a little too quickly. He'd heard all of the words, but in that order, it had taken him a few moments to process them all. "Are you sure, baby?" He saw the immediate nod of Hank's head. Scott had been prepared to wait as long as it would take before Hank would feel comfortable surrendering this last bit of himself to another man. Scott had discovered this the hard way when he'd first moved away from Duncan. He'd been so eager to get rid of everything he saw as the embarrassing mark of virginity that he'd never once considered what it would have meant to keep it to give to someone like Hank. "You want me to be your first?"

"And only."

Scott heard the words spoken so softly and sweetly. He felt the burning behind his eyes as he looked at the flush creeping up Hank's beautiful face. "I love you, Hank." He kissed Hank, cupping his face in his hands, letting him know how much he wanted this.

"How do I...." Hank's hands trembled slightly as he reached out to push down the sheet. "Should I lie on my back, or...."

"I think they say that lying on your stomach is easiest the first time...." Scott pulled the trembling hand up to his lips, pressing them against the flesh. "We'll go very slowly at first, okay?" He smiled when Hank nodded and turned on his stomach. "Remember to breathe, baby." Another nod. Scott laid his hand flat against the small of Hank's back and smoothed it slowly to the broad shoulders, trying to ease any tension or apprehension out of the big body.

Scott remembered his first time and wished he'd been a little more relaxed, that his partner had taken the time to loosen him up completely. He wasn't about to make the same mistake with Hank. Scott wanted this night to be burned into their subconscious, into their flesh. He wanted to be able to close his eyes forty years from now and remember every sound, every sight, every feeling, and every taste.

Scott reminded him to breathe and to relax. He didn't want to spoil this for Hank or for himself. He wanted more than anything for each moment of this night to be something that he would remember every time he looked at his lover. He breathed deeply as he pushed one finger against Hank's entrance. He offered soft words of encouragement and imagined what it would finally feel like to have someone give himself over so completely. He heard a sharp intake of breath as he touched and tapped at Hank's prostate. He studied Hank's face; his lover's eyes were closed, his brow furrowing and relaxing as Scott continued his ministrations. He was quite sure he would be able to come just from the sight of his lover alone.

Scott put two fingers inside of Hank's heat and closed his eyes at the feeling, the anticipation, the overwhelming desire to be even closer to Hank. Hank had been inside of him many times over the past two weeks, and each time had been more incredible than the last, the connection becoming stronger and deeper with each movement, each caress. He left a trail of kisses down Hank's spine, feeling the muscles relax and release with each touch of his lips. He kept murmuring words of love and encouragement as he pulled out two fingers and slowly, deliberately pushed forward with three, moving slowly at first and then stopping. "How does it feel?"

"So incredible," Hank hummed into his forearm. "So... I don't know." Hank lifted his hips and pushed back against Scott's fingers. He had been so certain that he wouldn't enjoy this much, but now all he could think of was having Scott inside of him, of letting go of this final piece of himself.

"Lift up, baby," Scott whispered as he pulled up against Hank's hips. Once he was on all fours, Hank looked over to see Scott reaching for the lube and a condom, his skin on fire and his nerves firing so rapidly that he wondered how Scott could do this two or three times in an evening. "I'm going to push in slowly and stop. You let me know when you feel relaxed enough for me to move."

Hank nodded and let his forehead rest against his forearms and felt Scott's lips against the small of his back. Hank couldn't help but smile at how attentive and tender his lover was being. It was so obvious to him that Scott wanted this to be special. He smelled the familiar scent of strawberry and then hissed in a deep breath when he felt the fingers return to soothe and encourage, stretch and release.

Scott rested on his knees, his fingers pulling out slowly from Hank's heat. He rolled on the condom and returned two fingers to slick some more oil across the tender hole before him. As he bent forward to kiss and lick Hank's hole, Scott reached through the muscular thighs, taking hold of the throbbing erection that was already leaking and leaving a growing wet spot underneath Hank's hips. He pulled gently on the foreskin, feeling it move back so that Scott could brush the tip of one finger over the slit and then into it. When he felt the tight muscle of Hank's sphincter contract against his tongue, he knew that his lover was ready.

Hank heard the words against the small of his back and understood the meaning behind them as the tip of Scott's sheathed erection pushed slowly against his hole. Hank was sure that he'd never felt anything quite so sensual, so personal, or so very welcome in all of his life. He closed his eyes and gave himself over to all of the sensations coursing through his body all at the same time. He listened to Scott's whispered reminders to breathe and to relax, willing his body to allow itself to be breached by something that had not felt this long and thick when it had been in his hand.

Scott pushed gently so that the head of his cock breached the tight ring of muscle, and then with a few words of encouragement, he waited, letting out a breath he hadn't realized that he'd been holding. He shifted his hips slightly from side to side, delighting in and memorizing the sweet gasps and delicious moans that he could feel vibrating all the way down to his dick. His hands smoothed their way to Hank's shoulders, prepared—when Hank wanted it—to latch on and begin the beautifully torturous feeling of pulling out only to push back in. The truth was that he much preferred bottoming, but just the mere idea of being able to bring this kind of pleasure for the first time to a man was so special…. There was no way he could describe what it was doing to him inside.

"Oh Scott." Hank lifted his head a few inches and reached around with one hand. He reached for Scott's right hip, his fingers encountering a different kind of tension in the muscle. It was like elastic, tight and taut but seemingly ready to spring into life at any given moment. "Please, baby, move. Need to feel you move."

"Jesus, Hank," Scott panted as he began pulling his hips back. "So tight, so fucking beautiful, baby." Scott felt the drag against the swollen head of his dick as it moved closer to the tight ring of muscle and had to remind himself to breathe through the exquisite sensation of being squeezed and held from all directions. It was so different than his hand— or anyone's hand. As he began to push forward again, he willed himself to last long enough so that his lover would know the incredible feeling of being joined this way with another person. But mostly, he wanted to ensure that Hank would also find release, that Hank would feel the powerful orgasm that came from being penetrated and massaged. He wanted every nerve ending in Hank's body to be on fire with lust and passion and love, just as his were every time he held Hank inside him.

The noises they made filled the room, each man calling out the name of the other as their bodies came together again and again. Scott's hands and arms reached out to touch skin wherever he could find it. His hands brushed and stroked, petted and patted Hank's thighs and ass cheeks until finally he let his body slump onto the muscled lats. He reached around and took a firm grasp of Hank's engorged cock, astounded at how hard and rigid yet silky smooth it was. He began placing lazy, wet kisses across Hank's back and neck, luxuriating in the feel of Hank's callused hands running their way up and down his thighs.

Hank gripped Scott's hip, his fingers too excited, too weakened by the pleasure he was experiencing to feel anything but the movements of a hip thrusting, creating a feeling of being filled by someone Hank loved, a feeling of being massaged from the inside out. Hank listened to Scott's breath, felt it across his back. He could feel his body responding to the insistent yet tender thrusts, could feel his balls draw up tight against his body, could feel the fire burning out of control all along his belly. But when he felt the draw and pull of those long, slender fingers against his painfully engorged cock, felt the swipe of a finger across the slit of his uncut dick, Hank cried out, his head falling back to rest against his forearms. The change of the angle allowed Scott to tap against his prostate, and Hank pushed back against his lover one final time.

Scott eased his way forward, sensing that Hank was close to finishing. He flicked his finger across the slit of Hank's awe-inspiring uncut prick and then began to feel the most intense pressure around his own dick. Hank, Scott realized suddenly, was coming. Scott threw his head back at the sudden rush of emotion. He had been responsible for taking Hank—for the first time—and had provided such pleasure that his big, beautiful logger was coming on his cock.

"Oh baby, baby, Hank," Scott grunted as he felt the hot liquid stream over his fist. "So tight, so sexy, so amazing." Scott stilled inside of Hank while the big man rode out his own pleasure.

"Jesus, fuck me, Scotty," Hank panted against the hot, sweating skin of his forearm. "I've never felt… I can't even begin to…." Hank felt Scott pull out slowly, the loss hitting him almost immediately. "What's…?"

"Flip over, baby," Scott whispered, his voice hoarse but patient. "I want to be able to kiss you when I finally come."

"Oh fuck yeah." Hank rolled onto his back and gripped the backs of his knees, pulling them up against his substantial chest. "Can't wait for you to fuck me like that the whole time. Your tongue and your dick fucking each end of me."

"Oh shit," Scott agreed, as he positioned himself once again at Hank's hole. Unable to restrain himself, Scott pushed inside and began to snap his hips. He braced his shoulders against the backs of the muscular calves and thrust a second time. He leaned forward to accept Hank's offer of a searing kiss. "So much… too much… so tight…." Scott could hear himself babbling but couldn't stop himself. His eyes made contact with Hank's, both of them finding an incalculable amount of lust and passion and love and tenderness.

"Come in me, baby," Hank muttered, his eyes closing slowly. "Make me yours."

"Mine," Scott grunted in time to his thrusts. "Love… love… love you so much, baby." Scott felt the pressure surround him, envelop him. He leaned toward Hank's lips one more time, stealing first one, then two, then three wet kisses. The words soothed his overworked nerves, soothed the burning desire to claim this gorgeous man as Hank caressed the back of his head and pulled his head beside his own. "Gonna come… can feel it, Hank." Scott snapped his hips, unable to control himself, and felt his balls slap against Hank's ass. He drove himself forward repeatedly, driving himself higher at the same time.

"Come for me, Scrappy," Hank whispered beside his ear. With a final tremor of his arms, Scott's hips thrust forward, losing any sense of rhythm, his seed filling the condom while Hank's arms wrapped around him, and Hank said, "Yes, yes, love you, love you so much."

He let himself be enveloped in Hank's embrace. The only thought that was in his mind was that they now belonged to each other. Scott let himself memorize the smell of strawberry, the feel of Hank's chest hair against his skin, the taste of Hank's kisses on his tongue, and the sound of the most perfect man reassuring him that he was loved.

CHAPTER 28

SCOTT and Hank had just sat down to enjoy the breakfast that Scott had made while Hank was finishing with his shower when the phone rang. Scott chanced a look at Hank, hoping that he would ignore it and let the machine pickup. He offered a smile and a shrug when Hank mouthed the word *sorry* and stood up from the table to walk the ten feet to the phone in the den. He could only hear Hank's end of the conversation, but he'd heard enough to know that it was Brian calling. It was nearing seven that morning, and Scott couldn't help but wonder what his brother could be calling about. Hank wasn't scheduled to supervise any jobs for another two days. As he heard Hank confirm that he would be "there" the following day, Scott consoled himself with the idea of finally finishing the finale for the musical.

"Anything serious?" Scott asked casually when Hank took his seat at the table again. He was hoping that it wouldn't be anything that he didn't want to hear—like that Hank would be leaving Scott alone for most of the day, or worse, that Hank had just agreed to several days away on another remote site on the island.

"Nah," Hank said as he shook his head and picked up his knife, more than hungry enough to eat the plate full of pancakes, sausage and toast. "Roddy and Hughy still haven't been certified in first aid yet, and Brian had planned on Roddy being at the next job as climbing supervisor."

"Meaning," Scott sighed, stretching the word to three times its normal duration, "that he wants you to go out and take his place."

"I'm sorry, baby," Hank offered as he reached out to clasp their hands together. "But I did make him a promise."

"How long?"

"It's a three-day run on the coast just north of Tofino." Hank gave the long, slender fingers a little reassuring squeeze. "You don't need to worry about me." Hank let go of Scott's hand and dug in to his breakfast. Around a mouthful of syrup-coated pancakes, Hank smiled. "I can be scrappy too, you know."

"I know." Scott pushed his plate a little further away and tried to smile. "It's not that." He rolled his eyes when he saw Hank's eyebrow shoot up and corrected himself. "Okay, okay," he sighed at last. "But I… it's just…."

Hank swallowed and took back Scott's hand. "Will you eat if I tell you that it's just a routine job and that I'll come back unharmed?"

"I know." Scott chuckled at the earnest look of reassurance that lit up Hank's face. "I know I sound like some worried old—"

"What you sound like," Hank whispered as he brought the hand to his mouth and kissed it gently, "is someone who loves me." "Promise me, Hank." Scott let his hand slide along the warm flesh of Hank's cheek, combing it through the still-damp chestnut hair. "Promise that you'll be careful."

"I promise, baby," he whispered, turning his head to kiss the cool palm of his lover's hand. Hank pulled gently on Scott's hand until the lithe body was sitting on his lap, neither of them seeming very hungry for anything other than skin-to-skin contact. He looked up, stilling his hands that had, just a moment ago, been caressing and soothing his lover's back. "I love you, Scott."

He saw the look in Hank's eyes, suddenly feeling as if those green eyes were promising him everything, anything Scott wanted. He closed his eyes against the burning sensation and leaned forward to press their foreheads together, the flutter of Hank's long, dark lashes against his cheeks making his chest a little tighter. "I love you, too."

"So," Hank whispered hoarsely, "do you love me enough to let me eat breakfast… finally?"

Scott swatted at Hank when he heard the little snort of laughter that escaped his lover's warm lips and stood to sit down in the seat he'd been pulled from just minutes before. "I'm sorry, baby, but… I mean, I don't mean to worry about all of this, but…." Scott picked up his fork and moved the food around on his plate, his eyes darting to Hank's almost-empty plate and his own untouched one. "I've spent my entire life wondering when I'd get a phone call telling me that Brian was... like a few weeks ago...." He heard the hitch in his voice, felt the invisible band around his heart tighten just a little more. He remembered all too well the sound of Kari's voice telling him that the only family he had left had been in an accident, that he was in the hospital.

"Shhh, baby." Hank stood and pulled Scott into his arms, rocking him slowly. "I'm not going to lie to you and tell you accidents don't happen, but we do everything we can, the good climbers, the careful climbers that is, to be sure that we'll come home to the people that love us."

"I know," Scott pressed his face against the warmth and protection that Hank's chest offered to him. He snorted a humorless laugh. "It's funny, you know. The one thing I always figured would never happen to me was what my mother had to live through...." He pulled himself closer to the security and the warmth of Hank's large, muscled frame and sighed heavily. "All those times when the weather would turn and she'd sit at the kitchen table telling me everything would be fine." Scott pulled away from Hank and brought his hands up to the handsome face. "I never understood what she was going through... until now."

"Why...?" Hank looked down, his face a study of confusion. "Why did you think you'd never have to worry about that?"

"I figured logging would be the last place I'd find a gay man." Scott shrugged and let go of a one-note laugh. "Let alone one that would fall in love with me and want to be with me."

"Who said," Hank teased as he let his hands fall to cup Scott's ass, "that I was gay?"

"Very funny." Scott slapped at the firm pecs and tried to pull away. He was held firm by the gentle, but firm pressure of those muscled arms.

"No," Hank continued to tease. "Seriously, this doesn't mean I'm gay, does it?" Hank could only school his amusement for a few seconds before letting Scott know that he'd only been teasing. "Listen," Hank said as he walked them back to the sectional. "Gay, straight, bi, whatever—I'll be whatever will make you forget all of this worrying and be my little Scrappy again, with the beautiful smile and the laugh that makes me feel like I'm listening to a symphony and the touch that makes me think I just want to crawl inside you and never come out."

Scott felt his calves hit the soft, velvety fabric of the sectional, and then he was on his back with Hank supporting his huge, hard body with just his arms. He felt Hank lower his own pelvis so that the two of them were lined up perfectly. He reached his hands under Hank's T-shirt, his eyes closing as Hank's hair fell forward to tickle his nose and forehead, his hands skimming across warm flesh covering granite-like muscles. When he felt Hank's legs work themselves in between his own, he let Hank take over.

Hank kneeled on the cushion of the sectional, Scott displayed before him, underneath him. He pulled himself to his knees and quickly removed his T-shirt, his hands reaching to undo the button of his cargo shorts. He stood momentarily so that the shorts fell away from his slim hips. He brought a hand to his hair, his fingers raking the chestnut waves up and away from his face. His eyes alighted on the toned body splayed out before him; his hand trailed down his own belly until it glanced over the heated surface of his growing erection.

Scott looked up, a finger finding its way between his lips as he watched Hank's shorts fall away, his eyes mesmerized—as always—by the sight of Hank's towering, chiseled physique. "God, you're breathtaking," he murmured as he watched Hank take his own erection in hand and pull back the foreskin. Scott moved to sit up, to get closer to the swollen purple head, but Hank was there in an instant, his thighs on either side of Scott's torso, offering himself to Scott's eager lips and mouth.

Hank threw his head back when he felt the heat of Scott's mouth engulf his swollen head, the hot, rough texture of that talented tongue working its way under the sensitive foreskin. He remembered how, a few nights ago, he'd discovered how his lover was fond of biting and pinching his foreskin as a way to help him become more excited, or a way of helping him to come down after orgasm, but Hank wished more than anything at that moment that he'd had even more foreskin so that even he was fully erect, there would be more for Scott to pinch, to bite, to pull on and drive him crazy with the two sensations at once. He growled softly, the sound seeming to come from somewhere deeper than his gut, when he felt Scott's hands on his ass, pulling Hank forward until he landed on the sectional, his hands planted above his lover's head. He felt one hand come to the side of his dick and ball sac, the thumb pressing into the sensitive flesh behind while the other rested on one ass cheek, two of the fingers pushing against his hole. He looked down and beheld a sight that would forever be etched in his psyche.

Scott felt himself straining against the thin, worn fabric of his boxers. He was still fully dressed in a pair of Hank's sweats that he had to keep pulling up and one of his T-shirts. He would have been hard-pressed to explain why, but the knowledge of Hank being completely naked while Scott was still clothed stirred something deep inside of him. He and Hank had made love and had spent marathon sessions using mouths, hands, and asses to bring each other to orgasm over and over again. But this, Scott realized, was different. It wasn't claiming. It wasn't sex. It wasn't even making love. This was something much deeper, primal. He wanted Hank to fuck his mouth, to claim every inch of him, take every part of him and make him remember every moment.

Hank gripped the cushions in his powerful hands and looked down one last time, the feeling of Scott's fingers inside him, the feel of his rock-hard dick touching the back of that moist heat, the sounds of Scott's moaning causing his cock to vibrate and sending him somewhere he'd never been before. Even with all the times they'd made love, Hank had never experienced anything as powerful or as consuming as what he was living at that moment. The thought and the feel of Scott pulling him deeper into that beautiful mouth made his balls pull up and tighten.

He called out Scott's name over and over until his vision blurred and he felt the explosion behind his eyes rush down his spine and radiate out to the tips of his clenched and sore fingers. His arms began to shake as he felt the base of his dick being held firm in those long fingers and experienced the sensation of Scott licking and sucking every last drop from his spent dick. He opened his eyes and saw that Scott had not been able to swallow it all, saw the traces of his spunk on his lover's cheeks and chin. He eased himself from his prone position over that beautiful face and settled himself between Scott's thighs, his hands threading through the blond hair at the back of his head as his mouth descended to kiss his own seed from Scott's flushed cheeks and chin.

"Yours, Scott," Hank whispered softly as his eyes settled on Scott's heavy-lidded gaze. "All yours, forever. Anything you want, baby."

Scott looked into those green eyes and recognized happiness staring back at him. It made his heart lurch in his chest, his toes curl, his fingers grasp at the strong muscles beneath warm flesh, and his voice stop in his throat. He closed his eyes and nodded just once and then heard the fabric of the borrowed boxers rip. He opened his eyes just as the strong hands tossed the shredded boxers to one side and gripped him behind his knees. He listened as his lover told him what he would do to him, for him, and then the words were replaced by the sweet sound of Hank's mouth kissing his inner thighs, Hank's tongue licking and probing until it found its way to his entrance, the muscles pinching and jumping at the warmth of the breath that seemed to promise bliss.

Scott threw his arms over his head. His fingers grappled with the cushions, struggling for purchase, but he was unable to do anything except scratch and claw along the velvety surface. He heard his own voice calling Hank's name as all of his blood seemed to pool in his painfully erect cock, the only nerve endings seeming capable of normal functioning being those below his waist.

Hank had wanted to do this since he'd felt the sensations of Scott's tongue on his hole, in him. He could recall how the rough texture pulling and lapping against the thin flesh of his entrance had made him see stars, had made him feel reduced to that single, tiny area of feeling. He could still taste himself on his own tongue, could still see the images of that beautiful mouth sucking and laving and pulling on his engorged dick. His brain seemed to be fixed on an unending loop of sights and sounds and sensations that he'd experienced with this man under him. He could taste the strawberry oil, feel the movement of his lover's cock in his ass caressing his prostate, and hear his own hoarse, raspy pleas for Scott to move. Hank was sure that even if he lived forever, he would never find anyone who would make him feel and see and hear what it truly meant to be connected to another human being. He was Scott's forever, and he would do whatever it took to make sure that he would never lose his Scrappy.

Scott's moans of pleasure gave way to feral grunts of ecstasy as he writhed, trying unsuccessfully to touch any available part of Hank's body. His thighs were spread apart, his cock and balls and hole were wet with saliva, and he could feel each of them in turn being licked and heated by his lover's hungry mouth. It was an exquisite pain. He wanted it to go on forever. He could feel the heat rising from somewhere at the base of his spine, could feel the delicious lick of fire at his balls and could still hear and feel the words of love and sex that emanated from his lover's mouth.

Scott lifted his head and blinked. Hank's hands were no longer holding his thighs. *But then why can't I move my legs?* The thought was quickly replaced by the feel of Hank's thumbs entering his hole, one on either side, coaxing him apart, opening him up. He listened as Hank spat, felt the warm saliva hit its target, and cried out when the thumbs sank in even further. When he thought he could take no more, one thumb pulled out and was immediately replaced with a finger, Hank's aim dead-on as he massaged the prostate.

Hank looked up and saw the sweat gleaming across Scott's forehead, a moment of regret flashing through him that he'd not taken the time to remove the T-shirt, and then returned his mouth to engulf his lover's swollen dick, taking it to the back of his throat while the callused pad of his finger pegged Scott's gland over and over. He felt Scott's body go tense, could feel the beautiful, silky dick in his mouth grow even harder, and pulled his finger away from the gland, teasing it with only a few more touches. He pulled Scott further into his mouth and nestled his nose in the soft, silky hairs at the base. When he brought a hand under the ball sac, gently lifting the sensitive testicles to rest under his chin, he heard Scott cry out his release.

The first jets hit the back of Hank's throat, and he swallowed them hungrily, massaging Scott's balls and prostate. He tried to imagine anything hotter than the feel of his finger clenched in his lover's tight, spasming ring of muscle or the feel of Scott's seed hitting the back of his throat or the way the sensitive balls tried to pull away from his touch, but he couldn't. In fact, the only coherent thought he had for moments afterward, even as Scott pulled on his arms so that they could lie together sharing languid but sloppy kisses, was that he needed to figure out how to ask Scott to live with him right away. *I'm just being selfish,* Hank thought as he brushed wet strands of blond hair away from his lover's face.

"When you do move back…live with me?"

Scott looked over at him and released an exhausted chuckle. "Oh thank God," Scott sighed. "I thought I was going to have to ask you."

Hank's exhausted arms pulled his lover closer. As he planted a gentle kiss on Scott's forehead, a smile ghosted across his lips. "My Scrappy," Hank muttered and stopped trying to keep his eyes from closing.

CHAPTER 29

HANK stood for a moment at the tailgate of his truck. He was trying to think of something snappy to say so that his Scrappy wouldn't worry himself into an early grave over the next three days. Coming up with nothing better than *I love you*, he slammed the tailgate shut on his equipment, took the stairs two at a time, and opened the door, finding Scott just where he'd left him only moments before. "Do I get a hug and a kiss?" Hank's smile was broad, happy, teasing.

Scott quit scuffing the hardwood floor of the foyer with his slipper and advanced toward Hank, the pout on his lips obviously not working. He leaned against Hank's chest and brought his hands up to encircle his waist. "You promised me. Don't forget."

"I remember." Hank laughed, slapping and then cupping his lover's ass. "If you get bored," he offered after kissing the petulant pout off of Scott's lips, "you can always start planning how we're going to fit all of our stuff in this townhouse."

"Already done that." Scott huffed into the soft cotton of Hank's T-shirt. "While I was doing that." Scott pointed out two double-lined grocery bags filled with sandwiches and Tupperware containers. "Remembered my mom always making meals for my dad to take with him."

Hank looked down at the bags and pulled Scott even closer. "Always wondered what that would feel like," Hank said after kissing the top of his lover's head.

"What?" Scott asked, his breath warm and welcome against Hank's T-shirt.

"Showing up to work with a bunch of food that someone had made just for me. I'd see the other guys show up with it, and... well." Hank closed his eyes, willing the heat to abate. "Always wondered what it would feel like to have the other guys know that someone thought enough of me to make my meals for me."

"Oh Hank." Scott sighed as he pulled away from the warmth of his lover's embrace. "I'll make your meals for you anytime." He leaned up for a kiss.

"Now," Hank announced suddenly. "What about this planning?" What did you come up with?"

Scott pulled himself against the hard body once more and growled playfully. "Your stuff is going on eBay."

"Okay." Hank chuckled and kissed his lover's forehead. "But not the couch. I have good memories of that couch."

"Me too." Scott smiled sweetly and squeezed the muscled ass in his hands.

"Yeah." Hank winked. "I can't remember her name, but—" He brought his forearms up to protect himself as he fought off the punches and tried to find a way to get Scott back in his embrace. "I'm just kidding, baby," Hank teased and felt the lithe body fall back against him. "Of course I remember her name." This time, he pinned Scott's arms to his side and put his warm lips against the tender flesh of his lover's neck, sucking, licking, and kissing until he felt the shorter man still. "Please don't worry about me, Scott." Hank's voice was soft but strong. "I'll never do anything that will keep us apart."

Hank saw his lover melt a little. He freed his arms and wrapped them around Hank's trim waist again, hoping that if he just held on tight enough, Hank wouldn't want to leave him. "Better not," he pouted.

"Okay, now." Hank relaxed his grip around the tall, slim body. "Give me one to go on... one that will last until I get back...." Hank brushed his lips against Scott's, tenderly at first; he pulled back slightly. "The one that will make me forget what's-her-name."

Scott pulled the T-shirt out from the back of Hank's cargo shorts and plunged his hands to rest in the warm, fuzzy crease of his muscled ass. He leaned up as Hank leaned down, and their tongues met, dueling first in his mouth and then in Hank's. Hands caressed naked skin, fingers probed the sensitive spots that each had memorized over the past two weeks, and the joking of moments ago was completely forgotten as each man tried to burn this moment into his gray matter. Scott brought his hands around to the front to rest against the waistband of Hank's cargo shorts. His fingers registered no boxer shorts—no underwear of any kind—and popped the button. He smiled against the soft skin of his lover's lips when he took hold of Hank's growing erection.

"Scott." His lover's name was but a puff of air against his lips, the feel of Scott's finger brushing over his slit once, then twice. Hank watched Scott fall to his knees, and at the same moment he pulled Hank's shorts down; he was speechless as he watched his uncut dick being swallowed by that beautiful mouth. He felt Scott's nose push against the coarse hairs and felt the engorged head of his prick hit the back of Scott's throat. Hank's gaze was fixed on him, his lips slightly parted and his tongue darting out to moisten them when Scott took him all the way to the back of his throat.

He brought a hand up to cradle Hank's heavy balls and squeezed gently at first, and then when the muscled thighs parted, he massaged them gently. He smiled and pulled back to lave at the head, and darting his tongue into the slit, he pulled back the foreskin all the way with his free hand to let his teeth trail along the enormous mushroom head, smiling again—or still—when Hank cried out a warning.

Relaxing his throat muscles one last time, Scott took his lover all the way in and moaned as he felt the balls in his hand pull up. He felt Hank's body lower and freed his hands to stroke up and down the tensed inner thigh muscles, his fingers nudging against the balls playfully on the upstroke. Scott groaned again, loudly this time, as Hank began to pant his release, the warm, musky scent of Hank's seed filling his senses. Scott swallowed every last drop that Hank shot into his mouth and brought a hand up to caress the tensed belly, bringing his lover down slowly. He felt Hank's hands on his head, his big body jerking slightly with aftershocks as Scott used his tongue to clean up, licking around the head. He released the foreskin and kissed the slit, lifting himself up slowly by pulling on Hank's wrists.

"Better than what's-her-name?" Scott's eyes twinkled as he caressed Hank's chest.

"Huh?"

"Good answer." Scott smiled and bent over to pull up Hank's shorts, fastening them as deftly as he'd unfastened them. He pushed his arms up to bookend Hank's flushed face. "I love you, Henry Isaac Ballam. And I'll be right here waiting for you."

Hank's arms encircled the slight waist and he let his reeling head rest on Scott's shoulder. "I meant what I said, Scrappy." Hank pulled back to kiss his lover, tasting himself on Scott's lips and tongue. "Everything... anything... all yours."

As they stared into each other's eyes, Scott knew that there were no words that would keep him from worrying. And Hank knew no words that could state any more clearly that in Scott's arms was the only place he'd ever want to be. Hank was the first to pull back, hating the look of loss that crossed Scott's beautiful features and wanting to stay there with his arms around his lover forever. The ringing of the phone took Scott's eyes away from Hank's briefly. "I bet that's Brian wondering where the hell you are." Scott tried to joke.

"I love you." Hank adjusted himself and offered a wink. "Better than all the what's-her-names combined."

"Smooth-talking bastard," Scott chuckled, trying hard to keep the pout on his lips.

Hank stole one last kiss and headed out to the truck, hoping that Scott wouldn't follow him.

Scott answered the phone, growling, "Yeah, yeah, he's on his way."

"And good morning to you, Scooter," Brian laughed.

"If anything happens to him—"

"Nothing," Brian harrumphed, sounding as annoyed as if he were sixteen again and having to deal with a ten-year-old little brother who couldn't sit still, "is going to happen to him. He's my best climber, for Chrissakes."

"Okay." Scott knew he was being incredibly infantile, but he didn't seem to be able to stop himself. He felt deprived of the three days that they'd planned on spending together, only to have his own brother steal Hank away because Roddy and Hughy were being more dickheaded than usual. "I'd better not hear of anything else happening to you, either!"

"Nice to see you remembered I'll be out there, too," Brian laughed. After a few moments of silence, he said, "I'll take care of him for you, Scooter." The tone of Brian's voice sent Scott immediately back to the days following their mother's funeral. Brian had been so strong and brave then. Scott could still remember the nights he couldn't sleep, waking up and padding out to the kitchen for some water. He would see Brian sitting alone on the sofa, his hands quickly swiping at the tears he'd not wanted his little brother to know he'd shed. "I promise, baby brother."

"I know," Scott sighed, feeling guilty now as well as ridiculously morose. "I'm sorry, Bri. I'm kind of fond of both of you, but, you know, for different reasons."

"Look on the bright side," Brian said, his voice seeming happier. "You'll get to find out what satellite phone sex is like."

"Ewww." Scott laughed despite himself. "You're a pig!" Of course, he would never admit that he found himself wondering if it were any different than landline phone sex or cell phone sex.

"Bye, Scooter," Brian offered, his voice full of reassurance and warmth.

"Bye, big brother. Be safe."

Scott hung up the phone and took the stairs quickly, headed for the bedroom, and threw himself on the cool sheets. He closed his eyes and inhaled deeply. He could smell Hank and strawberry and musk and sweat. He hugged a pillow to his chest, feeling sorry for himself, and thought of strong arms, muscled thighs, soft skin over rock-hard pecs, and the feeling of Hank inside him, beside him, on him, under him. Before drifting off to sleep, he thought about doing something about his sudden erection.

HANK looked across to his passenger, wondering if the silence was because of what he'd just said or because Brian was in shock. "You're not okay with this, are you?" Hank asked and continued to ramble, not really wanting to know Brian's true feelings. "I know you said that you were, but if you're not... I mean, if you're still thinking that I'm a fuck-up and that I'll do something to hurt Scrappy, uh, I mean Scott, then you need to tell me right now so that we—"

"Hank." Brian laughed as he reached out a hand to pat the big shoulder. "Relax, man, before you blow a gasket." Brian pulled his hand back and shifted in his seat to regard Hank seriously. "I think it's great that you two found each other. I mean, of all the men I've worked with over the years, I never would have guessed you for a... you know, but I guess it just goes to show that opposites attract, yeah?"

Hank let go of his nervousness with a snort and felt himself relax. "Really? You're okay with Scott living with me, of us living together?"

"You love him?"

"More than I ever imagined I could."

"You'll take care of him? Protect him?"

"'Till I'm dead and buried."

"Make him happy?"

"Every minute of every day."

"Well, then." Brian sighed, turning to look out his window and then back at Hank. "I guess I got no cause to worry, right?"

"No, you don't." Hank smiled and loosened his death grip on the steering wheel. "And for what it's worth, no one's ever made me feel so...."

"I know." Brian nodded. He didn't need for Hank to finish what he already knew. "Scooter's a pretty amazing person. Gives himself to everything and everyone, one hundred and ten percent all the way."

"I never met anyone who thought I was worth something, you know?"

"Listen, Hank," Brian started, "if I ever said anything that made you feel like—"

"It's okay, Brian," Hank soothed. "I know I've made some bad calls in the past, but I made you a promise, and I'm going to keep it." Hank took his right hand off the steering wheel and let it rest between them. "Friends?"

"Friends?" Brian barked and clasped Hank's hand in his. "Looks like we'll be related soon enough." Hank laughed and put his hand back on the wheel, looking back when he heard his boss take a deep breath. "Of course, if you do anything to hurt him... I'll have to kill you, you know."

Hank turned just in time to see Brian's playful wink. "Good to know."

CHAPTER 30

HANK rolled over when he heard the banging, his hand reaching out instinctively to pull the little, toned body to him. It took him a few blinking moments to realize that he was not with Scott. He was alone in one of the small, sterile rooms on some oversized houseboat hundreds of kilometers away from the man he loved. It wasn't that thought that made him close his eyes but the realization that he'd forgotten to bring anything with him that might remind him of his man's scent. His Scrappy. And as he listened to his boss shouting that they all had thirty minutes to eat, gear up, and meet out on the heli-pad, he realized that he wouldn't have time to call him either. *What a crappy way to start the day! No kiss, no sex, no nothing!*

"Hey, sunshine," Chris, the greenhorn, chirped and pushed an empty bowl toward him as he sat down and held his mug out for coffee. "Sleep well?"

"Just dandy," Hank grunted, rubbing his eyes with his free hand while he smelled the coffee, felt it weighing down his mug. "And you?"

"Well," Chris huffed, "I didn't have anyone to make two big bags full of meals for me, but...." The greenhorn didn't finish his sentence, but the smile on his face told Hank his mood needed improving.

"Not a morning person," Hank grunted as he sipped his coffee.

"I simply *won't* believe that." Chris said, his face a study in shock and surprise.

"Shut it," Hank warned as he fought the twitch at the corner of his lips.

"Seriously," Chris said, closing the cereal box and holding up the carafe to ask if Hank needed a refill yet. "I'm glad I'm working with you on this job."

"Me too, kid," Hank said as he shook his head, declining the refill.

"So." Chris winked and grinned. "What's her name?"

"Scott," Hank announced loudly and waited, studying the greenhorn's face for some sort of reaction.

"Sss—" Chris hissed, his face registering more confusion than shock. "A guy?" Hank nodded. "Well," Chris said after he realized Hank wasn't having one over on him. "Congratulations." He patted Hank's shoulder as he stowed the milk back in the fridge and stood at the door to the little kitchen. "Anybody else know, or is this something I should keep to myself?"

"Brian knows." Hank nodded as he stood and downed the dregs of his coffee.

"And?"

"Scott's his brother." Hank offered a lopsided smile as he patted the greenhorn's shoulder and passed by him to make his way to the landing pad at the other end of the building.

"Oh," Chris grunted through pursed lips. "In that case... good luck!" He stifled the laugh when Hank raised his hand in a wave and followed his coworker to the little chopper that would drop them at the work site.

HANK couldn't help but notice by the second day that Chris was turning into a mighty good climber. He was fast, unafraid of heights—or at least less afraid than he'd been last week—and was keeping up with Hank for the most part. "Yeah," Hank had said to Brian during their shared lunch together with a wink to the blushing greenhorn. "Give him another few years, and he'll be besting any of my times!" And Hank had meant it, too.

"And what about you?" Brian turned to Hank after he saw that Chris was far enough away. "Where do you want to be in another few years?"

"Right here," Hank stated as he nodded to the trees and the forest that surrounded them. "That is, if I can get your stubborn brother to agree."

Brian let out a little puff of air that Hank interpreted as laughter. "He is something, isn't he?" Hank nodded and wondered where this particular conversation could lead. "You have to understand, Hank, that Scooter is so much like our mother." Brian's voice was soft, Hank noted, when he was talking about his family. "He moved away to get away from all of this. He saw what it took out of our mom to be waiting up at night… to be away from our dad for days at a time… to be—"

Hank screwed the cap back on his thermos and looked back, squinting, at Brian. "So that's what the promotion was all about… keep me out of the trees so Scott stays happy?" He shook his head and looked away. "He made you make that offer, didn't he?"

"Hank," Brian chastised as he tilted his head, his eyebrows lifting in surprise. "You know better than that. Nobody tells me how to run my business, not even Scott." He rubbed his hand over his face, trying to stave off the frustration and possibility of Hank's temper. "You want to climb, I'll keep calling you for jobs. I was trying to show you… I offered you that promotion so that you'd see there were no hard feelings." Brian clasped his hands together and leaned a little farther forward. "Scott told me what Roddy and Hughy were saying while I was lying in that hospital bed, and I wanted you to know that I don't blame you either." Brian shook his head and let it hang for a moment before looking back up. "I need someone like you, with your experience—someone who knows how the business ought to work—to keep an eye on the climbers, keep the jobs on time, keep the money coming in." Brian stood, ready to leave before things turned ugly.

"Brian?" Hank stood as well and offered his hand. "I'm sorry." Hank smiled weakly when Brian took his hand and gave it a few hard pumps. "I guess I'm not completely changed yet, huh, jumping to conclusions, thinking those things about Scrappy—uh, I mean Scott."

Brian couldn't control his laughter. "Scrappy?"

Hank felt the heat slither up his neck and face. He shrugged, his eyes suddenly finding the label of the thermos very interesting. "Scott told me one day that he may not be as big as you or me, but that he could be scrappy." Brian threw his head back and laughed, the sound reverberating all the way to the tree tops. "What?" Hank felt like he was missing part of the story.

"Scrappy, huh?" Brian shook his head and reached out to slap Hank's shoulder. "I'll let him tell you his other pet name... other than Scooter," he chuckled, shaking his head again and calling over his shoulder as he walked back to his section of trees. "Scrappy... that's a good one."

By the time Hank got his turn on the satellite phone, the drizzle that had called a halt to their productive day had turned into a torrential downpour and was beating down on the corrugated metal roof so hard that Hank wasn't even sure he'd be able to make himself heard. "Hey, baby, it's your bunny," Hank called as he reached over to the office door and pushed it closed.

"Hank?" Scott's laughter felt like music to his tired ears. "I thought 'bunny' was off the table."

"It is." Hank laughed along with his lover. "I just wanted to make you laugh."

"Mission accomplished," Scott chuckled. "So, how's the job going?"

"What?" Hank growled, "no 'I miss you'? 'I wish you were here beside me'? 'I've already sold the couch'?" Hank closed his eyes when he heard more peals of laughter, letting it wash down his spine. The humming and whirring of the chainsaws were but a distant memory at that moment.

"I miss you," Scott soothed when he'd stopped laughing, when he'd realized that Hank needed him just as much. "I wish you were here beside me, *inside* me... and... that couch has very fond memories for me now too."

"Speaking of," Hank deadpanned. "I finally remembered her name."

"Asshole," Scott barked, trying not to laugh.

"That my new pet name?"

"Maybe," he said petulantly.

"Speaking of," Hank repeated, "your brother told me I was supposed to ask you your other pet name, the one besides *Scooter*." Hank waited, not hearing anything, and a silent dread filled him that the connection had been lost. "Hello? Scrappy?"

"I'm here," Scott said, his voice suddenly sedate.

"Thought I lost you there." Hank sighed in relief. "So, what is it?"

"I don't know what he's talking about."

Hank tried not to laugh while the only thought that was going through his mind was, *This has got to be a whopper then, if he doesn't want to tell me.* "Really? 'Cause he sounded real certain about another pet name."

"He is mistaken," Scott announced in a clear, crisp voice.

"Okay," Hank relented and held the phone a few inches away from his face. "Hey, Brian?" he called out to the empty office. "Scott says he doesn't know what you're talking about—" He pulled the satellite phone close to his ear again when he heard Scott barking at him.

"All right, okay, you win," Scott conceded, accepting defeat a little less gracefully than Hank would have imagined. "It was 'Tsmtowel'."

Hank laughed as he could just see Scott swipe his hand over his mouth. "I'm sorry, baby, I didn't catch that last word."

"I said, 'It was….' Oh hang on, my cell phone is r—"

"Scott," Hank warned.

"Tasmanian devil," Scott barked. "Tasmanian devil, okay, are you happy now?"

"How… you mean, as in…?" Hank sputtered through his laughter. All he could see was the little cartoon from Bugs Bunny reruns tearing up the scenery and chewing his way through boulders.

"Yes," Scott sighed. "As in."

"Ho-ho-holy," Hank's eyes were filling with tears as he imagined his little Scrappy tearing around the playground, completely wigging out on people that got in his way. "If it's any consolation, he was always my favorite cartoon." Hank closed his eyes and bit his tongue against the laughter that threatened.

"It was a very long time ago," Scott stated, and Hank could just see his pink cheeks and his clenched fists. "I didn't like being teased or picked on when I was at school, so…."

"You spun yourself into a frenzy and scared the crap out of everybody who got near you?"

"I have to go,"

"Wait!" Hank called out, his laughter suddenly dwindling to a whimper. "Baby, wait, please, I'm sorry, okay?" Hank took a deep breath and let it out slowly. "Please, baby, I'm sorry."

"I know you were just kidding," Scott said. "But I do miss you. I wish you were here with me."

"I miss you, too, baby." Hank didn't really feel like laughing anymore. He knew that sat-time was expensive and that he needed to end the call, but he couldn't make his fingers let go of the phone. "I'm keeping my promise, being safe. I'll be home in fewer than two days, baby."

"I love you, Henry Isaac Ballam."

"And I love you," Hank soothed. "Even if they'd called you Foghorn Leghorn. I say, now, I say I would," Hank barked in a moderately good imitation and closed his eyes when he heard his Scrappy laughing again.

HE REPLAYED that phone call in his head—well, certain sections of it— over and over as he worked the next day to catch them up on their quota for the job. The rain had stopped sometime during the night but had left the moss, ground, and leaves dripping with moisture. Brian had even anticipated a slow day due to fog, but by noon, Hank had made sure that they were only a dozen trees behind and had seen nothing but clear skies. It was their third and final day out here, and nothing was going to keep him from getting home.

It wasn't until he'd sat down alone for lunch that he realized that Brian and Chris were nowhere to be found. He poured himself a thermos-cap full of coffee, munched on his chicken salad sandwich, and then, when they still hadn't shown up, pulled on his walkie-talkie and announced he was entering their section. He waited for a callback that would tell him it wasn't safe, that there were falling tops coming down, but when there was no such announcement, he headed out to look for them, figuring it was something simple like a busted chainsaw blade or a bent boot spike.

He found them only fifty yards away and congratulated himself on predicting something simple. Chris had gotten his chainsaw pinched in a tree. As he approached the seasoned veteran and the greenhorn, he smiled at the memories of Brian coaxing and instructing him through his own first pinched blade. Over the past couple of weeks, he'd started to see Brian in a whole new light: devoted brother, coach, mentor, and business owner trying to help all of the younger, eager climbers find their way safely through the dangerous world of logging. It was a shame, Hank realized, that it had taken so long for him to see Brian as anything but the hardass that had always harangued him about his drinking. "Can I help?" He called from a safe distance, not wanting to startle either of the men.

"Nah," Brian offered, his hands planted firmly on hips as he continued to survey Chris's progress. "I think he's getting it."

Hank stopped beside Brian, his own hands finding their way to hook into the openings of his safety vest. He studied the flustered and jerky movements of the greenhorn and listened to the curse words when some other solution didn't pan out. "He far behind now?" Hank asked with a nod in Chris' direction.

"Down by ten or so," Brian sighed as his arms came to rest over his chest. "Get this fixed, and we can make 'em up by quitting time."

"Want me to go get my saw, help him out?"

"Nah," Brian repeated, tossing him a quick smile of gratitude. "Greenhorn's got to learn, right?"

"I hated being called that, man," Hank huffed as he shook his head at the memory of being low man on the totem pole. "That and the way Roddy used to ride my ass over every little thing."

"I know." Brian nodded. "But it helped you in the end, yeah?"

Hank nodded and opened his mouth to ask what Brian was planning on doing about his best friend when he heard a yelp of satisfaction come from the greenhorn. Instead of asking a question his boss probably didn't want to hear, Hank decided to pat him on the back. "I'll take it from here so you can go finish your work." Taking a few steps forward, Hank turned to look back at his boss. "You doing okay? I mean, the head's not giving you any problems climbing and topping or nothing?"

"No, thanks." Brian laughed. "Only thing giving me headaches is trying to bring this job in on time."

"We'll make it." Hank accepted Brian's nod and watched him for a few moments as he headed for the clearing to have a sit-down and something to eat. It wasn't until he turned back to the greenhorn that everything he saw seemed to move into slow motion. He pulled his foot up to run, but it was like he was walking in knee-deep water or quicksand. He knew he was yelling something, but he couldn't be sure that Chris was hearing him because the greenhorn was still focused on the chainsaw. And if he'd had the presence of mind to turn, he would have seen that Brian was coming back pretty quickly yelling a few choice words of his own.

Hank was probably ten feet away when he saw Chris yank the pull cord of his chainsaw one final time, saw Chris turn, saw the greenhorn's smile at finding his saw still working and then saw the smile fade as he realized both men were yelling at him. It would never be clear to Hank or Brian what exactly had happened, but Hank would never forget Chris's screams drowning out the buzz of the motor as the blade snapped, hit the thick base of the tree and bounced back to glance off Chris's neck and shoulder, the greenhorn's helmet helping to deflect some of the blow. By the time Hank reached him, the sight of Chris's stricken, panicked young face and the smell of the blood were making him awfully glad that he hadn't eaten yet.

Hank had his safety vest off and his shirt wrapped around the greenhorn's neck before Brian reached them. "Call Kari, get the chopper here so you can evac him to Tofino."

"I'm sorry," Chris sputtered. "I forgot to check the blade."

"You keep quiet now, okay?" Hank tried not to look too worried for the kid's sake. "We're gonna get you choppered out of here and to some medical attention." He yanked on the sleeves of the shirt that would have to do as a bandage, pressed on it to apply pressure and turned to see Brian yelling into the walkie as he ran back for the first aid pack.

"I'm sorry, Hank," Chris repeated.

"You need to relax, Chris, please." Hank looked at the frightened face and then back at his shirt that was already showing little patches of blood seeping to the surface. He applied more pressure. "Take deep breaths, okay?" He started to breathe in and out, like it was some sort of birthing class, showing Chris what he wanted him to do. He had to get the kid calmed down before he hyperventilated himself into some major blood loss.

"How's he doing?" Brian asked while looking down at the greenhorn, as if Hank was an actual doctor or something.

"I don't think he's cut anything major, otherwise I think he would have passed out already, but...." Hank looked from Chris' face to Brian's, not knowing what to do or say. "Ah, fuck, boss, I'm no fuckin' doctor here. Where's the chopper?"

"I feel...." Chris was losing consciousness fast. His words were slurred and his eyes were fluttering.

"Kari's doubletiming it, but it'll be about ten before she's here."

"Well, then," Hank said as he looked back down at Chris' face, the young kid's eyes already seeming too heavy to keep open. "We gotta get him into the clearing." Hank nodded towards Chris's head. "You take his legs so I don't have to release the pressure." Hank appreciated that Brian didn't argue with him. He would have been hard-pressed to justify his decision to anyone, let alone his boss.

They moved quickly to get Chris to the clearing, Hank realizing too late that no one had remembered to turn off the chainsaw. He could still hear it laughing at him from over two hundred yards away. Hank felt his arms starting to shake from the weight of this full-grown kid and the constant need to apply pressure to the wound. It wasn't until they made it to the clearing that Hank realized that the chainsaw had been deafened by the rotors of Kari's approaching chopper.

He thanked every god he could think of when she didn't exit the chopper to try and help but then cursed his boss for starting the argument.

"There's no room, Brian," Hank yelled over the roar of the rotors when Brian tried to order him in the chopper. "And there's no time."

"Hank," Brian barked. "Get your ass in here."

Brian had gotten in the chopper first so that Chris was half-on, half-off his large frame, and when he found himself wedged into the far seat pressing the shirt against the neck wound, he'd started barking orders at Hank about abandoning the job, had even grabbed on to his hand once he'd made sure that the greenhorn's head was safely immobilized inside the chopper.

"We're still down about fifteen trees," Hank yelled, the rotor wash tossing his hair about his eyes and ears. "Get going for fuck's sake before he bleeds to death. Kari'll come back for me when we know Chris is safe." Brian let go of his hand, and Hank grabbed the door and shut it tight. He grimaced at the bloody handprint he left on the crisp white paint. He waved them away when he was clear.

As he made his way back to the clearing, shrugging back into his vest, intent on gathering all of Chris' gear to load for his eventual pickup in the clearing, he felt an overwhelming need to hear Scott's voice. Chris was unlucky, that was for sure. The falling pants that all climbers wore were actually a couple of thick layers of cloth over a Kevlar-like lining meant to protect the legs from snapping chainsaw blades. Unfortunately for Chris, his blade had snapped just when the greenhorn had been holding it at such an odd angle that it ended up catching him across the neck and shoulder. Hank had enough first aid and experience to know that the blade hadn't cut anything major, but he also had enough common sense to know that Chris was the priority. They could come back for Hank later.

ALTHOUGH he'd spent about twenty minutes and almost all of his water washing the blood off of his hands, Hank could still smell it. After gathering all of their supplies into the clearing, Hank had spent the next four hours climbing and topping the remaining trees like a man possessed. He was determined to get the job done, have the trees jigged for the helicopter that would transport the stems the next day, *and* be home to hold Scott and tell him how much he'd loved the lunches. *Who knows,* he joked with himself as he clawed his way to the second-to-last tree. *Maybe he'll surprise me with a pet name that doesn't suck!*

He managed to avoid the marms and the widowmaker and top the cypress in record time. Brian would definitely be proud of him for getting this job in on time. *Maybe I'll ask for a raise,* he smiled as he pulled the ribbon from his pouch and bit off a good length. He had the ribbon wrapped around the top of the tree and was pulling it over the top, ready to staple it in place, when he looked up. His blood ran cold when he realized that he hadn't even noticed the fog roll in until just now. It wasn't uncommon for the island to be blanketed in fast-moving fog like this, but it was uncommon for helicopters to be able to fly in it.

The little voice in his head told him to finish the job, so he did, figuring that it might just look worse since he was two hundred feet in the air. As he hoisted his claw, ready to throw it to the next tree, he stopped again, suddenly realizing he couldn't make out the clearing. He'd been in such a hurry that he hadn't bothered to count steps or use any of his usual tricks to keep himself oriented. *Don't panic,* he warned himself as he threw his claw to the next tree.

Within ten minutes, he was back at the bottom of the tree and still trying not to panic. *Fuck, fuck, fuck.* He realized he'd have to pick a direction and hope he was right. He wasn't climbing now, and with the cold, dense fog against his skin, he realized that he no longer had his shirt. *Fucking idiot,* he chastised himself as he pulled out his cell phone. No signal. *Well, this just keeps getting better, doesn't it?* He stopped in his tracks and took a few deep breaths, hoping to clear his head. *The packs, the equipment*, he suddenly realized. *Find them, and I'm at the clearing.* He closed his eyes again, took a few more deep breaths, and tried to retrace his steps, trying to pick out the reverse order of the trees he'd climbed since the chopper picked up Brian and Chris. *Look up,* he thought as he slapped his forehead, sarcastic smile crossing his lips, *and you'll see which trees have been topped.* He slapped his forehead again as he looked up to see nothing but the dense water vapor hanging in the air, cutting off his view of the tree tops. *Fog, you stupid shit. The trunks!* He smiled to himself. Surely the big pink X's on the trunks would help him.

His stomach grumbled, and he checked his watch. Almost five in the afternoon. The chopper had picked up Brian and Chris just after noon, if his memory served. But…. Hank took a few deep breaths again, trying not to panic when he realized he'd topped his last tree almost an hour ago. He'd been fumbling around in the fog for over forty minutes and still hadn't come across the equipment. Cursing himself for being stupid enough to think he was smart enough to do it, he stayed where he was for a moment and then sat on the ground, jerking back to a standing position when he felt the water soak through the seat of his work pants. *Fucking idiot*, he cursed as he began to rub his upper arms. He reached into his pouch for his lighter, the idea to build a fire helping him to focus his nervousness.

He tried not to stray too far, searching for something dry enough to catch fire, but every time he came up empty, he decided to go just another ten or fifteen feet. He searched under fallen logs and between spaces he figured might have been protected from the rain but found nothing. He stood between two cypress trees and scrubbed at his face, wanting nothing more than to be home in bed with Scott right at that moment. *I made you a promise, baby, and I'm gonna keep it.* He closed his eyes and thought of the long legs, the pouty mouth, the infectious giggle, and the warm, sensitive skin of his boyfriend's back. *Boyfriend,* he thought. *What a strange word… couldn't any boy that's also a friend be a boyfriend, then?*

He shook his head at the idiotic thought and pictured Scott lying in bed, hugging the pillow to his body, waiting for him to keep his promise. *Want to hear the pet name you picked out for me, baby… Tasmanian devil, terror of the playground.* Hank laughed as he shrugged and headed out to continue his search for something to burn. He flicked his lighter absent-mindedly and looked down to see the slight wind—that he hadn't realized was blowing—sending the flame licking at his thumb. *How come I don't feel it?*

He released his thumb and brought it up to his mouth, the coldness of his skin not really worrying him. *Heat blanket,* he realized suddenly. *I'll find the heat blanket.* He headed off in another direction, not realizing that he was retracing his path back to the last tree he'd topped over an hour ago. *Where the hell is Scott?* He slowed his pace, the image of the warm skin and the kissable lips absorbing him so completely that he didn't see the tree branch sticking out of the fallen tree. *Finally,* he thought as he felt the sweat fall down his side. *Some heat.* He fumbled his hand over to swipe at the sweat, wondering for a brief moment how he could be sweating with all this fog and no sun. He reached over to his side to let the warmth soak into the blue-tinged flesh of his fingers.

And as he sank down to rest by the fallen log, his mind recalling the feel of Scott's hands and the smell of Scott fresh from the shower, he closed his eyes and wondered momentarily why his sweat was red.

CHAPTER 31

BRIAN was frantic.

His logical brain had reminded him many times that the chopper couldn't fly in that kind of fog, but the other part of his brain, the part that would have to explain this whole thing to Scott, kept screaming at him to do something.

It was just after four in the morning, and the fog had disappeared, so he'd woken up Kari—not that either of them had managed to get any sleep at all—and they'd headed out in the chopper to find the clearing empty. They each had a flashlight and fanned out on either side of the clearing, Brian heading out, backpack with supplies slung over his shoulder, in the direction of Chris's uncut trees. He called Hank's name over and over, trying to console himself with the knowledge that Chris's wound had been serious but not life-threatening. He was resting in a nice warm hospital bed in Tofino while Hank was probably freezing to death. He schooled his anger at having let Hank make such a stupid decision and called again, stopping every ten feet to listen for something, anything.

He tried to keep his mind off of what words he'd use to tell Scott why he'd let this happen, but he couldn't get his baby brother's face out of his head. He knew technically this wasn't his fault—no one could have predicted such a sudden fog—but Scott wouldn't care about the technicalities. Scott would never forgive him for not having forced Hank into that chopper. "Hank," Brian whispered, shaking his head. "You said the magic words—'finish the job'—and I let you stay out here." He veered to his right after shining his light up into the canopy, convinced he was seeing the flash of red ribbons.

"Blow your whistle, Hank," Brian muttered, his voice already going hoarse from yelling in the cool morning air. *Fucking hell,* he thought as he flashed his beam over and over, coming up empty each time.

He hoisted his pack again, and the beam of light caught something off to his right. He froze and pointed the light, finally seeing the flash of orange of a safety vest and running, flat out, until he was beside Hank's body. He saw the bloodstained hand first, the spots of flesh among the glistening red almost blue. The rest of Hank was beneath the log, and Brian figured he'd tried to find some warmth underneath.

"Hang on, Hank." Brian reached down and found a faint pulse. *Oh, thank fuck!* He pulled the whistle to his lips and blew it repeatedly, signaling Kari to return and start the chopper. "Hang on, buddy."

Squatting down on his haunches, Brian pulled Hank from underneath the fallen tree and then he saw what had caused the bloodstain on Hank's hand. Hank had somehow given himself a gash on his right side. Brian didn't have to wonder too hard how. They had just heard a couple of days ago how disoriented and confused hypothermia patients could become. He let the thought go as he brought his hand away from Hank's torso, a momentary surge of panic constricting his chest as he wondered why his hands were wet. He glanced down quickly to see if there was more blood, relief flooding him when he saw sweat. It took his brain a few moments to realize it shouldn't be relief he was feeling but a more urgent, pressing need for panic.

Sepsis, was the only thing that Brian could think when he saw that Hank's blue-tinged flesh was actually covered in a layer of sweat. *Thank Christ I helped Scooter study for all those bio tests.* Brian huffed as he hefted Hank onto the log, wrapped the heat blanket around his cold skin and then pulled him onto his shoulder in a fireman's carry.

He took the return path very slowly and carefully, his flashlight in one hand while the other hugged Hank's muscled thighs to his chest. He was careful not to jar Hank's injury as he found the clearing and heard the whir of the rotors. He pulled open the door, positioned Hank in the back and strapped him in, tucking the blanket around his big frame. He gave the thumbs up to Kari and sat back, releasing the breath he hadn't realized he'd been holding.

After what seemed like hours, Kari landed the chopper on the street, dismissing Brian's concerns, not caring that she might be inconveniencing motorists on the deserted road or that she might be arrested. Brian watched her turn and give a thumbs-up, and then, hoisting Hank onto his shoulder again, he cleared the rotors and waved as she took off again.

He practically ran to the small one-story hospital building and found two nurses waiting for him. He'd had Kari call ahead and alert them to a hypothermia patient with possible sepsis on his right side. The nurses held the gurney while Brian lowered Hank like a sack of potatoes, the blue-tinged arms flopping over the sides. He stepped back as the nurses moved into action, using words and acronyms that he'd certainly never learned while helping his brother. One nurse pointed him toward the admitting desk, and he found himself staring at an old-fashioned white phone, complete with protruding plastic buttons. He resisted the urge to call Kari and have her fly them both to Duncan or Victoria and started reciting Hank's statistics to the plump little nurse behind the computer screen.

"Mr. Alan?"

Brian looked up, blinking his eyes several times. He hadn't even been aware that he'd closed his eyes. "Yes, yes," he stuttered. "I'm Mr. Alan. Brian Alan." He was on his feet, his hands rubbing at his face and then fumbling to find a home while he stared at the short man with the stethoscope.

"I'm Dr. Lowen," the man smiled. "You're with…." The doctor looked down at his chart. "Mr. Ballam?"

"Yes," Brian replied, his heart somewhere in his throat. "Is he…?"

"We won't know until we've had the chance to do some blood cultures, but…." The doctor let the chart fall to his side. "He's very lucky to be alive and that you warned us about the gash on his side." Without waiting for any acknowledgement of his praise, the doctor continued, most of the explanation going right over Brian's head. But he did reach out a hand, stopping short of actual contact, when the doctor mentioned something about a cooling blanket.

"I'm sorry, doctor, but…." Brian rubbed his forehead. "Don't you mean heating blanket?"

"No." The doctor smiled again and tucked the chart under his arm. "If we were to bring Mr. Ballam's core body temperature back to normal, any infection in his side would spread that much more quickly." The doctor clasped his hands in front of him as if he was sure that Brian had actually understood any of that and nodded.

"Sorry." Brian reached out again to stop the doctor from walking away. "Again, sorry, doctor, but...."

"Until we can determine if there is an infection, and if there is, whether it's bacterial or fungal," the doctor explained patiently, "Mr. Ballam's best chance of survival is to have his core body temperature kept below normal."

"Isn't that just putting him in the fridge instead of the freezer?"

The doctor smiled, and to Brian's relief, resisted the urge to laugh in his face. "I've never heard it put like that, but... yes, I guess you could say that what we're trying to do is keep the germs from spreading to the fruit crisper."

"Fruit...?" Brian's eyebrows went vertical. "Crisper? You're keeping him fresh?"

"Exactly," the doctor stepped forward and touched Brian's elbow. "I know it doesn't make sense right now, but trust me. It's what's best for him until we determine if the wound has been infected."

"I see." Brian looked down at the doctor as he pulled his hand back. "But he'll be okay eventually?"

"That's the plan, sir."

Brian fell back into the chair and pulled out his cell phone, remembering at the last minute that he would need to vacate the premises before using it.

Steeling himself for a hysterical reaction, Brian punched in the number one and listened to the ringing. *Two... three... four.... Fuck, voice mail!* "Hey, Scooter, it's big brother. I need to talk to you, so when you get this, call me right away." He flipped his phone shut, wondering if he should have said something about Hank and then, convinced he'd done the right thing, headed back inside to ask for the nearest open coffee shop.

Tuff Beans, Brian thought as he pulled on the door. *If that doesn't say it all, I don't know what does.* He plopped down at the counter and ordered a coffee and the pancake special that was written on the chalk board behind the cash register. He thanked the elderly woman who smiled at him when she poured his coffee and had almost brought the colorful mug to his lips when his cell phone rang. He held up a hand to the woman and headed outside for some privacy.

"What?" Scott's voice was loud and frantic. "Are you hurt? Is Hank hurt? Who's hurt? You never call me from a job! Who's hurt? Answer me."

"Scooter," Brian started.

"Wait," Scott panted. "It can't be you if you're calling me. Where's Hank? What did you do with him? Where is he?"

"Will you just calm down for a sec?"

"I am calm," Scott barked.

"Hank's in the hospital in Tofino."

"What?"

Brian didn't repeat it.

"Wh... how... when...? Is he okay?"

"The doctor said—"

"Doctor!"

"Scooter," Brian soothed. "The doctor said that Hank is suffering from hypothermia, but he's also very optimisitic—"

"Optimistic!" Scott sounded as if he were running on a treadmill. "About what? How did he get hypothermia? Why are you in Tofino and not—"

Brian waited for the rest, but nothing else came. His chest hurt as he realized he hadn't even gotten to the worse part. *They've decided to keep him in the fruit crisper until they can figure out if he's got fungus or bacteria, or both.* Brian closed his eyes and resisted the urge to say anything else.

"You're in Tofino because you couldn't risk bringing him home."

Brian noted how calm Scott's voice was and wished, irrationally, that he'd go back to yelling. As long as he lived, Brian would never forget the sound of Scott's voice saying *home* and meaning the townhouse he'd been hoping to share with Hank. "Yes," he whispered, suddenly terribly aware of how quiet the streets of Tofino were at five thirty in the morning.

"Is he...? Is it...?"

"You need to get here, as quickly as possible."

"How long a drive is it?" Brian began to admire how well Scott was holding himself together.

"Four or five hours?"

"Fuck that," Scott laughed, but with no humor in his voice. "I'll pay for a charter flight."

"I'm sorry, Scooter," Brian whispered, not sure how he'd be able to tell Scott the whole story.

"What? I can't hear you."

"I said... I'll be waiting for you, Scooter."

"Did he...?" And now, Brian heard the voice of his nine-year-old baby brother, the same voice he remembered from all of those long nights he'd spent soothing away the nightmares. "Is he in pain? Will he know it's me?"

"He'll be okay, Scooter. He'll be okay, I promise. Just... get here, okay?" Brian closed his eyes when he heard Scott's voice finally break. In all the years he'd cared for and loved his brother, he'd only ever heard him cry once. Brian had had to sit his nine-year-old brother down in their shared bedroom and explain why Mom wouldn't be coming home anymore. Blinking up at the dawning light on the horizon, Brian promised his soul to the devil if only he wouldn't have to watch his brother go through that again.

Hearing the tap on the window, Brian turned and tried to smile for the elderly woman, not really sure he had the strength to stand up from where he sat on the bench outside the restaurant, let alone eat anything.

CHAPTER 32

THE chartered helicopter landed at the municipal airport, and then Scott found himself in a taxi, which was nothing more than a yellow car with an incapacitated meter attached, and on his way down a winding road to a small building that, at first sight, Scott assumed would have been a general store of some kind. But then he saw the outdated ambulance and had to take deep breaths so that he wouldn't storm in and demand an immediate transfer to a better-equipped facility. He told himself that he was being irrational as he handed over a couple of twenties to pay for a distance that he could have covered on foot. He reached for his duffle bag, accepted the profuse thanks from the driver—who was either tired or stoned, or both—for the sizeable tip, and exited the vehicle, his eyes focused solely on the little white lettering on brown siding.

For the second time in as many weeks, Scott found himself rushing into a hospital and approaching a busy nurse, demanding to see someone he loved. "Yes, hello," he offered as he finally got the nurse's attention. "I'm here to see Hank, uh, Henry Ballam."

"Are you family?"

"I'm Scott Ballam, his brother," he lied, not really caring whether she believed him or not. It might have been a more convincing lie if he wasn't so fair and slender. He nodded when the nurse pointed him towards a small room at the rear of the hallway. *Jesus,* Scott thought as he walked down the halls of what looked like a cabin from his Boy Scout days. *First thing we do is get him back to real hospital.*

The Intensive Care Unit consisted of exactly four beds, each contained within its own ring of pretty yellow-flowered curtains. Not that

Scott was an expert or anything, but all the sounds and smells seemed about right, so he decided to wait and hear what the doctors had to say before he started making any arrangements to have Hank moved. He pulled back the only curtain that was drawn and noticed the man sitting in the chair first.

"Brian?" He saw his brother's eyes open and focus on him while his own eyes took in his lover. "Why is he wrapped up like a mummy?" Scott asked, looking to his brother for an answer. Without waiting, he walked over and felt the cool plastic. "These aren't even bandages. And they're cold!" Scott's voice was loud and getting louder. He looked back at his brother who didn't seem interested in anything other than the volume of his voice.

"Scooter," Brian reached out and took hold of his duffle bag and placed it on the floor beside the chair. "They have to keep him cold so they can figure out if his wound is infected."

"Keep him... wound?" His eyes widened as he looked at his brother's pained expression. "What the hell happened out there?"

"I guess—"

"You guess? What the hell do you mean—"

"Scott." Brian tightened his grip and pulled his brother towards him. "You have to keep your voice down." Scott repeated his question in a whisper, finishing it this time. "One of the other climbers," Brian began "was injured and had to be flown here to the hospital. Hank decided to stay behind to finish the job and then the fog rolled in and we couldn't fly back to get him—"

"You left him out there?"

"Scooter, please." Brian pulled his brother against his chest; whether he was doing it to comfort him or to keep him from turning into the Tasmanian devil, Scott wasn't sure. "It's my fault." Brian heard the strain of holding it all in finally break. "I'm so sorry, Scott. I let him stay out there because I didn't want the job to fall off schedule... I knew better but—" Brian braced himself as Scott managed to push his way free of his brother's grip. He threw his hands out to the side, surrendering himself to what he knew he deserved.

"I think you should go," Scott said, almost too softly. *You selfish prick.* Scott couldn't get the thought out of his brain. *I know he's not but....* Whether the anger toward Brian was actually because of his brother or because Hank had made such a stupid decision to stay out there all alone, Scott couldn't know at that moment. The only thing he did know was that he felt betrayed, as if he'd just come to realize that Brian was capable of making decisions that could ruin people's lives.

"What?" Brian wasn't sure he'd heard correctly.

"I said get out." Scott made sure to keep his voice calm and low.

"Scott," Brian pleaded, his eyes blinking, as if it would help him understand what he knew he'd heard. "Please? I didn't mean for any of this—"

"Brian," Scott said, closing his eyes and fisting the hem of his shirt. "You're my brother, my only brother, and I love you and always will." Scott looked over at Hank's handsome face and tried to smile through the anger, but the anguish and the frustration needed an outlet. "But if you don't get out of my sight right now, I'll make sure there's nothing left of that fucking company." He stepped aside to let his brother pass, wanting to reach out and tell him he didn't mean any of it, that he was sorry that Brian had had to be the one to tell him, that he loved him more because he'd been the one to tell him. But he couldn't bring himself to do it. He let his brother go in silence because he wasn't absolutely sure that he didn't mean what he'd just said.

He pulled the chair up until it was close enough for him to sit and still hold Hank's hand. "Hey, baby," Scott whispered against the cool flesh of the hands that had held him only days before. "It's me, Hank. It's Scrappy." He tried to concentrate on Hank's handsome, peaceful face, leaning over and kissing the back of the cool hand, but the only face that kept popping up in his mind's eye was the one he'd just sent away, with a threat to ruin his business no less. He fought back the tears that stung his eyes and hung his head, in shame or fatigue Scott couldn't be sure. *After all he's done for me. Fuck.* He released his lover's hand and went in search of his brother.

It was a short search; Brian was sitting hunched with his head in his hands in the little waiting area. Scott walked slowly, thinking of what he'd said to the man who'd always been there for him, until he stood directly in front of him. He was startled when Brian looked up, saw him, and jumped to his feet.

"What's wrong?" Brian's eyes were huge, his intense but tired gaze fixed on Scott's sad face.

"I'm sorry." The words were barely out of his mouth before he gulped a lungful of air, as if he were stranded at sea and holding on, clawing at any chance of survival. He felt the tears sting his eyes as he realized that even after what he'd said to his brother, Brian's first concern was for him. He walked until he felt the forgiveness wrap around him with the embrace that Brian offered, no questions necessary.

"Come on, Scoot," Brian whispered, his own voice cracking. "Let's get some air."

When Scott felt the cool air on his moist cheeks, he turned and looked into Brian's eyes. He felt comfort and love as Brian brushed his hand up and down his back, telling him that it would all be okay, that Hank would be okay.

"I'm sorry," Scott sniffed. "I didn't mean what I said." He'd tried so hard to hold it together all the way here, tried to remind himself that he'd only been with Hank for two weeks. Standing in front of his brother, he couldn't help but realize that he'd been the selfish prick during all of this. He'd consoled himself with a few phone calls to ensure that his brother was all right, was recovering well from his own injury. And now he forced himself to confront how he'd allowed himself to treat the one man who had unconditionally offered kindness and acceptance and love. "I know it all seems sudden to you," he sputtered, his hand wiping away the spittle that flew from his mouth. "But I love him, and—"

"And," Brian said as he drew him into a bear hug, "he loves you."

"I was cruel to say that to you—"

"Shhh," Brian whispered against his ear. "I know you didn't mean it, Scoot." Brian waited for the huffing and the spasms to calm a little. "And I know it's not sudden." He pulled away but kept a hand on each shoulder, peering down into his brother's tear-streaked face. "When you know it's right, you just know." He smiled and offered his brother a wink.

"Kari?"

"Yeah," Brian sighed. Scott couldn't help but notice the blush sweep across his brother's cheeks. "I always knew, but I was just being safe, you know."

Scott huffed a little laugh and wiped his face with the back of his hand, his other hand still clutching the side of Brian's shirt. "You should get back... you know, to your company. Make sure everything's okay."

"Not a chance, baby brother." Brian laughed as his hands smoothed over Scott's hair. "Besides, Hank got us all caught up. We're just waiting for the Virtol, and"—Brian jerked his arm forward, crooked his elbow and look at his watch—"it should be finishing up right about now."

"He wanted...." Scott closed his eyes and told himself he would not start crying again. "He was so worried that you were going to fire him." He remembered that day in the hospital, the morning after Hank had slept in the spare room, and how worried he was that he might lose the job he loved. "You should have seen his face, Brian. He was just so sad and looked so lost. All he's talked about is making you proud of him."

"I know." Brian closed his eyes and let his head hang. "I've been a real bastard about all of this, but—"

"No," Scott interrupted. "No, you haven't. That's just it." His brain scrambled to find the right words. "He was glad that you'd been so hard on him." Scott squeezed his eyes shut again. "He said it was what he needed to quit fucking up his life and to realize why he'd spent so much time drinking and banging every chick he met."

"Sounds like Hank," Brian laughed. "So, then, he was trying to fight who he was?" Scott nodded. "Poor guy."

At the now-familiar cry of the car that sounded like it was long overdue for some sort of overhaul, both of their heads turned to see the taxi coming down the long, winding road. Kari was out of the vehicle before it had fully stopped and held out a twenty to the driver through the passenger side window. Scott chuckled to himself when he imagined that the driver had to be wondering how he'd suddenly gotten so lucky.

"I brought the chopper." Kari huffed as if she'd run the short trek from the airport. "I've got it for a couple of hours, no questions asked." She came close to Brian, and he found himself with both arms full of what he was quickly seeing as his family.

"The Chinook?" Scott's brows knitted in confusion. Surely they didn't need something that big just to transport one patient.

Kari smiled patiently as she said, "No, the smaller one." Scott was grateful that she'd used simpler terminology. He'd never been very good at remembering the names of cars or planes or anything remotely mechanical. "How is he?"

"They're keeping him in a crisper," Brian said, trying to interject some levity.

Scott rolled his eyes, certain that he might—one day—be able to find something about all this amusing, and then said, "It is called induced hypothermia, and they're keeping him cold until they can figure out if his wound, the one on his side, is infected."

"Are there other wounds?"

"I don't know." Brian shrugged and pulled each of them a little closer. "I was just waiting for my brainiac brother to get here. Maybe he can understand the doctor." He guided his two armfuls towards the entrance of the hospital, letting Scott go in and be with Hank while he stayed outside for a moment with Kari.

Scott knew that Brian needed some comforting of his own and went ahead into the hospital to be with his lover. Brian and Kari, he knew, would be in when they'd found whatever comfort the other had to give.

By the time Kari and Brian entered, his arm around her petite shoulders and hers around his trim waist, Scott was sitting in his chair beside Hank's still frame. Brian gestured to the seat, and Kari sat for a few moments until the curtain was pulled back.

"Doctor?" Brian called as quietly as he could and turned to see Scott was now standing. "Ah, this is Hank's, ah...."

"Brother," Scott offered and extended his hand. "Scott Ballam." They may be living in Canada, bastion of equality, but this was still a small town, and Scott didn't want any unnecessary complications that may arise from telling the whole truth.

"Could you go through that explanation one more time?" Brian looked down at his brother and winked. "Mr. *Ballam* here is a lot more knowledgeable about medical stuff than I am, so maybe he'll get it the first time."

Brian listened, his eyes ping-ponging between his brother's face and the doctor's, and did not seem to gather anything more than he had the first time he's listened to the doctor's explanation. His chest threatened to burst with pride as he watched Scott ask a few questions, but then he saw Scott put his hand up in the air, halting the doctor's words.

The doctor stopped his explanation when he noticed Scott's blank expression and the wave of a hand in the air.

"Doctor," Scott said through a strained smile. "I failed high school biology. Could you use English, please?"

"We're administering a broad-spectrum antibiotic so that we can eliminate as much infection as possible, but we won't know for another couple of days whether there is, indeed, an infection, and if there is, whether it's bacterial or fungal... or both."

Scott noted the pleased look on the doctor's face and couldn't help but wonder if he was waiting for a pat on the back. "And?"

"We'll need to keep his core temperature low until we can administer the anti... the medicine, and then when the blood cultures show that he's improving," the doctor said with a sweep of his hand across Hank's prone body, "we can warm him up, and he'll be as good as new."

"Thank you, doctor," Scott sighed. He kept the smile on his face until the door closed behind the doctor. He turned to regard Brian and Kari out of the corner of his eye. "Warm him up?" Scott grunted. "What is he, a pizza pop?"

"You didn't fail biology," Brian stated urgently, his thumb crooking to point towards where the doctor had stood only moments ago. Turning to look down at Kari, their hands now joined, "He didn't fail anything. He was a straight-A student. I made sure of it."

"This isn't about you, sweetie," Kari told him and smiled when Scott looked at her in confusion. She pulled on her boyfriend's hand to settle him in his chair again. "Scott, honey?"

Scott turned to see the look of relief on both of their faces. Hank would be okay. He hadn't lost anything with the man he loved except a couple of days. "I'm never letting him leave the house again." Scott announced, his arms folding across his chest as he turned to look down at Hank's handsome face.

"I think he might have something to say about that," Brian laughed and looked to Kari, the smile dropping from his face as she shook her head briefly.

"No," Scott said, his eyebrows finding their way to his hairline. "No, he won't."

"Well, there, Brian," Kari said as she patted the back of Brian's hand. "We should go get a room...." She glanced at Scott when his head turned. "Rooms... and leave these two in peace." She approached Scott, touching his shoulder and pulling him in for a soft hug when he turned.

"Brian?" He released Kari's slight frame and reached into his back pocket. "Will you get three and put them on my credit card?"

"No," Brian puffed. "Absolutely not. I can get the rooms." He walked to stand beside his brother. "You need me, need anything," his brother whispered when Scott fell against him. "You call me, anytime... day or night."

Scott nodded and watched them leave, the absence of voices in the room making him feel suddenly lonely for Hank's rough growl. He stood for a moment and looked down at the sleeping face of his lover, and he had an uncontrollable urge to get in the bed with him, to tell him the news, to tell him they'd be together again forever.

But then the door swung open, and the nurses came in carrying more of the IV bags that made a crunchy sound when the nurses loaded them on the metal stands, and he knew that was his cue to step out of the room. He waited in the hall for what seemed like an hour and tried not to glare at the nurses when they left Hank's room.

Hoping they'd be alone for several hours now, Scott shucked his shoes and climbed onto the bed beside his man, settling his head on the pillow and reaching to place a kiss beside Hank's ear. Before he pulled back to let his eyes close, he delivered the good news that the doctor had explained, quick to point out that he had not, in fact, failed anything in high school, and then sang "But for You" softly beside his lover's ear.

And he wouldn't swear to it, couldn't promise that it wasn't just wishful thinking, but he was sure that before sleep finally claimed him, he saw Hank's lips twitch a little.

CHAPTER 33

THE second day had been pretty much the same as the first, as had the third except for meeting Chris. He was on his way home after getting a clean bill of health.

"Oh, I'm sorry," Chris had stammered upon discovering Scott in the chair, his hand clasped with Hank's.

"It's okay." Scott got out of the chair and took a step closer. "You're Chris?" Scott noticed a panicked and strained look cross the young man's face as he nodded. "You're going home, I see." Scott pointed to the backpack that he'd assumed had been brought by Brian during one of the most recent jaunts between the worksite and the hospital where two of his loggers were being treated. "I'm Scott," he added after a few moments of silence.

"Scott?" Chris's eyes darted from Hank's face to Scott's and back again. "You're Scott." It wasn't really a question, Scott noted, and he nodded. "I'm real sorry that I caused all of this, and—"

"Chris?" He interrupted the young man, seeing that same hurt and confused look that he'd seen on Hank's face only weeks before. "It's okay. I grew up in a family of loggers. Accidents happen, okay?" He didn't think he'd done a very good job of convincing the young man, so he added, "No one will blame you for this." Scott smiled and winked. "Unless you're telling me that the fog was your fault." He was suddenly aware of how similar this conversation was to the one he'd had with Hank only weeks ago.

Chris seemed to relax a little at the lame attempt at a joke. He stood, his fist tightening and loosening around the handle of his backpack, and then looked back at Scott. "That's a real great guy you got there, Scott. He's a good man, none better."

Scott's head swiveled. "How did—" Chris nodded at Hank. "He told me where the lunches came from." Chris bowed his head, and when he looked back at Scott, his eyes were red-tinged and glistening. Scott took another few steps and placed a hand on his shoulder, squeezing gently, the way his father had consoled his boys after their mother had died. "Never forgive myself if he doesn't...."

"Now, Chris," Scott quieted him. "Nothing is going to happen to him. He's strong, he's healthy...." Scott smirked a little. "And he'd never miss a chance to drive me insane with all his teasing."

"He teases you?"

Scott was glad to see the tears had abated a little, calm settling in again when a smile ghosted over Chris's dark expression. "All the time." Scott rolled his eyes. "Drives me mental." Scott noticed the smile get a little bigger and the eyes continue to dart between his face and Hank's. He imagined that Chris was hearing about a side that Hank rarely showed in public.

They said their goodbyes then, Scott feeling a little big lighter than he'd felt in days. But then, the fourth day came.

He'd not had much use for the room that had only ever seen his duffle bag sitting on the double bed, but Scott didn't care. He washed his face in the little bathroom, and he had deodorant in his pocket and a chair that was becoming more comfortable, although what made it so, he really didn't know. Perhaps it was just the closest thing he had at that moment that allowed him to stay close to the man he'd fallen for.

The problem with falling, Scott realized that fourth morning as he sat up in the hospital chair and looked over at Hank's peaceful, sleeping face, was not the sudden stop at the end but the exhausting journey all by himself back to somewhere even remotely near where he'd been before he fell. He searched for those moments of bliss just before he was fully awake in the morning, before his mind had a chance to remind him of the many mistakes he'd made. He searched for those long-ago but well-known moments when waking up didn't mean another long, tedious day of trying to slog his way back to a time when happiness was more than just the hope of having a life with Hank. It was a place he remembered but only vaguely, as if it were one of those dreams that he always used to like, the ones just before waking, the ones that seemed so real but had an element of the unreal in them.

Scott didn't complain, and he got up every morning as he always had with a facsimile of a smile on his face, even though he caught himself staring at his own reflection some days and wasn't sure who or what he was staring at. Still, seeing the confusion and pain in his own eyes always served to remind him that he had voluntarily given up his old life in favor of this one. And in some of those wistful, elusive moments just before he awoke fully, just before he remembered that he'd had the chance to walk away, that he'd had the chance to stop it all in that little pond near French Beach, he saw Hank's green eyes and playful smile, felt their lips touch again and thought, maybe, it had all been worth it.

He padded to the little bathroom, wet a cloth, and returned to the side of his lover's bed, lovingly washing that handsome face and noting with some amusement how quickly Hank's beard seemed to grow. He let his fingers remember how it had been to comb through the thick chestnut waves during those achingly beautiful moments of passion. It had only been a week since they'd made love, but it may as well have been a lifetime ago.

Hank was on his third round of antibacterial and antifungal medicine drips, and the doctors had switched over the Kool-Kit hypothermia system to begin warming Hank back to a normal core temperature. As long as Scott lived, he would never forget the feeling of how cold Hank's skin had been for those two long—so very long—days. The doctor had been kind enough to stand patiently and explain everything to Scott—and Brian or Kari when they were there. But for almost twenty-four hours, Scott had been alone with Hank in the hospital room. He'd had to fight the urge to hug the doctor when he'd announced that Hank was out of danger and it would only be a matter of assessing any residual damage that the infections might have caused.

At Scott's insistence, Brian had finally managed to track down Hank's parents in Coquitlam very late that first day and deliver the news. It hadn't been easy to track them down, since Hank had not listed them as emergency contacts, having listed only the younger of his two sisters. She'd not made it to the hospital yet, and she said she would "try" to make it out once Hank was moved back to Duncan. Scott didn't really blame her. She had a husband, two kids, and a life of her own—a life that, according to her, hadn't included Hank for almost three years.

As he stood by the bed, one hand giving Hank the tummy rub he enjoyed and the other sweeping the lemon-flavored mouth swab between Hank's cheeks and teeth, Scott wondered what could have gone on in the family to keep them apart for so long. He remembered that Hank had not really felt comfortable speaking of his family and had only mentioned a few incidents during which one or all of his family members had expressed disappointment in how Hank lived his life. He wondered, while tossing the mouth swab in the garbage can, if any of that would change now. Hank was a hero. He'd saved someone else's life, although almost at the expense of his own.

Scott let himself fall back into the chair. He'd had good moments and bad moments in between fitful bouts of sleep. During the good moments, he would know deep down that Hank would wake up, make some silly remark, and be as good as new. During the bad, however, Scott couldn't keep his mind from dwelling on any and all of the possible scenarios that the doctor had described. But right at that moment, as he stroked the silky hairs of Hank's forearms, Scott was having a good moment.

And tomorrow, when he would be allowed to charter a helicopter so he could med-evac Hank back to Duncan, would be the best moment so far. As he leaned back in his chair, his long legs stretched out in front of him, he realized he'd forgotten during all of their one-sided conversations to inform Hank that he'd finally finished the big finale for the musical. Scott was officially free to move back to Duncan, to his brother and to Hank.

He closed his eyes briefly. When he opened them again, feeling the insistent hand on his shoulder, it was dark outside. He'd slept in the chair beside Hank for almost six hours.

"Mr. Ballam," the nurse was saying. "Your brother's awake."

Even in his exhaustion, Scott had not forgotten the charade. "Hank?" He turned from the nurse's broad smile, and there they were, those beautiful green eyes he hadn't seen in almost a week.

"Hank," Scott whispered as he brought his face to lie beside the forearm he'd practically stroked bald over the past three days. "Are you in pain?"

"Scrappy?" Hank's voice was weak and lethargic as if he were trying to speak through a mouthful of food. Scott turned at the pet name, already preparing an explanation for the nurse, but she was no longer there. He hadn't even noticed that she'd left the room.

Scott got up, closed the privacy curtain against the only other bed in the room, wondering why he was doing it since the other bed hadn't been occupied since Hank had been transferred to this room, and leaned over his lover's groggy expression to plant a few tender kisses to his lemon-flavored lips.

Hank smacked his lips and tried to smile. "Hate lemon."

Scott smiled through his tears, bowed his head for a brief second out of relief, and then teased, "What? No 'I missed you. I wish you were here. Why haven't you sold the couch yet'?"

"Tired," Hank whispered, his voice gravelly and strained.

Scott let his hand rub lazy little figure eights over Hank's belly.

"Love," Hank croaked as his eyes fluttered closed. He struggled to open them, but failed.

Scott leaned over one more time and kissed the warm lips. "I love you, Hank," he whispered before taking his seat again, his heart doing flip-flops and threatening to bounce its way up to his stomach. It was only a few words, but Scott decided to make this a good moment too.

HANK awoke to the sound of beeping machines and the sight of a water stain on the ceiling. He wondered when his townhouse had developed that and then closed his eyes. When he opened them again, he heard water running and saw Scott step out of the bathroom and come to his side.

"Hey, Scrappy," Hank said. His voice was still a little fuzzy, but the smile on his face was positively bright with possibility.

"Hey, baby," Scott said as he stroked the hair back from Hank's forehead, his fingers teasing their way through the shiny strands. "Time for your bath." Scott waggled his eyebrows.

"Shower?"

"Not at this particular establishment," Scott teased. "Perhaps next time, you'll let me make the reservations."

"Establish... huh?" Hank closed his eyes and tried to get up, his body feeling like a lead weight.

"Whoa, there, handsome." Scott pushed gently against Hank's chest, his palms rejoicing in the return of the warmth that they had always found there. "You're in the hospital, Hank."

"I'm in...?" Hank brought his hand to his forehead slowly, the exertion seeming overwhelming. "Chris was hurt but not me."

Scott reached out and held the long, thick fingers between his own hands, bringing Hank's hand up to his mouth for several long kisses. "Yes and Chris is fine. He's gone home, as a matter of fact. He thinks you're a good man. None better, I believe he said."

"Nice kid," Hank croaked, "Why am I...?"

"You had hypothermia, and you cut your side, so"—Scott kissed Hank's hand again—"you're in the Tofino hospital. You had a couple of infections, bacterial and fungal infections, and they had to keep you four days until they could figure out how to treat it."

"Tofino?"

"Yes, central part of the island, west coast," Scott offered.

Hank released a puff of breath through his dry lips. "I know where.... Why not Duncan?"

"You were too ill. They couldn't take a chance on flying you all the way there."

"Am I okay?"

Scott's smile grew broad. "You will be once your body has had a chance to regain some its strength. The infections took a lot out of you."

"When can we go home?"

Scott turned when he heard the two words in the same sentence. "I guess when the doctor says you're strong enough to travel." Scott sat down on the bed beside his lover. "I'll charter a chopper to get us back to Duncan."

"Brian?"

"He and Kari are both doing fine. I finally had to make them go home so the company wouldn't fall apart." Scott figured he'd have to tell Hank how he'd overreacted and threatened Brian, but at that moment, all he wanted to do was look into those green eyes.

"Did you...?" Scott thought that Hank was going to ask about making the arrangements to move back to Duncan. "Did you stay with me this whole time?" Hank cleared his throat, his eyes fixed squarely on his lover's.

"Of course." Scott leaned over the railing of the bed, kissed Hank's lips, and then pulled back, reaching for the nightstand. Using the lip balm the nurse had given to him yesterday morning, he squeezed a little dab onto his finger and then ran it along the full lips. He leaned down again and kissed Hank a little more passionately this time but kept his tongue to his own mouth. As he pulled back a little, he felt Hank's hand land heavily on his own hand. He looked down and then smiled back at Hank's attempt at a mischievous grin. Scott gave another quick peck and then slipped his hand under the white sheet that covered Hank to touch his muscular chest. He couldn't help but wonder what was going through Hank's mind, the green eyes going wide but the husky, bass voice remaining mute. Scott let the hand trail down and gently allowed his hand to find its way under Hank's hospital gown. He saw the big man's eyes close when he began to rub little circles over the flat, warm belly.

"Sorry." Scott leaned over and kissed Hank quickly, letting the tip of his tongue reacquaint itself with the deliciousness of Hank's warm lips. "Didn't mean to tease, but," Scott shrugged, "we'll get to that when you're all better."

"Can't wait," Hank smiled as his eyes grew heavy. "Love you, Scrappy," Hank breathed as his eyes closed. "Love... tummy... rubs."

"I know," Scott whispered and kissed Hank one last time.

EPILOGUE

H ANK woke up alone.

After a few moments, he rolled out of their bed. *Our bed.* He still couldn't believe it sometimes. Scott had moved in, although they'd had to put some of his stuff in storage back in Toronto because it simply wouldn't fit in his townhouse. They'd toyed with the idea of having a house built just for the two of them, but for now, they were home.

They'd had a few disagreements about what to do with some of Hank's older furniture, but they'd compromised, and now their home was a strange mix of sleek, minimalist Asian-inspired antiques (Scott's contribution) and overstuffed comfort (Hank's contribution). Hank didn't know much about decorating, and to his utter surprise, neither did Scott, but it all worked for him. After the first night that he and Scott had exhausted themselves arranging and rearranging, every possible combination and permutation set in place, adjudicated and either discarded or accepted, Hank had left their bed to pad to the kitchen for a glass of water and had found himself. He had stood in the living room and imagined a Christmas tree in the far, empty corner, adorned by blinking multicolored lights and a pile of festively wrapped presents underneath. Two stockings—initials embroidered on each—would hang over the fireplace; there might even be a little get-together for Brian and Kari and Chris and any other people who might be lucky enough to become part of their little extended family.

In the bathroom, as he turned the faucets to shave the beard he'd grown over the past several weeks since his return to Duncan, he heard the familiar rattle of pots and pans—one of the perks of having a boyfriend who could cook. Hank smiled as he realized that if Scott kept feeding him, trying to put the weight he'd dropped since his bout with hypothermia, he was not only going to gain what he'd lost but then some. He splashed his face with warm water and dabbed the towel over his face and throat. Today was a celebration of sorts; they were going back to French Beach. Scott's contribution to the musical was finished, and the whole thing promised to be a big hit, and Hank would be back at work on Monday. That was the other disagreement they'd had, but Hank had put his foot down and explained that it was what he loved to do and that he would promise to be safe. He would make decisions knowing that he was part of a couple, but he would not give up logging. "Sure," he'd said to Scott calmly, rationally. "When I'm not getting anything out of it anymore, I'll give it up, but it's what I want, baby."

"Baby?"

"In here," Hank called as he pulled the trigger to spray some shave foam into his palm. Hank looked up into the mirror when his lover appeared in the doorway and turned immediately when he noticed the look on Scott's face wasn't a happy one. "What's wrong?"

"What...? Are you shaving it off?" Hank thought that his little Scrappy looked close to tears.

Hank rinsed the foam off his hands, tossed the can back in the medicine cabinet, and turned off the faucet. "No," he assuaged, tongue planted firmly in cheek. "Of course not."

"Good." Scott smiled as he walked forward and leaned his body against his lover's warm skin, his hands dipping behind the broad back and falling to rest against the cheeks of Hank's ass. "I promise I'll make it worth your while."

"You already have, Scott."

Scott reached up and took Hank's bearded face between his hands. "I am the luckiest man in the world." He leaned forward and stood on his tiptoes, planting a gentle kiss that seemed to say *I love you* while promising so much more. "I love you, Henry Isaac Ballam... with all my heart. You are absolutely perfect."

Hank smiled and leaned down, stealing another little kiss from Scott. He trailed his hand up his side, the backs of his first two fingers trailing over the three-inch scar. "Not anymore."

"If anything, baby," Scott cooed and licked his lips, "that just makes you even sexier."

"So," Hank teased as he bent to lift his lover and set him on the counter. "You have a thing for bad boys with scars."

"No." Scott wiggled forward on the counter, Hank's growing erection finding his. "Just you."

"I'm not sure what to make of that." Hank squinted in mock confusion. "Should I go out and get a bunch of tattoos and more scars, then?"

"Wouldn't matter." Scott leaned forward and flicked his tongue against one nipple and then the other. "I'd still think you were perfect." Scott slid off the counter, Hank's grip on his shoulders softening when he realized Scott was going down on his knees. Scott took him in his mouth fully, right to the back of his throat, and groaned. With his hands guiding Hank's slim hips, he turned slightly so that Hank would be able to lean against the counter. Scott had become concerned ever since Hank's release from the hospital about moments like this. He was never completely sure that his lover would be as strong or have as much stamina as before.

Hank always insisted he was fine, but then Scott would see him moving slowly or take a little break when they were out for walks. Pride, he'd just assumed. Hank was too proud to let him know that he wasn't back to his old self yet. *One day soon we'll be back to our usual routine of hours and hours,* Scott promised silently, thrilled by the low, guttural sounds of Hank's lust.

His hand cupped Hank's testicles, massaging them just the way he knew his lover liked it to be done, and ran his tongue along the underside, alternately kissing and licking his way up to the sensitive head. He took a few moments to squeeze the foreskin between his lips, dipping his tongue into the opening each time he wanted another moan of pleasure from Hank. He freed his hands, using only his mouth to take his lover in right to the base of his thick erection, and slowly trailed his fingernails up and down the tender flesh on the inside of Hank's lean thighs.

"Scott," Hank panted, his head thrown back and his chest heaving with the desire to come.

"So pretty, baby," Scott said as he brought one hand up to rub Hank's sensitive belly. "Come for me, Hank. Want to taste you."

"Oh fuck, yeah, Scrappy,"

Scott wasn't sure when the pet name had become a lustful pet name, but if Hank liked it, he wasn't going to complain. He liked thinking of himself as Scrappy. He'd been by Hank's side every minute during his recovery, questioning the doctors, asking for second opinions, and being a general pain-in-the-ass. Hank still liked to tease him about it, but if it meant his lover was safe and getting the best, then Scott would take the teasing as it came.

"Come for me, baby," Scott pleaded as his finger moved around to tease Hank's entrance. "Watch me swallow."

Hank opened his eyes when he heard the words; it never failed to get him off, watching that beautiful mouth on his dick. Until he built up his stamina, Hank had taken to closing his eyes and tilting his head back. But when he was ready to come, wanting it to be at the same time as his lover, all he had to do was look down and see himself inside Scott. Then he knew it would be mere seconds before his balls pulled up, his spine tingled, and his eyes were seeing stars.

"Love you, Scott. Love you so much," Hank grunted, and then his belly flexed, his ass cheeks thrust forward repeatedly, and he was crying out his release as his lover swallowed every drop, those long, soft fingers still making little circles over his belly.

Scott was still cleaning and licking when he felt Hank's big hands around his wrists. He let himself be pulled up and let Hank guide his hands so that they were now resting on his lover's broad shoulders, his fingers finding their way into the chestnut curls. "I love you too, Hank, very, very much."

Hank's arms encircled his waist, and he stretched languidly against the solid body, pulling his lover even closer against his sated body. "Your turn," Hank said between gentle kisses.

"No." Scott giggled as he felt Hank's full lips plant a kiss on the end of his nose. "I want to wait until we get to French Beach." He waggled his eyebrows. "There's a little clear pond near there that has some fond memories."

"You hoping for a repeat?" Hank slipped his hands underneath the boxer shorts and squeezed and caressed his lover's firm ass cheeks.

"I was hoping," Scott whispered against Hank's ear. "For a lot more than a repeat."

"Oh yeah?"

"Yeah," Scott confirmed. "I've been having this fantasy lately and…." He pulled against Hank's hair, bringing their lips together.

"Really?" Hank grinned as he felt his lover's dick jump against his "Do I get to know any of the details?"

"All of them," Scott promised.

When D.W. MARCHWELL is not teaching future generations the wonders of science, he can usually be found hiking, writing, riding horses, trying new recipes, or searching for and lovingly restoring discarded antique furniture. A goofy and incurable romantic, D.W. admits that his stories are inspired by actual events and that he has a soft spot for those where boy not only meets boy but also turns out to be boy's soul mate. After almost fifteen years of working his way across Canada, D.W. has finally found the perfect place to live at the foot of the Canadian Rockies. He still can't believe how lucky he is, and, as his grandmother taught him, counts his blessings every day.

Visit his web site at http://www.marchwellbooks.ca/. You can contact him at dwmarchwell@hotmail.com.

Don't miss

http://www.dreamspinnerpress.com

Also by D.W. MARCHWELL

http://www.dreamspinnerpress.com

Try these Contemporary Romances from
DREAMSPINNER PRESS

http://www.dreamspinnerpress.com

LaVergne, TN USA
03 June 2010
184840LV00003B/33/P